"Just what are you doing here?" she asked, wondering where the outrage had gone in her voice.

He leaned his forehead against hers. "There was a small argument that needed settling."

The very scent of him wrapped around her like smoke, pulling her inexorably toward him. She thought her throat would close with mingled fury and arousal. "What argument?" she managed, lying perfectly still, as if that could protect her.

"The one about whether I want you or not."

Grace gasped. She itched to hold on to him and never let go. She ached for the taste of him.

"What does this prove, Diccan?" she asked, struggling to hold on to her sense.

She couldn't simply succumb to him again. She would be putting herself back on her own path to ruin. But it was so hard to stay strong when she realized that what she heard in his voice was urgency, need. Sweet Lord, he was all but trembling, as if he hadn't had a woman in years.

"I want to be in you, Grace," he growled into her ear, lifting his hand to pull away the covers. "I want to feel your body melt around me. I want you laugh again."

Praise for Eileen Dreyer's

Barely a Lady

One of *Publishers Weekly*'s Best of 2010

A Top Ten *Booklist* Romance of the Year

One of *Library Journal*'s Five Best
Romances of the Year

"Dreyer flawlessly blends danger, deception, and desire into an impeccably crafted historical that neatly balances adventurous intrigue with an exquisitely romantic love story." —*Chicago Tribune*

"Vivid descriptions, inventive plotting, beautifully delineated characters, and stunning emotional depth."
—*Library Journal* (starred review)

"Romantic suspense author Dreyer makes a highly successful venture into the past with this sizzling, dramatic Regency romance. Readers will love the well-rounded characters and suspenseful plot."
—*Publishers Weekly* (starred review)

"*Barely a Lady* is addictively readable thanks to exquisitely nuanced characters, a brilliantly realized historical setting, and a captivating plot encompassing both the triumph and tragedy of war. Love, loss, revenge, and redemption all play key roles in this richly emotional, superbly satisfying love story." —*Booklist* (starred review)

Also by Eileen Dreyer

Barely a Lady

Never a Gentleman

Eileen Dreyer

FOREVER

NEW YORK   BOSTON

This book is a work of fiction. Names, characters, places, and incidents are the product of the author's imagination or are used fictiously. Any resemblance to actual events, locales, or persons, living or dead, is coincidental.

Copyright © 2011 by Eileen Dreyer
Excerpt from *Always a Temptress* copyright © 2011 by Eileen Dreyer
All rights reserved. Except as permitted under the U.S. Copyright Act of 1976, no part of this publication may be reproduced, distributed, or transmitted in any form or by any means, or stored in a database or retrieval system, without the prior written permission of the publisher.

Forever
Hachette Book Group
237 Park Avenue
New York, NY 10017
Visit our website at www.HachetteBookGroup.com.

Forever is an imprint of Grand Central Publishing. The Forever name and logo is a trademark of Hachette Book Group, Inc.

The publisher is not responsible for websites (or their content) that are not owned by the publisher.

Printed in the United States of America

First Printing: April 2011

10 9 8 7 6 5 4 3 2 1

It's been too long since I've done this.
To Rick, because without you, it wouldn't
mean anything.
Let's go to Machu Picchu next, okay?

Acknowledgments

I'd like to thank everyone who encouraged me on this road to the past: the Divas, of course. Members of the Convocation, members of my long-suffering family, who put up with a lot in the name of deadlines. My family at Rotrosen, especially Andrea Cirillo, and my family at Grand Central. Thank you, Amy, for always making me think harder, and Beth, for your support and friendship. To my copy editor, Isabel Stein, who cleans up my continuity glitches and makes sure each character has only one name; to the art department, especially Clare Brown, for my luscious covers; and everyone in sales, marketing, and PR, especially Samantha Kelly and Anna Balasi.

I would also like to thank everyone who helped make my research trip to India a reality, from my lovely Rick to everyone at Larsen & Toubro for their hospitality, especially Mr. and Mrs. A. P. Misra, R. S. Kapur, and Sangeeta, who was not only a wonderful hostess, but managed to create a western sari for me. Thanks to our friends Saurabh and Ghitika Kant, and to Rick's brother, Manmohan Chowla;

and Ruchi and Chintoo Mohanty, who welcomed us like family to their wedding. Thanks to Michele and to Travel and Leisure Elite, and to Bhankaj, driver extraordinaire, who went out of his way to actually find Lohagarh Fort in Bharat-pur when I asked. And thanks to all the wonderful hosts who welcomed us into their inns and B & Bs (and who are listed on the Travel for Fun page of my Web site, www.eileendreyer .com), and taught us so much about their country. I will never forget my visit, and hope I can return soon.

Thanks to the real Barbara Schroeder, who donated money to the Brenda Novak Auction for Diabetes Research to have a character named after her. Good choice. You'll be seeing her again. To the generous friends on the Beau Monde loop, Ninc, Teabuds, MoRWA, and all the friends I've made on Facebook. Knowing you're there makes it feel less as if I'm sitting all alone in my office wringing words out of a soggy brain.

Never a Gentleman

Prologue

The room stank of whiskey, sweat, and despair. Tucked away on the top floor of an aging hotel on the rue de Seine in Paris, the suite still bore remnants of its past glory. The torn wallpaper was gold-flocked. The tatty furniture betrayed elegant lines, and the windows, too grimy to see through, stretched up ten feet. Age and time had worn away the elegance. The current inhabitant had destroyed the rest. His half-eaten food and liquor bottles littered every surface. Dirty clothing lay piled on the floor. A table had been shattered against the door, and red wine dripped down the wall.

Bertie Evenham, the one responsible for the mess, balanced on the balls of his feet, as if listening for the sound of pursuit. An unprepossessing blond, he had fine aristocratic features, wide blue eyes, and a hawkish nose he hadn't yet grown into. His hair was greasy and unkempt, his linen soiled, and his hands shaking. His eyes darted impatiently between his guest and the door.

Across from him, Diccan Hilliard lounged in a faded blue brocade armchair, legs crossed, his quizzing glass spinning from his left hand. It was all Diccan could do to hold still. He hated confessions, and Bertie seemed compelled to make one. It wouldn't do to seem anxious to leave, though. Bertie had vital information to impart. He also had a gun pointed at Diccan's head.

"But why should I believe you, old chap?" Diccan asked the pallid, unwashed boy. "You must admit it sounds a bit fantastic. A gang of British nobles trying to overthrow their own throne."

Bertie scrubbed at his face with his free hand. "Don't you understand? You're in danger. *England* is in danger."

"So you've said." Leaning back, Diccan shot his cuffs. "Why not inform the Embassy here?"

Bertie's laugh was sharp. "Because I'm sure some of them are members."

Diccan nodded. "Of this group of yours that calls itself the British Lions. But you've also just told me that you helped Napoleon return to France. That's treason, old son. You're asking me to believe a man who betrayed his country."

If possible, the boy looked even more desperate. "Don't you think I know it? But they were blackmailing me. They're going to blackmail you, too, damn it. Why won't you believe me?"

"Maybe if you tell me what it was about you they thought worthy of blackmail."

The gun began to wobble in the boy's hand. Diccan couldn't help but notice that it was a finely crafted Manton dueling pistol. It wouldn't take much for the lad to make a mistake. He was too unstable. Too desperate. Sweat was dripping down his temples.

Bertie actually turned his face away, and Diccan couldn't help feeling sorry for him, no matter what he'd done. "You don't understand," the boy whispered. "You can't. You're not...*unnatural*."

Ah.

Diccan kept his voice gentle. "Tristram Gordon."

Evenham's face crumpled. "You know?"

"That you and Lady Gracechurch's cousin were lovers? Yes. You're right, though. Most don't."

"Her husband murdered him!"

"Not murder," Diccan suggested quietly. "A duel. I know. I was there."

The boy began to shake harder. "So was I. And I couldn't even go to him...."

Diccan didn't like tearing wings off flies or torturing children. Evenham couldn't be more than twenty-five. "What do you want me to do, Bertie?"

"Warn the government. Make them believe that these people are dangerous. These people really think they can do better." He shrugged and sat abruptly on a straightback chair, as if he had used the last of his energy. "We have a mad king and a profligate heir," he said, sounding like a recitation. "Riots from the lower class and threats to power from the middle class. Unemployment, crime, failed crops, rising prices. They believe that they can cure it all by taking power back into noble hands."

"What about the king?"

He shrugged again. "I don't know. They aren't stupid enough to share that kind of information with someone who's been coerced." He shrugged. "Besides, the way the

Lions are organized, only a few people know all. Five or six, maybe. Each of those has a specific area of responsibility, and recruits and organizes individually, so no one can betray the whole group. Even those who believe in the cause only know who their immediate superiors are."

"So you don't know who your group is headed by?"

He shook his head, rubbing now at his eyes. The gun, sadly, was still leveled on Diccan. "I know who controlled me. I've told you their names. They funneled gold and men to Napoleon. The Lions believed that if he won on the Continent, the Lions would control the British government."

"How do you know *I'm* in danger?"

"I overheard them. They think you might be susceptible. And that you have contacts they want."

Diccan shook his head, wondering whether someone might have peeked beneath his facade. "Honored they think I live such an interesting life. Can't think why. The most interesting people I meet are chefs and fishmongers. They do know that my most challenging diplomatic task is organizing parties, don't they?"

"I don't know. They'll succeed, though. If they can't blackmail you, they'll use threats. If threats don't work, you'll suffer a fatal accident so you can't expose them. When they came after me, they told me that even if I slipped from their net, they could drag me back by hurting my mother or sisters."

Diccan gave a bark of amusement. "I would buy a ticket to watch them face off with my mother. She'd eviscerate them without bending a nail."

He did not, however, speak of his sisters. Deciding that he had to take control of the situation, he made a move, as if to get to his feet. Immediately Bertie jumped up, gripping the gun more tightly.

"I will shoot you. If you won't help, I'll kill you. Don't you see?" There were tears in the boy's eyes. "I've risked everything."

Yes, Diccan knew. He had. The boy hadn't just put himself at risk from the Lions. His love for another man was a hanging offense.

"And there isn't anything else you can tell me?" Diccan asked. "I mean, I appreciate your concern for me, but I'm not sure that's enough to interest Whitehall."

"Well then, what about this? The Lions are looking for something they've lost. I don't know what, only that they'll hand it off as a signal to set a plan into motion. When they find it, they will act."

"Act how?"

"They're going to assassinate Wellington."

Diccan felt the air leave his lungs. "Yes," he mused, "I imagine that would get the government's attention."

"The group that aided Napoleon has already been reassigned. They are to assist the Surgeon."

Diccan all but stopped breathing. "The assassin?" Images of the Surgeon's work flashed before his eyes; bleeding, raw wounds draining life. Fish-white bodies. "But he's in Newgate."

Bertie shook his head so hard droplets of grease flew. "Not for long."

Diccan's instinctive reaction was to argue. Nobody got out of Newgate Prison. But if the Lions were as well-placed as Bertie said, nothing was impossible.

"All right." This time he gained his feet without challenge. "You have my word, Bertie. I'll ride *ventre à terre* to London to warn them. We'll stop this long before it involves Wellington."

The boy laughed. "Don't be so sure. They won't stop. If you get one of them, another will step in to take his place. You really don't know how committed they are. You don't know how well-placed."

If Diccan hadn't already been investigating this very plot, he would have scoffed at Bertie's charge. But a few traitors had already been unearthed, and they had indeed been well-placed.

"Thank you, Bertie," he said, hoping the boy knew how sincere he was. "You have done your country, and me, a great service. If you ever need assistance, find me."

It was as if Bertie had held up on will alone, and Diccan's concession had stolen it. The boy literally sagged, tears streaking his gaunt cheeks. The gun drooped in his hand. Diccan thought to make a try for it, but he believed Bertie had lost any reason to hurt him.

"Thank you," the boy said, free hand over his eye. "You're kind."

Diccan knew he was nothing of the sort. He nodded all the same and turned for his gloves. "Then if you don't need anything else from me, I believe I'll be off."

Bertie nodded. He took a breath. "No. Nothing more. I've done what I needed to."

Diccan was still pulling on his gloves when he saw Bertie raise the gun again. Instinct kicked in and he dove to the side. He was just about to hit the floor when he realized that Bertie had no intention of hurting him. He meant to hurt himself.

"No!" Diccan screamed, lunging for him.

He was too late. Smiling, as if relieved, Bertie turned the gun on himself. Diccan could do no more than hold the boy in his arms as he died.

Chapter 1

Canterbury, England
Three days later

Grace Fairchild was confused. She was dreaming; she knew that. But she couldn't make sense of it. Oh, she'd had dreams like it before; vague, anxious fantasies of a man making love to her. But usually her dreams were indistinct, more suggestion than fact. Visual rather than visceral. After living with the army her whole life, she knew what copulating looked like. In India, she'd seen graphic depictions of it painted and carved into temple walls, parades of couples writhing in ecstasy in each other's arms.

Her dreams, predictably, mirrored them. She saw what happened; she didn't feel it. Even as her dream lover took her, she did no more than watch, a voyeur in her own boudoir.

This time was different. In this dream, she could feel her lover tucked against her back like spoons in a drawer. Skin to skin, heat to heat, pounding heart to pounding heart. His clean scent filled her nostrils. The harsh rasp of his breathing fanned through her hair. He was nuzzling the base of her neck, releasing a shower of shivers that cascaded down her body. His callused fingers traced each vertebra in her back. She swore she could feel the abrasion of hair against her legs and bottom; she heard the syncopated sounds of breathing.

She shuddered before the onslaught of sensations she'd never known: an almost painful sweetness, heat like a Madras sun, shocks of pleasure that skittered through her limbs like lightning. Her skin seemed to have caught fire, the scrape of his palm igniting her like flint against too-dry tinder. An exquisite, anxious thrill snaked through her, curling along her legs, the sensitive skin of her nipples, the deepest recesses of her belly to touch her womb, like the sun warming a dormant seed. Her insides felt as if they were melting, and she couldn't seem to hold still.

She smiled in her sleep, where it was safe to dream a bit. Where she could remember that beneath the gray dresses and pragmatic mien everyone saw, she was a woman. And that even a plain woman wanted the same things other women took for granted. Touch. Comfort. Pleasure. She wanted to *be* one of those temple paintings.

In her head she pleaded with him to hurry. To stoke the fire; to ease it. To pull her closer, closer yet, so she would never again have to be alone. She stretched, a cat in the sun, closer to his hard, lithe body. She gasped at the hard shaft that pressed against her bottom. Such an alien pleasure, so intriguing. So deeply erotic.

She heard a moan, a gravelly, low threnody that resonated right through her. A sensuous, mesmerizing growl of pleasure. It made her chuckle. His one hand was teasing her breast, flicking the nipple until it ached. His other was drifting lower, stealing her breath. Her heart was pounding; her skin was damp. She heard another moan.

Abruptly she stiffened. Her eyes popped open.

She really *had* heard a moan.

Desperately she tried to think. She could see the early morning light seeping into the inn room. Yes, that was right. She had stopped at the Falstaff Inn at Canterbury with her friend Lady Kate the night before. Drawing a careful breath, she tested the air, expecting to smell woodsmoke, fresh air from the open window, her own rosewater scent. Instead she smelled brandy and tobacco and a subtle scent of musk. She smelled man-sweat.

Her heart seized. Her brain went slack. She had dreamed him; she was certain. Why could she still smell him? Then she felt his hand move toward the nest of curls at the juncture of her legs, and she knew. He wasn't a dream at all.

Shrieking, she lurched up. The bedclothes were tangled around her legs. She yanked at them and pushed with her feet, trying to get away. She pushed too hard. Suddenly she was tumbling off the bed, arms flailing wildly for balance. She shrieked again when she landed with a thud on the floor.

For a moment she lay where she was, eyes closed, pain shooting up her bad leg, her stomach threatening revolt. All the heat that had blossomed in her died. She was dizzy and dry-mouthed and confused. And, evidently, lying on the floor of a strange man's bedroom, trapped by his sheets. Christ save her, how could that be?

"Bloody hell!" she heard from the bed, and knew without opening her eyes that the disaster had just become far worse. It was not a stranger at all in that bed. It was Diccan

Hilliard, the single most elegant man in England. The one person who never failed to turn Grace into a stuttering fool.

Still cursing, he sat up. The early morning sunlight gilded his skin as in a Rembrandt painting, limning muscle and sinew and bone with a molten gold. Shadow etched the sharp ridges of jaw and cheekbone and shuddered through his tumbled sable hair as he dragged his hands through it. He was shaking his head, as if to clear it. Rubbing at his eyes. Grace knew she should flee before he spotted her. She couldn't seem to look away from him.

Could he have been more compelling? Not handsome, precisely. His features were a bit too broad, his nose a bit bent, his eyes too ghostly gray. But tall and elegant and aristocratic to his toes. The perfect antithesis for the hopeless spinster sitting like a lump on his floor.

"*Merde*," she muttered in despair.

He turned at the sound, and his jaw dropped. He had obviously just recognized who it was he'd been fondling.

"Miss Fairchild," he drawled, his voice like ice. As gracefully as a god, he climbed out of the bed and stalked over to stand before her. "If I might be so bold. What the deuce are you doing here?"

She couldn't draw breath to answer. Sweet Lord, he was naked. He was breathtaking, with solid shoulders, and arms that had worked hard. His chest was taut and lean, and shadowed with curling hair that arrowed down his torso right to...She flushed hotly. Sweet, sweet Lord. He was magnificent. He was an ancient statue come to life... well, except for one small difference.

Well. Not so small at all. And it wasn't as if she could miss it. Not only was she at eye level, but, if her old temple art hadn't lied, he was magnificently aroused. Just the sight of his shaft, jutting straight up from that nest of dark hair, sent shivers cascading through her. It made all those two-dimensional watercolors pale in comparison.

Of course, the minute he got a good look at her, his erection wilted like warm lettuce.

"I'm still dreaming," she muttered, shamefully unable to look away. "That's it. A nightmare. I should never have had that second piece of pigeon pie last night."

She should shut her eyes. She should make a grab for her clothes and run. She should at least defend herself. She couldn't so much as blink. She could still feel his hands on her skin, the unbearable pleasure of his body against hers. His expression of horror made her want to wither with shame.

"I expected better of you, Miss Fairchild," he said, his voice dripping with disdain, his hands planted on sinfully lean hips. "Never did I think you'd be the kind of scheming, brass-faced hussy who'd force her way into a man's bed. Just what did you slip into my drink?"

Suddenly furious, Grace clambered to her feet, grabbing a bedpost to steady her when her bad leg cramped. "What did I slip into *your* drink?" she demanded, outraged. "Why, you insufferable, self-centered, overweening park saunterer. You're the last person on earth I would *ever* let—"

Instead of apologizing, he shut his eyes. "For the love of God, madame, cover yourself."

Grace looked down and squeaked in dismay. She hadn't considered her state of undress. She'd grabbed the covers because it was frigid in the room. Not because she was... oh, *bugger*. She was as naked as he was, providing him with a view of every bony inch of her chest and shoulders.

"Where are my clothes?" she cried, trying to cover every unlovely jutting angle of her with the voluminous blanket.

"Don't waste your time," he snapped. "Just hide yourself."

"You could do the same," she snapped back.

Cocking an imperious eyebrow, he considered his status. "No, could I? But I thought this was what you were after."

Grace felt panic shutting off her air. Her head hurt. She felt sick. "I told you," she insisted, her voice unpardonably shrill. "I wasn't *after* anything."

Suddenly the door to the room slammed open and bounced against the wall. At least half a dozen people peered in, all clad in nightclothes and gawking like pit rowdies. Grace did the only thing she could. She dropped to the floor and yanked the covers over her head.

"Isn't that General Fairchild's daughter?" a woman who sounded like Lady Thornton demanded from the doorway. Grace shrank down even more.

"How delicious," another, thinner voice answered with a delighted giggle. "The feather-brained antidote obviously thinks she's nabbed Diccan Hilliard."

Grace heard laughter and wanted to die. How many people were out there?

"Good to see everyone," Diccan was saying, as if they had come to tea. "My apologies for presenting myself to you *en deshabille.*"

More salacious laughter. Grace squeezed her eyes shut, her thundering heart almost drowning out the sound of Lord Thornton and some unknown man taking bets on her future. She was terrified she was going to disgrace herself. Her stomach was lurching as if she were back on the channel packet.

"Well, well," she heard a new and welcome voice intrude. "Letitia Thornton. I had no idea that this was what you wore to bed. Amazing color, really. You must have been dragged right from your sleep. Not a very attractive time of the day for you, is it? And Geoffrey Smythe. What an interesting banyan. Are those roosters on your chest? Hmm. I must admit I've never seen a puce chicken before."

Lady Kate had arrived.

If this had been happening to anyone else, Grace might have smiled. Leave it to Kate to send the cream of the *ton* scurrying away like embarrassed debs. But it was happening to *her*. She was the one crouched on the floor, naked beneath a blanket as an audience laughed.

She must not have heard the door close, because suddenly she felt a gentle hand on her shoulder.

"Grace?"

If it could be possible, she felt worse. She had so few female friends. Only three, really: Olivia Wyndham, Lady Bea Seaton, and Lady Kate Seaton, who had taken her in after Grace's father had died at Waterloo. It had been Lady Kate who had seen her through those terrible days, who had provided safety and support as Grace adjusted to civilian life. Grace couldn't betray her friend this way. Even a notorious widow like Kate had no business associating with a ruined spinster.

"Grace, tell me you're all right," Kate said, sounding distressed.

"I'm fine," Grace managed, huddled miserably on the floor.

It didn't occur to her to cry. Soldiers don't cry, her father had always told her. At least not after their seventh birthday.

"Is this some joke of yours, Kate?" she heard Diccan demand, sounding like a petulant child.

Lady Kate huffed. "Don't be demented. I'm even more stunned than you are. I know for a fact that Grace has better taste."

"Why, you repellent brat," he snapped. "Your *friend* just arranged to make an appearance in my bed before the worst gossips in the *ton*. Naked."

"Really, Diccan? She must be amazingly sly, then, since neither of us expected to see you or them here."

"She *must* have, damn it! They're here. And she's... here."

Lady Kate sighed. "Your arguments might carry more weight if you were dressed, Diccan."

"What about *her*?"

Still crouched beneath her blanket, Grace winced. Her leg hurt. The blanket was beginning to scratch, and a draft had found its way underneath to bedevil her. And yet she wasn't about to move.

"Grace can dress after you leave," Lady Kate was saying over Grace's head. "From *her* bedroom, by the way."

"*Hers*?"

"The miniature of her father in regimentals on the bedside table should be a dead giveaway."

Grace heard the rustling of clothing. He must be dressing.

"What *are* you doing here, by the way?" Lady Kate asked as if she were addressing him over tea. "We were supposed to meet you in Dover tomorrow."

There was sudden silence. "This isn't Dover?"

"Canterbury," Grace answered, before she thought of it.

"*Canterbury*?" Diccan echoed, the sounds of movement

ceasing. "Deuce take it. How the devil did I get here? The last I remember I was on the Dover packet. Where's Biddle?"

"Your valet?" Kate said, sounding absurdly amused. "Undoubtedly looking for you in Dover. We'll send someone after him, once we're all dressed. Are you still all right under there, Grace?"

Grace felt another miserable blush spread over her. "Do you see my clothes?" she asked.

"Strewn over the floor as if they'd been on fire," Kate informed her. "Another reason I know you are not the culprit here. Even during those awful days we spent caring for the wounded from Waterloo, you never once failed to fold your clothing like a premier abigail."

"She could have been anxious to get into bed," Diccan suggested dryly.

"Not with you, she wouldn't," Kate said, sounding positively delighted. "She doesn't like you."

Grace made a sound of protest. It wasn't polite, even if it was true. She didn't like him. It didn't mean she was immune to him. He was like a broken tooth Grace couldn't resist running her tongue over, a sharp reminder of everything she wasn't and never would be.

"Don't be absurd," Diccan was saying. "Everyone likes me."

"Would you *please* get your pants on and leave?" Grace demanded, finally losing her patience. "I'm about to catch the ague down here."

And damn him if he didn't chuckle. "Anything you say, Boadicea."

Which made Grace feel even worse. A few months earlier, Diccan had nicknamed her after the English warrior queen, undoubtedly because he couldn't think of another female tall enough to look him in the eye. Which, as Grace well knew, was not necessarily a compliment.

"Why don't you secure a private dining room?" Kate said to him. "We'll meet you there."

Grace heard some inarticulate grumbling.

"Trust me," Kate said with a laugh. "They're changing. See if you can get to the parlor before they make it back out of their rooms. I would remind you that one of those people is Letitia Thornton, and you know she doesn't consider a day complete unless she's destroyed a reputation or two."

This time it was Grace who groaned. The news of her ruination would be all over London before dinner. Diccan, it seemed, had no more to say. Grace heard the door open and close, and knew without being told that he'd left.

"Come out, little turtle," Lady Kate said, her voice too gentle for Grace's mood.

Grace poked her head out of the blanket to find Kate laying her clothing on the bed. "I truly didn't try and compromise him, Kate."

Kate's smile was beatific. "My darling Grace, I never thought it." She tilted her head. "It has been a revelation, however. Who knew our Diccan had such amazing…attributes?"

Grace almost retreated back under the blanket. Kate hadn't even seen one of the attributes at its most amazing.

Kate evidently didn't notice Grace's reaction, for she wandered over to settle onto the window seat, where the sun warmed her primrose skirt and set fire to her hair. The thick mahogany curls framed a piquant face enlivened by slyly amused cat-green eyes and set off a perfect form on a tiny frame. Grace, of course, felt like a Clydesdale in her presence.

"I must confess, though," Kate continued, a shadow flitting across those magnificent eyes. "There is no getting around the fact that we're in a pickle. What do you remember about last night?"

Carefully, Grace climbed to her feet and recovered her clothing from the rumpled bed. Grace couldn't look at the untidy linen without remembering those few moments of bliss. She knew her skin was flaming all the way up from her knees. Redheads blushed. Grace went blotchy.

"I remember arriving here," she said as she struggled into her chemise and petticoat. "I remember dinner."

Kate nodded. "Excellent roast. The turnips, on the other hand, needn't be mentioned."

"I remember us having that glass of cognac after dinner."

"Did it taste odd?"

Grace couldn't help but smile. "Cognac always tastes odd to me, Kate. I never developed the liking for it you have."

"And after I left you here?"

Grace paused with her gray walking dress in hand. She tried to remember entering this room, placing her candle on the small dresser, unbinding her hair from its tight knot.

She shook her head. "I don't even remember climbing the stairs. You really did leave me here?"

"Oh, yes. I assume if Diccan had already been within, you would have alerted me."

"I would have made more noise than one of Whinyates' rockets."

"As you did this morning?"

Grace sighed, wondering how she could feel more miserable. "How could this happen?"

Brushing off her skirt, Lady Kate stood. "An excellent question. Finish dressing, dear, and we'll see if we can find out."

• • •

Diccan Hilliard was in a rage. No one could see it, of course. Diccan had long since perfected the mask of bland sophistication that was his trademark. But as he strolled down the hall toward the private dining room fifteen minutes later, he seethed. How could this have happened? He wasn't a greenling to be caught with his pants down. And yet somehow between Paris and Dover, he'd been drugged, shanghaied, stripped, and set up. And not by Grace Fairchild. No matter how hard he tried, he couldn't make the facts fit his accusation. Grace Fairchild had been with Kate, not sneaking aboard a packet boat with a bottle of laudanum tucked into her chemise.

Could it really have been the Lions? Could Bertie have been right? Diccan fought the urge to rub at his head. He was still wobbly and dizzy from the laudanum, and his skull felt too small for his aching brain. He could barely form his thoughts, which was damned inconvenient. Because if he didn't think fast, he would find himself stuck in Canterbury when he needed to be in London as quickly as possible to pass on Bertie's information. He needed to redeem the poor, sad boy, whom he'd left lying in that fetid apartment. He needed to redeem himself for failing him.

He wanted to curse. London had to wait. He was stuck here until he unraveled this latest disaster. He had to locate his valet, who should have been with him. He had to learn how he got here, and how his horse had ended up in the stables. And he needed to deal with Grace Fairchild.

Sweet Christ, he thought, his head hurting even worse. Why her? Grace Fairchild had to be the most honorable, well-respected spinster in England. She was also the most unfortunate. Taller than most men, she was, to put it baldly, plain. His Aunt Hermitrude looked better, and she was sixty and slew-eyed. To make it worse, Miss Fairchild didn't walk. She lurched like a sailor on shore. Whoever named her Grace must have been blind. Whoever put Diccan in her bed had been cruel.

He liked her. He really did. That didn't mean he wanted to wake up next to her for the next forty years. His cods shriveled just at the thought. He refused to even consider the fact that he'd woken hard and ready, with only that bony frame to entice him.

He looked down the half-timbered hallway to the front door and thought how easy it would be to just leave. Walk out the door, climb on Gadzooks, and not stop until London. Maybe not even then.

Which was, he suspected, exactly what his enemies hoped for. If he failed to marry her, his reputation would be blown wider than Byron's. Any accusations he made would become immediately suspect. If he did marry her, he would be delayed and distracted, which might just give the Lions time to find their lost object and attack Wellington. It was an impossible choice.

Damn it. *Damn* it! He didn't deserve this. Not now, when the war was over and he could finally come out of the shadows. Not when his future finally looked promising.

A shuffling noise alerted him that he was no longer alone. Looking toward the public room, he saw that he'd been joined by almost all the witnesses to the morning's debacle. Of course it would be Thornton who would be the first to speak. The porcine peer and his knife-thin wife were no friends of Grace's.

"Wasn't there anything better in town to entertain you,

old man?" Thornton asked with a simper and a nudge to his friend Geoffrey Smythe. "I know you regretted leaving that pretty little mistress of yours behind in Belgium, but even that sway-backed bone-rattler of yours out in the stables would be a more cozy armful."

The malice in those words brought Diccan to a halt. "Pardon?"

Proving his dearth of intelligence, the overstuffed peer chortled, leaning close enough to inflict his bad breath on Diccan. "Although they do bear a certain resemblance to each other."

Diccan deliberately slowed his breathing. He had to remember that smearing this worm all over the floor would only delay him further. "My friend," he said calmly. "I know that you're sensible."

Suddenly Thornton looked a bit less assured. "Why, of course."

Next to him, the slickly elegant Geoff Smythe leaned against the wall, arms across his chest, as if settling in for a play. Diccan ignored him.

"Good." He nodded to Thornton. "Good. Then you would never do anything that would force me to face you across a dueling ground. Knowing, of course, that I have already stood up four times." He gave a measured smile. "And walked off alone each time."

He thought Thornton might have gulped. Even so, the man raised his chin, leaving him only three. "Doin' it too brown, ain't ya? Not going to marry the chit, after all."

Diccan froze. Of course it was what Thornton would think. The Lions, he suddenly realized, had counted on it. Diccan had never been shy about announcing his sexual preferences, and there wasn't a person who would dare to claim Grace Fairchild fit the bill. And, truthfully, hadn't he just been standing here, plotting escape?

But he couldn't offer Grace up to this pack of jackals. He wouldn't give Thornton the satisfaction. Nor would he give Thornton's wife a vulnerable soul to shred. Grace deserved better.

"I won't marry her?" he asked, twirling his quizzing glass. "Why not?"

It was Geoff Smythe who answered, his classic blond English features coolly amused. "Why *not*? You really mean to face the prospect of that across the table every morning just because she winkled her way into your bed?"

"Actually," Diccan said, turning away so no one saw the impact of his decision, "I do."

"No, really," Thornton protested, grabbing Diccan's arms. "You can't marry the chit."

Diccan saw a faint sheen of sweat on Thornton's forehead.

"What alternative do you suggest?"

But Thornton couldn't seem to think of an answer. *Good Lord*, Diccan thought, *was Thornton involved in this, too? He certainly wasn't the one who'd planned it. Thornton wouldn't know how to schedule breakfast. Maybe, however, he was supposed to have been the witness. The blackmailer.*

As for Geoff Smythe, Diccan wasn't so sure. Deep waters was Geoff Smythe. Something to investigate. When he got out of here.

"The pater's been nattering at me to settle down for years," Diccan said, plucking Thornton's hand from his sleeve. "I imagine Miss Fairchild will do as well as any. If I do marry her, you'll understand that I can't tolerate any disparagement of my wife."

Now Thornton looked sick. "But of course," he mumbled. Smythe was still smiling.

Diccan had once again started on his way when he stopped. "By the way, Thorny," he said, as if he didn't notice the fat man swiping his forehead with an embroidered handkerchief, "I know why I'm here, but what in blazes brought you to a place as boring as Canterbury?"

Thornton startled, the cloth floating from his fingers like a linen leaf. "Looking at horses. Old Brickwater has a string to sell."

Considering Thornton's size, Diccan hoped Brickwater was selling draught horses. He kept his silence, though, sparing no more than a nod before leaving.

The staff of the Falstaff must have known his need, for by the time he reached the parlor, a coffeepot and cup were on the table. Plumping himself down in a chair, he drank cup after cup until the cobwebs began to dissipate.

The situation looked no better with a clear head. Only a week ago he had looked to his future with anticipation. After all, he'd been promised recompense for all his hard work. A plum position in one of the newly opened embassies, perhaps. A position at the peace talks. He could finally enjoy himself, doing what he did best, savoring the best the world had to offer.

He hadn't even considered marriage yet. It would come, when he was ready. He would probably marry a diplomat's daughter, someone like his cousin Kate: sharp, intelligent, elegant, and challenging. A woman who could help him plot his course and celebrate the success they'd both dreamed of. Instead, he would have to figure out what to do with Grace Fairchild.

The frustrating thing was that he loved redheads. He

couldn't think of any more exotic treasure than that burst of fire right at the juncture of a woman's legs, more promise than color, a hint of the delights that lay beneath, a flash of whimsy and heat and lust. He loved every shade of redhead. He loved their milky skin and their vivid personalities and their formidable tempers. He even loved the color of their freckles. In fact, he loved redheads so much that he'd suggested that his last two mistresses dye their thatch with henna, just to please him. He could get a cockstand just thinking of it.

Except for the freckles, though, Grace Fairchild could boast of none of that bounty. To call her a redhead was to exercise unforgivable license. Her hair was virtually colorless, the kind of faded, dismal hue one might see on an old woman. Her skin was almost swarthy from all her years spent under the Iberian sun, and her blushes unfortunate. She had no shape to speak of, no temper, no spark.

The sharpest reaction he'd ever gotten from her had been the day he had dubbed her Boadicea. For just a moment, a spark of fury had lit her eyes, a spirited defiance stiffening her spine. But as quickly as the fury had risen, it dissipated, almost as if there were no place on her for it to gain purchase. Word was that she'd never even wept when she'd carried her father's body back from Waterloo.

As if called, the door opened and in she walked, clad in one of her ubiquitous gray dresses, her hair scraped back into a tight bun. Diccan wasn't surprised that she couldn't quite look at him. He couldn't believe what had happened that morning, either. His balls still ached, heavy and thick with unmet expectations. Seeing her again now, he couldn't figure why. His body seemed completely disinterested in the lanky antidote who limped into the room with the briskness of a wounded cavalry officer.

Almost betraying himself with a sigh, Diccan climbed to his feet and gave his best bow as Kate followed Miss Fairchild in and shut the door. "Kate. Miss Fairchild. Let me ring for breakfast."

Miss Fairchild went almost chalk white. "Not for me, thank you. Some tea and toast."

Diccan tilted his head to assess her. "Stomach a bit unsteady?"

"A bit."

"Muddled head? Dizziness?"

She looked up briefly as she reached the table. "Indeed."

Diccan held out her chair and waited for her to sit. "I thought so. I have the exact same symptoms. I don't know if you tipple to excess, Miss Fairchild, but I rarely do, and never on a packet boat. So in the absence of other evidence, I believe we were both drugged."

He was disappointed when Miss Fairchild failed to react. "You're not surprised?" he asked.

She looked calmly up at him. "It would explain much."

He shook his head, a bit disconcerted by her poise. "Kate," he said, turning to seat his cousin. "Who sent you the message to meet me?"

She sat down. "I thought you did. I assume I was wrong."

"You were. Where did you receive it?"

"We were at a country weekend at Marcus Drake's. We got as far as Canterbury last night."

That brought Diccan's head around sharply. "Drake? Who knew you were there?"

Kate gave him a grin. "Everyone, I imagine. The notice was in the society pages."

Even so. Marcus Belden, Earl of Drake, was the one who had asked Diccan to meet with Evenham. Could he somehow be involved in this latest debacle? Diccan didn't want to think so.

"The note did look to be in your hand, Diccan," Kate said, bringing his attention back. "Do you know why?"

"I have been involved in some delicate negotiations. The postwar map of Europe and all." He shrugged, hoping he looked convincing. "Someone might have wanted me to stumble."

Kate raised her head. "They finally gave you a real job?"

Diccan flashed her a smile. "Purely by attrition, my dear. The usual suspects are too busy."

She gave him a brisk nod. "Well, then, I believe an apology is due."

Diccan flinched from the thought. He tried one last time to believe that Grace Fairchild had orchestrated her own runaway marriage. One look at the high color on her ashen cheeks put paid to that. She was, just as he'd suspected, a pawn. So he stood, and he gave Miss Fairchild a credible bow.

"I had no right to cast aspersions on your character," he said. "I apologize."

And oddly, he got a smile in return. "Thank you, but I wouldn't be too hard on yourself. I can't imagine your having any other reaction to finding a woman you didn't expect in your bed. I would be happy to help any way I can to find out how. And why."

Diccan nodded, already focused on the quickest way to settle the business. "Of course," he said. "Now then, my schedule is tight, so we must get on with making plans. Propitiously we're in Canterbury, and the good archbishop is one of those ubiquitous cousins. I should be able to obtain a special license by the afternoon. Do you wish to stay here, or repair to London for the ceremony?"

Kate looked toward Miss Fairchild, who sat suddenly silent. "Oh, London," Kate said. "It will make it look less like a hole-in-the-wall event."

Diccan nodded absently, beginning to pace. "Good. I have to get there as quickly as possible anyway. I can send someone ahead to reserve rooms at the Pulteney. When Biddle finds us, he can begin to move my things from the Albany." A sudden dread had him eying his cousin with disfavor. "You don't expect the pater to preside over the nuptials, do you?"

Kate sighed. "It would look odd if your father were excluded, Diccan. He is a bishop, after all."

That was the last straw. All he needed to complete this farce was to see his father in one of his bouts of self-righteous indignation. When the maid came, Diccan would ask for hemlock in his coffee.

"Excuse me," Grace spoke up.

Diccan stopped. The deuce. He'd all but forgotten her sitting there. "Yes?"

"Am I involved in these plans?"

He blinked. Surely she wasn't that dense. "Of course you are. What did you think?"

"I thought you might have consulted me."

The expression on her face was serene, but Diccan could see the pulse in her neck quicken. "What? You'd rather be married in Canterbury? Don't blame you. The pater's a regular tartar."

"I'd rather not be married at all."

It took a second for that to sink in. "You have no choice," he snapped, thinking of Thornton.

"Of course I do," she said with a slight smile. "And my choice is that you go on about your business, and I'll go home to mine."

Diccan wasn't certain just why he was so furious. She had just given him a way out. He'd offered marriage, and she had rejected him. The onus now rested on her. But he resented the hell out her blithe dismissal of his sacrifice.

"You just promised to cooperate."

"I promised to help. By that I meant I could disappear into the country where nobody cared about what happened in Canterbury, and you would be able to avoid a marriage neither of us wants."

She was exacerbating his headache. "Don't be absurd," he said. "Every gossip in London is waiting outside. You can't leave this room without announcing an engagement."

Her eyes had gone flat. "An engagement? Oh, is that what we're talking about?"

"Of course it is."

Kate gave him a quick kick in the shins. "An actual proposal might come in handy, Diccan."

Diccan sucked in a breath. He didn't have time for this. The longer Miss Fairchild balked, the farther behind he got. Evenham's confession weighed on him; he swore he could still smell the boy's blood on his hands. "Oh, hell," he muttered, digging the heel of his hand into his eye, as if that could ease his throbbing head. "Fine. Miss Fairchild. Will you do me the honor of marrying me?"

It might not have been the most romantic proposal ever. It certainly didn't warrant Miss Fairchild's reaction.

"If you want to insult me," she said in deliberate tones as she rose majestically to her feet and approached him, "You might as well do it behind my back. I have too much to do to waste my time."

"Damn it—"

She never let him finish. Winding up like a premier

boxer, she punched him in the nose and walked out the door.

In her wake, the room echoed with a thick silence. Diccan was surprised his nose didn't bleed all over his cravat. Miss Fairchild hadn't spent her life with the army without learning how to hit.

Kate, too, got to her feet. "Well," she said, sounding suspiciously amused as she settled her primrose dress about her. "Now I understand why you're thought to be the suavest man in England."

Diccan knew he had no right, but he felt aggrieved. "I'm marrying her, Kate. What do you want?"

She gave him a sad look. "Courtesy would be a good start." And she walked out too.

Diccan was still standing slack-jawed when the maid finally came in to answer his call. He slumped back into his seat and dropped his head to his hands. "Coffee," he growled. "And see if you have any hemlock."

Chapter 2

Grace was folding her clothing into her portmanteau when Kate strolled into the room.

"May I come in?" she asked, closing the door.

Grace didn't bother to look up. "As long as you haven't brought anyone else with you."

Kate laughed. "I believe he's downstairs making sure his nose is intact." Before Grace could respond, she raised a hand. "And don't you dare apologize. I've known that scapegrace since my christening, and I have never once seen him bollocks up a situation like he did just now. If it had been anyone else, I would have said he was overset."

"I imagine he was," Grace allowed, shaking out her gray moiré evening gown. "I'd think the very last place he would expect to find himself was in bed with an antidote like me."

"Grace," Kate warned, settling herself back on the window seat. "That is unworthy of you."

As miserable as she felt, Grace smiled. "Dearest Kate," she said, smoothing the drab silk with her hand. "I was not looking for sympathy. I know perfectly well who I am. *And* who I am not. And I am definitely not a woman Diccan Hilliard would notice if he hadn't met me in your parlor."

"He likes you perfectly well," her friend protested.

"Of course he does. To tip his hat to in the street. Not to bed."

Feeling the heat of yet another blush, she decided she was tired of always being uncomfortable. But the feel of his hand had been so delicious...

"Here," Kate said as if she heard the turmoil inside Grace's head. "A wee nip might be in order."

Grace looked up to see her holding out a chased silver flask. "Do you still have that?"

Kate looked at it with an impish smile. "Oh, yes. I never forfeit anything I steal from a friend."

Just the sight of the thing incited a flood of memories for Grace. Those terrible days of Waterloo; the search for her father, and finding Jack Wyndham, Earl of Gracechurch, fighting for his life. The days that followed, when a band of traitors threatened the women who sheltered him. In fact, Diccan Hilliard had helped save them all.

That had been what had opened Grace's eyes to him. Until then, she had seen Diccan as a bit of a lotus-eater. Brilliantly witty, devastatingly sarcastic, and publicly devoted to pleasure, even his vague position in the diplomatic corps no more than an excuse to entertain. But when called to help, he had not only been efficient and discreet, he had stunned Grace with the uncommonly gentle care he'd taken of Jack's desperate wife, Olivia. Even more, for one amazing moment, the man nicknamed "The Perfection" had befriended Grace, the ungainly daughter of an old soldier.

Those days and weeks after Waterloo were mostly a blur to her, especially after she found her father dying on the bloodsoaked cobbles of Château Hougoumont. But one image stood out: the sun slipping through the trees in Brussels' Parc Royale to warm Diccan as he laid his hand on her arm in sympathy, the ruby in his signet ring flashing fire. It had been the first time he had voluntarily touched her; not the obligatory meeting of fingers in greeting or accidental brush in passing. He had seen her in the park that day and made it a point to stop. The most enigmatic man in the *ton* had smiled as he told her what a good man her father had been, and she had realized that those chilly gray eyes could be kind.

She looked again at the flask. It had been Jack's, but Kate had blithely confiscated it for herself. For one mad moment, Grace almost grabbed it from her friend's hand and emptied it.

"Couldn't you see your way to marrying him?" Kate asked.

"No," Grace said. "Nor does he really want me to." Turning to her packing, she picked up the old red Guards jacket she'd worn all across war-torn Spain. She knew she should put it away, just as she should her father's uniforms and her nursing apron. But it comforted her to wear it when she rode. She had a growing suspicion that she was going to be needing that comfort often in the coming days.

Without so much as knocking, Diccan Hilliard pushed open the door and stalked into the room. "We need to talk."

"Are you certain you're still in the diplomatic service?" Kate asked wearily.

He huffed. "I don't have time for diplomacy, Kate. I

have to get to London, and every moment Miss Fairchild dithers, she puts me further behind schedule."

Grace was clutching her jacket so tightly she knew the braid would imprint on her hands. She couldn't bear to face the fury in his eyes. "I fail to understand what's keeping you, Mr. Hilliard," she said, struggling mightily to keep her voice level. "Certainly not me."

Kate once again offered the flask. "Drink, Diccan?"

Flashing Kate an impatient glare, he strode right up to Grace. "You bewilder me, Miss Fairchild," he said, sounding more furious than bewildered. "Surely you know the way of the world."

He was too close. Grace stepped back and bumped into the bed, beset by the sense that he was sucking the air from the room. All she could do was comfort herself with the familiarity of that well-worn jacket in her arms.

"Quite as well as you, sir," she said with what she thought was admirable calm.

"Perhaps it isn't clear to you how much you would profit by this marriage," he said, his voice tinged with condescension.

Immediately her body reacted, heat blossoming deep in her belly and snaking along her limbs. She knew perfectly well what she could gain with this union; it burned her. And yet, it wasn't enough.

"I gain nothing I want, Mr. Hilliard."

He looked stunned. "A proud name."

"I'm perfectly happy with my own."

"A fortune."

"I have one, thank you. An eccentric aunt died and left her estate divided between me and her pet monkey. So you see there are others who value me as they should."

He raised a wry eyebrow. "You would have me."

For the first time, she felt almost like smiling, even as her heart battered against her rib cage. "An almost irresistible temptation, to be sure. And yet, I must refuse."

"You will be ruined!"

She tilted her head, assessing. "Is it ruin to be ignored by a society that has ignored me all along? Or would it be worse to bind myself for eternity to a man who can't even look at me? Have done, sir. I am content. You need not offer yourself up on the altar of matrimony to save me."

He looked oddly irritated by her answer. "And what about me?"

She forced a smile. "After having spent time with you at Lady Kate's salon, I feel certain you feel nothing but relief at my refusal. Enjoy it with my blessings."

Even though her heart shriveled with shame at having to baldly state the truth, Grace returned to her packing, praying no one saw her tremble. Was she a fool? She could have this man in her life. She could bear his children. She could see him every day, teach him to find happiness with her. By all that was holy, she could have him in her bed.

And watch him wander off to every other bed in the realm.

Grace didn't have much. She did have self-respect. She would be betraying herself if she sold herself for such spurious comfort. Even to have the right to have those elegant, clever hands on her.

She knew he still stood behind her: she had never been able to share a room with him without knowing. She could feel it now, a persistent hum along her skin, as if the two were connected by some kind of magnetic force, stronger now that he had touched her. Hoping he would never know how much he affected her, she picked up another gown and folded it, the routine keeping her from running away. Or worse, begging him to ignore her protests and marry her out of hand.

"Miss Fairchild," he warned, his voice lower, harsher. Not the smooth tones of a town buck. The sound, she thought, of a man who had fought duels. "You have no family to protect you."

She stiffened. "As a point of fact, I do."

Kate flashed a quick grin. "She's related to half the great houses of Britain," she said. "Including the Hilliards."

Grace shrugged. "My grandmother was a Cavendish."

"I mean close family. Not third and fourth cousins."

Grace looked up a moment. "There is my Uncle Dawes. He was a general with the Hussars."

That seemed to make an impact. "General Wilfred Dawes? The Hero of Tarrytown?"

She allowed a smile. "Yes, indeed. He'll surely stand by me."

"He'll turn you out on the streets."

"Oh, do go away, Diccan," Kate snapped, waving him off like a pesky gnat. "Somewhere between Brussels and Canterbury, you seem to have lost that silver tongue of yours. Until you can recover it, you won't help matters at all."

"You don't understand, Kate," he insisted, sounding sharp. "I really don't have time to waste."

Kate didn't answer. Grace was terrified that they were communicating silently, undoubtedly concocting some kind of conspiracy against her. It didn't matter. She had too sharp an image of what her life would be like with Diccan to change her mind.

She actually let out a sigh when Diccan opened the door and walked out. She didn't think she could have withstood him much longer.

"It's not you who will be ruined, you know," Kate said to Grace after the door closed.

Grace paused, the silence in the room throbbing in her ears. She couldn't bear to look at her friend. "I'm sorry."

Kate went on, her voice soft. "Twelve years ago," She said, "Diccan defied his father by refusing to take holy orders. Once you meet the bishop, you'll understand what an unparalleled act of courage that was. He immediately cut Diccan off, and he hasn't changed his mind. But Diccan talked his way into any low-level position he could obtain in the Diplomatic Corps. He says it was so he could get away from his parents. I think it was so he could be his own person. And he has. But his career balances upon his good reputation."

Grace's heart was beginning to thud painfully. Somehow her Guards jacket was in her arms again. She clutched it to her chest, as if it could help shore up her defenses. "How good can the reputation be of a man who's been in four duels?" she demanded.

Kate smiled sadly. "Certainly better than that of a man who destroys an innocent woman's name." Briefly her gaze dropped to the bundle of scarlet Grace had clutched to her chest. "You have every right to give Diccan his marching orders," she said gently. "He's been ungracious and rude. But think of this, Grace. Someone made sure he would be found in a compromising position with one of the most honorable young women in Britain. Do you really think Diccan's enemies will let the *ton* believe you were the one to break this off?"

Of course not. Who could think that a plain, uninteresting woman would shy from the chance to marry The Perfection? Certainly no one in Diccan's circle. "I'd happily take an ad out in the *Times* to say that he asked and I refused."

"It would be too late. Letitia Thornton will have already spread her poison. You would both be ruined. I couldn't bear that for you."

"And so I should offer myself up to that vicious pack of jackals, so they can make the rest of my life miserable? I did not do this, Kate. I shouldn't have to pay for it."

"No, you shouldn't. And yet, you know the world as well as I. Someone made sure you, a respected spinster, were Diccan's partner."

Grace almost sneered. "You know perfectly well I wasn't picked because of my work with the wounded. I was picked because of my looks. My leg. Whoever wanted to hurt Diccan made sure he was compromised with the last woman on earth he would—or should—marry. If I accepted, I would only further humiliate him. I can't do that, Kate."

Grace had known Kate through terrible times. She had never seen her look so regretful. "You really couldn't see yourself being married? I don't think it would be long before you could lead your life just as you want. You only need to wait long enough to protect both of your names."

Grace laughed, surprised at how bitter it sounded. "I have spent my entire life waiting to lead my life just the way I want," she said, finally dropping her Guards jacket into her portmanteau. "Every military post, every battle, every whim of the government and the Army and the general took me farther away from the life I wanted. But I went along, because I knew they needed me. Well, Kate, nobody needs me now. I don't want them to. I want to go home to my little estate and raise horses. Alone. I want *finally* to become the Grace Fairchild I've always dreamed of being."

Grace knew Kate couldn't understand. She could never know what it was Grace had hidden away there. What she had waited so long to uncover. And she was almost there. She was almost *there*!

Kate looked at her with palpable regret. "And those negotiations Diccan was talking about that could affect postwar Europe? What if his disgrace destroys those?"

Grace could feel the noose tightening around her throat.

"If there were any other way," Kate said, those luminous green eyes suspiciously bright as she finally stood, "I would carry your luggage out of this inn myself and give those busybodies a piece of my mind. But what happened wasn't an accident. It was very carefully planned. And if you're right, if it is your looks the dastards were considering, then they might have been counting on Diccan to ruin himself by walking away."

"He'd never do that," Grace retorted instinctively.

"No," Kate said, softly. "He wouldn't. But most people don't bother to look past Diccan's facade."

Grace wanted so badly to get far away from this inn, these people, this disaster. To run all the way back to her home at Longbridge, where she would be safe. Where she would never again be tempted by Diccan Hilliard's proposal.

"It's happening so fast," she objected, looking out the window toward freedom. "I need to think."

"What if we simply announced the engagement?" Kate offered. "Work out the rest later."

Grace's heart leapt. She turned to her friend with an anxious smile. "Do you think it would be enough to save Mr. Hilliard's reputation?"

"I'd certainly think it worth a try."

Grace tried not to succumb to hope. "By spring no one will remember who I am. I can cry off, say we don't suit. No blame could ever be attached to him." She turned pleading eyes to Kate. "Surely it would give him enough time to finish his important work."

"The plan certainly has merit. Let's ask Diccan." Kate flashed one of her ineffable grins. "And Grace. After this morning, I think you have the right to call him by his given name."

Grace gave way to a small sigh. "I don't suppose I could simply call him 'nodcock.'"

Kate's laugh was bright as sunshine. "Of course you can. But I recommend 'cork-brained cod's head.' Much more satisfying."

"Good-for-nothing jackstraw."

"Totty-headed twiddlepoop."

Laughing now as well, Grace shook her head. "No. I'm afraid of all the names you could call Diccan Hilliard, twiddlepoop is not one of them."

Kate nodded and picked up another of Grace's dresses. "Let's get this bit finished, then, and we can inform Diccan of your decision."

Grace was more than happy to comply.

"Did your aunt really leave money to a monkey?" Kate asked as the two walked out of Grace's room a few minutes later.

Grace smiled. "Oh, yes. I made the mistake of bringing him home to her from India. I wasn't entirely truthful about the will, though."

"Indeed?"

"It wasn't really equally distributed." She even managed to giggle. "The monkey got more."

They were both laughing as they stepped into the front hallway. One look at the redheaded Hussar striding their way wiped the smile from Grace's face. "*Maldição*," she muttered, stopping.

"Tell me it isn't so, Gracie," the young soldier begged, his handsome face screwed up in distress as he came to a perfect military stop before her. "That rum-touch actually sullied your good name?"

"What are *you* doing here?" she demanded.

"On our way to reassignment. Now, spill, Gracie."

Grace had no idea what to say. Hoping to buy herself a few minutes, she made introductions. "Lady Catherine Seaton, may I present to you Captain Lord Phillip Rawlston? Phillip, this is the Dowager Duchess of Murther."

His expression one of awe, he executed a perfect bow over Kate's hand. "An honor, ma'am," he greeted her, kissing the air above her knuckles. "I've heard of the great service you offered during Waterloo. You cared for several of my comrades in your own home."

Kate waved away his praise. "I cannot say nay to a handsome soldier, Captain, which left me with a surfeit of them littering my floors."

Phillip smiled, his austere face lighting. "Be assured at any rate, Your Grace, that you are now an honorary member of Grace's Grenadiers."

"Grace's Grenadiers?" Kate asked.

A quick blush stained his high cheekbones. "An old club from the Peninsula. The little colonel here kept us all in line. Made sure we were fed and tended, like an orphanage full of scrubby brats. We are her devoted servants." He gave another bow. "And now, yours as well."

"Thank you, Captain. I am honored to accept."

"We were just on our way out," Grace said, trying to take a tentative step by him.

Her escape was short-lived, as Phillip blocked her way. "Not unless I escort you both. I will not have you suffer any more insults."

Grace laid her hand on his silver-braided sleeve. "All is well, Phillip. Mr. Hilliard has asked for my hand in marriage."

"Good," he said with a brisk nod. "Then I'll stay to walk you down the aisle. The other lads will make sure Hilliard is waiting for you."

Grace tried not to panic. Other lads? Just how many Grenadiers could there be in Canterbury? "Oh, no, Phillip. Lady Kate and I are going back to London to plan the wedding."

Young Rawlston stiffened, making all the silver frogging on his blue jacket shimmer in the morning light. "The wedding will be before you leave town," he insisted. "I don't trust Hilliard."

"Don't be silly," Grace objected stiffly. "He is an honorable man."

Phillip laughed. "Much you know."

"He is also Lady Kate's cousin."

The young man immediately dropped another bow. "Apologies, Your Grace. But you know the scapegrace better than I. Not good tactics to let him get too far."

"Phillip!" Grace protested. "I'm engaged to Mr. Hilliard. Isn't that enough for you?"

"No, Gracie. It's not. There's many a slip between cup and lip, my dear. And I don't put it past Hilliard to slip right away before the deed is done. Which is why unless I see you two before the vicar by the time we leave, I'll have to issue him a challenge."

Grace hadn't noticed that they had company, until she heard the two new voices proclaim in unison, "Us, too."

Oh, no. Two unbearably young men in full Guards regalia, one tall, blond, and thin, the other short, even blonder, and elegant, were marching up the hall as if on parade.

"We're just one cannon shy of a military review," Kate mused.

Grace sighed. "Lady Kate Seaton, may I present Ensign William Tyson and Lieutenant Charles Grim-Fisher. They're going to try and intimidate Diccan."

The two bowed in unison.

"He needs to see that we're serious," Phillip said.

"You can be no more serious than I," Grace insisted. "I want you to stop this nonsense."

"Nonsense, Gracie?" Billy Tyson asked, bending his lanky frame to frown on her. "Do you know the man's reputation?"

"I know he's been the victor in four duels," she snapped. "And I don't want to see anyone hurt."

Phillip lifted an auburn eyebrow. "Has he charged the guns at Mont-Saint-Jean?"

"I sincerely doubt Diccan would resort to artillery," Kate offered dryly.

"For me," Grace begged, straightening so they could see she was taller than all three of them. That as grateful as she was for their support, she did not need their protection. "Do not challenge him."

"Course not," Grim-Fisher said with a big grin. "As long as he stands up with you today."

"I know this suggestion is belated," Kate said next to Grace, "but why don't we take this discussion into the parlor?"

Appalled, Grace realized that they had once again drawn an audience of both maids and guests. "Indeed," she said and took hold of Phillip's arm to turn him toward the private parlor.

"I'll just follow along, shall I?" a new voice asked.

Grace knew her goose was cooked when she turned to see that Harry Lidge had joined them. Her favorite Grenadier, he was in his sharp green Rifleman's uniform, a shako under his arm.

"Harry Lidge," Kate growled quietly behind her.

Grace looked around, astonished at the venom in her friend's voice. Harry caught sight of the duchess and gave a bow that was stiff with disdain. "Ah, Duchess. Why am I not surprised to find you at the heart of this little fiasco?"

"Where would you expect me to be, Harry?" Kate drawled. "Waiting for you to start the show?"

"You never waited for anything, my girl."

Grace whirled around on him. "Enough, Harry. She had nothing to do with it."

Harry hadn't taken his eyes off the duchess, who Grace could see trembled with rage. *Good God,* she thought. *Now what?*

"You obviously know each other," she said.

"Quite well," Harry said, his voice cold.

"Obviously not as well as I'd thought," Kate retorted.

Heads in the lobby swung back and forth as if following a game of badminton.

"I think Kate's right," Grace demurred, taking Harry's arm. "Let's take this into the parlor."

Harry immediately opened the door, where Grace suffered another setback. Inside, methodically making his way through a breakfast that would have satisfied a teamster, sat Diccan Hilliard.

"I am always pleased to see the military arrive on the scene," he said, setting down his cutlery, "but I refuse to share my breakfast with that lot behind you."

At the back of the pack, Phillip waited for the interested parties to enter before slamming the door on the curious who would have followed. "A word, Mr. Hilliard," he said, stepping up.

Diccan was already on his feet. Grace couldn't help but notice that he had taken the time to complete his toilette. He looked neat and elegant from his Hessians boots and biscuit leathers to his hunter green jacket and coachman knot. His hair, which she now knew had a tendency to curl wildly first thing in the morning, had been tamed to thick sable waves, and his ice-gray eyes were inscrutable. The perfect town buck.

"It seems you have the advantage of me, Captain," Diccan said, coming to his feet. "Harry I know. Hello, Harry. You part of this sparkling delegation?"

Harry grinned. "Just a concerned observer."

Having no choice, Grace made introductions all around. "Please, won't everyone have coffee? Lady Kate has an idea to solve this dilemma that I believe will suffice."

Diccan gave her a lazy perusal. "Are these gentlemen the Greek chorus in this little farce?"

More than one of Grace's friends growled at the term.

"Please," Grace objected, feeling unutterably weary. "Could we dispose with the clever banter and address this situation with some purpose? These gentlemen are friends who only seek to see my good name protected."

"Which I have already attempted to do," Diccan answered.

Ignoring him, Grace took her seat alongside Kate so the men could follow. Her Grenadiers hemmed Diccan in on both sides, but it was Grace who felt surrounded.

"Put simply," Kate said, reaching over to steal a rasher of Diccan's bacon, "Grace does not wish to be married today." She got another growl from the men, whom she stared into silence. "Why don't Grace and I travel on to London, where she can be seen with Diccan, and I can sponsor a ball to announce the engagement? Give them time to get to know each other before saying their vows."

Grace saw Diccan's features tighten and wished like the devil she could have told him that the engagement would be a sham. But with her Grenadiers glaring at him as if they had personally caught him debauching her, she knew to keep her silence.

"It's the most sensible thing to do," Grace said instead, addressing her friends. "Don't you see? It would give me a bit of time."

"You agree to that," Phillip warned Diccan, getting to his feet, "and you'll meet me at dawn."

Tyson and Grim-Fisher stood as well, grim-faced and silent.

Grace was suddenly on her feet as well. "Oh, sit down," she snapped. "You'll do nothing of the kind. I am not asking for your protection."

"You don't need to, Gracie," Phillip said gently. Phillip, who was three years her junior. "We all pledged it back in Spain. You expect us to betray our word?"

"She does not," Diccan said mildly. "Neither do I. Your actions do you credit."

His words were met with stunned silence. Before Grace

could even protest, he'd risen and taken her by the hand. "Miss Fairchild," he said, sounding as exhausted as she felt. "I know you'd as lief wish me to Jericho. But you can't argue with the inevitable. Or, I might add, with these good friends who only have your best interests at heart. Will you allow me to obtain a special license so we may marry before we leave Canterbury?"

She opened her mouth to tell him no. But she heard the expectant silence. She felt the regard of her friends. She felt smothered by Diccan's clasp. She felt stripped bare before his enigmatic gray eyes. She felt small and insignificant, which should have been amusing, considering she stood six feet in her stockings. Most of all, she felt incapable of what he asked.

He couldn't expect it of her. None of them could. But when she looked around, she saw the grim determination on her Grenadiers' faces. She saw the certainty in Kate's eyes. She saw no emotion at all in Diccan's.

At least she didn't see the disdain she'd expected. If she said no, she could still escape to Longbridge. No one would care. No one would chase her or remember her. She would be no more than that unfortunate antidote who had once run afoul of the renowned rake Diccan Hilliard.

But if she did, Diccan Hilliard would find himself out on the heath at dawn facing these accomplished soldiers. And it wouldn't matter who won. Diccan's future would be destroyed. Her dear Grenadiers could be ruined. And someone, maybe someone she loved, could be killed.

She looked at them all, her own heart shriveling in her chest, hope for her quiet life wavering.

"Answer him, lass," Harry suggested quietly.

"Leave her alone," Kate muttered.

Eileen Dreyer

Grace couldn't face Diccan's reaction to her words. So she closed her eyes. "I would be honored to accept, Mr. Hilliard."

And with those eight words, the dreams that had sustained her since her childhood died.

Chapter 3

For Diccan, the day only got worse. He didn't even get to finish his breakfast before he was ushered from the parlor by a contingent of surly soldiers.

"Send someone to the Old Coaching Inn at Barham," he told Kate on the way by. "Biddle is undoubtedly there, wondering what's become of me. I refuse to be married without aid of my valet."

Diccan thought Kate might have nodded, but his military escort didn't let him wait to find out. In a phalanx, they escorted him out onto St. Dunstan's Street and past the River Stour to where the square spires of the cathedral rose above the jumbled roofs of Canterbury.

Diccan spent the forced march formulating his argument for expediting a special license. He even managed a smile when told that His Grace the Archbishop of Canterbury would be pleased to see Mr. Hilliard.

Smile and eloquence vanished the minute he stepped into his cousin's office. Cousin Charles did, indeed, wait inside for him with a welcome smile. But he didn't wait alone. Seated in one of the archbishop's leather chairs, as if it were a seat on the high court, was the very upright person of the Most Reverend Lord Evelyn Richard Garwood Hilliard, Bishop of Slough.

As etiquette demanded, Diccan first greeted the Archbishop. "Cousin Charles," he said, taking the dignified man's hand. Then he bowed to the archbishop's guest, his diplomatic face hiding his dismay. "Pater. I bid you good day."

"What business could you have with His Grace?" his father demanded, his face folded in its perpetual frown. It occurred to Diccan that he wouldn't recognize the man without it. "Can't you see we are in a meeting?"

"So you must be, to be so far from home," Diccan acknowledged easily. "How is my mother?"

The frown intensified. "Who are these people with you?"

Diccan turned, as if surprised to find himself still flanked by a contingent of soldiers. "Moral support," he said. "They have offered to wait outside for the outcome of our meeting."

"We have indeed," Harry Lidge agreed, herding his little group back into the hallway. "We'll have a seat in the parlor."

"Why?" Diccan's father demanded. "Are you under arrest? What have you done?"

"Nothing that warrants arrest, sir, I assure you." He flashed a wicked grin for his cousin, who was far more understanding than his own father. "At least this time."

Cousin Charles settled back into his chair. "Nonetheless, Diccan, you have made a rather startling appearance. I imagine you would like to explain."

Diccan took his own chair across from the archbishop's

desk. "It seems I need a very special favor from you, Cousin," he began, doing his best to pretend his disapproving parent was not in the room. "A special license. Quickly, I'm afraid."

"Good God!" his father protested, popping up like an outraged matron. "What have you done?"

Diccan brought out his snuffbox and took a pinch. "I believe I have been involved in an attempt to discredit the negotiations in Vienna. I was bringing back some sensitive information. While on the packet boat, it seems I was drugged and shanghaied. I won't bore you with the sordid details, except to say I woke in the bed of a respectable young woman. There is a hue and cry for a speedy marriage."

"I assume that is what the military is present for?" Cousin Charles said with gratifying *sangfroid*.

Diccan gave him a wry smile. "My reputation preceded me."

"Don't dress this up, you ingrate," his father predictably raged. "This is just another chance for you to shame your family. Well, I won't have it. Pay the chit off and move on."

"Evelyn," Cousin Charles chastised quietly.

"I won't have his disgraces bruited about like some sordid nursery rhyme," Diccan's father protested, pointing at his son as if he'd managed to foul the floor. "And I won't be party to having some loose-moraled trollop for a daughter-in-law. He's a Hilliard, by God. He should remember it."

"He happens to be sitting in front of you," Diccan reminded his father in deceptively gentle tones. Suddenly he resented his father using almost the same words he had earlier about an innocent woman. "And the lady I am to wed is Miss Grace Fairchild." His voice dripped ice. "You might know the name."

It was what finally cost Cousin Charles his smile. "Know it? I believe I'm related to her."

"We all are," Diccan informed him with a listless shrug. "So yes, Father, she will be your daughter-in-law. And if I were you, I would be on my knees in gratitude before the Almighty."

"She's a cripple," his father sneered.

And you're an ass, Diccan thought uncharitably. "I'm afraid I cannot have even you speak of my future wife in that manner."

"I'll speak of her as I choose. Your mother and I have tried for ten years to make you see your duty. And *this* is how you answer?"

Again Diccan shrugged, knowing how it irritated his father. "At least I am doing my duty. You win. Can we please move on? My military escort out there call themselves Grace's Grenadiers. They will not be satisfied until they see her married. And Father, before you vent your views on this marriage to them, please remember that they're armed. And that Grace evidently saved each of their lives at least once over the course of the last ten years."

Cousin Charles rang for his secretary. "In that case," he said, suddenly sounding very much the Archbishop of Canterbury, "I believe we have a wedding to arrange."

Lady Kate was standing at the window of Grace's bed-chamber when she saw Diccan and his retinue return. "If I leave you a moment, you won't throw yourself out the window, will you?"

Seated by the fire, Grace smiled. "I'd only succeed in breaking my legs. No fun in that."

"Good girl."

Lifting her gown, Kate skipped downstairs. She had to

see Diccan. She needed him to convince her that everything would be all right. It was Kate's opinion that Grace had already been through too much. Her father had only been dead for two months. Her celebrated connections were all distant, which left her with no real family. Kate decided it was up to her to take on the job.

She was so focused on seeing Diccan, she actually forgot who had accompanied him. She had just reached the front hallway and was making for the front door, when she heard a step behind her.

"So, you're still here," she heard.

The hair lifted on the back of her neck. Her stomach clenched with dread. *Why hadn't she anticipated this?*

"If you wish to say something, Harry," she said, turning to the tall, sandy-haired Rifleman who frowned at her, "say it. Otherwise I'd be happy to pretend we'd never met."

"I would, too," he told her, his sky-blue eyes as cold as midnight. "But it seems we're going to be thrown together, at least for today. Grace has only one chance to come out of this business intact. I'm here to make sure you don't ruin it. The poor girl has been through enough."

Well, if he'd wanted to outrage Kate, he'd done it. Pulling herself to her full height of almost five feet one inch, she gave her childhood friend the most glacial glare in her repertoire. "She has?" she asked. "Really? I didn't know. She must have forgotten to mention it to me during the three months she's lived with me. Especially that day we traveled the twenty-five miles down to Waterloo to bury her father." She tilted her head, the picture of bemusement. "But then, I didn't see you there. I didn't see you the entire time we were in Brussels, or when we came home to London. You can imagine my confusion that you know so intimately what she's been through."

She managed to strike him speechless. His handsomely rugged face went scarlet, and his fierce blue eyes narrowed. Oh, she'd loved those eyes once. Once a very long time ago.

Finally, he snapped off a perfect bow. "Of course Her Grace must be correct in all things."

"How good of you to realize it."

He said not another word, just stalked off, his boots ringing on the hardwood floor. Kate was left breathless and shaking. Damn him. *Damn* him. How could he goad her into bad manners? How did he always succeed in making her feel a failure?

Thank heavens it was Diccan who saw her first, because Kate knew she was red-faced and rigid. He didn't say a word, just slipped his arm through hers and walked her back out the front door.

"You continue to amaze me, brat," he told her, leading her down the narrow cobbled street. "I can't remember ever seeing Harry Lidge that color. And I've seen him atop everything from whores to cavalry horses."

"Shut up, Diccan."

His grin was unabashed. "Didn't he grow up near the Castle?"

She sighed and looked up to where the morning sky beyond the half-timbered houses reminded her of a certain pair of eyes. "His father was squire. He and my father enjoyed playing chess."

Diccan laughed, shaking his head. "A sad want of consequence for a duke. No wonder my father thinks he should have been the heir instead. He says hello, by the way."

Kate swung around, stunned. "Your father? He's here?"

"Oh, yes. Simply seething with righteous indignation.

Delighted to his toes that I have once again proven his low opinion of me."

"He's a sapskull. And he never sent me greetings. He loathes me even more than he does you."

Diccan lifted her hand and kissed it. "We are a pair of reprobates, aren't we?"

Taking a long moment to study Diccan's saturnine features, Kate found herself furious for him. "It's not fair," she said. "To either of you."

"Ah, sweetheart, you know better than that," he said, continuing down the street.

"Yes, I do," she said, matching his easy stride. "Cousin Charles has agreed to marry you?"

"He will officiate at our service himself, this afternoon at four."

She nodded. "I'll arrange a little wedding breakfast." She paused, her focus on the half-timbered houses they passed. "Diccan. About Grace..."

Diccan looked over. "She hasn't bolted, has she?"

"Of course not. If there is one thing Grace has had beaten into her over the years, it is her duty. She certainly wouldn't turn her back on it now. Which brings me to my threat."

Diccan's smile was unbearably sweet. "I'm afraid you'll have to stand in line for that, old dear."

She stopped, bringing her much taller cousin to a halt at the edge of the River Stour. "Grace gives everyone the impression that she's made of iron," Kate said. "She's always the first one to help. The person everyone goes to. But I have a feeling Grace is more fragile than we know. She hasn't even had the time to grieve for her father. I know you better than anyone, Cuz, and I know that as much as you would protest to hear it, you are as honorable as she."

She looked up at him, her favorite person in the world, and she did something inconceivable. She begged. "Promise me you won't hurt her."

Diccan lifted a lazy eyebrow. "You make me sound like a savage."

Kate snorted. "All men are savages, Diccan. You're just more elegant than most. Promise me."

For a moment, she thought he wouldn't answer.

He looked away to where swans floated by on the narrow ribbon of water. "I can't."

Kate would have railed at him, if she just hadn't seen his eyes. Fathomless, icy gray, rimmed in blue, usually as opaque as mirrors. Suddenly, here on a street in Canterbury, she could see uncertainty, dismay, pain. She saw that her cousin, the man the *ton* called the Perfection, was vulnerable as well.

"Can you at least tell me you'll try?" she asked softly.

He sighed and shifted his shoulders, as if the weight of his promise were almost too heavy. "Yes, Katie. I promise I'll try."

Kate lifted up on her toes to kiss his taut cheek. "Then I am satisfied. Just remember. I'm always there for you both."

Giving her hand another kiss, he turned them back toward the inn. "Well, that should keep you busy for the next fifty years or so."

Grace was married with a full military honor guard in Canterbury Cathedral. And not in a side chapel, where she could have at least felt inconspicuous. No. The Most Reverend Charles Manners-Sutton, Archbishop of Canterbury, insisted that his cousin Diccan be married right at the high altar, as if it would help impress on him the gravity of the moment.

And then, as if Grace weren't uncomfortable enough, Diccan's father joined them at the altar. A tall, thin, balding man, he would have disappeared into his rich ecclesiastical robes except for the icy disdain in his eyes—the same glacial gray eyes his son possessed, but infinitely more inhospitable. He stood just behind the archbishop and glared without once blinking.

Diccan seemed to find the whole thing entertaining, his face set in a knowing half-smile. Grace found it overwhelming. The great church was frigid, the stone beneath her slippers unyielding. Clouds had rolled in to obscure the glorious light from the Trinity Chapel windows above the high altar. Candles flickered, but the stone walls rose dim and distant, the archbishop's plummy tones rising into their shadowy recesses like incense.

Even the attendees conspired to unnerve Grace. Diccan sported his customary faultless black and white, with a silver-threaded ivory vest. Pristine to a tee, he had tied his cravat in a perfect *trone d'amour* and secured it with a ruby of obscene size that matched the one that gleamed in his ring.

Bewigged and mitered, the two bishops were arrayed in vestments that shimmered, and Kate wore her best peacock lutestring and Oldenburg bonnet. A contingent of Grace's Grenadiers had gathered in the choir, their uniforms a bouquet of color, each restless shift setting up a clattering of swords and spurs that almost drowned out the archbishop's words.

And Grace? Given only six hours to prepare, and with no modiste available who carried ready-made dresses for an Amazon, Grace stood up in her gray serge traveling dress and bonnet, a moth among the butterflies.

Indeed, they had all come in their uniforms, Grace thought, so they could be easily identified. Her soldiers, her dilettante husband, her notorious friend. The stately bishops and the unwanted bride.

"Repeat after me," the archbishop intoned. "I, Richard William Price Manners Hilliard…"

Grace was sure she should be paying attention. But she couldn't seem to focus on anything but Diccan's cool amusement as he repeated the words that would bind them, as if this were some parlor game. She couldn't drag her eyes away from the unearthly pale gray of his eyes, or feel anything but the warm strength of his hand. She couldn't think of anything but the fact that here on one of the highest, holiest altars in Great Britain, she was making a pact with the devil. By taking these vows, she was committing herself to a life of grief and loneliness and regret.

At least, she thought, she would reap one benefit. Soon Diccan's elegant hands would be on her again. Soon she would be initiated into the mysteries of lovemaking by the greatest master of the age. For the first time in her life, she wouldn't be outside looking in, a scrubby brat with her hands on a high fence. She would be wrapped in the amazing sensations only hinted at that morning.

Diccan would take her, and her life would be different. Suddenly she couldn't quite concentrate on anything else.

"Miss Fairchild," the archbishop said in patient tones.

Trying hard to hide the chills that chased through her, Grace snapped to attention. She looked up to see an expression on the archbishop's face that let her know he was repeating himself.

"I, Grace Georgianna Fairchild," she echoed, her voice dissolving into a tiny white cloud of chilled air, her hand caught in Diccan's surprisingly gentle grip, "take you, Richard William Price Manners Hilliard..."

The next thing she knew, the archbishop was blessing her ring. She had no idea how Diccan had found it, a plain gold band to match his plain gray wife. The archbishop handed Diccan the ring. Diccan deliberately stripped off his gloves and handed them off before accepting it.

When he once again took hold of Grace's hand, she flinched. She couldn't help it. She thought his fingers must hold lightning. She was shocked to the soles of her feet, the hot energy spearing right into her belly. He slid the plain gold band onto her ring finger, and it felt as if he were pouring warmth into her, life, energy. It felt as if the odd magnetism between them had solidified into physical light.

"A wife wouldn't shy at her husband's touch," he murmured, his eyes dark.

"A husband wouldn't speak so to his wife before a priest," she retorted just as quietly.

Suddenly, he went still. Grace looked up to see the words had suddenly registered. *Husband.*

Wife.

Diccan Hilliard was one of the most elegant gentlemen of his age. No one had perfected ennui as well as he. Yet just for a moment, Grace saw the truth register on his face. She saw horror flash in his gray eyes. She saw him try to hide it. She felt it strike her anyway, harder than the lightning from his fingers, colder than the glare from his father. More fatal than a wound from a rusty blade.

Too quickly for anyone else to note his lapse, he regained his patented smile. But not quickly enough for

Grace. If he hadn't had such a firm grip on her, she would have disgraced herself by bolting right down the cathedral aisle. For in that fleeting moment of honesty, she had seen her future.

"For as much as Diccan and Grace have consented together in holy wedlock," the archbishop intoned, his hand over their joined ones.

No! Grace thought wildly. *He'll destroy me.*

"...I pronounce that they be man and wife together, in the name of the Father and of the Son and of the Holy Ghost."

Too late. She saw it in Diccan's eyes. She heard in her own heartbeat, surely the only sound in the stark silence of the cathedral.

"Amen."

Grace wanted to pull away. She wanted to close her eyes, as if it would help her escape the inescapable. She wanted anything but the bleak acknowledgment in her new husband's eyes.

And then from behind her came Harry's voice. "Well, kiss her, you clunch!"

And Diccan, with a wry smile for his audience, bent to kiss her. She knew he hated it. How could he not? But how could he know that it was her first kiss? And oh, it was a kiss a maiden could dream of, gentle and slow and sweet. It was the kiss that sealed Grace's fate, for the warmth of it settled too deeply into her heart for her to ever let it go.

"Well, wife," Diccan whispered against her ear, "shall we greet our loyal supporters?"

She could do naught but nod, so he bowed to the bishops and turned her down the aisle.

"No," she suddenly said, seeing all the steps she would

have to take. They had come in by the side door. Now Diccan pointed her toward the massive doors that had been opened at the far end of the great nave, spilling light along the long, dark aisle. Grace realized she would have to make a painful, lurching progress all the way to the door. "Can't we go back out the side?"

Diccan held more tightly onto her hand. "And disappoint your Grenadiers? I believe they're waiting to honor you."

She looked over to see that the choir was empty. Only Kate and a man Grace suspected to be Diccan's valet occupied the chairs in the presbytery. She wished with all her heart that she could have had all her friends here to support her, Olivia and Lady Bea and Breege and Sean Harper. But Olivia was in Sussex, and Lady Bea was waiting at Kate's home. Even Breege and Sean weren't there, because she had sent them on to Longbridge to prepare it for her.

She wouldn't need it done now, of course. Her new husband would probably tell her that she wouldn't need her home, or a one-legged Irish ex-regimental sergeant and his big, loud wife. And God alone knew what he would think of her cook.

She would have quite enough time to deal with that later. Right now she had to focus on a successful exit. Laying her hand on Diccan's arm, she turned toward the door. She was ungainly, and her knee hurt. She tried to ignore both. Her attention fixed on that great, gaping door four or five miles away, she limped down stairs worn hollow by generations of pilgrims' feet and started down the aisle.

"A smile might be in order," Diccan reminded her as he guided her past the ornately carved choir screen into the soaring nave.

She did her best, even though she knew it looked like

a rictus. She was shivering now, and decided to blame it on the cold. The church seemed to expand around her, the shadows whispering its magnificence, the great west door a mile away. She was sure it must be raining. It seemed only fitting.

And then she and Diccan stepped through the great doors into the clearing afternoon, and she saw where her Grenadiers had gone. They were lined up down the steps, five officers on either side at full attention, Guards and Hussars, Dragoons and Riflemen. The minute they saw her, the order was barked, and they swept up their swords to form an arch. Harry even called for three huzzahs.

Beyond them, a crowd had gathered in the yard, attracted by the ceremony. Grace barely saw them. She saw only her friends, gathered at attention to honor her. She only heard their cheers. Emotion clogged her throat, and she was suddenly afraid she would humiliate herself before them. But they were all smiling. They meant the best for her. So she smiled back. And with every ounce of dignity she could muster, she limped through the arched swords, head high and her hand on Diccan's arm.

"Stand down, men!" she called gaily. "My husband has just declared that no soldier will pay for a drink this day."

The cheer that met her words was full-throated. With another command, they turned with a snap and followed the wedding couple as if on parade.

"Impressive," Diccan said, never looking back.

"Do not," she warned, very serious, "make light of them."

He shot her a look of pure astonishment. "You wrong me, madam. I was just thinking of the kind of person who would warrant such devotion. And wonder at the fact that she is my wife."

It was Grace's turn to look astonished. She turned to her husband, expecting to see that familiar sardonic gleam in his eye. But his his eyes were clear. He lifted her hand and kissed it. Behind them, the men again cheered. Grace didn't know what to do but walk on.

Chapter 4

The wedding breakfast was boisterous and fun. Lady Kate set the tone when she gifted every soldier with a glass of champagne and a kiss. Diccan circled the room as if at a diplomatic reception. The Grenadiers, knowing well how to celebrate, celebrated well.

Grace never moved from the wing chair Diccan had positioned for her between the great brick fireplace and mullioned windows. It was a thoughtful gesture, as if he could tell how much her leg ached and her head spun. Her Grenadiers lined up with hugs, congratulations, and promises of support. She smiled and she sipped her warm champagne and balanced a plate of uneaten food on her lap, battling a growing sense of dislocation, as if she had been dropped into a play and didn't know her next line.

She was completely unprepared to have Diccan slip up behind her and lift the plate from her lap.

"If I might steal my wife, gentlemen," he greeted them. "I'm feeling just the slightest bit jealous of the military right now."

"Don't be daft, man," one of the men objected. "You have the bonniest lass in England."

His smile seemed genuine. "Yes, but I feel I must perform some impossible feat to have her smile on me as she does you all."

Grace knew that he was proffering his *ton* face, but she couldn't help blushing. If only it were true. Allowing Diccan to help her to her feet, she dipped a curtsy to the men she had always considered to be her family and took the arm of the man who now actually claimed that privilege.

"I don't wish to drag you away from the party," he told her, his head bent close enough that she could feel the tantalizing whisper of his breath against her hair. "But I must be in London."

For a moment, Grace stared blankly up at him. Was he leaving her?

"Kate's dresser has packed for you," he went on. "I need you to bid farewell so we can leave."

He spoke as if her acquiescence was a foregone conclusion. She found herself stammering. "But we haven't even seen your father."

His smile was dry. "Oh, he won't be here. He doesn't hold with drinking. Or revelry. Or happiness."

Just then, Lady Kate sidled up, Grace's pelisse and bonnet in hand. "Looks like you managed to winkle her away."

"You knew about this?" Grace demanded, feeling betrayed.

Kate's smile was rueful. "He did tell us he had to go. I offered to have you return to London with me, but I think he's right. You two need to present a united front right now."

Grace sighed. "You're right, of course." The sense of dislocation growing, she accepted her plain gray bonnet. "It was just a surprise."

"I have to collect Bea from home," Kate said. "But the minute we reach London, Diccan has promised that Bea and I can help you look for a house. Bea will be so excited."

Grace couldn't help but smile at the thought of sweet, loyal Lady Bea. Grace was not as certain as Kate, however, that Lady Bea would approve of this sudden marriage.

Grace was tying the ribbons of her bonnet when a sharp voice stopped her cold.

"Where are you going?"

She turned to see Phillip striding over to her.

Diccan took gentle hold of her elbow. "I'm taking my wife back to London." he said.

"Tonight?" Phillip demanded, drawing attention. "Don't be ridiculous. It's already gone six."

"Tonight," Diccan repeated. "I have business there that cannot wait."

"Business."

"With the government."

Phillip crossed his arms and planted his feet, a living barrier. "This marriage needs to be consummated."

By the abrupt hush around her, Grace knew that the entire room had heard him. She felt her stomach go hollow. "What?"

Diccan let go of her long enough to grab the young Hussar by the arm and drag him into a side parlor. The occupants, a brace of Guards who had been throwing dice, took one look at the expression on Diccan's face and fled. Her own heart skidding around in shock, Grace followed with

Kate and shut the door, just in time to hear Diccan berate young Phillip.

"If your aim is to humiliate my wife," he said, his voice dripping with disdain, "you're doing a bang-up job."

But Phillip wouldn't back down. "You know what I mean. What good does it do if you're allowed to set the marriage aside? Give me your word."

"I'm standing right here," Grace reminded them both, through the sudden constriction in her throat. "And while I sincerely appreciate your help, Phillip, this is no longer your concern."

He swung on her, and suddenly she realized that even after his years on campaign, he really was still a very young man. "I promised to protect you, Gracie. He might not want to bed you, but he must, or the marriage could be overturned."

Grace literally lost her breath. She knew it was probably true. But to have it stated so baldly stripped her pride bare. She felt all her insecurities gather in her chest like sharp-taloned birds.

"You have my word," Diccan said abruptly. "The minute I have concluded the pressing business I have, I will gladly bed my wife."

Another duty to be performed, Grace heard in her head.

"My, you two certainly know how to make a woman feel attractive," Lady Kate drawled, her eyes cold. "I'm certainly glad you aren't courting *me*."

No one was courting her either, Grace wanted to remind her.

"This is too important," Phillip insisted. "I don't trust him."

Feeling oddly superfluous, Grace sighed. "He gave his word," she said, laying a hand on Phillip's arm. "You cannot ask more. You should be happy for me." And then, because there was no other way to end the argument, she perjured her soul. "*I am.*"

Still, Phillip glowered at Diccan. "She has friends, Hilliard."

Diccan delivered a perfect, courtly bow. "And a husband."

Grace felt Phillip's hand tense, as if he would strike Diccan down. Lady Kate must have noticed too. "Oh, good," she said, blithely taking his arm and turning him to the door. "That's settled. Now, Captain, let's celebrate with a bit of that smuggled champagne. I vow I have a prodigious thirst."

And out the door they went, leaving Grace behind with the bitter truth lingering in her mouth.

She was still staring after Phillip when, out of the corner of her eye, she saw Diccan rub at his temple. "I'm sorry, Grace," he said quietly. "That was quite uncalled for."

She shook her head as if it didn't matter. "I'm the one who should apologize. I think you've had your word questioned one too many times today."

"Blast my word!" he snapped, and she thought she could actually see pain in his ghostly gray eyes. "It's you who've been insulted beyond bearing. And I can't even stay to mitigate the insult."

Grace couldn't believe it. He was sincere. That alone could have made her fall in love with him. "Thank you," she said, lifting up on her toes to brush a kiss against the temple he had been rubbing. "But we have to go." Pulling on her gloves, she smiled. "Besides, there is a sizable pile of coin on the floor waiting for those soldiers to return. Let us give them a chance to finish the game."

She turned so she couldn't see the expression on his face and swept out the door. And that, she thought, would be that.

She couldn't have been more wrong. Whether it was to counter the insult Diccan felt had been dealt her, or to dissipate the gossip, he left the parlor with a far different expression than when he'd entered. Once again laying her hand on his arm, he smiled at her, as if the two of them had a secret. Grace smiled back, hoping he couldn't tell how much that simple gesture meant to her.

No matter how quickly he had to leave, he strolled through the room as if he wanted to do nothing more than spend time with his wife. He even laughed when he caught sight of the gamblers, who paced in agitation outside the door. "Not a ha'penny is lost, gentlemen," he assured them.

The soldiers promptly slipped back into the parlor and their game.

"I've arranged a post-chaise," Diccan was saying, his head bent to Grace's. "I hope it will be comfortable enough."

She found it even easier to smile. "My dear Mr. Hilliard," she said. "I am accustomed to traveling by bad horses and worse feet. I can bear anything as along as I am sheltered from the weather."

He shook his head, evidently amused. "I must accustom myself to having an intrepid wife. And you must accustom yourself to using my given name. It would look passing strange if you addressed me with the same familiarity as the postman."

She nodded. "That is just what Kate said." She couldn't help but grin. "Although she had a few rather more colorful suggestions as to what else I could call you."

Diccan chuckled. "I'm sure she did."

They had made their good-byes to the crowd and had just reached the door, when Diccan brought her to a halt. She looked up to see a smile in his eyes.

"Well, kiss her, you clunch," he murmured, echoing the command they'd heard in church.

Grace felt as mesmerized as a rabbit sighting a hawk. His touch froze her and his eyes warmed her. She thought her heart would tumble right out of her chest. Lord, what would happen when he touched all of her?

"Yes... ahem, um, thank you."

This kiss was different than the last. Longer, deeper, slower. Grace felt Diccan's fingers against her face and caught the faint scent of tobacco and sandlewood soap. She tasted champagne on his lips and thought, distractedly, how soft they were. How clever, nipping and seducing and testing her own lips, as if staking claim. There was a spark, a glow, a delicious fire that seemed to live in his lips, and it swept through her, winding through her chest and belly. She felt as if her feet were melting to the floor.

He must have felt it too, she thought, her heart tumbling in her chest. How could he not, when it flared so hot?

And then, Diccan stepped back. Grace opened her eyes to see him straightening, his expression perfectly composed. She was still caught in a web of pleasure, humbled by the gift of his kiss, and he'd felt nothing. A lesson she should take to heart, she imagined, the glow abruptly dying into ashes.

It was only then she heard the cheer go up around them. Diccan blinked, as if pulled abruptly back from somewhere, and delivered a smile of surprised delight to the crowd. "Well, now I know that I have something over most of His Majesty's soldiers," he said, sounding triumphant.

"None of you lot were smart enough to snatch my Grace up before I did."

Ignoring the howls of protest, he gave them all an insouciant tip of the hat, wrapped his arm around her, and led her out the door. The evening air was cool against Grace's heated cheeks. The light was softening, so that even the crowded, noisy inn yard seemed more elegant. The postchaise stood a bit off to the side, the door open, a square, balding man in livery standing beside it.

Hours in a coach with Diccan, she thought, her heart once again skittering around. What would he do? What would she say?

Nothing, evidently. Diccan was accepting saddlebags from a groom, and a saddled horse stood in the shadows. "By the time you reach London," Diccan said, leading her over to the carriage, "I will have arranged everything to your satisfaction. Try and rest if you can."

"You're riding?" she asked stupidly, looking up at the lowering sky. "It's going to rain."

His smile was lazy. "Which is why I'm riding. You know how bad the Dover Road is. I can't afford to get stuck in the mud. Biddle will be with you, and he knows the road better than the highwaymen. He'll make sure you're comfortable."

As long as they weren't stuck in the mud in the middle of nowhere, she thought, resentment thickening her chest. With a quick peck on her cheek, Diccan swung into the saddle and rode off, leaving her to stand alone in the inn yard, staring after him in stunned silence.

Chapter 5

Bastún," she hissed.

"That doesn't sound complimentary at all," Lady Kate murmured as she came up alongside her.

Grace sighed. "Your cousin could use some manners, Kate."

Lady Kate laughed. "Oh, no, my dear. Manners he has. It's courage he seems to lack. It's nice to see that my handsome Diccan is as subject to a normal husband's fidgets as anyone else."

"Hmmph."

With a lilting laugh, Kate reached up to sweep Grace into an enthusiastic hug. "Oh, but I'm going to miss you, my little colonel. Promise you'll still recognize me when you're a proper matron."

Grace hugged back, suddenly feeling as if she were losing everything familiar. "I won't be far," she said. "In fact, I have a feeling I'll be by quite frequently, asking for advice on marriage."

"Good Heavens, don't expect *me* to know." Wiping her

eyes, Kate pushed Grace into the coach. "Now, get along. The sooner you go, the sooner you get there."

The door shut, and Grace gave her friend a final wave. It was when the coach lurched into motion that she realized she wasn't alone in the carriage. Diccan's valet sat opposite her.

"Oh. Hello," she greeted the mournful little man. "Biddle, isn't it?"

He regally bowed his head. "Indeed. You have no maid, madame?"

"No. Lady Kate offered hers, but I don't usually use one."

His opinion obvious in the pursing of his lips, he kept his silence. He looked very much like a hound, all jowls and sad eyes, even his ears pendulous. Most amazingly, though, Grace realized that his feet didn't reach the floor. He was probably no taller than Lady Kate.

Grace spent a fruitless hour trying to get to know the dour little man. But no matter what conversational gambit she used, Biddle answered with no more than monosyllables. And she didn't have the courage to ask the question she really wanted answered; how in the world the diminutive valet managed to get a jacket over the six-foot two-inch Diccan Hilliard's shoulders. Did he use a stool? Stand on a hatbox? Bounce on Diccan's bed?

She must have given herself away, because without looking away from the view out his window, Biddle spoke. "I jump, madame. Like a bunny rabbit."

Grace was startled into a laugh. "Thank you, Biddle. I'm impressed. Mr. Hilliard's coats never show a crease."

Without looking at her, he rewarded her with a small nod.

"You don't approve of Mr. Hilliard's marriage to me, do you?" Grace said.

He kept his gaze out the window. "I don't approve of anything my master does, madame."

She blinked. "Then why valet for him?"

Finally she got a reaction, and it was pure shock. "Not do for the first gentleman of fashion? What can you be thinking?"

So, Grace thought, as Biddle turned back to the scenery. No cozy conversation about Diccan or valeting or the diplomatic life. What else could she do to keep herself occupied for the next fifty miles?

She should sleep, but the ride was too uncomfortable. The Dover Road was living up to its reputation, knocking them about like tenpins. And the rain would surely come, making it worse. Every other time she'd been in a coach since her return to England, she'd spent her time watching the passing landscape. It had been a revelation to her. In her life she had lived in India, in Egypt and America, and the West Indies. She'd been to Ceylon and Turkey, Italy and Spain, and had enjoyed every exotic sight and sound. But she'd never really had a chance to enjoy her own country.

She consumed it like food for a starving soul. Green and hilly and peaceful, it was a land of neat farms and whitewashed thatched villages, quaint half-timbered inns and solid stone castles, all arranged as if by a master gardener to emphasize the beauty of the land. She swore it was the tidiest country she'd ever seen.

But this wasn't the time to simply watch out the window. If she did, she would be left with too much time to think about what had just happened. About what *would* happen.

Suddenly she could feel Diccan's last kiss again. How

surprisingly soft his lips had been, how smooth his cheek and calloused his thumb. How she'd almost been overcome by the need to lean into him, mesmerized by that hard, fascinating body against hers, the heat that radiated off his skin.

Didn't he know how he tortured her by delaying the consummation of their marriage? Didn't he know how frightened she was? How anxious? How hopeful? She certainly knew the mechanics of what would happen. She knew how to describe it in Hindi, Portuguese, French, Latin, Spanish, Urdu, and Cree. She knew what went where. After all her time tending soldiers, she certainly knew what the *what* looked like. She even knew what men called it when they didn't know a woman was listening.

Cock. Prick. Dick. Tallywacker. Bagpipe. Bayonet. John Thomas. Some men were even contrary enough to name the thing, as if they could hold discourse with it. Her favorite had been a sergeant in her father's company who, not knowing she could hear him, admitted that he called his Mr. Pickle. How, she'd thought at the time, was a girl supposed to take it all seriously?

· She had taken it seriously when she'd seen Diccan. When she'd seen *his* bayonet upright and rigid and throbbing. She'd always thought that those phalluses on the temple walls had been exaggerations to make a point, like ages in the Bible stories or the strength of Irish heroes. After seeing Diccan, she had to admit that she'd been wrong. Just the thought of it sent another shower of chills spilling down her spine. Her fingers itched to touch it, to learn if it was as mystifying as it looked. As soft *and* hard.

Quite without her permission, her body began to heat up. She battled a sudden need to move, as if it could ease the ache that had blossomed at the juncture of her legs. Her skin felt stretched too tight, and her breasts, her small, practical breasts, tingled and ached. She was restless and impatient and humming with tension. She tasted an unfamiliar flavor on her tongue and recognized it as anticipation.

She knew how to ease all those feelings, of course. Her friend Ghitika had showed her one day in India. Laughing at the incomprehensible British reserve, the Indian girl had used the temple art as a tutorial in how to ease...tension. Not, though, Grace thought, in a moving carriage with a witness.

Abruptly she shifted in her seat. This wouldn't do at all. She needed occupation.

Lists. She needed to make lists. It had always been her job to make sure her father had a comfortable bivouac. She would simply consider this another move. A new *haveli* in India. A farmhouse in Portugal. The difference would be that she wouldn't be planning for her father, but for her husband. Her husband, who had surprisingly calloused hands and a mouth that wove magic. Her husband, who opened a door she'd long since thought closed: the chance for a home. A family. A life no longer lived at the periphery, but deep in the core of life.

Staff, she thought, almost desperately rummaging in her reticule for her ubiquitous notebook and pencil. She would need staff. Breege and Sean, of course. Sean had always been there, first as her father's batman, and then, after losing his leg to a stray cannonball, their man-of-all-work and Grace's good friend. Breege had come along later. But it been Breege who had taught Grace the basics of good housekeeping. As for the rest of the staff at Longbridge, they could stay there, where they were safe and comfortable. She couldn't imagine Radhika and Banwar liking London.

So. Staff. She assumed water and safety were taken care of. That left shelter, provisions, comfort. Furniture. Wardrobe. She underlined *wardrobe*, and then added *night rail*. Surely she should get a new one. Diccan wouldn't want to see her old nightgown. It was worn, plain, and practical.

Diccan wouldn't really want to see her, either, though. She hadn't forgotten the distress on his face when he'd seen her naked. She shuddered. Sometime in the next few days, Diccan Hilliard would make love to her. But if she kept thinking of that, she would never survive the hours until then. So she purposefully bent over her paper. She had lists to make.

He was going to have to have sex with Grace Fairchild. No, Diccan thought. *He was going to have to have sex with his wife.* Christ, his head hurt.

He should be planning his meeting with Marcus Drake. He was late, he'd been compromised, and he failed to keep Evenham alive. He was going to need every diplomatic skill in his kit to impress the government with how dire the situation was. Instead, he loped along on the indefatigable Gadzooks and thought about the woman he'd just left. The life he'd just stumbled into. The chore he'd been set. He shuddered just thinking about it.

If she only weren't so bloody nice. He liked her. But it was inevitable that he'd end up hurting her. Oh, he'd get the job done. After all, he'd been without his mistress for two weeks now, which was not a good state of affairs for him, as evidenced by the fact that he'd woken up hard as a board this morning. More than morning-piss hard. More than, there's-a-body-with-breasts-in-my-bed hard.

Even wrapped around that long, painfully thin frame, he'd been blue-balled-I-need-my-sword-in-that-sheath-this-minute hard. Pump-my-eyes-blind hard.

And that last kiss. He had meant to give Grace a chaste salute, just to counter her Grenadier's insult. But sometime between the offer and actually putting his mouth to hers, something had changed. The kiss had softened, slowed, and he'd felt as if he were sipping a cool, sweet lemonade. A surprise he blamed on the waning effects of the laudanum. A memory that made his cock stir, even now.

But even if he managed the thing so well that Grace took out a notice in the *Times*, it would still be a travesty. He shouldn't be married. He'd be a disaster at it. And Grace...

He shook his head, actually distressed for her. The idea of her becoming part of his life was ludicrous. He was a diplomat. A diplomat's wife had to be a social animal: clever and witty and cool. Grace was honest and ungainly and shy. She wore her gray dresses like a uniform and her hair so ruthlessly tied down it seemed invisible.

If only she'd been a real redhead. If she'd been blessed with a redhead's fire, or even his cousin Kate's outrageous self-confidence. Kate could navigate the waters of a diplomatic function like a frigate in full sail. Grace Fairchild would stand out like a frog in a fishbowl.

Beneath Diccan, Gadzooks snorted and shook his head, as if chastising him. Diccan knew he was being cruel. But it was beginning to rain, the road was getting sloppy, and he was wet and cold. And he'd just had a too-clear image of what life would be with Grace Fairchild at his side.

Maybe the best thing he could do for them both was to bed her, secure her reputation, and then find a way to live apart. She certainly didn't need him. He could return to his post in France and leave her to set up house in London. Her and the monkey. It would be enough, wouldn't it?

Excellent. Problem solved. Suddenly beset by an odd frustration, he kicked Gadzooks into a canter. He didn't have the time for this. He had more urgent problems to deal with. He had to redeem poor Evenham by warning the government that the Surgeon was going after Wellington. And then, because he had made a vow, he was going to have sex with his wife.

The rain came in buckets. It disrupted traffic on the Dover Road and filled the coaching inns to overflowing. It rained all night and into the next morning, the clouds low and thick and unending. When Grace climbed back into the coach after a cold, damp night, she was armed with the travelogue she'd been reading when she and Kate had stopped at Canterbury.

Usually she was a quiet reader. This time, it seemed, she muttered.

"Is there something wrong, madame?" Biddle asked.

Startled at the sound of his voice, Grace looked up to find the morning advanced. She had been reading for hours. "No, thank you, Biddle. I simply find this account of Egypt to be quite incorrect."

"Have you been to Egypt, ma'am?"

"Yes. But I don't think this Mr. Pettigrew has. He has quite misplaced the Valley of the Kings."

"Then why read it?"

She smiled. "So I know what not to do when I write my own travelogue."

Biddle frowned. "Write . . . oh, I see. You are jesting."

She couldn't help twitting the valet a bit. "Of course not. What would have been the point of all that travel, if not to share it? I believe that it is the one disappointment I have in Hester Stanhope. She has so far left her adventures unrecorded."

He actually sputtered. "Lady...Stanhope?" he squeaked, his opinion of the woman who had taken to living among Bedouin obvious. "You don't know her."

"But I do." She tilted her head. "Does that put me beyond the pale?"

He opened his mouth, but couldn't seem to find words.

"My association with Hester should greatly increase my notoriety," she said, her eyes brightening with mischief. "Why, it might even lead to a speaking tour, don't you think?"

Biddle pursed his lips. "Mr. Hilliard would never allow it. Much too dangerous for a lady."

Grace's laugh was soft. "More dangerous than fighting off French *voltigeurs* or Algerian pirates? My, I must get to know my country better. Or purchase another pistol."

He blanched. "Another...you joke again, madame."

"About my pistol? Oh, no. I never go anywhere without one."

"Unthinkable. You must rely on the very excellent protection Mr. Hilliard gives you."

Grace almost asked the obvious, how he could think that a hired postilion would be concerned enough to lay down his life for a stranger, but one look at the valet's ashen features told her he would not appreciate it in the least. Let him rest in pleasant ignorance. She would keep her pistol primed.

A moment later she wondered if she had wished trouble

down on them. The going had been slow, but as they struggled up a steep hill, the mud seemed to take complete hold
of the wheels. *Slow* became *stop*. The driver yelled. Horses
whinnied. The coach began to slide backwards.

Grace grabbed the strap and braced herself. Biddle
moaned. Grace could feel the horses strain against their
collars. The coach lurched. The coachman yelled, and she
heard the crack of a whip. They suffered no disaster, however. They were simply stuck.

Retying her bonnet against the wind, Grace pulled her
pistol from her reticule and slipped it into her pocket. Then
she kicked open the door and stepped out into the quag-
mire, her boots sinking to the ankle. "Mr. Wilson! Stop!"
she called up, blinking against the blowing rain. "Pull off
our luggage. We'll get out and you can try again."

The coachman's astonished visage peered down from
beneath a dripping slouch hat. "Happen y'r right, missy.
We'm stuck solid." Tying off his reins, he jumped down.

"Come along now, Mr. Biddle," Grace urged, leaning
inside the open door as the postilion trudged back to the
luggage compartment.

"But the mud..." the valet protested in dying tones.

"Will be all that much worse, the longer we stay. Believe
me. Without a bit of help we'll be here all day. Do you think
there is a farmhouse nearby, Mr. Wilson?"

"The Browns'll answer," the postilion, a weedy little
man, lisped through missing teeth. "They well know the
perils of Shooter's Hill."

"Shooter's Hill?" the valet echoed faintly. "Oh...no."

Grace looked an inquiry at the driver. His smile was
too satisfied by half. "Highwaymen. Love this neck o' the
woods. But don't fret. Han't seen one in weeks."

It was like an announcement. Suddenly there were hoofbeats and the report of a gun.

"Stand and deliver!"

Grace sighed. Of course. Without checking Biddle, she edged toward the high coach box, where she hoped Mr. Wilson kept a gun. Everybody else was frozen. Two horsemen could be heard approaching the far side of the bright yellow coach. Maybe she could surprise them.

Another shot rang out and Biddle screamed. The postilion crumpled. Grace saw that he'd drawn a gun of his own. Her heart sped up, but she also felt the unnatural calm settle over her that always accompanied crises.

"Get out of the coach, you!" a rough voice yelled. Horses stomped impatiently on the other side of the coach. Grace didn't think she'd been seen. ·

"Open the door and climb out, Biddle," Grace urged quietly. "And give them what they want."

Biddle's moan sounded like a woman in childbirth. But the more distracted the robbers were, the better Grace's chances. Stealthily, she reached up and slid her hand along the floor of the coachman's perch. Yes, right where she'd hoped. A blunderbuss, tucked beneath a rain cover. She just hoped the powder was dry.

Pulling it toward her, she stealthily cocked the hammer and peeked past the crosstrees to assess the situation. There were two highwaymen, both large and masked, both with guns. Except that the one man had already discharged his. Off his horse now, he was making for the back of the coach.

"Appreciate y'r savin' us time," he was saying to Mr. Wilson, who had already pulled Grace's bag down. "Now, open it. And you inside the carriage. Ain't gonna tell you agin. Climb out."

Grace could hear Biddle wheezing, but he pushed the door open on the far side and slowly climbed out. For that brief moment, both men were distracted. Grace pulled the blunderbuss from the high perch. She aimed it at the man on the horse. Suddenly the man by the rear yelled.

"There's another one!"

Grace leaped to the side, firing as she fell. She landed on her bad leg with a grating thud. The horses whinnied and shied. She heard a curse from the mounted highwayman and cursed herself. She'd only winged him. She pulled her pistol from her pocket and rolled beneath the coach. The robber was off his horse. His gun was up. He was shouting at his friend to finish off Mr. Wilson.

"Move, Biddle!" she yelled.

Biddle promptly fell on his face. The armed robber saw Grace and swung around. He fired. She fired. He fell. Biddle screamed again. The horses reared, almost succeeding in getting the carriage unstuck with Grace still under it. At the back, the other two men were still fighting. Grace pulled herself out of the thick mud and ran over to retrieve the gun from the fallen postilion. Then she shoved it against the other robber's head before he could strangle Mr. Wilson.

"I think you should stop now," she said, her voice preternaturally calm.

"Gor," he breathed, letting go of Mr. Wilson's throat.

"Crikey," Mr. Wilson echoed, coughing as he jumped to his feet.

Grace didn't move. "See how the postilion is, please, Mr. Wilson. Biddle, make sure that thief is dead." She nudged her robber with her pistol. "And please, sir, don't underestimate me because I'm a woman. I have shot far better men than you."

"Jeb's alive!" Mr. Wilson called. "But 'e's bleedin' bad. The other robber's got a new hole right between 'is eyes. Blimey."

"Get Jeb into the coach," she said. "Then hold this man while Biddle ties him."

The minute Jeb was stretched across the seat, Grace handed off her gun. Then, retrieving the portmanteau with her medical supplies in it, she limped toward the coach, already reaching for a petticoat to rip. "Biddle," she said, quietly. "Once the robber is secured, it might be best for you to go to the farm. We'll definitely be needing help now."

For the next forty minutes Grace directed the scene, using her voice to calm the frantic victims and unsettled horses. When the farmer arrived with his cart, they were able to transport Jeb, who would have a devil of a head when he woke, and then managed to get the poor horses unstuck from the mud. Grace was all set to follow the farmer, if for nothing more than the chance to clean the mud from her hands and face, when Biddle let out another screech.

"Your arm! Oh, madame, you're bleeding!"

And Grace made her first mistake of the afternoon. She looked to where Biddle was pointing. "Oh," she said bemusedly. "It seems I've been shot as well."

And then without even a moan to warn them, she pitched face-first onto the grass.

Chapter 6

Diccan Hilliard was not used to being kept waiting. He had been back in London since five that morning. He had delivered his information to his contacts and been told to wait on their answer. He'd returned to the Albany to organize his eventual move, and checked into the Pulteney Hotel. He had even stopped by to see Barbara Schroeder, lingering over cognac and comfort as the two of them negotiated a change in their arrangement in response to his marriage. He bathed, slept, and ate, expecting his wife by noon. It was now almost eight, and there was no sign of the post-chaise.

His initial instinct was to wonder if she'd bolted. It was an unfair thought, but he wasn't sure he'd blame her if she did. God knows there were moments he still felt like bolting.

There was a scratching on the door, and he jumped to answer. It was only one of the hotel's maids, who bobbed nervously. "Since madame has not arrived yet, sir, shall we hold your supper?"

He'd even arranged a *dîner à deux* to make up for his

abrupt departure the night before. "Yes. I'm sure they'll be along in a bit. They've probably been caught on that beastly road."

The plump young girl was just bowing when Diccan caught the sounds of tumult in the lobby below. A new guest, from the sounds of raised voices. He was following the maid out into the hall, just to check, when he heard the petulant tones of his valet.

"Madame, you have suffered a gunshot wound. For the love of Heaven, let us help!"

Diccan was down the stairs in an instant.

"Gunshot?" he demanded, not even noticing the raised eyebrows of other guests at the sight of the most elegant man in London raising his voice like a staff sergeant. "What the hell is going on?"

And there was Grace, her drawn features pulled into an expression of strained patience as she leaned on the shoulder of the coachman he'd hired. Wet and bedraggled, with mud from head to foot, she looked as if she'd taken a header at a hunt. Following behind like a nervous acolyte, Biddle looked only marginally better.

"I tried to tell them, Diccan," Grace said, her voice sounding perilously thin. "I suffered no injury. I'm limping because I landed on my bad leg when I fell. The gunshot wound is nothing."

"Nothing?" Biddle retorted in high dudgeon. "Madame, you fainted dead away in the middle of a public road!"

"I told you," she said, as if this were a very old refrain, "I faint at the sight of blood."

Barely regaining his legendary control, Diccan raised a wry eyebrow. "Fainted? A woman who nursed her way through the Peninsula?"

She looked up and he saw the strain in her eyes. "*My* blood," she corrected. "A sad failing, but there it is. I can be up to my knees in gore, but one glimpse of a trickle of my own blood, and over I go."

So, his Boadicea had a weakness. Diccan found himself caught off guard by the sudden urge to grin. One look at her expression kept him sober, though. That and the crowd that had gathered to hear all the lurid details. He'd had his fill of interested crowds the last two days.

Instinctively knowing that his calm would help her keep her composure, he strolled over to take her from the coachman. "A sad failing, madame. Thankfully, Biddle is more valiant. He faints for nothing less than grass stains on my breeches."

There. He got her to smile. Everyone else looked like panicked animals. He understood. He'd felt a jolt of something himself when he spotted the thick white wrap around Grace's upper arm.

"You will, of course, have a physician called," he told a loitering bellman in bored tones. "My wife will also need a bath and a maid, since hers was unable to make the trip, which undoubtedly explains her resemblance to a mudlark." Oddly compelled, he tucked a loose hunk of hair back from her mud-streaked cheek. "And you, wife," he said, turning her to the stairs, "will explain the gunshot."

She nodded, taking slow breaths, as if to stanch pain.

"Highwaymen," Biddle gasped, his hands fluttering like birds, as he trotted after them.

"It was a lucky shot," Grace said, sounding disgusted as she limped along. "I'd just gotten hold of the blunderbuss—"

Diccan stopped. "Blunderbuss? You thought to wield a *gun*?"

Behind him the coachman laughed. "Wield a gun, is it? She didn't just wield it. She shot the lights outa one cove and brought t'other to pissin' his pants."

"She saved our lives," Biddle insisted, and Diccan was stunned to see an abject light of devotion in his valet's eyes. Good Lord, what was the world coming to?

"We'll discuss this upstairs, Grace," he said grimly, "if you can climb the stairs."

She huffed impatiently. "My leg is sore, sir. Not missing."

"And your arm?"

She flashed him a wry grin. "Is sore, too." Then, turning back, she smiled for the coachman who stood dripping, hat in hand, in the middle of the Pulteney's elegant lobby. "Mr. Wilson, thank you. I know my husband will be happy to compensate you for your help."

The big man blushed like a boy, his slouch hat twisted into rope in his hands. "Nay, my lady. 'Tis you I owe. Hope everything works out. An' you can call on Tom Wilson you ever needs anything."

"Biddle," Diccan called.

Pulling out a purse, the valet followed the man out the front door. Once they had gone, Grace turned for the stairs. "Thank you. He's a nice man. I think I frightened him."

Diccan shook his head. "You terrify me, madame."

Her features scrunched up. "Do you suppose you could cease calling me 'madame' in that perfectly odious way? I thought we had agreed on *Diccan* and *Grace*. Although," she admitted with a chagrined smile at her destroyed attire, "I admit I don't bear any resemblance to that particular appellation at the moment."

He made it a point to look her up and down. "A mistress of euphemism, I see. Think nothing of it. I'm sure you'll feel more the thing after scraping an inch or two of Kentish mud off of you."

Wearily trodding up the steps, she nodded and sighed. "I hate to disoblige you, but I believe this might set back our plans a day."

"You mean fulfilling Captain Rawlston's kind suggestion?"

Grace blushed, and Diccan thought how unfortunate it looked. "That was no suggestion, sir. That was blackmail."

"Ah, wife," Diccan said, as he guided her up the wide staircase, "What is life without a bit of blackmail? Certainly the *ton* would go quiet. For myself, I believe I will survive the wait. As long as it is not too long. A man has his needs."

The truly confusing bit of that speech was that he meant it. How could he be relieved at his reprieve and disappointed at the same time?

The message reached White's at ten o'clock that night. The Surgeon had escaped prison. The most feared mercenary agent on the Continent had been incarcerated in Newgate, awaiting trial for murder and espionage. According to their best reports, he had vanished sometime the night before, leaving behind two guards with slashed throats and the words *au revoir* carved into their foreheads.

Reading the report over his Chambertin brandy in White's reading room, Marcus Belden, Earl Drake, cursed quietly and pithily. As if they needed anything else right now. "Do you know why we're just hearing about this?" he asked the man who had just delivered the news.

A score years older than Drake, Baron Thirsk was a moderate man, so nondescript that people were hard-pressed to describe him after he'd gone. He occupied the other leather armchair, swirling his own snifter of cognac. "The officials at Newgate are not anxious to broadcast their peccadilloes."

Drake lifted an eyebrow. "A working girl caught servicing the warden is a peccadillo. The escape of one of the most dangerous men in Europe is a disaster. Especially now. You heard about Hilliard's *contretemps*?"

Thirsk shrugged and sipped his own brandy. "Got caught sniffing up the skirts of the most notorious virgin in the realm, I hear."

Drake was shaking his head. "He was set up. He told us that Evenham warned him about it."

"Convenient for Hilliard to notify us after the fact, don't you think?"

Drake lifted the report in his hands. "He also warned us about the Surgeon."

"Too late to do us any good."

"You think he made all this up, even the plot to blackmail him? For Heaven's sake, man, Hilliard brought back enough information to take down the under-secretary of the Treasury. Do you think the opposition would not go to any lengths to stop him?"

Thirsk sniffed. "He was married, not waylaid and murdered. Besides, no one but a very select few know about Hilliard's activities. You're certain Hilliard didn't just make up his accusations to deflect attention from his mishandling of the boy?"

"I've never known Hilliard to lie. Not in these matters."

"I've also never known an Evenham to commit treason."

Out in the foyer, the door opened to a fresh blast of rain-driven wind as two of the club members left. Drake watched the comings and goings out beyond their little corner of isolation and considered the missteps that had dogged them. He thought of what kind of access it would have taken to arrange them. Any of the men walking into this door could be involved.

"Sidmouth thinks this is all misdirection," Thirsk said, staring into his drink. "Revolutionaries throwing smoke in our faces. By the time we realize this is all a diversion, they'll have pulled down Parliament. God knows they've made a start, what with the blasted Luddites destroying looms and the rabble rioting over the Corn Laws." Drake tried to answer, but Thirsk was well into a familiar rant. "And then we have those returning soldiers wandering the streets, just looking for trouble. I say we look to them for our traitors."

Drake shook his head. "I'm sure the Home Secretary would like to think so. But both Hilliard and Jack Gracechurch came across the same information, and it didn't point toward disaffected soldiers. It implicated men of property." He huffed impatiently. "*British Lions*. Imbecilic name for a group of traitors."

Thirsk glared. "You're talking about men in the peerage, the highest levels of government. What could possibly make them want to imperil their own positions?"

Drake fortified himself with a drink. "You read the report. They want the throne. Don't forget. Evenham told Hilliard that the group actually helped Napoleon, thinking he'd give it to them."

He shuddered at the cost of that betrayal. Wellington might have held sway at Waterloo, but the loss of life had been catastrophic.

"Hilliard *says* Evenham told him," Thirsk reminded him tersely.

Drake looked over to see the suspicion that never quite left those nondescript brown eyes. "I believe him. After what I saw with Gracechurch, I have no question that powerful forces are behind this, and that they mean to take over this government. And we don't have much time to stop it."

He saw that Thirsk's first instinct was to protest. Instead, the older man shook his head and looked around, reassuring himself with the normalcy of the club. "Well, until we can better assess Hilliard's information, we're at an impasse."

Drake had to agree. "If only his best source hadn't moved on."

"The mistress?"

Drake nodded. "Madame Ferrar. I know how hard he tried to convince her to follow him here."

Thirsk chuckled. "After seeing her, I understand why. Quite a charmer. Seems Hilliard is losing his touch. Did Schroeder at least come home with him?"

"Babs? You know he wouldn't move without her. As for Madame Ferrar, I've sent another gentleman over to see if he can make any headway with her. In the meantime, it might behoove us all to keep our information close to the vest. After all, the Surgeon's capture was a state secret. Whoever is involved had enough power to set him free."

That didn't sit well with Thirsk. "Look to your own little group, Drake. Remember. We still don't know everything Gracechurch did in France."

A remarkably indifferent comment about a man who had sacrificed four years of his life and his memory in the service of the Crown.

"Jack doesn't know, either," he said. "He's still at his estate in Sussex, recovering from Waterloo."

And helping his wife recover from injuries she suffered

at the hands of the Surgeon, Drake thought. Injuries Drake blamed himself for. It was he who'd sent Jack to France to infiltrate the government, and he who had been responsible for Jack's and Olivia's safety after Hillard got them out of Belgium. And even after all that, Gracechurch had still only remembered some of the information he'd risked his life for and then lost to an exploding shell on the battlefield.

"We need to warn him," Drake said, setting down his drink.

"A courier will be sent."

"No. I'll go down. As you said, the members of Drake's Rakes are my responsibility. Maybe I'll take Diccan with me."

"No." Thirsk peered into his cognac. "I'd rather not put Hilliard near any delicate information right now."

Drake frowned. "Then you *don't* believe him."

"Let us say simply that Hilliard is not in good odor with Whitehall at the moment. The Fairchild chit's great-uncle is old General Dawes, and he's raising a ruckus. Almost as much of a ruckus as we'll get from Viscount Bentley when he hears about Evenham's suicide, I imagine. The boy was his only heir."

Drake wanted to argue. Whitehall was playing right into the enemy's hands by marginalizing Diccan Hilliard. But Drake had no real power there. So he would carry out his own mission and do his best to ease Diccan's way. At least with the government.

Thirsk was already getting to his feet.

"If another attempt is made on Hilliard, should he allow himself to be compromised?" Drake asked, following.

Thirsk paused, his gaze unfocused. "I hate to take the chance."

"They *will* go after him again. If he doesn't seem to cooperate, he'll be putting others in danger. Evenham said the Lions would follow blackmail with threats to those Hilliard loves."

Thirsk snorted. "Well, they'll catch cold at that. There isn't a soul in England who doesn't know that his family cut him off."

"What about his wife?"

"Difficult to threaten a man with danger to a woman he never wanted in the first place. Hell, they'd be doing him a favor."

"To let the Surgeon have her?"

Thirsk actually paled. "The threat will come first. When we hear it, we can act. For now, there is a rather troublesome German princeling we're depending on for port rights, who is anxious to sample Newmarket. Hilliard will be the perfect nanny."

Drake shook his head. "He won't thank you."

For the first time, Thirsk smiled. "Oh, I think he might. You forget. I've seen his wife."

It was the definition of ambivalence. The last thing Diccan wanted was to ride herd on a petulant royal. He would enjoy the horse racing, but not with the prince along. There were only so many times a man could hear improbable sexual exploits in German before he committed homicide.

On the other hand, he was guiltily relieved that he had an excuse to put off his wedding night. He did not like to be confused, and Grace Fairchild confused him. He had worried over her yesterday. He'd been relieved when she'd turned up safe, and delighted when she'd shown such unexpected vulnerability. He'd even been surprised by a stab of fear at the sight of that bandage.

It hadn't changed his mind about their future, though. In fact, it had cemented it. He didn't have the time for that kind of worry in his life right now. He didn't want to always wonder about her. Hell, he didn't even want to bed her.

Yes, he had suffered brief episodes of arousal around her. But it hadn't happened again. He couldn't imagine that it would. Not for a woman who dressed like a nanny, fought like a hussar, and couldn't be coy if her life depended on it.

Two weeks ago, Diccan had had his hands full of Minette Ferrar's magnificent, creamy breasts. How in God's name could Grace Fairchild compare? Wasn't it a better idea to wait until he could feel more enthusiastic about the whole thing?

It didn't help that Biddle kept sniffing as he packed. Diccan knew Biddle disapproved of him. No one had a repertoire of resigned sighs and disapproving sniffs quite like Biddle. These particular sniffs, though, were beginning to sound like a certain defensiveness for Diccan's wife, who had taken the news of his leaving with quiet acceptance.

"If you are so unhappy, Biddle," Diccan said, shrugging into his drab surtout, "I can certainly give you a good recommendation."

"I'm sure that won't be necessary, sir." Sniff.

Diccan took his beaver hat from Biddle's hand. "While you're sighing away, don't forget to keep alert. The Surgeon is on the loose, and I know how you hate surprises."

"You have not mentioned his escape to Mrs. Hilliard?"

Diccan shrugged. "I'd hate for her to worry. She will be watched. Besides, she's already played her part in this farce."

Biddle's answer was another sniff. Diccan gave up and

left. He was going to ride. The sun had finally come out, making it unnecessary for him to try and squeeze into a coach with his corpulent young charge. His mind on the next few days, he walked out of the Pulteney's front door only to come to an abrupt halt. His wife was there before him, cooing and stroking Gadzooks' nose. The horse, usually as foul-tempered as Biddle, was whuffling into her hair like a besotted suitor.

"God's teeth, madame," Diccan drawled, pulling on his gloves. "What are you about with that reprehensible beast?"

She looked up, and he saw that her face was glowing. Oddly, his chest tightened at the sight. "I believe I've just recently seen this fine gentleman," she said. "Is he yours?"

The groom who held the horse's reins struggled to keep a straight face. Diccan laughed out loud. Gadzooks was surely the ugliest horse in Christendom. A raw-boned, jug-headed, dirty roan, he was the laughingstock of the diplomatic corps.

"Methinks you have spent too much time with soldiers, if you call this cart horse a gentleman," he protested dryly. "Gadzooks' phiz has been known to frighten children and startle crows."

Grace laughed, a pleasant, throaty chuckle that did uncomfortable things to his cock. "Gadzooks?" she echoed, leaning her forehead against the horse's. "But how perfect! For he would be a complete surprise on a race-course, wouldn't he? He has the heart of a champion, this one. I can see why he means so much to you"—her smile widened—"in spite of his common looks."

Diccan swore his own heart stumbled. "This piece of dog meat?" he retorted, feeling oddly disconcerted. No one had ever seen Gadzooks' potential on meeting him. No one realized what a loyal and ferocious friend he was. "How could you think that?"

Her eyes sparkled. "I am quite well acquainted with unbeautiful horses, Diccan. After all, Wellington's Copenhagen would put this gentleman's unpretty looks to shame, and he has the greatest heart I've ever known. Your Gadzooks has that same look about him. Tell me you mean to breed him. I have the perfect mare for him."

Diccan blinked. His heart beat faster. "You?"

She nodded. "A person who has grown up around the cavalry must know her cattle. My Epona would complement Gadzooks to a tee."

"Don't tell me. She's swayback and blind in one eye."

Grace chuckled again, and damn it if Diccan didn't smile back. "She's a solid black beauty my father acquired for me in Spain for my birthday. Do you know the Andalusian?"

Diccan's heart all but stopped beating. Did he know Andalusians? He had lusted for one for years, with their great arched necks and thick chests and intelligent eyes. "But they aren't allowed out of Spain without approval from the king."

Her smile grew impish. "My father saved much of the royal herd from conscription into the French Dragoons. The king was grateful."

An Andalusian. Diccan's mouth was watering. Gadzooks would die of happiness.

He shook himself to attention. "We'll see, madame. We'll see. Right now I must focus on keeping an overweight toddler from unintentionally mucking up an important treaty."

He thought she would step back and fade away. Instead she walked right up to him and straightened his coat, then gave it a pat. "I'll be busy while you're gone. I am in need of an abigail, a wardrobe, and a list of available houses to tour."

For a dangerous moment, he fought the urge to stay where he was. What was it about her domestic send-off that made him want to step into her arms?

Before he could be tempted, he stepped away with a brisk nod. "I have seen to your abigail. She arrives today. As for the rest, wait for Kate. I trust her taste. She has an unerring eye, you know."

Grace went very still. Diccan felt suddenly unsettled by her silence. "You know," she said quietly, "there is a difference between preference and necessity."

He found himself blinking again. "Pardon?"

But she was already walking into the hotel. "Have a safe trip, Diccan."

Left standing on the street, Diccan was still struggling with his incomprehensible new wife, when Gadzooks gave him a shove. "Yes. All right. Let's be off." Diccan glared at his horse. "If you don't mind my riding you, that is."

Gadzooks snorted, and all Diccan could think was how much it sounded like one of Biddle's sniffs.

It might have been easier on Grace if Diccan hadn't disappeared almost as soon as she arrived. Or if he hadn't looked quite so relieved to be leaving. She had been nervous enough the night she'd reached the Pulteney. Even the ministrations of a first-class staff hadn't soothed her, although they had eased her physical aches. The doctor had pronounced her injury minor, and the maids had helped her get about three pounds of mud out of her hair. She'd slept the clock around and awakened ready to face her husband's attention, only to find him on the verge of leaving again.

She knew her duty. She tried to see him off with every appearance of sympathy and support, only to have him insult her taste, her judgment, and her capabilities. Disappointment inevitably darkened to anger, and she spent the first day questioning his parentage in six languages.

And then, to make matters worse, her abigail appeared. When Grace opened the door on Barbara Schroeder, her fragile confidence crumbled even further. The woman looked no more like an abigail than Grace did a diplomat's wife. Comfortably past her immediate youth, the abigail was curvy and blond and blessed with immense blue eyes that seemed to always be laughing.

"My husband hired you?" was all Grace could think to ask.

"Oh, yes, ma'am," Schroeder answered with a hint of a German accent. "My Dieter, you know, was a sergeant in the 20th Foot, lost at Vittoria. But no one wishes to hire a woman with my...accent."

That seemed to amuse her, too. Grace was not nearly as sanguine. She didn't really believe that it was the woman's accent that kept her out of the homes of jealous women. So if Schroeder's story was true, it might mean that Diccan had done a laudable thing. If not...

This new to her marriage, Grace chose to think the best of him. She let Schroeder help prepare her for bed, another new experience she wasn't sure she liked. But she wasn't sure whether that was because she suddenly had an abigail, or because it was *this* abigail.

On the second day, Grace woke to a profound feeling of loss. Nestled amid acres of cotton and goosedown in a warm room in a lovely hotel, she wondered why. Certainly she'd suffered quite an upheaval, but she had become quite adept at handling upheavals in her life. Yes, she missed her father, but in truth, she had been preparing for his loss from the moment she realized what soldiering meant. Her old life was gone, but that, too, was inevitable. Her every need was met, her feet were dry, and her belly full. What could be wrong?

And then she heard it. Silence.

It surrounded her, cushioned her from the rest of the world. Far below her window, the city clattered along, cart wheels and mongers' cries and horse hooves, but the noise sounded almost unreal. It was the silence that was real, throbbing in her ears like a living thing.

She was reminded of those moments before battle: the minutes when lives balanced on the edge of a frightening future. When every man and woman paused between preparation and action, waiting for the storm to break over their heads.

At least then she'd known what to do. She'd been able to recognize the threats and respond. She didn't even have that anymore. Even after living with Lady Kate, she had no idea what to expect from this new world, and she hated it. Worse, she hated the feeling that she was unprepared. That no matter how hard she tried, or well she performed, it would never be enough. And how could it be? Even her abigail seemed to fit into this world better than she.

She wished her mother were here to advise her. To reassure her. Even though she knew her mother would not have been of any help, whether she'd still been there or not.

Huffing in impatience, Grace threw back the covers and climbed out of bed. She had no patience with people who wasted time wallowing in their own misery. It was much better to take action.

It would be easy. She had spent her life being what people expected: daughter, friend, nurse, housekeeper, guard, birth and burial attendant. She would just have to learn what it was Diccan needed, and be that. She had no idea how to earn Diccan's love. But she was very good at being needed.

Slipping on her wrap, she limped over to her portable desk and pulled out the lists she'd begun in the coach. It was time to get on with things.

By the end of the afternoon, she had drawn money from her account at Hoare's Bank and arranged for a list of available properties. She gathered information on furniture warehouses and galleries and dependable workmen. She set up an account at the Parker Employment Agency. then, bolstered by these small successes, she donned her best gray bonnet and pelisse and set forth to do battle with Lady Kate's modiste, the great Madame Fanchon.

"You are Her Grace of Murther's companion, you, yes?" the elegant woman asked in suspicious tones when Grace requested a full wardrobe.

"I am her friend," Grace answered, matching her height against the little Frenchwoman's disdain. "I am also now Mrs. Diccan Hilliard."

The modiste let go a surprised bark of laughter and turned to leave.

"You may, of course, wait to ask the Duchess of Murther when she returns to town next week," Grace said quietly to the modiste's stiff back, "but I doubt the delay would please Mr. Hilliard. He was the one to suggest you to me, after all."

He hadn't, of course. But if there was anything Grace had learned after years of foraging, it was how to brass it out. At least she succeeded in bringing Madame to a halt.

"Even I know there is a marked difference between dressing as a soldier's daughter and a diplomat's wife," Grace continued. "I was hoping I could count on you to advise me on the best way to go about it."

Madame turned back around, an eyebrow raised in disbelief. Grace paid no attention. Her gaze had been caught by a bolt of fabric near the top of Madame's shelves. Hot orange, the color of a desert sunset. So brilliant it would look like a jungle flower in a room of pansies. She could almost taste the tartness of it on her tongue. And next to it, a sharp aqua, the shifting shade of the Caribbean Sea. Searing, whimsical colors that made her think of adventure and joy.

"Not," Madame said in tones of supreme disdain, "those."

Grace smiled placidly down at her. "Of course not." And pushed aside her hopes yet again.

It took two full days of fittings and consultations, but the order was placed for everything from chemises to court dress, all in bronzes and greens and blues. All uniforms of respectability, appropriate for a proper *ton* matron who had never been tempted by the exotic hues of India.

Grace was on her way out after the last fitting when Madame caught her by the arm.

"I do have something special," the Frenchwoman murmured, leaning in as if imparting a state secret. "Something to entice the oh-so-particular gentleman. The color of a moonless night, soft against your pale skin. The most delicate aerophane gauze silk, all illusion and seduction."

With no more than those words, Grace could see it.

She could see herself wearing it, this scrap of indecency Madame was proposing. She could almost feel the slither of silk against her skin as Diccan removed it, exposing her to cooling air and heated touches. She knew she was blushing, because Madame was smiling.

"A wife needs every advantage, yes? Especially with such as Monsieur Hilliard."

Out of the corner of her eye, Grace caught sight of a small, secret smile upon her abigail's face. And she knew there was only one answer.

"Yes," Grace said. "She does."

Chapter 7

Grace tried to keep busy for the next two days, but it wasn't enough. Once Madame put the image of that negligee in her mind, it wouldn't go. It followed her to Hatchards and the milliner's. It followed her down the aisles of the Army Hospital where she volunteered. It followed her to sleep. Whatever she did, she kept hearing that whisper of promise in Madame Fanchon's voice. She kept thinking of the magic in a simple swath of fabric. She found herself hoping for a miracle.

By the time Diccan finally returned, she was wound up tighter than a top.

"Well, Grace," he greeted her, shrugging out of his surtout as he swept into the sitting room. "I see you're still waiting for Kate."

Grace bristled. "It will be nice to see her, but I have been agreeably busy."

He lifted an eyebrow as he took in her gray Indian mull dress.

She kept her calm. "Even for so accomplished a modiste

as Madame Fanchon, it takes more than two days to sew a wardrobe for Boadicea, sir."

She was rewarded with a grin. Quickly, though, it turned into a small frown Grace could read like the *Times*. *Oh, Lord, what kind of disaster would the plain Grace make of her wardrobe?*

"I was just about to have a sherry before dinner," she said, turning away. "Will you join me?"

He nodded and took the chair across from her.

They shared a sherry and then dinner, tucked away in their parlor above the city, both firmly in control of their manners, their conversation prescribed by custom; weather and acquaintances and Diccan's recent trip. And finally, over fruit and nuts, his position in the diplomatic corps.

"You're posted in France right now?" Grace asked, nibbling on an apricot.

"I hope so. We'll see what happens when the dust settles from our little drama."

She set her fork down. "Then you've suffered for it?"

"No. Just cautioned, I'm sure. Nothing to worry about. Now, finish your dinner."

"Will you stay in diplomatic service?" she asked instead. "Seeing Gadzooks, I thought you might be interested in breeding."

"Gadzooks is more friend than investment," he said after a moment. "I wouldn't mind getting foals off of him, but I don't mean to put him to stud. He'd go distracted."

Thinking of the rangy roan, she smiled. "A terrible way to suffer."

She actually got a bit of a smile out of Diccan. It was the closest they came to addressing their future, as if they could indefinitely put off the inevitable. As if they were tablemates at a *ton* dinner, barely acquainted and buoyed only by social convention. Perhaps it was only she, Grace thought, who felt suspended in midair. Diccan might not even care that he'd made a vow to bed her as quickly as possible. That unless he was called out on an emergency, this would be the night it would happen.

Grace cared. Every time she caught a whiff of his sandalwood soap. When he reached up to run his hand through his hair and she caught sight of the ruby, a dark drop of blood on his hand. When he laughed, his voice a honeyed rumble that seemed to resonate in her belly.

She thought she was doing an excellent job of keeping her nerves under control, but she didn't seem to have as much sway over her body. Each time Diccan's hand came near her, her skin began to hum. Every time he smiled, as impersonal as it was, she fought the urge to smile back. To preen, even knowing it would be as pointless as it was ridiculous. He betrayed no intention to bed her, but her body hoped. Anticipation built right alongside uncertainty. She was beset by a shivery, anxious feeling that made her feel alien and alive. And all the while, Diccan acted as if he were doing no more than babysitting another minor royal.

It wasn't until the covers were removed from dinner that he finally betrayed himself. He had been sharing his impressions of the St. Petersburg court, when the door closed behind the last waiter. Suddenly faltering to a stop, Diccan looked around, as if surprised to see an empty table between them. He stood and straightened his coat, his movements jerky.

His distraction actually made Grace feel a bit better. "Diccan?"

Pouring a glass of brandy from the drinks cart, he

walked over to the window and looked out. Left behind at the table, Grace had no idea how to progress. *He* was the one who was the expert here. He should have the easy words, the quick smile that would signal the next stage of the evening.

"I believe your abigail will be waiting for you," he said without turning.

Grace was surprised by a flash of irritation. Annoying man. "She was really married to a soldier?" she couldn't help but ask.

Diccan gave her a fleeting look. "She was. You won't find fault with her."

She already had. But Grace had no idea how to express the vague unease Schroeder gave her. So, without another word, she gained her feet and disappeared into her bedroom to find Schroeder there, as promised, a particularly smug smile on her face. Grace was about to chastise her when she saw why. Laid out on the high tester bed was the most outrageous length of material she had ever seen.

Definitely the color of deep night, a blue so dark that only movement betrayed the real color, the sheen of a blackbird's wing.

Grace realized she was shivering. "*Sapristi,*" she breathed almost reverently.

"If this does not turn his eye," Schroeder promised, "he is already dead."

Grace couldn't quite get in a breath. She was supposed to *wear* this thing? She would be all but naked, and that certainly wasn't something she was used to. In fact, in all her years following the drum, she'd become quite the expert at remaining covered.

But this was for her husband. Her husband who didn't

really want to bed her. Maybe this could help change his mind.

"Well," she said with a abrupt breath, "let's get on with it, shall we?"

Barbara's grin grew bright, and the two women went about taking down Grace's thick hair and divesting her of her plain clothes before slipping Madame's creation over her head. And then, feeling peculiarly hot in a cool room, Grace sent Barbara off and waited for her husband.

And waited.

She refused to climb into the bed like a sacrificial virgin. Instead she curled up in a wheat damask wing-back chair and laid the Egyptian travelogue on her lap, as if preparing to read. She looked out the window. She flipped pages. She counted chimes from the sitting room clock. She counted them four times, and still Diccan did not come.

She was mortified. She was terrified. She was swamped by memories of the last time they'd shared a bed. The seductive warmth of his body, the maddening path of his hands. The regret that she had stopped him before he'd reached that hot, hungry place between her legs. The place that now anticipated Diccan's return, as if attuned to his scent. His attention. His command. He hadn't even opened the door, and she was already wet for him.

When she heard the clock strike midnight, she decided she'd had enough. Diccan might be uncomfortable with this, but he could be no more uncomfortable than she. Did he think she would be pleased to be treated like the only thing worse than a fat prince?

Before she had the chance to change her mind, she climbed to her feet and opened the door. The fire in the sitting room had burned low, and the table was cleared away.

Diccan was nowhere to be seen. Grace looked toward the closed door of his bedroom and cursed. He'd better be in there. If he'd escaped completely, she would follow him with a fire poker.

Hand to her suddenly tumultuous chest, she padded across the rug in her bare feet and tapped on his door. She heard a mumble. She decided to take that as permission and entered.

The sight of Diccan almost sent her running. He was slouched in a wing chair to the right of the dying fire, his bare legs protruding from an elegant black banyan. It seemed to be the only thing he was wearing, if the sight of his naked chest was any indication. Hair curled at his throat and arrowed south, bisecting muscle and rib. His legs were strong and long, the hair on them oddly fascinating. But what Grace couldn't take her eyes from were his feet. They were so long and elegant and sensual.

How could feet be sensual? But they were. Grace's midsection tightened even more. Her womb seemed to melt. She knew what was under that robe, and she wanted it. She wanted this disheveled, delicious libertine to introduce her to the mysteries of love.

It took the sound of a cognac snifter thudding to the carpet for her to realize that he was gaping at her. "What the bloody hell do you think you're doing?" he rasped, his eyes stark.

She was trembling and terrified, wanting to do nothing more than hide. Which meant she became very calm. "Why, I was looking for my husband," she said quietly. "I had been under the impression I would be seeing him tonight."

He ignored her insinuation. "Did Kate lend that to you?"

He was looking at her gown. She was surprised that she

didn't blush all the way to her feet. "Don't be silly. I would have destroyed anything of Kate's trying to get it over my shoulders. Do you like it?"

More indiscretion. A lady never mentioned body parts. But then, a lady never forced her way into a gentleman's room. Even if that gentleman was her husband.

As if in a trance, Diccan rose to his feet. "Where did you get all that hair?"

Grace blinked. "It's been there," she managed, breathless at his approach. "I didn't think tonight would be a good night for a braid."

He was shaking his head, as if he didn't believe her. Or as if he didn't believe what he was seeing. "Come here."

Grace fought mingled surges of frustration and delight at the growl in his voice. But the last thing she needed now was to limp across the room. "I did," she said. "It's your turn."

She couldn't believe she was being this forward. But she could smell the brandy on him, and saw that the decanter at his elbow was almost gone. The dastard had needed to get half seas over just to face her. And then, apparently he'd drunk so much he'd completely forgotten to do it at all.

He tilted his head, and Grace thought he looked faintly satanic. His gray eyes seemed to catch the light and incandesce. His face, not handsome, but virile with its broad forehead and strong chin, seemed drawn in bold slashes. His body, so beautifully proportioned, so blessedly taller than hers, exuded power. Her knees were weakening and he hadn't even touched her.

"You are a surprise, Grace," he said, reaching out to run a finger down the length of her arm and setting off showers of chills. "I didn't think you'd be this cool about things."

She shivered. She could feel heat radiating off him. Please, she almost begged out loud. *Please*.

And then, just as she'd hoped, he caught his hands in the hem of her gown and began to lift it. For a second she panicked. Wasn't he supposed to snuff the lights? Weren't they supposed to be in bed? How could she hide when she was standing in the middle of the floor?

She kept silent. One protest and he'd be out the door. And she simply couldn't bear that.

"You have small feet," he murmured, and sounded surprised.

"For my size, yes," she answered, paralyzed at the sensation of air swirling up beneath the lifting negligee. Praying that the shadows would mask the shriveling of her bad leg.

Diccan didn't seem to hear her. "I think I'm going to enjoy having a tall partner."

And then he looked down, and everything changed. He froze, his hands still caught in the shimmery material, just above her pelvis. She was holding her breath. She wanted to squeeze her eyes shut. She could feel how wet she was, and it frightened her. Not as much as his sudden laugh.

Her eyes flew open to see a cynical smile on his face. He was staring right at the juncture of her legs, as if he could see the betraying moisture that wet her curls. He was shaking his head.

"Christ, am I a fool," he muttered, his voice harsh. "I can't believe I didn't see this the other morning. I might have at least had *some* enjoyment out of that little fiasco."

She curled her hands to keep from yanking her night-dress away and covering herself. "Pardon?"

He was paying no attention. Closing his eyes, he shook his head, which seemed to overset his balance, because he wove a bit. "And here I thought you had been the victim," he said, sounding disgusted. "Well, that'll teach me."

Grace was totally lost. "What do you mean?"

His laugh grew harsh. "Good trick, Grace. How in the devil did you manage to hold on to your nickname?" He looked up at her, his eyes suddenly hard. "Notorious virgin indeed. Notorious, all right. But exactly how long has it been since you've been a virgin?"

As he spoke, he was backing her inexorably toward the bed. Grace opened her mouth to protest, but her mind refused to function. What was he talking about?

"How did you know?" he asked. "Did Kate tell you? No. I never told her. Not exactly the kind of thing you tell your favorite cousin. One of your military friends, then. How convenient."

"I don't..."

Without warning, he grabbed her around the waist and tossed her up onto the mattress. She sprawled back, stunned into immobility.

"Diccan?"

"I'll have to thank him, whoever he is. And, of course, I thank you for going to the trouble. I was so afraid I couldn't do this. But now that you've been so obliging as to accommodate my favorite little fetish, I might as well enjoy it." He was sliding his hands up her legs. "Where'd you learn it? A nautch girl? Somebody in a port town? Tell them thank you."

Grace tried to scoot away from him, her heart now speeding. "Diccan, I don't understand."

"Of course you do, my dear," he said, and wrapped iron hands around her legs. "But it's all right. I never waste a red thatch, especially since you went to all the trouble to dye it."

She opened her mouth to protest, but he didn't notice. Dragging her to the very edge of the bed, he bent over her. Over the juncture of her legs. She couldn't breathe. She couldn't think. He was putting his face right up against her wet, red curls, and she would swear he inhaled. *Inhaled* as if sampling perfume, and his face was only inches from...

Oh, sweet Jesus.

Desperately she tried to clamp her legs closed. What was he *doing*? It was all happening so fast. Her brain was screaming, but her body, her hungry body, went pliant.

"Open for me," he growled, "there's a good girl. Let me see the prize that lovely flame hides."

She felt his hands wrap around her knees, and she sobbed. She saw him smile down at her, at the nest of hair between her legs, and she finally, finally blushed. She was crimson with it. Hot and cold and crawling with shame. With outrage. With anticipation.

And then he opened his mouth and placed it right against her. Pleasure speared her. She bucked almost off the bed. The cool wash of his breath stroked that exquisitely sensitive flesh and sent lightning shearing through her. His tongue unleashed unimagined needs. She grabbed fistfuls of linen and fought the urge to cry out. Dear God, what was he doing? He was sipping at her, licking her, nibbling...ah, *oh*! His teeth, scraping against that most sensitive bud, tormenting her. Touching her only there. Only there and on her knees, her body still draped in midnight, her hair spread across the bed.

She closed her eyes, unable to watch. Her heart stumbled, and her lungs seized. She should move. She should kick him. Run. Scream.

Oh, she'd scream. She was terrified she would wail like

a banshee. He was chuckling against her, humming. She could feel the sleek line of his cheek against her thigh and thought he must have shaved. She felt the unbearably sweet pressure of his lips, urging on the pleasure that swelled in her; hot pleasure. Sharp pleasure. Sensations she had never felt before, never even imagined.

"And you're already wet," he said, almost conversationally, and laid a finger against the petal he had just been licking.

She jerked away again. It was too much. "Stop, please . . . *please . . .*"

He must not have heard her. He slid his finger into her, deep into her, and pulled it out. In again, out. She felt her body bow to it, speaking its own language of want. She felt his finger return, and then, his mouth. She felt lightning sweep through her, fire, maelstrom, and it terrified her all over again. And still she couldn't move away.

All the sensations that careened through her began to center. Her eyes opened to see his tousled black hair just above the flare of her red nether hair. She thought it the most unbearably erotic thing she'd ever seen. Until he stroked down with his finger and up with his tongue.

His tongue. Sweet Jesus, his tongue. It was an instrument of torture; dipping, lapping, circling, compelling her flesh to swell, her body to glow, to burn, to begin to disintegrate.

"Oh, yes, my little doxy, come apart for me," he murmured against her. "Scream."

He kept murmuring endearments, salacious suggestions, harsh orders. "Don't play about," he ordered, his breath unbearably delicious against her wet flesh, "I don't have the patience. You're about to be fucked and fucked good, and you know you can't wait."

She couldn't. That was what was so humiliating. She wanted him to do all those things he said. She wanted him to do them *now*. She wanted her body to cooperate. She just didn't know how. She was panting, whimpering, tossing her head, as if she could somehow locate whatever it was she sought. What she desperately wanted. The lightning collected, slithering up her legs, down her arms, through her chest. It centered and it swirled, and beyond her, Diccan's voice became indistinct. Her body, her willing, wanting body, stilled, as if pausing for a battle to come.

And suddenly, from one heartbeat to the next, she disintegrated into light. Into sound and color and music. She could hear Diccan laughing, and knew it was because she screamed. Screamed because she couldn't contain it, not something this huge, something this violent. Her body convulsed around his hands. Her heart hammered against her ribs, her eyes filled with tears of amazement. And then, before she could collect herself, he drove that huge, hard cock into her. And she screamed again.

He went abruptly still. Grace, fighting the sudden, searing pain, looked up to see an look of utter shock on Diccan's face. He looked appalled, and suddenly Grace wanted to curl up into a small ball and disappear. He pulled out of her as if she'd just betrayed him.

"Goddamn it!" He yelled. "You're a virgin!"

Chapter 8

He felt like the biggest idiot alive. He felt like a ravisher. He felt...

He felt like a fool standing there with his cock still rock-hard and Grace looking confused and hurt and as debauched as a whore. He had hurt her. But how the hell was he supposed to know she was a virgin? Nobody who knew how to dye a thatch like that could be an innocent. Not that color, the color of sin and seduction. His favorite color of fire and lust. Red. No, not red. Flame. Sunburst. Sex.

Yes, that was it. Sex red. And he'd fallen for it.

"You're a *virgin*," he repeated, as if that would help cement the fact in his still-reeling brain.

"Not anymore," she said with unbelievable calm, not moving from where she lay on his bed, her hair spread out across the pillows, that obscene excuse for a gown hastily tugged back down.

It was another reason he'd thought her experienced. She'd sashayed into his room in a scrap of silk that would have made Minette blush, and then challenged him like the most experienced of courtesans, not once pulling away. Oh, she'd said *stop*, but then she'd said *please...please*. She'd been wet for him. She'd been wet before he'd ever touched her, and she'd climaxed. She'd climaxed so loudly they should have heard her in the kitchens four floors below. Virgins never climaxed.

Frustrated and furious, he scrubbed at his face, as if that would help dissipate the rest of the brandy that blurred his thoughts. "I'm sorry." He couldn't even look at her. Seeing that he was still fully aroused, he yanked his robe closed and knotted the belt.

"But not satisfied," she said, this time sounding faintly upset. "Won't you come back?"

He stared at her. "No gentleman..."

But he couldn't finish the thought. It was too disturbing to think that he'd just treated Grace like a two-penny whore. He might be worldly, but he had standards. And one of those standards was that one didn't initiate a chaste woman this way. For God's sake, he hadn't even kissed her. He'd just...

"I'm sorry," he said again, backing away.

Slowly she sat up. "Why?"

He scowled. "If you don't know, then you've spent too much time with the military."

She shrugged. "Undoubtedly. But I'm still confused. Shouldn't we...um, finish?"

"No. We're finished. *You're* finished."

She looked down at the obvious tenting on his banyan. "Please, Diccan. Don't turn this into a melodrama. We knew this was going to be...uncomfortable. But if we don't at least try for normalcy, we're already doomed."

She was right. He rubbed his face again. He took a

breath. Of course, all he had to do was stand here a bit longer, and he'd wilt like high collars on a hot day. But he had the odd suspicion that such a result would only shame her more. So he nodded. She laid back down. He climbed up onto the bed. Lifting her nightgown up just far enough that he could get a peek of fiery red, he parted her legs and settled himself between them. Then, eyes closed, he laid his elbows on either side of her head and went about finishing the task.

He hated himself, but once he slipped back into her, he couldn't seem to stop. He pumped into her tight, hot sheath until he climaxed, and the force of it stunned him. He found himself straining into her, deep, deeper, until he threw his head back and shouted. And when he finally fell onto her, his face against her neck, he realized that she wasn't completely shapeless after all.

It was too late for that, though. He was spent, and he was ashamed, and damn it, he was resentful as hell. Why couldn't she have been that wanton she'd seemed? Now he'd never be able to do all those wonderfully perverse things he'd been promising himself as he had dined on her.

Shamefully, he found himself blushing. Diccan Hilliard, the Perfection, had just acted like a randy second termer with a woman who deserved better. But what could she expect after she'd dyed her thatch the color of sin? He rolled off her and lay looking at the ceiling. "Where *did* you learn the trick of dyeing your...maiden-hair?" he asked. "India?"

She paused, but he didn't look over at her. "Yes," she finally said. "India."

He nodded. "You might want to stop. You see what happens."

That just earned him silence, which crowded him. Accused him. "Are you all right?" he asked.

"Yes. Thank you."

He nodded. He didn't know what to do now. He'd never had a virgin. He wasn't sure what reassurances she might need. What care or comfort. It didn't help that he'd had five days to think about this and hadn't come up with anything. "I'll, uh, go downstairs for a bit, shall I?"

He could hear the slither of her hair against linen as she turned her head. "Is that how it's done?"

For a moment he could do no more than close his eyes. "I imagine so."

Then, without waiting for her reaction, he climbed out of bed and into his pants. He didn't once look back at his wife, who still lay in the center of his four-poster while he dressed. He did take a moment to wet a cloth in the still-warm water in his ewer.

He wished he knew what she was thinking. But when he turned to hand her the cloth, she appeared as she always did, calm and collected and curiously invisible. How could this be the same woman who had writhed under his touch only moments before?

"This won't happen again," he promised, not sure why.

That brought her back to a sitting position. "At all?"

He looked down, the taste of her still strong on his tongue. He had to get out of here before he threw her back down on the bed. His wife.

Good God. What had he gotten himself into?

"Not if you don't want it to."

She frowned. "Why wouldn't I?"

He gave her an abrupt nod. For some reason, that was when he realized that he was looking at her legs; long, strong legs. Well, the left, anyway. The right was a bit thinner, the muscles not as pronounced. And that was when he made his next mistake. He flinched.

"How could I have forgotten about your leg?" he said. "I hope it wasn't affected."

And he looked up to see that he had finally gotten a reaction out of her. She sat frozen at the edge of the bed, the cloth still clutched in her hand, her face ash pale and taut. Her eyes suddenly seemed huge and deep, and he realized that they were gray, like his. But not like his. Hers were soft, like storm clouds. Except for now, when they were bleak. He was obviously making a right bollocks of this. He shook his head, not knowing how to apologize.

"I won't wear this gown again," she offered, as if it would relieve him.

He shook his head again. And then, not knowing what else he could possibly do that wouldn't hurt her worse, he grabbed the rest of his clothing and left.

Grace sat for a long time, the cloth cooling in her hand, her leg aching from rough usage, her throat clogged with humiliation. Her father had been right. No decent woman should have hair that color. Good men wouldn't stand for it. Other women would disdain it. She just hadn't thought.

She wished she knew what to do now. She felt as if she'd been battered by a strong surf and tossed up on a cold beach. She felt hollow and sad. It had been the most shattering experience of her life. A door had been opened, a lamp lit. And then Diccan had brutally doused that wonderful light by turning the most magnificent experience of her life into one of shame.

If only her skin didn't still hum. If she could forget the stunningly wicked smile on his face as he'd bent to...to *taste* her. She could still feel it, like being laved by fire. She could still hear his throaty chuckle. Her body felt lit up like an evening storm. Her heart still hadn't slowed. It had been so wonderful, right up to the moment he'd realized she was a virgin.

He hadn't meant to hurt her; she knew that. In fact, he'd endeared her with his shock at his own actions. But it didn't change the outcome. She had been given a revelation, a peek into a far country into which she'd never been invited. And then, quickly, brutally, it had been snatched away again, and she didn't know how to recover it.

Not knowing what else to do, she finally got up. It was pointless, after all, to waste the rest of the night agonizing over what had happened. She might as well get on with things. Taking a few minutes to clean herself with hands that shook, she returned to her room and traded her gown for one of cotton. Then, careful not to snag the beautiful silk on her still-rough hands, she folded the gown and stowed it beneath her practical gray clothes, where she wouldn't be faced with the miscalculation it represented. Where, hopefully, she could forget how close she'd come to happiness.

She had thought that maybe, with Diccan, she could step outside the plain gray life she had always led. She'd been wrong. He had been appalled by what he'd done. What he'd thought she had tricked him into. Well, it was a mistake he would never make again.

She found herself standing before the mirror above the little vanity staring at the ghost-pale woman who stared back and wondering whether she would ever find her way past what she was. A plain woman. A useful woman. A competent nurse and loyal friend. A woman who hungered for intensity and settled for silence.

If only her body didn't ache. If only he had left before he'd taken her virginity. It had hurt. She had never had anything hurt as much. She couldn't imagine getting used to that sense of fullness, of invasion, of complete surrender. She couldn't imagine *wanting* to get used to it. She would want it to be a surprise every time, an explosion of wonder and possibility and belonging. For those few moments, she had been part of him. He had been a part of her, as inextricably bound as two humans could be. For that brief, hot, exquisite instant, she had not been alone.

Deliberately, she turned away. Braiding her hair into order, she built up the fire and pulled out her lists. She would never be able to sleep tonight. She might as well be busy.

He hadn't known where else to go. He certainly couldn't stay in the Pulteney. *She* was there, calling up every lascivious moment he had spent with her. Confusing him with the urgency with which he'd taken her. Infuriating him with her air of innocence, when he'd seen the proof himself that she couldn't have been. Just what the hell had she learned in India?

For just a moment, he considered finding out. If she'd learned to dye her nether hair, what else had she picked up? Would she do it with him? Ignoring his shaking hand, he shoved a key into the door to his rooms. She would *not* do that with him. God's blood, he couldn't imagine wanting her to. It would be like disporting with a nun. A horsey nun. A dull horsey nun. The fact that he was being completely unfair only made him angrier.

He'd simply been celibate too long. He should have just thrown a bag over Minette's head and carried her off with him back to London. Not only would he have continued to get his intelligence, he could have avoided what had happened tonight. He would have been too sated to even think of debauching his wife.

His wife who had dyed her goddamned thatch. Hell, he'd had to *ask* Minette to do it.

He was thankful he hadn't given up his rooms at the Albany. He needed a bit of distance tonight. Someplace to bathe off Grace's scent and the evidence of his mistake. He needed to be alone.

"Hello, old man. Didn't expect to see you here."

Diccan came to a screeching halt in the doorway. His sitting room was full of people. Briefly he wondered if he'd walked into the wrong room. But no. There was his brown leather sofa, the hunting prints the last tenant had left on his walls. Tidy stack of *Edinburgh Journals* sharing his end table with the sketch of Gadzooks that his sister Winnie had drawn. Those were even the etched brandy snifters he'd brought back from Ireland. Yes, definitely his place, being used, evidently, as the clubhouse for Drake's Rakes.

While Diccan was orienting himself, Marcus Drake unwound himself from his chair and stood. "Didn't think you'd mind. We needed someplace out of the public eye and all."

Marcus might have been blond and blue-eyed, but Diccan had always thought of him as a wolf. Cautious, predatory. A natural leader, both as Earl Drake and as founder of the Rakes.

Not so Chuffy Wilde, who followed Marcus to his feet. Round and bespeckled and still prone to spots, Chuffy was the group's tentative hold on innocence. It was Chuffy who offered a hand, as if Diccan had invited them all over. "Good to see you, old man."

The rest of them simply lounged on his furniture, fouling his air with cigarillos and draining his supply of alcohol. Ian Ferguson. Alex Knight. Beau Drummond. Nate Adams, which made a quorum, even if Nate was snoring off an evening spent among the champagne bottles at Madame Lucille's.

Usually Diccan would have been pleased to see any of them. But tonight he wasn't sure he was up to it. He had the most disconcerting feeling he reeked of sex. Of debauchery. Of Grace.

"One hopes you've at least saved a bit of my own brandy for me," he drawled, taking Chuffy's pudgy hand. "Come to celebrate my nuptials? I might have expected you at the ceremony, Drake."

Marcus Drake smiled. "I was as surprised as you, old thing."

Diccan cocked an eyebrow. "Not *quite* as surprised, I imagine."

"All the same," Drake said, his expression knowing, "celebration is in order. I like her."

"The lady could have done better," Diccan answered.

"Quite so," Chuffy said, completely oblivious to the undercurrents as he plopped back down on the sofa. "Wonderful woman. Saved m'brother's leg after the Battle of Cornwall, don't ya know."

"I believe that's Corunna, Chuff," Alex Knight advised, from where he lay sprawled in the armchair, brandy and cigar in hand, white-blond hair straggling over his undone collar.

"Is it?" Chuffy blinked, then laughed. "Course it is. You should know. Incomprehensible names. Should fight someplace a man can pronounce."

"Like Cornwall?"

"Exactly!"

Diccan strolled over to get his own drink. "What brings such *bon vivants* together?"

"I've been bringing them up to speed on the news," Drake said, sitting back down.

"Bad luck about Evenham," Chuffy said, the light glinting off his glasses. "Poor sod."

It was Beau Drummond who finally spoke up. "He was a traitor," the saturnine viscount said in an uncompromising voice. Beau had lost a brother at Talavera. "He was lucky it wasn't me there."

"Would he have been any more dead?" Diccan drawled, sipping at his brandy. Oddly, the discussion settled him. This was something he knew. A familiar problem to be solved.

Ferguson shook his massive auburn head. "Even for a wee Sassenach, he didn't seem the type."

"If you can spot a traitor just by looking at him," Drake suggested, "please let the Home Office know. It would save so much work."

The Scot frowned, his usually open face dour. "You know what I mean. The boy was a bloody choirboy. How did they turn him?"

"Don't know," Diccan said, with no qualms about lying. "He took it to his grave."

"Are you sure the Home Secretary isn't right?" Alex asked. "That Evenham isn't part of a smokescreen the real revolutionaries are throwing up?"

Ferguson let loose a hard laugh. "Sidmouth sees revolutionaries under the bushes. He might not be so paranoid if he'd spend more time actually dealin' with the real problems instead of tryin' to arrest anybody who complains." His smile was grim. "Save that for us radical Celts."

"We can discuss politics later," Marcus suggested. "Let's focus on the matter at hand. You seem to be the target, Diccan. Any idea what they're after?"

"Not a clue. I imagine I do look ripe for a fall, but I can't imagine what they think I know."

"Do you think they know about us?" Drummond asked as he passed through, refilling glasses.

"That the Rakes are government agents cleverly disguised as aristocratic wastrels?" Drake asked dryly. Without opening an eye, Nate Adams raised his glass in tribute. Drummond refilled it.

Diccan shrugged. "Only one way to find out. We need an eye into their organization."

For a moment, there was a thick silence in the room. Then Drake stirred. "If nothing else, we need to employ your household army to infiltrate the homes of some of the people Evenham named."

"Household army?" Chuffy asked.

"Oh, that's right," Ferguson said, looking up. "You weren't on the Continent. Diccan here collected a store o' maids and such to listen at keyholes for him."

Chuffy nodded wisely. "Nobody knows what's going on faster than the house staff."

"The information they were able to bring him in Vienna changed the course of negotiations," Alex said. "Have they followed you across the Channel, then?"

Diccan shrugged. "Some of them. I've been trying to

get a couple into Bentley's. It's a long shot, but maybe Bertie Evenham left something behind in his father's house that could prove useful."

Drake nodded absently. "What about you? Are you going to let the Lions have at you?"

Diccan studied his own liquor, the brandy turning in slow eddies that gleamed in the light. "I don't know. According to Bertie, after blackmail come the threats. I don't want to put Grace at risk."

"Shouldn't be a problem," Drummond suggested. "It's not as if it's a love match between you two. Just make sure everyone knows it."

"They may go after another Rake," Alex Knight offered. "There are ten of us, after all."

"And if our reputations are to be believed, all susceptible to blackmail." Chuffy grinned. "Wouldn't mind them coming after me. An honor. Never was quite as notorious as you other lads."

For another hour, they considered plans and contingencies. In the end, though, they agreed to wait on events. The bells of St. George's were tolling the hour of three when Drake shook Nate Adams awake so the Rakes could depart. But when the others walked out, Drake stayed behind with Diccan.

"One thing, old man," Drake said in a suspiciously calm tone. "I assume you arrived here from wherever you and your lady are staying."

The key in his hand, Diccan went still. "And if I did?"

"I detect signs that lead me to believe that your bride is no longer a maiden."

Diccan stiffened like an outraged matron. "That's not your goddamned business."

"It is if it gets you or your wife killed. I agree with Beau. Your best protection is a show of indifference. At least for now. You don't want make her a target."

Diccan resented the hell out of Marcus's intrusion. Blast, wasn't he having trouble enough with this marriage without other people poking their noses in? Glaring at Drake, he downed his brandy and set the glass down. "Fine. From this moment, my thoughts will be pure and my hands kept to myself."

How odd that what he felt was not relief.

Not too many blocks away in a townhouse on Bruton Street, the Surgeon watched from the shadows as two of the senior Lions faced off across a desk. They were sequestered in an oak-paneled library while a ball could be heard being enjoyed a floor away.

"Why does it have to be Hilliard?" the gentleman on the visitor's side of the desk demanded. "Surely there's someone better placed we can attract."

"Your only job was to compromise him," his superior reminded him in a scathingly dry voice. "Since you failed at even that, I doubt anyone is interested in your opinion."

The visitor huffed. "Well, how were we to know he'd actually marry the chit? Good Lord, have you seen her?"

"It no longer matters. We must move on, and Hilliard is still our best option. Our source in France says he can be turned."

"Not with blackmail. At least, unless he kills his wife."

"We haven't discounted that option. For now, just keep an eye on them both. I have someone due over from France who will help catch Hilliard for us. Hilliard is our conduit.

He is also the last person to see Bertie Evenham alive. I need to know if the boy said anything."

"He didn't have the verse?"

"Not when our people got there. Evenham's father still insists that Bertie never took it, but it hasn't turned up anywhere else."

"You're sure? Could your informants have lied?"

"Not when I was the one who questioned them," said the Surgeon, stepping out of the shadows.

One sight of him caused the visitor to blanch. "Of course. Of course. You are most thorough."

"Most," the Surgeon assured him, stepping just a little too close to the man before taking a seat. Easing back in his chair, he slipped out his favorite knife and began to run it across his palm. "I would be more than happy to deal with Hilliard for you."

"Maybe later," his superior promised, with a curiously sensual smile. "If things don't work out. Or, indeed, if we need to leave an...example to him to prove our threats aren't baseless."

"Lady Kate?" the visitor asked.

"Too problematic. She may be notorious, but the duchess is curiously well liked. Hilliard's wife, I think. After all, who would protest the loss of a soldier's daughter?"

The visitor laughed. "Take a good look at her and tell me Hilliard would care. To be frank, you'd be doing him a favor."

The superior smiled. "I believe the Surgeon is...proficient enough to keep her alive."

The Surgeon frowned. "She would not be my first choice, certainly. She is flawed."

"I imagine you'll find a way to overcome your aversion."

It was the Surgeon's turn to smile. "I will devote myself to finding the perfect quote to carve across her breasts."

The superior nodded. "Fine. In the meantime"—those long fingers were tapping again, this time atop an unfolded letter—"get more information on Hilliard. He seems curiously well-breeched for a man whose father cut him off. I've heard rumors that he isn't averse to exchanging information for gold."

The Surgeon turned his knife just to watch the light spill down its edge. "Which would make you wonder why he'd sacrifice the chance of an heiress for that fright. I'll go bail she dies a virgin."

"I hope not," the superior said. "Or we won't be able to use her."

The Surgeon sighed, impatient. "You sure we can't just kill him and move on?"

"Not yet. It does not mean, however, that we can't destroy him."

Chapter 9

Diccan rose the next morning still unsure what to do about his wife. He knew he should check in on her before he left for the day. He needed to share his decision with her about their marriage. But surely she was still too embarrassed to face him. Better to give her some time. He was just slipping out of his room when he stumbled over a surprise that immediately lightened his day. Barbara Schroeder was tidying up the sitting room.

"Well, Babs," he greeted her with a smile. "You succeeded."

Straightening at the sound of his voice, Babs turned to him with a delighted smile. "Well, if it isn't Dandy Diccan," she greeted him, her voice soft as a secret.

Diccan couldn't help but compare her to Grace. Grace was all angles and pragmatism. Babs was soft curves and smiles, the perfect size to fit comfortably beneath a man's arm.

"You were right," she said, stepping close so they couldn't be overheard. "All I had to do was raise the specter of being a war widow, and I was in. I'm afraid she really is a nice lady."

"So I hear."

He was surprised at the scowl she gave him. "I mean it."

He could smell the lemon verbena Babs always wore, and it calmed him. "I know. Was that little number last night your idea?"

Her smile as old as time, she shook her head. "Are you going to tell her the truth about me?"

He scowled. "Good God, no. Why would I?"

Babs stared as if he were the greatest fool in history. "She'll find out. She has that air about her."

"Not if you don't tell her. Now, be a good girl and see to your mistress." And with a swift pat on her bottom, he walked whistling out the door.

Grace must have fallen asleep after all, tucked up in the armchair by the dying fire. She woke to the murmur of voices out in the sitting room. Rubbing the sleep out of her eyes, she stretched out the kinks and climbed out of her chair.

It took only one foot on the ground to prove how ill-advised her sleeping position had been. Her knee seized up and sent a lance of pain shooting down her leg. For a moment she could do no more than stand where she was, her hands clawing at the back of the chair.

As always, the cramp passed. This time, though, she couldn't pretend it was nothing. It was a reminder of what it had cost Diccan to marry her. He hadn't only been saddled with a plain woman, he had been tied to a cripple.

The cramp had long since passed before she could move on with her day.

By the time Schroeder scratched on the door and

entered, Grace was carrying out her ablutions as if it had been any other morning. She ignored the raised eyebrow at her cotton nightgown. She was too busy planning her next meeting with Diccan. They had to get past what had happened the previous night. And if there was one thing Grace knew, it was that men hated to be faced with their mistakes. So it would be up to her to set the tone for their future.

"Has Biddle woken Mr. Hilliard yet, do you know?" she asked as she finished pinning her hair.

The pretty blonde frowned. "I believe Mr. Hilliard has already gone down to breakfast, ma'am."

Grace sighed. She would much rather have faced him alone, but she wasn't about to pass up this chance to ease his mind. Thanking Schroeder, she gathered her lists and carried them down to the dining room to find Diccan reading the *Times* over coffee and a beefsteak.

"Good morning, Diccan," she greeted him, relieved that she could sound so prosaic.

Just the sight of him sent her heart stumbling about in the most alarming fashion. He was perfectly groomed in tobacco brown jacket and biscuit breeches, his hair tamed to a soft wave rather than the half-wild curls of the night before. This handsome man had been hers, she thought, even if only briefly.

"My dear," Diccan greeted her, jumping up to pull out her chair.

Grace almost flinched at the strain in his eyes. He could barely look at her. For just that pregnant moment, what had happened hung between them, and Grace couldn't breathe. She felt him inside of her, she swore, that wondrous, stunning sensation of completion. She was flushed with every forbidden feeling he'd ignited. But he looked so distressed.

"Thank you," she said, trying to sound unaffected as she sat. "Oh, that steak looks wonderful."

A waiter materialized at her side. "Steak, madame?" He sounded faintly alarmed.

Setting down her lists, she smiled. "Oh, yes. Rare, please. And eggs. And, oh, scones, with clotted cream and jam. Tea, and...hmmm, possibly some fruit. Do you have oranges? I became very partial to oranges in Spain."

The waiter bowed and departed. Diccan retrieved his own seat with a dry smile. "Are you certain you don't want the man to simply drag a steer over to the table and be done with it?"

She chuckled. "I fear I'm not one of those frail beauties who eats like a bird."

"Oh, I don't know. I've seen Andean condors consume almost as much."

She chuckled. "Sometime I would love to hear about it. But for now, please feel free to finish your paper. If you have a few minutes later, though, I would appreciate your opinion on a list of available properties I've obtained. I had hoped to begin visiting them today."

Anyone else would have seen only the droll amusement in Diccan's eyes. Grace saw the initial distress flicker into surprise and then relief. She had a feeling he had chosen the dining room for their first meeting so she couldn't confront him about the night before. Hopefully, he was reassured. She had no more interest in discussing what had happened than he did. Her body was enough of a reminder of how foolish she'd been. Her breasts actually ached, and her limbs still felt weak.

"You simply exhaust me, madame," he drawled with a nod toward the pages she'd laid out on the table. "What shall you do after lunch? Plan an invasion?"

"Not yet, I think. At least, not until my wardrobe arrives."

"You should be seeing Kate today or tomorrow. I can have her look over the properties, too."

Returning, the waiter poured her tea. Grace focused on the taste of the bitter liquid rather than the unfairness of Diccan's words. "Why wait?" she asked. "Don't you trust your own taste?"

"It's not me..." Abruptly, he stopped, and she saw that she'd flustered him. He thought his wife was a bumpkin, and he didn't want to tell her. Well, suddenly his wife wanted to force him into it.

"It's not me, either," she said briskly, rifling through her lists. "I understand that you're more used to Lady Kate's taste, but she isn't going to be living there. We are."

She looked up, expecting to see irritation. She felt her heart stumble again, because what she saw was regret, loss; and it was sharp. Brief, of course. Diccan was a master at shielding his emotions. But she'd seen it, and it hurt.

But Grace also had long experience of masking her own hurts. Fortunately, her breakfast came, the waiter depositing a laden plate before her. It was a good way to fill the next few minutes, even though she'd lost her appetite. Diccan returned to his *Times* and she returned to her lists.

"I have an appointment this morning at Whitehall, or I'd check the properties with you," he eventually said. "I only suggested you consult Kate because she knows London. I meant no insult."

Grace bit back a sigh. "Of course you didn't. How could you know that my taste wouldn't make you bilious? I will wait for Kate if you prefer, but I hate to wait. A hint about your taste would help."

"You first," he countered, setting down the paper. "Do you have an idea of what you want?"

For a heartbeat, she fought a surge of grief. Oh yes, she did. She'd spent her entire life preparing her home at Longbridge. But she'd meant it to be hers, and hers alone, a place where she could be herself without fear of ridicule.

Considering the sparse black-and-white attire Diccan usually preferred, though, she didn't think he would be ready for the home she'd dreamed of. She wasn't sure he ever would be. Maybe when she knew him better, or trusted him more, she could bring out her majolica or golden Ganesha. She could introduce him to Banwar Singh and test his palate with curries. For now, she needed to remember that her plan was to be what Diccan needed.

"Well," she said, buttering her last scone, "I would prefer that our house doesn't look like a cow byre or bombed-out church. I can't say I preferred either decor."

He lifted a wry eyebrow. "A cow byre?"

She smiled. "Very warm in the winter. And cows make most undemanding houseguests."

"No cows, no matter how complaisant they are. Mayfair hostesses tend to frown on livestock."

"Ah, something we agree on, then. Anything else?"

He looked as if he were actually considering the matter. "With my job, I haven't had a chance to put down roots. But I imagine that if you use Kate's style as a template, it would serve."

"Clean lines, not too much fuss."

"Precisely."

She nodded, scanning her list of furniture makers. "I agree. Crocodile feet belong in a river. Not on sofa legs. Any family treasures you want to have a place of prominence? I understand you have an estate in Gloucestershire. Is there something there you'd like to transport here?"

"Heavens no. It's a dark, grim place, and the only painting is of my Great Uncle Philbert, who was even darker and grimmer than his house. I was always certain he'd shove me in an oven and roast me for dinner. I can't imagine what effect he'd have on another generation of children."

Grace began to chuckle. When she looked up, though, she realized that Diccan was silent. He was staring at her, his expression stark. And suddenly, she understood.

"Children," she said, knowing she sounded stricken. "I hadn't considered..."

Certainly not before he had visited her the night before. Just the thought incited fresh blushes.

"Do you *want* children?" he asked as if he meant to say *bedbugs*.

She blinked, a war of emotions set loose in her chest. Hope, dread, fear, amazement. "I never..." *could have hoped for children*, she thought. She had long since understood that no man would want to father a child on her, and had pushed the idea away where it couldn't hurt her. She didn't know what to do with it now. "What about you?"

He scowled. "Thank you, no."

She wondered what his response would have been if she'd been a different woman.

"At least for now," he suggested, sounding pained, "It might be better..."

Firmly quashing the hope she'd briefly courted, she nodded and returned to her lists. "Of course. I'll take care of it."

Oddly, she seemed to have shocked him. "My dear Grace, that is a most indelicate notion."

She tilted her head, suddenly amused. "That I would know how to prevent pregnancy? Did you think only soldiers ever needed my help? Believe me, there are few things more dangerous than giving birth on the march. The more sensible women do their best to prevent it. I helped where I could."

He slowly shook his head. "You are a constant surprise."

"I'm not certain why. You know I didn't have what is considered a normal upbringing."

"I'm beginning to appreciate that."

For a moment, she thought she caught the memory of the night before in his eyes. She wished he hadn't seemed so revolted by what had happened. But it wasn't something to discuss in a public room. No more than preventing childbirth, anyway. Suddenly, she found herself chuckling.

"Something amuses you?" Diccan asked.

She shook her head. "I was just thinking that I can't think of another couple who knows less about each other than we do."

He offered an arch smile. "No such thing, madame. You know that I have unequaled taste in all things, and that in my hands a quizzing glass can be more lethal than a saber."

"And that your father considers all other mortals to be lacking in moral fortitude." She'd no sooner said it than she was blushing again. "My apologies. That was rude."

"Never apologize for telling the truth, Grace. It is most fatiguing."

He had reverted to his public persona, Grace realized, eyes hooded, posture languid, tone droll. *Was that a good thing or a bad thing*, she wondered. It had always intimidated her in the past.

"Even if the truth is unpleasant?" she asked.

"Especially then. But only to me. I'm not sure the *ton* matrons would appreciate it as much as I."

I want you. She had no idea where that thought had come from. No, she knew perfectly well. It came from the sudden memory, a flash of his tousled hair between her knees, his fingers trailing fire, his eyes wicked and laughing as he'd done unspeakable things to her. She desperately wished last night had ended differently.

She might as well wish she were a different person. One who could truly attract a man as sophisticated and vital as Diccan. One who could match him equally. She might as well wish for her father back. Or, come to think of it, her mother.

"What truth has you blushing now?" he asked as the waiter swept away her empty plates.

She couldn't remember eating a thing. "My appetite."

"Well, yes. That is worthy of a blush or two. I must admit I am in awe. How do you not weigh more than Lady Cornley?"

Grace sipped at her tea. "A friend of yours?"

Diccan shuddered. "God forbid. I swear the woman devours her mates. She's had five, I think."

Grace found herself laughing. "You do know the most interesting people."

Diccan picked up Grace's lists and perused them as she sipped her tea. "Pugs," he said suddenly. "I categorically forbid those loathsome creatures in my residence, no matter which of these it will be."

Grace smiled. "A pug once offended you?"

"They must offend all civilized persons, madame," he said, looking affronted. "They *snuffle*. My mother has made it her life's work to breed the little monsters."

Grace nodded. "You must be the authority on pets, then. I have no experience with them."

Diccan looked up at her, his face curiously still. "No pets at all. What about the monkey?"

She smiled. "I have yet to live with him. From what I've heard, though, he is less pet than nemesis."

"Unheard of, madame. I'd suggest you didn't like animals, but you managed to find favor even with my reprehensible horse."

She smiled. "I never said I didn't want one. I said I never had one. Horses and hunting dogs are the only animals that survive a forced march, and those are notoriously bad lap pets. Did you have pets as a child? Besides the pugs, of course."

"Pugs are not pets. They are vermin. And of course I had a pet. I had a goose."

Grace almost spit out her mouthful of tea. "I beg your pardon?"

He looked severe. "A goose. Surely you have made the acquaintance of a goose or two."

"Of course I have. I ate them."

He flinched. "I would prefer not to hear the details. My goose was a stout defender of small boys and barnyards. Her name was Mildred."

Grace felt laughter burbling up in her chest. "An estimable name, I'm sure."

Diccan shot her a look that would have seemed threatening, if his eyes hadn't been twinkling. "This information is not for public consumption."

"Dear me, no. Since you are such an arbiter of fashion, it might become all the thing to have a goose perched up alongside one in the carriage, and then where would Christmas dinner be?"

His lip notched upward. "Precisely. Now then, do you have a pencil? There are several houses here not worth the look."

Grace handed him her pencil and he began to scratch through certain addresses. "Bentley?" he mused to himself, frowning. "How did I not hear about this?"

"Viscount Bentley? The agent said that he is also selling his string. He sounded as if it was of some import."

Diccan looked up, still frowning. "He just lost his son. What else, I wonder?"

"Pardon?"

He started, as if called back from far away. "Do you drive?"

She couldn't help wondering what he wasn't telling her. "Do camels count?"

"Not unless they're attached to a curricle."

She nodded. "In that case, I will limit my boast to being able to drive anything from provisions wagons to phaetons. I once attempted to move a piece of field artillery, but General Picton objected." When Diccan raised his eyebrow, she smiled. "There was a lot of time to fill between campaigns. It was a favorite pastime of my father's men to test my skills."

"You had phaetons at Talavera?"

"Calcutta."

He shook his head. "And I thought riding camels to the pyramids qualified as accomplished. Bentley has a matched pair that would be good for you. And you said you already had a mount."

She nodded. "I had hoped to have Harper bring her up when we found permanent lodgings."

"Where is she now?"

"Longbridge. In Berkshire."

He flashed a wry smile. "Residing with the monkey?"

"Indeed."

"Don't feel compelled to include him in the invitation. I have a particular aversion to fleas."

She chuckled. "I'll have you know that Mr. Pitt is more fastidious than half the peers I've met."

"He has all my admiration. He still does not have a place in my house. It is my second pet law."

"What about the Harpers? They are as close to family as I have left. Is there a place for them?"

"I remember them. Feisty little Irishman and fiercer big Irishwoman?"

She nodded. "They are also at Longbridge. They've looked after me since I was seven."

"I assume they are also unafflicted by fleas?"

"Breege would box your ears for even suggesting it."

"Have you informed them of your change of status?"

Uncomfortable, she set down her cup. "I...um, thought I would let them know when I had an address. Silly to have Harper bring Epona to a hotel just to move her again."

He nodded. "Well, have them come. Although I think they might feel stifled in a townhouse."

She hated it that he was right. Sean and Breege would wither in this rarefied atmosphere. They had barely survived Lady Kate's. Better they stay at Longbridge to help the Singhs fit in. But she didn't know how to go on without them.

"Come to think of it," Diccan said, "I would feel better about leaving you here if they are with you."

For the second time in moments, he'd brought her up sharp. "Leaving? Where are you going?"

He waved a hand. "Paris, for now. But who knows? I could find myself in the wilds of Siam."

She was assailed by a fresh surge of loss. Wasn't that what she wanted? To be on her own? But to once again be left behind with no more thought than a forgotten umbrella?

She must have betrayed her distress, because Diccan seemed to go very still. "You've known this about me."

"Indeed I have." Grace managed a wry smile. "I was just thinking that I've never been to Siam."

Diccan scowled. "I thought you preferred to stay here."

Grace tried not to look hurt. "Would you *prefer* I not accompany you? This is a quite a new situation for us both."

He took too long to answer. Grace's heart began to drop. Finally he gave her a stiff smile. "How can we know what we want to do? We're still strangers. I say we spend an hour each day sharing information: likes, dislikes, favorite people, foods and such. Do you like the color blue? Does Shakespeare make you weep? Would you walk across broken glass for the last lobster patty? It should only take a few months to know enough to be able to revisit the question, don't you think?"

Grace tilted her head, as if considering. "Favorite people will take a while. But the other questions? Yes, yes, and absolutely. I'd drag you across with me if there were also *gulab jamun*."

He lifted an eyebrow. "I do hope that is a food and not some heathenish religion."

She smiled. "It is a delicacy of India. My friend Radhika makes them for me. Fried dough in rosewater, sugar, and cardamom. It puts English syllabubs to shame."

Diccan had not given up his arch look. "Rosewater is for perfume, not the sweet course."

"Come now," she argued. "Surely you've had more exotic foods than roast and kippers."

"And counted the hours until I returned to the land of bland and boring. There are enough surprises in life, madame. I don't need them at my table."

As often happened, Grace couldn't tell whether Diccan was still jesting or not. She hoped he was, because if not, theirs would be a greater mismatch than even she had feared. Even more so because she suddenly realized that whatever else happened between them, she didn't want to be apart from him for months or years at a time. Even at the risk of forfeiting her home and all her dreams, she wanted a chance at a full life with this man.

She thought she'd been frightened before, but this thought terrified her. She knew better, though, than to let Diccan see. "I suppose I'd better add a good English cook to my list of tasks."

"Some red-faced woman with hams for hands and a way with a joint."

She smiled. "I know this marriage isn't the one you would have wanted, Diccan," she said. When he moved to instinctively protest, she raised a hand. "Don't dispense with the truth so easily; you might not get it back. What I want to say is that I will try my best to be an asset to you. I might not yet know how to seat formal dinners, but I can guarantee you the best accommodations in Bangkok."

She wasn't sure what reaction she'd expected. She knew for certain his wasn't delight. She thought Diccan might have even paled.

"I think it would be better to wait at least a week or two

before deciding the future, don't you?" he asked, leaning back a bit, as if afraid of some contamination.

Grace berated herself for letting her tongue run on so. She knew that men didn't like to be pushed, and Diccan would certainly consider her words pushy. As if happy to prove her point, he tapped his fingers at the edge of the table.

"Until we do know each other better," he said, his voice oddly strained, "I think it also might be better for us if we postponed the…physical side of the relationship."

Grace felt as if her stomach had dropped away. *No!* She wanted to cry. *Don't take that away, too.*

"I don't want you to suffer for my misconceptions again," he said before she could quiz him.

Her instinct was to argue. How could he think she'd suffered? One look at the distress in his eyes silenced her. She could only give him a jerky nod, as if he hadn't just pulled her feet out from under her. Again.

He never waited for her answer. Gathering his newspaper, he got to his feet. "I'm afraid I'll be busy the next few days," he said, at least having the decency to look uncomfortable. She hoped he felt like hell. "I simply have too many urgent meetings. And then there are two embassy balls…"

Again he faltered to a stop, certainly aware that he'd once again insulted her. He was going to embassy balls that he didn't wish her to attend. Because she would humiliate him. Because she would never be worthy to be his wife, no matter how she tried to camouflage her inadequacies with Madame Fanchon's handiwork.

Maybe it was just as well he didn't want physical relations, Grace mused. She suspected that if she ever got him naked, she'd pour alcohol on him and light him like a plum pudding. But she never got a chance to tell him that either. Not even facing her, he threw off a stiff bow and left.

She had obviously displeased the Fates, because she was still gathering her lists up when Diccan reappeared in the doorway, looking decidedly unwell.

She instinctively came to her feet. "What's wrong?"

"We didn't escape quickly enough, madame wife," he said, holding a calling card between finger and thumb like a dead rat. "We have a visitor. My sainted mother has arrived."

Grace found that it was suddenly hard to breathe. "Is she as bad as your father?"

Diccan's laugh was sharp. "Oh, no. She's far worse."

Grace's spirits hit her half-boots. She looked down at another of her practical gray gowns. She knew her hair was insipid, a tight bun meant to get her hair off her face. And her leg was still stiff from her night in the chair. Not exactly the way she would want to meet her new mother-in-law.

"I don't suppose she'd be satisfied with seeing only you," she suggested, with a sickly smile.

His answer was to hold out his hand. "Come, my girl. She is but an old woman. I'd put my blunt on Boadicea any day."

Considering the look on his face, Grace didn't think she believed him. She knew she had no choice though, so, putting her hand on his arm, she allowed him to guide her across the hall into one of the private parlors.

Lady Evelyn stood by the fireplace, where the morning light would not betray her age. Not tall or short, not especially beautiful, not quite blond. But regal. Regimental sergeants would have wept at her posture. Debutantes undoubtedly quailed before those cold gray exopthalmic eyes. And the devil himself must have envied the self-satisfaction in that tight smile. Clad in a deceptively simple cream *indienne* walking dress with matching green spencer and bonnet, she was the picture of elegance.

It was obvious that Diccan favored his mother in looks, although the square lines and broad forehead better fit his masculine frame and darker features. The expression on Lady Evelyn's face convinced Grace that she had also taught him his more offensive affectations. Grace was convinced of it when Lady Evelyn caught sight of her. There was a keen intelligence in those ghostly gray eyes, a well-honed air of superiority. A well-seated sneer of disdain.

"I see," that lady drawled, slowly raising a quizzing glass with the same ruthless precision as Diccan. "Your father did not exaggerate, then."

She offered neither of them a chair. Grace had the feeling it was her method of asserting superiority. It must have worked a champ on terrified debs. Unfortunately for Diccan's mother, Grace had survived generals who could give the older woman lessons. Not only that, Grace towered over her, which made it deuced hard for Lady Evelyn to look down on her.

Diccan proffered his mother a most correct bow. "The Lord Bishop undoubtedly said what a lucky man I am. Mother, may I present your new daughter, Grace Fairchild Hilliard. Grace, my mother, the Lady Evelyn Hilliard. How lovely that you couldn't wait to see us. I assume that is why Winnie and Charlie don't accompany you. My sisters," he explained to Grace, who kept her gaze on his mother.

Lady Evelyn's reaction was classic Diccan, a measured sigh that spoke volumes, although without the spark of humor that leavened his best set-downs. "Winifred and Charlotte," she answered in long-suffering tones, "are at school, as you well know."

"It is a pleasure to meet you, My Lady," Grace said, dropping a precise curtsy.

Diccan's mother never acknowledged her. "If this is your idea of rebellion, Diccan," she drawled in a flat, almost lifeless tone that was more chilling for its mildness, "I am not amused."

Grace had meant to let go of Diccan's arm and sit, permission or not. She could feel the tension in his muscles, though, and refused to abandon him to this...creature.

"I'm disappointed," his mother went on, dropping the quizzing glass as if it were too heavy. "You have been raised to better standards."

Diccan's smile was sharp. "Grace and I are delighted to accept your good wishes."

His mother's nostrils flared, just a fraction. But then, her faintly feral smile grew, and Grace felt a *frisson* of alarm snaking up her back. "Good wishes?" Lady Evelyn echoed, her soft voice amused. "Yes, I imagine you would. I believe the more appropriate sentiment would be that you have finally received your just deserts. Does he know who your people are, dear?"

Grace felt that dread gestate into fear. "He had the privilege of meeting my father, My Lady."

"And your father of course told him all," the woman said with another tight-lipped smile.

Grace could only stare, a mouse paralyzed by the eyes of a snake. *Why hadn't she ever anticipated this?*

"What are you getting at, Mother?" Diccan asked. "Are you saying that Grace's family is unacceptable? I will remind you that she is related even to the exalted house of Hilliard."

"Yes," his mother almost hissed with a dip of her head.

"She is. But you don't know exactly how, do you, Richard? It is my suspicion that you didn't compose the notice for the papers."

Diccan flinched. "The notice..."

Grace felt herself deflate. Lady Kate must have taken care of it. But how had she done it? She had no information about Grace's family.

Lady Evelyn chuckled, and the sound crawled over Grace's skin. "You don't even know who her mother was, do you, Richard?"

Diccan looked over at Grace. Grace fought against a new, miserable flush. "Should I?"

Again his mother laughed. Nodding to herself, she gathered her reticule and parasol. "Not by looking at your wife, I assure you. But you will, I think. Please come see me when you find out. I don't wish to miss a minute of your reaction."

And without another word to either of them, she swept from the room.

Grace plopped unceremoniously onto a chair. She wanted to curl into a ball and disappear. How had she not anticipated this new, even more spectacular humiliation? How could she have assumed that no one knew of her mother?

"I need to tell you," she said to Diccan, and knew she sounded as miserable as she felt.

Diccan sighed, and she could see that his hands were clenched at his side. "Why? Do you number felons among your family?"

"No."

"Your grandfather was a costermonger."

Her own laugh was abrupt. "Worse. An admiral."

"How long has she been gone?"

"My mother?" Grace swallowed. "Since I was seven."

Slipping his quizzing glass beneath his waistcoat, he held out a hand. "Then the point is irrelevant."

Grace looked up at him, knowing that his mother was right. Someone would figure out who her mother was. And they would delight in telling Diccan at the worst possible moment.

"I'm afraid it's very relevant. I think you should know."

"And I don't." He flicked his hand at her, urging her to move. "Come. I'm already late."

Grace knew that she either told him now or never. And his mother would never allow that. Better to at least get it over with in private. Taking a calming breath, she returned to her feet.

"Before she married my father," she said, feeling the cold of inevitability seep into her bones, "my mother was Lady Georgianna Hewitt."

His reaction was everything she'd dreaded. Of course he knew of her mother. Everyone in the great cities of Europe knew of her mother. But especially men. Especially *handsome* men.

For the longest moment, Diccan just stared, obviously stripped of all cogent thought. "Glorious Georgianna?" he finally demanded in tones of absolute shock. "*She's* your mother?"

Grace knew she should have been used to this reaction. But it had been so long since she'd let anyone know. "Unless fairies switched me at birth," she said. "Although it has been suggested."

Mostly by my mother.

He was flummoxed; she could tell. No more than any

other person who made the inevitable comparison between Glorious Georgianna and the Little Colonel. But of course, the real humiliation came when Diccan, the smoothest man in the British Empire, plopped down on the chair she had just vacated and stared at her in aghast silence. It seemed that he had finally found something that appalled him more than his marriage.

Chapter 10

Diccan knew there was a considerate answer he should have given. Something kind or noncommittal. It seemed all he could manage was to blurt out, "But she's alive."

Grace, poor Grace, merely nodded, her expression passive and her hands clenched at her waist as if she were literally holding on. "Yes," she said very quietly. "I know."

"Not only alive," he insisted, as if she really didn't understand, "but she was the most popular hostess at the Congress of Vienna."

"A perfect place for her."

He kept shaking his head. Well, if he hadn't already known that God had a strange sense of humor, this was proof enough. Grace Fairchild the daughter of one of the most celebrated beauties of the age. Reynolds had painted Georgiana Hewitt no fewer than half a dozen times, as had Romney and Raeburn, each portrait imbued with that rare otherworldly glow that marks true beauty.

Glorious Georgianna was the definition of English loveliness: blond, blue-eyed, with a delectable peaches-and-cream complexion. As petite as a porcelain doll but with womanly proportions.

And her smile. Sonnets had been written to that smile, odes to a face at once gamine and sweet and seductive. The last time Diccan had set eyes on Georgianna, about a year ago, she had been lavishing that smile on the Hapsburg court; she was still, in her fourth decade, head-turningly lovely.

Now that he thought about it, he remembered that she had once married a handsome soldier. The legend was that disappointed swains had left a veritable mountain of flowers on her doorstep the day of her wedding. How had no one ever known about Grace?

Looking at her now, standing before him like a suspect in the dock, her excruciatingly plain face carefully composed and her almost colorless hair scraped back from her high forehead, he simply couldn't take in the absurdity of it all. Grace was smiling, but Diccan wasn't foolish enough to think she was amused. Oh, Lord. How many people had reacted just as he had?

He damn near made it worse by apologizing again. Instead, he stood, as if it could diminish his reaction, and let out a low whistle. "I have to admit I thought it impossible living up to the world's most perfect arbiter of morality. I can't imagine growing up in the shadow of Helen of Troy."

Grace still looked bleak. "Legends are never easy, I think."

"Why did you say your mother was dead?"

"But I didn't. I said she was gone. And she has been."

"Since you were seven."

She actually looked sympathetic. "Some women simply aren't made to follow the drum. She tried. She really did. But in the end, it was just too much for her."

But what about her daughter? Had the Glorious never even thought to take her child with her? It didn't sound as if she'd even seen her again.

"You're an only child?"

She couldn't quite look at him. "A stillborn sister. I think that was the last straw, actually. She was the most perfect baby I've ever seen, and she never drew breath."

And the perfect beauty was left with a girl child who could never be called perfect in anything. Kate had told him once that Grace had been born with her lame leg. Had Georgianna ever favored such a child? Or had she year by year stripped that small girl of her sense of self-worth? Was that why Grace seemed sympathetic to the woman who'd abandoned her? Didn't she even have enough self-respect left for anger?

Not knowing what else to do, he stepped up and took her cold hand in his. "Not everyone is as valiant as you, Mrs. Hilliard," he said, hoping like hell it was the right thing to say.

Her smile became more genuine. "Oh, I'm very hardy, Mr. Hilliard. Virtually indestructible. I apologize for having put you in such an uncomfortable position with your mother. I vow I have no more surprises. You already know my full name. Grace Georgianna. A bit of wishful thinking on my mother's part, I believe."

"She was far more insightful than she knew," he assured her, kissing her work-roughened hand.

And oddly, he meant it.

"You're kind," Grace said, her blush deepening to an unpretty brick color.

"No," he said, smiling back. "I'm not."

He knew he was embarrassing her again. Surely he wasn't the first to ever pay Grace such compliments. Yet she looked as flustered as a girl at his paltry words, which angered him all over again.

Signaling an end to their tête-à-tête, Grace gently pulled her hands away. "Now then, don't you think it's time to get on with the day? I believe you said you had an appointment."

He nodded, still feeling upended. "As long as I am assured you have survived your collision with my mother."

Grace slanted him a sly look. "I don't suppose it is a Christian sentiment to hope her pugs devour her?"

She surprised a full-throated laugh out of him. "I believe we understand each other better than we thought, wife." Laughing again, he turned to open the door. "Sadly, I can't wish that kind of indigestion even on a pug."

"May I ask one question?"

He stopped, his hand on the door. "Of course."

She tilted her head, which made her seem curiously smaller. "What did you ever do to deserve such acrimony?"

He smiled, knowing how grim it looked. "I survived. Now, I truly do have a full day today. But perhaps you would join me for dinner this evening. We can begin our orientation sessions."

Grace blushed like a girl being asked to dance. "I would like that very much."

He'd never suspected he was a coward. He did when he saw that blush. It made him want to take her into his arms and hold her, just that. Just let her know that she deserved more than her mother's rejection. But that would signal a new, closer relationship, and that could put Grace at risk. At least that was his rationalization.

He ended up retreating as quickly as he'd advanced. "Good. I shall see you then, shall I?"

And before he could see her reaction, he left.

· · ·

Grace prepared for dinner that night with particular care. She was still in gray, of course, one of her ubiquitous gray *moiré* evening gowns, which she'd begun to hate. The dress wasn't vile. It was forgettable, which had once been her goal. After all, a woman at an army post in Portugal had very different wardrobe needs than one entering the main dining room of the Pulteney Hotel in London.

Diccan greeted her with a curious formality before seating her himself and ordering the meal.

"Now, then," he said as he sipped his clear beef broth. "Where shall we begin?"

His smile was constrained. Grace couldn't fault him, really. After her revelation that morning, she was sure he was bracing for other surprises, like a fondness for whisky or unnatural habits in the bath. She didn't even think he realized how tense he looked, as if bracing for disaster.

"Well, we can begin with the social basics," she suggested. "Do you like opera?"

He seemed a bit set back by the innocuous question. "If there truly is a definition of purgatory," he said, finally, his social mask firmly in place, "it is opera. Save me, please, from shrieking sopranos. But please don't share that with anyone. It would be deadly to my reputation."

Grace smiled. "Then it must be a sore trial for you, since I imagine a diplomat is forced into the opera house on regular occasions."

"Too regular, in my opinion. What about you? Are you an aficionado of the aria?"

Grace smiled. "I'm not yet sure. Opera is not something I've had much time for."

"Not even while you've lived with Lady Kate?"

"She likes opera no more than you."

He nodded, thoughtful. "True. What about other forms of entertainment? What do you do in your leisure time?"

She had always sewed and cooked and cleaned. "Well," she said instead, as the waiter traded the soup for sole, "my father always made sure we had a library with us. I enjoy the classics."

His fork poised over his fish, he scowled. "Not, please, in the original texts."

"And why not?"

He groaned. "My dear, you are unnatural, and it shouldn't be mentioned. Your erudition is quite lost on me. You would have made a much better bride for my brother Robert."

She blinked, surprised. "You have a brother?"

It was only a moment, but he hesitated before smiling. "Had." Grace saw pain at the back of those cool gray eyes. "Lovely chap. Up and coming churchman, being groomed for great things."

She wanted to hold his hand. She held herself still. "What happened?"

Another pause. A sip of wine. "Oh, nothing worth remark. He simply wasn't up to the bishop's weight." Before she could continue, he flashed a bland smile that closed the door. "What about other interests?" he asked. "Theater? Ballet? Anything that would constitute proper dinner conversation?"

She dug out a smile. "Harry Lidge once organized a production of *School for Scandal*. Harry played Lady Sneerwell."

"Who did you play?" he retorted easily. "Truehearted Maria?"

He had to know how ludicrous that was. Maria was beautiful.

"The troupe was made up of soldiers," she said, turning her attention to the *relevé de poisson*. "My role was that of appreciative audience."

For a long moment, the only sounds between them were the desultory clinking of silverware and glasses as they picked at their food.

"That was in India?" Diccan finally asked, his voice uncommonly hesitant. "The play? I know Harry said that he met you there. Over an elephant, I believe?"

"In Hyderabad. He saved me from being trampled." She smiled at the memory. "I believe the fact that he was the one who got the elephant drunk in the first place weighed in his actions."

Diccan cocked an eyebrow. "How much ale does it take to inebriate an elephant?"

"Not ale. Whisky. And pretty much all of the commandant's supply."

He chuckled. "No wonder Harry's still only a major. How long were you there?"

She shrugged, suddenly uncomfortable again, wondering what Diccan really thought of her vagabond life. "I was born there, in Calcutta. We returned twice, once with Wellington and once with General Lake. As a matter of fact, I was inside Bharatpur when he put it to siege."

She wasn't sure why she said it. Maybe just to see Diccan's reaction. She wished she could have been surprised. He stared as if she'd said she was a member of the Hellfire Club.

"You were inside an enemy city in India during a military siege? Weren't you terrified?"

She thought back to those lazy days in the sunwashed rooms high above the fighting and smiled. "I suppose I should have been. I was fourteen and had been saved by the locals from bandits on the road to Deeg. Sadly, it was just before our army advanced. The only reason I was spared was because Ranjit Singh thought I was Irish, and he said it was a fact that the Irish hated the British."

"It must have been an immense relief to have been rescued."

She could see the assumption in his expression: she'd gone from hell to heaven by the mere act of walking out the great gates of Lohagarh Fort. In her mind, though, she saw how the latticed stone window embrasures of the *zenena* had woven sunlight into lace. She heard the chuckling fountains fill the marble halls with music. She could almost smell the jasmine again, hear the chatter of the brilliant, birdlike women who had pampered her, feeding her sweet-meats and honey. And, intruding like the stalking approach of a great giant, the syncopated thuds of the big guns as Lake threw his cannonballs against the massive mud walls down the hill.

Some days she had stood at the high windows trying to find her father across the great moat, where the army endlessly scattered and reformed, like industrious ants in crimson. Some days she'd wondered if she really wanted to be saved at all.

But was that something she could share with Diccan? Her chest tight, she tried. "Of course I was glad. My father worried himself sick. But I cannot say I was abused in any way. I spent the time teaching the ladies of the *zenena* to dice. They gave me henna tattoos. I thought it quite an adventure."

Behind her, someone gasped. Grace looked over to see that a woman at the next table was leveling an expression of delighted horror at Grace through her lorgnette. In fact, there were others watching, their hands stilled over cutlery or cups as if too interested to remember to eat.

Grace blushed. She sought support from Diccan, but he must have heard the woman, too. His attention was on her, his expression suddenly tight. "Something you might think twice about sharing," he said, his gaze swinging back to Grace, distaste suddenly chilling his voice.

Her fragile hope fluttered back to earth, once again a spent balloon. "Why is that?"

He cocked an eyebrow and lowered his voice. "You truly think stories of time spent in a heathen harem are appropriate for polite conversation?"

Grace opened her mouth to protest, but Diccan had already turned back to his dinner. She was so tempted to blurt out what other knowledge the women had imparted behind upraised hands and eunuch-guarded doors. She wanted to assure him that if she had applied the lessons taught there, she could never have dyed her nether hair any color. She wouldn't have had any to dye.

"I thought you of all people would be amused," she said, unable to surrender.

"I'm not sure why." His smile was cool as he watched the waiter switch courses. The thick scent of beef replaced the memory of jasmine and sweetmeats. "I hardly espouse the unusual."

Grace peered at him, praying to see his sly humor peek through the stuffiness. She couldn't find it. "Didn't you join the diplomatic corps to experience the world?"

He picked up his fork. "I joined the diplomatic corps

to be as far away from my father as I could get. So far, it's worked a treat."

"If I can't talk of my life in India," she asked, "what am I allowed to speak of? As your wife."

His voice was mild, a teacher with a slow pupil. "Anything that would not shock a proper British woman."

And a woman who had enjoyed her time in *zenenas* wasn't a proper British woman. Or a woman who read Greek or shot bandits or made snowshoes. Grace's enjoyment of their conversation died after that. Expounding on the difficulty of living abroad as a British man, Diccan focused on his *boeuf tremblant*. Grace wasn't even certain that he knew she'd stopped eating.

Could Diccan truly be as hidebound as his black-and-white uniform implied? Grace thought of the treasures she'd hoarded back at Longbridge. The treasures that now might never see the light of day.

By the time Diccan left for the embassy ball, she was almost glad to see him go.

Diccan was still thinking about that dinner an hour later as he did the pretty at the Belgian Embassy ball. Standing by the balcony doors with a champagne glass in his hand, he watched the guests whirl past in a waltz and thought of the wife he'd left back in the hotel. He tried to imagine the most invisible woman in the *ton* fitting in among this rarefied company.

He couldn't. He couldn't imagine a day when Grace would feel comfortable in this atmosphere. It was too bright, too cutthroat, too exclusive. She was a soldier's daughter with a limp.

A soldier's daughter with a wicked sense of humor and

better stories than he'd brought back from his travels. He smiled to himself. He wished he could have heard the rest of that *zenena* story. She had looked so happy recounting her memories. He wondered what other lessons she'd learned.

Thank God he hadn't found out. It had been such a close call. If that old harridan at the next table hadn't gasped, he wasn't sure what would have happened. He was sure that observers would have seen him lean in toward Grace, as if he could ingest her words more easily. They surely would have seen them smiling at each other, maybe touching. She'd come close when he'd told her about Robert. They might have looked like a couple intent on growing closer.

Just the thought sent a *frisson* down his spine. If Bertie had been right, that was a sure recipe for disaster. Diccan had recognized several people in the restaurant. He couldn't have named any as Lions, but the minute he'd looked up, he had felt that odd tingling at the base of his neck that warned him of a threat. Someone in that room had been far too interested in Diccan's table.

"Heard you've been caught in the parson's mousetrap," a sultry voice purred next to him.

Diccan looked over to see Lady Glenfallon standing alongside him, sipping from a flute of champagne. Bette and he had been lovers once, back in Vienna. He hadn't regretted her loss at all. She was the very kind of harpy he would have to protect Grace from.

"I did. General Sir Hillary Fairchild's daughter. Will you congratulate me?"

Her drawn black eyebrows headed north. "I believe I'll congratulate me," she said with a sly smile. "With a wife like that, it won't be long before you're looking for...diversion."

He wanted to tell the bitch that the last thing he would

do was betray an honorable woman. He knew he couldn't.
He lifted his glass in a toast. "I am in awe of her industry
and compassion."

Bette's laugh sparkled. "Oh, a worthy woman, is it? I
can only hope I can meet this paragon. Will she have you
going to church, do you think? Supporting indigent widows
and climbing boys?"

"Of course. Can I count on a contribution?"

Eventually she wandered off. He watched her go and
felt his spirits sink even more. He couldn't expose Grace to
women like Bette. They would destroy her. They wouldn't
be crude, of course. They were far too subtle, their weapons words and glances and the fine art of silence. But those
were much crueler weapons to a woman like Grace. They
would wear at her like poverty until there was nothing left
of the woman he'd called Boadicea but misery. He had to
keep her from them for her own good.

He nodded to Lord Castlereagh. Across the room, Sir
Charles Stuart smiled and waved. Diccan didn't want to
hurt Grace. She was a nice woman. She *was* worthy, damn
it. But this wasn't her world. It was his. He felt alive when
he was swimming in these waters, where policy was woven
and futures staked. He was damn good at it. But what
chance of success did he have with a wife like Grace?

Just then, Marcus Drake stepped up, an intent look on
his face. "I need to speak with you."

Diccan felt that tingling at the base of his neck again.
Without a word, he stepped outside onto the balcony.

"You were seen being very friendly with your wife
tonight," Marcus accused without preamble.

Diccan sighed. "The entire report should have mentioned
the fact that we left each other in a less felicitous manner."

Drake looked over at him, as if assessing his veracity. "I know this is difficult, but you must realize that we're not the only people watching you."

It took Diccan a moment to answer. "Do you know that for sure?"

Drake looked out onto the darkened garden. "One of Thirsk's men has seen them."

Diccan hated the idea that he hadn't seen his shadows. "Anyone I know?"

"No. I'll have him point them out for you."

"Good. I think I might be for an early evening tonight then. Fill in my people."

"Not 'til you hear the rest."

Diccan heard the portent in those words and stopped cold. "What rest?"

Marcus looked down the balcony, but it was empty. "Bentley is dead."

Diccan froze. "What? Not suicide."

"No. Not like Evenham."

Not like Evenham; in an explosion of gore that he could still smell in his sleep. "Then how?"

"His throat was slit."

Diccan felt the air go out of him. "I don't suppose . . ."

"That there was a message carved on him?" Drake shoved a hand through his hair, and Diccan could see the distress in his eyes. "This information is privileged. The story will be that he was set upon by footpads. But yes. It was down his torso. *It is a wise father who knows his own son.*"

Diccan rubbed at his forehead. "The Surgeon. Does that mean the old man was involved?"

"We don't know. Did you manage to get your person stationed in his house?"

Diccan nodded.

"I need you to come back with me. We have to bring your people up to snuff, and then we need a more experienced eye on the situation. Bentley was last seen with Thornton."

Diccan was already shaking his head.

"Thornton? He doesn't have the brains to plot a birthday party, much less a revolution."

"Yes, but he is close as inkle weavers with Geoffrey Smythe, who does, and who works in Sidmouth's office. We think it's time for you to reacquaint yourself with that crowd."

Diccan bristled, suddenly furious at all the duplicity. "Why not let the professionals do that?"

Drake leaned close. "Evenham said there was a leak in Sidmouth's office. I think he's right. Which means that we can't trust them to investigate their own people."

Diccan rubbed at his temple. "I'll send Grace a message to say I'll be late."

"You'll send Grace nothing."

Diccan looked at his friend and mentor and cursed. Of course he was right. He couldn't tell Grace. He couldn't afford her the most basic courtesy. He was liking himself less and less.

Grace didn't sleep that night. She kept listening for Diccan's footsteps and feeling foolish for it. Was this what her marriage would be? Would she be forever waiting for her husband to return? She wished she didn't care. But she did. She was bound to a man who would never appreciate her. A man who saw her more as *aide-de-camp* than lover.

Oh, she couldn't expect him to ever love her. But suddenly, in the thick silence of a strange room, she wanted him to *want* her. To need her. To miss her when she was gone and be glad when she returned. She wanted to belong to him.

And that was what troubled her the most. Not that she wanted to belong. She knew that feeling all too well. But she couldn't remember ever wanting it this...*fiercely*.

She couldn't understand it. Of course he was handsome; he was witty and intelligent, honorable, and often kind. But so were most of her father's officers. What could be the indefinable something that set him apart? Why, of all men, was she so susceptible to Diccan Hilliard? And what could it lead to?

Chances were, he would never let her close enough to find out. He had made that perfectly clear tonight. His marriage would mirror his society, polite and amiable, no more. No surprises, no flights of fancy. No lessons from the *zenena*.

It was silly to ask if she could settle for that. She would have to, of course. She had no choice. She just wished she had something left of her own to hope for. Treasures collected in an empty house that would be hers if she only waited long enough. Independence, peace, beauty. But she would never grow out of marriage, or be able to count the days 'til it was over. It would be over when she was dead. And she had to find a way to accommodate herself to it. To him.

Impatient with herself, she walked over to the window that overlooked Green Park. It was dark, with only a few gaslights to push away the night. It was too late even for the *ton* to be out, so she was surprised to see a man standing across the street looking directly up at her.

For a second she froze, surprised. He looked like a gentleman, but he wasn't in evening attire. He was smiling, as if holding some private joke to himself. And he was watching her, head back, hands in pockets. She felt a chill snake down her back. Was he watching the hotel, or her specifically? He couldn't have seen her by accident, because he'd been facing her when she'd opened her second floor curtain. Could he have something to do with Diccan's mission? Not knowing what else to do, she closed the curtains and decided to tell Diccan when she saw him. Whenever she saw him.

He wasn't home by the time she and Schroeder cleaned out her wardrobe the next day.

"Take what you want, Schroeder," she told the abigail as she folded her gray gowns into neat piles on her bed. "Sell them with my blessings. I'll keep these for the Army Hospital."

Grace ran a finger over the gown she'd worn the day before, when she'd sat by a boy dying of infection. She could still see the glassy distance in his shrunken eyes, hear the death-rattle in his chest. She could smell the thick miasma of that hospital and feel the hard edge of the stool beneath her thighs. She thought of all the bedsides she'd attended, the amputation tables and littered battlegrounds. Her problems, after all, weren't important. Even if Diccan never learned to abide her, she faced no catastrophe larger than loneliness. She had no right to grieve.

She was so preoccupied with the thought that she didn't hear the knock on the sitting room door.

"Did no one bother to tell you that you should be lazing on a chaise longue, munching bonbons and reading Minerva Press novels?" a laughing voice demanded from the doorway. "This is not how a society matron comports herself."

Grace swung around to find Kate and Lady Bea standing in the doorway. "Oh, Kate!" She ran over to greet her friends, shamefully thankful to see them. "And Lady Bea! Oh, it's so good to see you."

Kate accepted her hug with raised eyebrows. "Heavens. Of course it is always a privilege to see me, but you sound positively frantic. Diccan hasn't been beating you, has he?"

Grace couldn't prevent a blush. "Of course not. It's just that I need your particular help."

Kate clapped her hands. "Excellent. I love being useful. What is it you need? Tips on how to land in the scandal sheets? How to handle more than one lover? Where to find the best erotic art?"

Well acquainted with Kate's delight in shocking others, Grace smiled. "I spent ten years in India, Kate. I know perfectly well where to find erotic art."

Kate's laugh was like music to Grace's ears. "And you haven't told me?"

It was the sound of a dry cough that brought Grace to her senses. "Oh, Kate, Bea, this is Schroeder, my dresser. Schroeder, we'll finish later."

Schroeder gave a credible curtsy. "Of course, madame."

Bea squinted at her. "Provenance?" she asked.

Grace smiled. "References?" she translated, long since used to Lady Bea's unique style of communication. "Diccan found her."

Now both women stared at the amazingly unruffled Schroeder. Grace intervened before there was a full-scale inquisition. "Schroeder is helping me pack away my old clothing."

Kate considered the piles on the bed. "Ah, yes. The uniform of the Peninsular nurse. Excellent timing. Since we're here and it's a glorious day, you can come to Fanchon's with us to order a new wardrobe. I don't know why Diccan hasn't already thought of it."

For the first time in what seemed like forever, Grace beamed. "Because I already did. I'm only waiting now for delivery."

Kate's eyebrows comically raised. "Brave girl. She saw you herself?"

"After I invoked both your name and Diccan's."

She finally had the chance to receive her hug from Lady Bea. At first sight, Lady Bea would remind one of Diccan's mother. As regal as a royal, the elderly daughter of a duke seemed to be looking on the world with stern judgment. After only moments in her company, though, one couldn't help but realize that her mien was protection for an uncommonly gentle heart. After a day, one could also begin to interpret her tangled speech, which had been left permanently affected after a bad injury.

"Forget-me-not," Bea said with a soft smile, lifting her beringed hand up to cup Grace's cheek.

Grace brushed a snowy curl back from Bea's cheek. "I've missed you, too. Promise you'll visit frequently. And that you'll help me find a place to live."

"She wouldn't miss it," Kate assured her. "Neither, come to think of it, would I. And you can tell us all about it as we ride through the park." She gave Grace a little push. "Bonnets, now."

"Oh, I don't…" Grace demurred, looking down at her dress.

Kate gave a gusty sigh. "Don't tell me I've wasted my time with you, Grace. Begin as you mean to go on. Besides, you'll be with me, and who will even see you in the shadow of my glory?"

Kate was in her typical daywear. Green and cream, just as Diccan's mother had been. But all resemblance ended there, as Kate wore a carriage dress of striped sarcenet, an apple green spencer with slashed Spanish sleeves, and a massive chip straw bonnet, heavy with fruit.

Kate was right, of course. "As usual," Grace said, "I bow to your wisdom."

Donning bonnet and pelisse, Grace led the way down to where the barouche waited out front.

"Where's Thrasher?" she asked, seeing a tall, middle-aged man standing in the place of Kate's twelve-year-old tiger. Moon-faced and slow-moving, the man looked out of place in Kate's livery.

"This is George," Kate announced with a pat to his arm. "He asked to see London, so I brought him back from the estate with me. George has been with me since I was ten. Haven't you, George?"

George had a smile like an oversized child. "Yes'm, Miss Kate."

Handing the women up, he took his seat at the back and the barouche set off. It was a day of rare, cloudless skies and soft breezes. The neighborhood gardens showed off the last of their flowers, and the breeze carried the scent of roses.

The park was crowded, with strollers meandering the paths and vehicles slowly circling the lanes. It was a scene of color and laughter and beauty, the *haute ton* at its best.

"Now then," Kate said, nodding to Lady Yardley and her two daughters as they slipped by in a pink carriage that matched their dresses. "Before we get to you, we have news."

Reaching into her reticule, she pulled out a letter and handed it over. It was franked by Jack Wyndham, the Earl of Gracechuch, and held an invitation that Grace read with delight.

"Olivia and Jack are getting remarried!" she cried. "Oh, I hope we can go."

"Of course you're going," Kate huffed. "You can't think that this wedding would be complete without the Three Graces."

Grace ran a finger across the invitation, as if it could help resurrect those fraught days after Waterloo, when three complete strangers, summarily dubbed the Three Graces, had formed a true friendship. Grace didn't even want to contemplate what her life would have been without her friends.

"There isn't any way of knowing what Diccan will be doing in another month."

Kate shrugged and waved to a group of handsome men on horseback. "It doesn't matter in the least if Diccan is there. You will be."

Grace managed a quick smile. "Who am I to argue with you?"

"Exactly. Now then, Grace," Kate said. "If Fanchon doesn't have you in a dither, who does?"

Grace instinctively looked around for eavesdroppers. A lot of people were focused on the carriage, but none were close enough to overhear. "I need lessons."

Kate lifted an eyebrow. "Considering the things I know, I'm not at all certain I want to hear what in. Shall I be forced to resort to my vinaigrette?"

"I doubt it. I need to learn how to be a good enough wife for Diccan."

Both women stared at her. "Are you mad?" Kate retorted. "You're too good for him already."

"You know I'm not, Kate. I'm not nearly what Diccan needs. I've spent my life with the army, which isn't exactly a world of formal dinners and small talk. No one ever taught me tact or etiquette or taboos. Good Lord, the only order of precedence I know is military. I don't fit in, Kate."

"Nonsense," Kate said, sounding very serious. "You've lived in my house for three months. I wouldn't exactly call you a bumpkin. You count Lady Castlereagh and the Duke of Wellington as friends, and have spent time in some of the most exotic places in the world."

Grace sighed, suddenly hating that word. "In barracks. Not drawing rooms."

"You know twelve or thirteen languages."

"Eight, actually. But only curses, drinking toasts, and how to buy a fat chicken. Not exactly polite discourse."

"You have one of the most insightful minds I've ever known."

Next to Kate, Lady Bea snorted, giving her hand a little wave. "Fur on a chicken."

It took a second, but Grace finally pulled out Bea's meaning. "You mean, you don't need much insight to mingle with society."

Bea giggled.

Kate considered Grace, uncharacteristically serious. "There's more to marriage than being introduced to ambassadors," she suggested.

Grace nodded. "I know there is. But it's all of a piece, don't you see? If I don't learn to fit into his world, he'll never be comfortable with me."

An image flashed through Grace's mind of Diccan's head thrown back above hers, his face taut and his muscles straining. She could feel him inside her again, for that one moment, perfectly comfortable. She wanted that moment again and didn't know how to achieve it.

Lady Kate must have seen something on her face, because she snapped open her umbrella as if it were an offensive weapon. "That blind fool," she growled. "I'll slice his heart out."

Grace laid a hand on Kate's arm. "Need I remind you that he neither wanted nor anticipated this marriage? He's doing the best he can."

"Bollocks. His best would be realizing that he's been given the gift of his life. Why, you need do no more than be yourself for him to fall in love with you."

"I've tried being myself, Kate," she said with a wry smile. "Even my mother couldn't abide me."

Grace realized her mistake when she saw pity briefly flare in Kate's eyes. Her face burning, Grace looked out to where the Serpentine glistened beyond the trees. They were completely stopped now in the middle of the lane, as around them landaus and curricles waited behind high-blooded horses, and acquaintances called out like birds on a tree. All people who knew each other, who knew how to dance the society minuet, when Grace couldn't even figure out how to gain entrance into the room.

"He's attending embassy functions without me," she said, not able to face her friend. "I can't let him get used to that, or he'll never think to include me."

This time there was no mistaking Lady Bea. "Idiot."

Kate had also taken on a militant look. "In that case, we need to change his mind. I love nothing more than to surprise a man with what's right under his nose." She laughed and patted Lady Bea on the knee. "What do you think, Bea? Will I make a good governess?"

Bea just laughed, which made Grace finally smile back. Kate's words eased her panic. She had a plan. She had friends to help her. She had a goal in sight. So what if it wasn't the goal she'd hoped for? It would serve. She hoped it would keep her from simply existing at the far reaches of Diccan's life.

Kate clapped her hands together. "Excellent. We'll begin tomorrow. Anything else?"

Grace looked down to her hands. "You put the wedding announcement in the papers."

Kate grinned. "You figured that out, did you?"

"Diccan's mother did."

Bea made a most rude noise, rather like a snorting horse.

Kate scowled. "You've met her? Vile woman. Did she crush you with her vast superiority?"

"She made a valiant attempt. I wanted to ask you, though, about what you put in the notice."

"You mean that your mother is Glorious Georgianna Hewitt? No. I just said General Sir Hillary and Lady Fairchild. The rest is no one's business but yours."

Grace felt the air thin out. "You knew?"

Lady Bea raised a gloved hand. "Cousin."

"You never said anything."

"What should we say?" Kate asked nonchalantly. "Unless she shows up in my sitting room, I doubt the problem of dealing with her will crop up."

As simple as that. Grace almost laughed out loud. And Kate, ever practical Kate, was already waving to an old woman in a landau. "Miss Dix," she said. "Lovely lady. Thinks she's Galileo."

"I do have another question," Grace said, straightening

her gloves. "About Diccan. Well, about his older brother. How did he die? Diccan just said that he wasn't up to the bishop's weight."

Both women wore identical scowls. "It's no secret," Kate said. "The bishop thought he'd fashioned the perfect Hilliard in him. Groomed him for greatness. Until Robert drank himself to death."

Grace swore she felt the loss herself. "Were he and Diccan close?"

Kate shrugged. "Difficult to tell with those two. Diccan never talked about it, except when his parents then turned their sights on him. He was supposed to fill the gap. He told them to go to hell."

Grace, wasn't surprised. He must have grieved badly.

"Mushroom," Kate muttered at a passing gig. "Have nothing to do with her. Beats her abigail."

Grace followed Kate's gaze, only to stumble over another person entirely. A mounted Harry Lidge was waving to her from down the lane. Oh, dear. What should she do? Kate and Harry seemed to loathe each other. But she hadn't seen him since Canterbury.

"Do you want to get down?" Kate asked without acknowledging him. "I may not be able to tolerate the saintly Harry, but I know you're friends."

Grace felt like squirming. "If you don't mind."

"We'll circle the park and pick you up."

Grace wished Kate would tell her what was between her and Harry, but she didn't have the right. So she let George hand her down, and she limped over to where Harry was dismounting from his bay.

Giving her a pointed look, he kissed her cheek. "You're well, Gracie?"

"I am, Harry. What are you doing in town?" She reached up to stroke the star of white on his gelding's velvety nose. "And you, my lovely Beau. Has he forced you to show off for the peacocks?"

Beau, who knew her well and had more than once carried her, whuffled into her hand.

"Hilliard doesn't accompany you today?" Harry asked.

How many times, Grace wondered, would she have this conversation? "He is in meetings."

"He's just married," Harry protested, and succeeded in making Grace feel worse.

"And that marriage interrupted serious responsibilities he must now fulfill," she answered. "Now then, have you been reassigned yet?"

It took a few minutes for Harry to relax, but in the end he and Grace walked, talking of nothing much, friends once again. Even if he had been complicit in her marriage, she was glad to be on his arm.

It wasn't enough to offset the uneasiness that grew as they strolled along. People were blatantly staring. Considering the fact that most were smiling on her with the same sly disdain as Diccan's mother, she was fairly sure they knew who she was. The tall, gawky girl with no looks and a limp who'd snabbled the elegant Diccan Hilliard.

"I hear his father tried to pay her off," she heard a young woman say.

Someone giggled. "I heard she paid *him* off."

"Ignore them," Harry advised, his hand tight on hers as they walked. "They're just jealous."

Grace managed a too-bright smile. "Well, you do look dashing in your Rifleman's green."

But his expression hadn't eased, even for her clumsy

humor. "Lady Kate is back from her jaunt around the park," he said. "Would you like me to walk you to her?"

"And have you two come to blows in the middle of the park? No, thank you. Someday you're really going to have to tell me why you two are always at daggers drawn."

His answering smile was tight. "Someday maybe I will."

Giving her hand a kiss, he vaulted up onto Beau. Grace waited until he was well away before heading back to Kate. She hadn't noticed the pair of strollers coming her way. They had obviously noticed her. An exquisite blonde dressed in an abundance of peach ruffles and a wasp-waisted tulip.

"Well, I must say I'm glad I got a good look at her," the girl was saying to the young dandy as she twirled her peach ruffled parasol. "Otherwise I wouldn't have ever imagined how bad it was. Poor Mr. Hilliard."

"Indeed," he said, patting her fair hand. "You'd think she'd have a sense of shame."

The girl sniffed, a picture of derision. "I just hope he doesn't succeed in bringing her into fashion. Lurching about like that would be so dreadfully tiresome."

Grace fought the urge to cringe. It was bad enough that she heard them. What was worse was that she began to blush, that ugly, splotchy red that so humiliated her. They were no more than ten feet away now. Calling upon old pride, she straightened her shoulders and walked on.

She wasn't sure how it happened. She had looked up to smile at Lady Bea where she waited in the carriage as the couple neared.

"I feel ill at the sight," the girl sneered. "She shouldn't be allowed to walk in public."

"Well, then," the dandy said with a smirk, "she won't."

And before Grace could react, he stuck his cane out and tripped her. Her bad leg twisted beneath her. She reached out to catch some kind of support; the couple stepped backwards, smiling as if watching a trick at Astley's. Arms windmilling in a last desperate attempt at balance, Grace sprawled face-first onto the gravel.

Chapter 11

For what seemed like forever, all Grace could do was lie there in the middle of a Hyde Park path, an untidy lump of gray and shamed red.

"See what I mean?" she heard the girl ask, and had to look up to see if such a pretty child was really that venal. The girl's smile was beautiful. One had to look close to see the glint of malice.

Just then Grace caught sight of Kate's groom George trundling her way, his face screwed up with worry. Kate was climbing out of her carriage, her expression ominous. *Oh, dear*, was all Grace could think, bowing her head in frustration. She'd better get up before Kate turned this into a circus.

She was looking down at her hands, gathering strength for a try, when she heard gravel crunch.

"I'm sorry, George," she apologized, unable to face him, "but I seem bent on imitating a tortoise. Might I have your hand?"

"But you already have my hand," she heard, and almost

crumpled right back to the ground. "My fortune, such as it is, and my heart."

Diccan. Ah, *merde*. She might have known he would arrive just in time to see her at her most inglorious. "And I am the richer for it," she answered with a stiff smile up at his coolly elegant features. "For now, though, I think your hand will suffice."

He eased her to her feet, his sure grasp on her arms surprisingly gentle. "Well met, wife." Straightening her bonnet, he smiled. "I was hoping to see you today."

She fought to keep from blushing. "Not so precipitously, one would hope."

"Any meeting is a pleasant surprise."

Impatiently brushing off her dusty clothing, she glanced at Diccan's pristine coffee brown jacket, biscuit pants, and gleaming boots. Of course he looked elegant and unruffled. She looked as if she'd been sweeping the stoop. "I don't suppose you could be kind enough to look a bit mussed."

An eyebrow lifted. "I would do almost anything for you, wife. But wrinkle my Weston coat? How could you think of so distressing Biddle?"

She smiled. "I must have been consumed by my desire to leave the park."

"I'll accompany you," Diccan said. "Right after I speak to young Mr. Palmerston behind you."

The boy preened. "A pleasure, sir," the boy spoke up, suddenly nervous. "May I introduce . . ."

Diccan raised his quizzing glass. "No," he said in flat tones. "I don't believe you can."

The girl went pale. The boy tried to bluster it out. "Doing it up too brown, sir, surely?" he asked, clutching his own quizzing glass. "It was an accident, after all."

Diccan went perfectly still. Grace heard someone gasp. She caught her own breath as Diccan lowered his quizzing glass. His languid expression had suddenly turned cold as death. "Odd," he said, and Grace shivered. "I saw something very different. Something no gentleman could excuse."

The young man finally realized the danger and began to babble apologies.

"See, Chuffy?" Grace heard from behind her. "We didn't have to run over here after all. Told you he wouldn't murder anyone in the park. He'd hold up traffic."

"Never stopped him before," was the answer.

Grace looked over to see two gentlemen approaching at a fast clip, one tall and broad, with a thick head of auburn hair and a parade-ground voice, the other shorter, wider, and balder, with spectacles that slid down his nose. They were in Kate's company and were leading their horses.

"Oh, but he's much older now," the tall one said. "Don't have the energy. Besides, he knows that grass stains are the devil to get out of superfine."

"When have I ever been brought low enough to worry about grass stains?" Diccan drawled. "No, this young gentleman has accepted my invitation to spar at Jackson's tomorrow. Haven't you?"

The boy grew even paler, and Grace knew that Diccan had picked the perfect punishment. Not only public humiliation, but time for the boy to consider the actions that had induced it. Diccan had truly frightened the boy. He was sweating, and Grace understood why. Diccan had frightened her, too.

In that one moment, almost too quickly to comprehend, his eyes had gone eerily blank. The urbane gentleman she'd come to know had vanished, and someone else entirely appeared. Someone as hard and ruthless as death. Someone she didn't know.

She wondered, suddenly, if she knew her husband at all. Even at his angriest, she had never seen this side of him that made her think he could draw blood with just his eyes. Yes, he had gotten them all out of war-torn Belgium only steps ahead of an assassin. She had always thought he'd used his diplomatic skills. For the first time, she wondered if that were true.

"Grace, see?" Lady Kate said as she stopped. "I've brought more company."

And giving one glacial look at the ashen couple, Lady Kate deliberately turned her back. Grace saw the girl sway. She had just received the cut direct, and from a duchess. A fitting punishment for her as well. Without another word, she and her beau fled.

"You must let me make known to you Diccan's particular friends," Kate was saying. "Charles, Viscount Wilde and Mr. Ian Ferguson. Gentlemen, my dear friend, Mrs. Grace Fairchild Hilliard."

The courtesies were exchanged. "Pleasure to meet you, ma'am," Viscount Wilde said, his head bobbing so much his glasses slid down his nose. "Call me Chuffy. Everyone does."

He was Diccan's opposite; plump and rumpled and altogether comfortable. Grace found that smiling with him was easy.

"Thank you," Grace said. "That is very kind."

Giving her own crumpled skirts another surreptitious shake, Grace looked around for a quick, inconspicuous escape. Chuffy evidently had other ideas.

"You're uninjured, ma'am?" he asked, hat off, not seeming

to notice that his horse was nibbling at his neckcloth. "Took quite a tumble."

"I am, thank you."

His blush was even more unfortunate than Grace's. "Trumps, ma'am. Trumps. Can't have anything happen to you, after all. Saved m'brother's life at Cardiff, don't ya know."

"Corunna," Diccan and Mr. Ferguson chorused gently.

"Just so," Chuffy said, his sudden grin infectious. "Conundrum."

"You truly suffered no injury?" Diccan asked, taking her hand.

Grace saw real concern in his eyes and flushed with pleasure. "Only to my pride. But it is an old campaigner like myself, so it is certain to recover."

He had no gloves on, she thought inconsequentially. His skin was rough and warm, his grip gentle. His eyes crinkled at the corners. Grace couldn't look away. For that exquisite moment, Diccan couldn't seem to look away from her either.

It was left to Lady Bea to hurry things along. "Treacle!" she called from the carriage.

Grace started, her attention snapped. "I should let Lady Bea know I'm all right."

Diccan looked surprised to find himself standing there. "Of course," he said, and let her hand go.

She wanted to protest. She wanted to reach out and reclaim his warmth. It was the bubbly, oblivious Chuffy Wilde who stepped up. "Honor to escort you, ma'am," he said, arm out, his other hand holding the reins of his well-formed chestnut, who was now nibbling his hat.

Grace waited a heartbeat for Diccan to protest. He didn't, of course. Trying not to sigh, she turned a smile on

Chuffy. "Your brother wouldn't by any chance be Brock Wilde, would he?"

Chuffy beamed. "You remember him!"

"Who could forget 'Wilde and Ready'?" she asked, laying a hand on Chuffy's arm. "Why, he singlehandedly kept us in stewed cony throughout the Siege of Burgos."

Behind them, she could hear Diccan sigh. "Yet another heart conquered. I tell you, Ferguson, it's enough to shake a man's confidence."

"Just friends, Hilliard," Chuffy assured him with a nod. "Not in the mood for a duel. Would displease m'mother."

They proceeded back to the carriage in pairs, as if it had been arranged. The attention Grace had garnered faded away, softened by Diccan's proprietary behavior and his friends' good humor. Grace knew she should be grateful. She should be delighted. She was. Selfishly, though, she wished Diccan's concern stemmed from more than courtesy. She wished that when he said she had his heart, he meant it.

Ah, Grace, she thought as Diccan helped her into Kate's coach with a flourishing kiss of her hand. *You always were a greedy girl.*

"Thank you, Mr. Hilliard," Gentleman Jim Jackson said, his thick face folded into a wry smile. "That was an excellent exhibit in the art of the fancy."

Diccan grabbed the towel Ian Ferguson tossed at him and wiped the sweat that dripped from his face. Across the room, his young opponent was struggling to stay on his feet. Blood poured down his skinny torso from his broken nose, and his right eye was puffing out. It could have been much worse. Diccan had been surprised at how ready he was to murder the little bastard. If the boy hadn't stood up to his punishment like a man, he would have crushed him. But the lesson had been administered.

"Thank you, sir," the boy said in nasal tones. A towel pinched to his face, he offered Diccan a formal bow. "I believe I understand what you were trying to show me."

Diccan still wanted to pummel something. It couldn't be this chastened puppy, though. He returned his bow. "See you don't make the same mistake again. Look what it did to your nose."

"Excellent science," Diccan heard to his right. He turned to see Geoffrey Smythe strolling his way, smiling. "I'm glad I've never had anything but the greatest respect for your lady wife."

Diccan felt his gore rise. He did not like the slick blond younger son. There was just something too cunning about him. It didn't take a warning look from Ian for Diccan to hold his tongue, though.

Slipping into his shirt, he shrugged. "These little lessons are tiresome," he drawled, "but necessary to a gentleman's education." Throwing off another shrug, he flashed a weary smile.

Ian looked troubled. Smythe looked amused. Diccan felt sick to his stomach. Hadn't he just been warned to ignore Grace? To not betray any partiality? And here was Smythe, probing for a weak spot. Expecting that weak spot to be Grace.

"I have some lovely *uisce beatha* back at the club," Ferguson suggested as Smythe strolled off.

Nodding, Diccan headed for the door. He had to do better. He had to protect Grace. Next time a spoiled stripling tripped her in the park, he'd have to look away.

It might not make a difference, though. He might have already made a fatal mistake.

Diccan didn't come home that night. Grace knew she shouldn't have noticed. But she was growing tired of having her hopes raised and then dropped again. She was weary of being unable to receive attention from Diccan with ease or demand his attention with authority. And she hated the fact that after hearing about his brother she wanted to forgive him any thoughtless behavior.

At least her wardrobe had finally arrived. She returned from a solitary breakfast to find her bed quilted in attire of all colors and shapes. Her heart took a great leap. Finally. Another move forward. A chance to...what? Get her husband's attention? Face the *ton* with impunity? Humiliate herself by trying to make a silk purse from a sow's ear?

"The pomona green, I think, ma'am," Schroeder said without looking up from where she was arranging underthings in the press. "I've laid it out for you. And I hope you don't think me presumptuous, but Lady Kate gave me the name of a hairdresser. He will attend you this afternoon."

Grace instinctively reached up to touch her scraped-back hair. It had been so long since she'd thought to do anything but keep it out of the way. "That would be lovely."

Before she had the chance to change, though, there was a knock on the door. She opened it to find a footman waiting outside.

"'Scuse me, ma'am. There's a man wants to see you downstairs."

"Let him come up."

"Er, no. He, uh, can't. Said to meet him out front."

Grace followed the boy downstairs, not exactly certain what to expect. She certainly didn't expect what she found. Standing in front of the hotel on Piccadilly was a short, bandy-legged man with a shock of red hair, the grin of a devil, and two prime horses on the rein.

"Harps?" she whispered, overcome.

A grin split his face. In his hands were the reins of a piebald gelding and a coal-black Andalusian, who knickered the minute she caught sight of Grace. Tears welled in Grace's eyes. She caught herself just shy of throwing herself into the little man's arms.

"Harps!" she cried, grabbing his hand.

"Ah, good, then," he growled, his eyes suspiciously bright. "You remembered. The missus and me thought maybe now you're flittin' about with them fine folk, you'd be after forgettin' your friends. Not a word do we hear. Not even an invite to your wedding. And then didn't we get that fine note?"

Passing pedestrians stopped to stare at the little man who stood glaring at her.

"Note?" she asked, paying them no mind. Harps was here, and he'd brought her girl. She struggled mightily not to cry as she laid her cheek against the mare's great neck. "What note?"

Sean Harper tilted his head. "Ah well, let's see now. Didn't he say somethin' mad about him not allowin' any pugs 'r monkeys near him, but a girl should have her horse."

She lifted her head. "He who?"

"Your husband, lass. And didn't he say for me to bring your lovely Epona myself so's I could personally give me blessing to the marriage, like I was your da and all."

"As close as makes no difference." Her throat felt

unbearably tight as she stroked the mare's velvety nose. "He really asked you to bring Epona? Diccan?"

"That snooty fella what was cousin to Lady Kate? Oh, aye, that's the one. Now, are ya gonna stand here entertainin' all the swells in London, or are ya gonna take y'r little lady out for a ride?"

"Wait right there."

Spinning around, she ran up the steps. Diccan hadn't come home last night. But he'd taken the time and thought to send Harper and Epona to her. How could she not fall in love with a man like that?

Chapter 12

Diccan saw her across the park. How could anyone miss her? For the first time since he'd met her, he was finally seeing his wife in her element. She was riding the Andalusian. Glossy black and as sweet a goer as he'd ever seen, with big liquid eyes, an elegant arch to her powerful neck, and the most delicate of heads. Grace had been right. Breeding her to Gadzooks would produce magnificent foals.

But the horse only took part of his attention. Grace took the rest. Clad in an old Guards jacket and split skirt, she rode like a Hussar, as fluid as her horse, her hands light, her posture strong. She was poetry in motion. And she glowed. It was the only way he could think to describe it. The brisk air tinted her cheeks, and her eyes were laughing and bright, the angles of her long face somehow softened. If this was how she'd looked on the Peninsula, no wonder the men had doted on her.

He'd once nicknamed her Boadicea. He'd been more right then he knew. She was magnificent. A goddess; a warrior queen clad in a tattered old scarlet Guards' jacket, sensuous as summer. And he wasn't the only one who saw it. Heads turned. Men smiled. Ladies straightened in saddles, unwilling to be shown up. He felt himself swell with unfamiliar pride. He had always respected Grace. For the first time since he'd run from her bed, he thought he understood why she had so thoroughly aroused him.

He knew he shouldn't. Still, he called to her, hand up. "Greetings, lady wife!"

If he thought she had been striking before, it was nothing to the sight of her smile when she saw him. "Diccan!" she called back, laughing as her horse danced beneath her. "Come meet Epona."

Diccan almost lost his reins in shock. Good God. Grace Fairchild had a dimple. A big, saucy one, just to the left of her mouth that only peeked out when she laughed. Had he seen her laugh before now? He must not have. He was sure he would have remembered something that sly and seductive.

Beneath him, Gadzooks seemed to have a similar reaction to Grace's mount. The stallion suddenly began to prance, head up, nostrils flared, mincing toward the filly like a park saunterer.

"Gadzooks, my lad," he said, patting the roan's neck. "You have an excellent eye."

Pulling to a halt, Grace leaned forward, her gray eyes alight. "You are my hero, sir."

Diccan raised a dry eyebrow. "Gadzooks? I admit he is a handsome fellow, but I'm not sure heroism is in his nature."

"Don't let him slight you like that, Gadzooks," she admonished, leaning over to pet the animal's nose. "But you know perfectly well, I don't mean him. How can I thank you for my surprise?" she asked Diccan, her hand out to him. "You can't imagine how this brightened my day."

"I know how it's brightening mine," he responded, oddly affected. "I can think of nothing more stirring than a brilliant horsewoman, except a brilliant horsewoman on a magnificent beast. Your Epona is everything you claim her to be, madame. I am in awe."

Beneath him, Gadzooks knickered and nudged the filly's head with his own massive one. Epona danced coquettishly away, pulling Grace's hand back, and Diccan was beset by a surprising desire to follow. To prance like Gadzooks for his mate's regard. Suddenly he wanted to see her again as she had been in his bed, her skin flushed and her eyes deep and languorous.

Was this how Grace Hilliard was revealed? Was it enough to afford her respect in his circles? And how would he hold out against her, knowing that magnificence lurked beneath her plain facade?

"Will you be home later, my dear?" he asked easily as if he hadn't just been picturing her spread out before him, dripping with arousal. "I think I'd like to match the paces of these two."

"I would be delighted. I believe Harper has a mind to interrogate you."

"Oh, aye," Harper agreed with a steely nod. "I do that."

Diccan nodded. Suddenly he found himself wanting to get to know this new Grace. This surprising Grace. He wanted to match her stride for stride, and see how she came alive on a galloping horse. He had to figure out a way to enjoy a ride without giving away his game.

He'd just turned away when an old man thundered toward them on a barrel-chested gray.

"Halloo, Grace!" the old man yelled, hand up as if calling a charge.

Grace stopped and stared. "Uncle Dawes?"

The old man pulled his horse up inches away, spraying gravel. "Where have you been, girl?" he demanded. "I've been wasting my time on these riding paths for a solid three days looking for you."

Tall, as barrel-chested as his horse, and clad in the broadcloth of a country squire, the old man was red-faced, with merry eyes and an excess of snowy side whiskers. Obviously a cavalryman.

Grace was leaning over to buss the old man on the cheek. "Oh, I didn't expect you in town. I wrote to you and Aunt Dawes at Marchlands. I'm so glad you've come!"

"And where would I be when I found out you'd been chased down like a fox by some man milliner?" Without hesitation or apology, the old man lifted a monocle in Diccan's direction. "Good God, girl! He's a nancy boy!"

Diccan couldn't help laughing. Grace joined him. "I believe you seriously underestimate him, my dear," she told the old man. "Did you know he's won four duels, a dozen horse races, and a bout with Gentleman Jackson himself?"

Diccan was surprised, not so much at Grace's correct history of him, but at her air of pride. "You put me to the blush, wife," he protested.

"Nonsense," she retorted with a bubbling laugh. "You wouldn't have done any of those things if you didn't want them spoken of."

Her uncle let loose a bark of laughter. "Never waste time fencing with her, lad. She's deadly."

"I know that only too well, sir."

Laughter lit her face. "Uncle Dawes, may I present my

husband, Mr. Diccan Hilliard. Diccan, this is General Lord Wilfred Dawes."

Dawes peered at Diccan as if he were a new recruit. "Princess Royal's Heavy Dragoons, sir. You?"

Diccan bowed. "King George's Light Diplomacy. It's good to see my Grace has a defender. Well, besides the eight thousand or so troops she seems to have saved on the Peninsula."

The general's glare grew even fiercer. "You makin' light of soldiers, sir, or my great-niece?"

"Myself, sir. Only myself."

That seemed to sit well with the old tartar. "Well, at least you have that much sense. And by the looks of that bonerattler you sit, you have an eye for horseflesh. Is he as bad-tempered as he looks?"

"Worse. And he's just now added to his sins by become enamored of my wife's lovely Epona."

Diccan had no sooner spoken, then Gadzooks lunged at the general's horse. The general cursed, his horse screeched and backed away, and Gadzooks tossed his head, very satisfied with himself.

Diccan smacked him. "Cease, you ill-tempered brat. I'm trying to impress the lady's family."

"That's the way of it for us unfortunate men," the general announced with a booming laugh. "Always pining for a pretty filly."

Gadzooks shook his head. Calmly watching him, Grace chuckled. "Oh, he'll have wonderful babies. All the fight in the world. Uncle Dawes, you must promise to come for dinner."

"Once we find a home, sir," Diccan offered, "you must consider it yours as well."

General Dawes shot him a trenchant look. "Oh, I will, lad. I will."

Diccan gave a bow. "And now I will leave Grace in the capable hands of two of her champions. Seems to me that just before I saw your niece on her horse, I was thinking how nothing could make me late for my meeting."

Grace flushed. The general barked and nodded, as if delighted. As he turned away, though, Diccan saw the steel in those old eyes and wondered just what it was he would have to face there.

He only gave the general a passing thought, though. He had more important things on his mind, such as whether he should have brought Grace's horse to town after all. It might be the bridge they needed to make a real marriage. But did he want that? Did he dare chance it, especially now?

Diccan got his first glimpse of the new Grace later that afternoon. Pulling up before the Pulteney, he found her standing with her loyal Harper alongside their horses. She smiled at seeing him.

"Oh, good," she said, her gloved hand resting on her Epona's gleaming neck. "I was hoping you'd remember."

"Of course I remembered," he answered, trotting up. "And as my reward, I'm given a chance to see you in your new glory. You have my abject apologies for ever doubting you, wife. You and Madame Fanchon have indeed triumphed."

Grace did benefit from Fanchon's dressing and a new hairstyle. Her riding habit was a symphony of tailoring, a sharply cut green kerseymere with frogging *a la militaire*, matching shako, and scarf that flirted with the breeze. Beneath, her hairstyle had been softened into a chignon, with a light fringe. The look complemented her lithe frame and contrasted perfectly with the glossy black of her horse. Diccan couldn't stop staring.

"Well, at least you have that much sense," Harper muttered.

"Hush, Harps," Grace chastised as the little man gave her a leg up. "How was Diccan to know that I could clean up? I thank you, Diccan. I have to admit that I am feeling unpardonably smug. I'll never be Kate, but at least I no longer look like a paid mourner. Now, then," she hurried on, gathering her reins, "Where shall we go? I'd rather not return to the park. Epona needs to stretch her legs."

"My thoughts exactly." Diccan turned them into the street, the indomitable Harper at their backs. "Besides, I'd be fighting off every Hyde Park soldier within a mile just to talk to you."

Even Grace's blushes seemed softer, her carriage somehow more ladylike. Diccan kept getting distracted by the sight of her hands on the reins. She had the perfect feel for her horse's mouth, a gentle touch that certainly translated well on a man's skin.

He was beset by memory again, this time of the moment he'd collapsed onto her, panting and spent from an astonishingly hard climax. She had wrapped her arms around him, stroking his spine with fingers he now realized were long and elegant, with just enough callus to intrigue. He felt a small *frisson* snake down that same area, and wondered what those fingers would feel like stroking his cock.

Beneath him, Gadzooks kicked out at a passing cart, calling him to account. Squeezing with his knees, he guided him away. He hoped like hell he hadn't betrayed himself.

He heard a suspicious snort from behind him and had a

feeling it wasn't from Harper's gelding. He was definitely going to have to watch himself around the Irishman.

"If you'll be patient," he told Grace, "we'll head out toward Kensington, where we can have the road to ourselves." *And where he could more easily spot a shadow.*

"That sounds perfect," she said, with a bright smile.

Just then a beer dray cut them off, sending Grace's horse rearing and spinning in a circle. Epona whinnied. Grace laughed out loud. Diccan didn't realize he'd reached out, ready to intervene, until Grace neatly settled her horse and received an apology from the carter, who tipped his hat.

"Sure, there's no need to hold my girl's hand," Harper said quietly from behind him. "Taught her myself afore she could climb steps, then, didn't I?"

Diccan turned around to see that fierce, protective light in the ex-sergeant's eyes. "Were you the one who taught her how to ride a camel?"

That earned him a bark of laughter. "Saints praise us, no. Didn't she do that all on her own, the little witch? Not even four when I lost her in the bazaar and found her up there chattering away with the driver, like he was a long-lost cousin and all." He shook his head. "Faith, and wasn't I always pullin' her outa one scrape or another, so? Truth be told, it's a relief to have some help."

Diccan had a wonderful time that afternoon. He and Grace rode hell-bent cross country, jumping fences and hedgerows, their laughter floating away on the wind as they tested the mettle of their horses. Gadzooks won, of course. But Diccan couldn't discount the Andalusian. She certainly held her own. So, he admitted, to himself, did her rider. The gray ghost he had met in Brussels had transformed into a red-blooded woman, and he thought that maybe he wouldn't mind this marriage so much after all.

His temper improved even more when he returned back to the Pulteney to find one of his operatives waiting with Babs in his bedroom.

"This is Sarah." Babs introduced the girl, a round-faced, round-bodied maid with lank yellow hair and sturdy arms. "She's been working for Viscount Bentley."

Diccan invited them both to sit, and adjured Biddle to make sure Grace was kept busy.

"The Bentley funeral was yesterday, wasn't it?" he asked.

The girl bobbed her head. "Yessir. Both the master and the son. Were a lot o' people."

Diccan nodded. The word had been put about that Bentley had been attacked down on the wharves when he went to collect the body of his son, who had died in a duel on the Continent.

"What can you tell me, Sarah?"

"My lord's lawyer, Mr. Melvin, spent yesterday at the house with a Mr. Geoffrey Smythe, goin' through the late master's things. Kept sayin' that they had to make sure Bentley didn't 'ave the verse after all. Said it were Bentley's responsibility and it were missin'."

His heart picked up a bit. "A verse? Like poetry?"

"Don't know, sir. Don't think they found it, neither. Fair tore my lord's office apart, secret-like."

Diccan considered what she'd said. "Anything else?"

"Yessir. Said that time was runnin' out. That things were getting desperate. Said somethin' about the Duke o' Wellington, but I couldn't catch it. I had to hide so's they didn't find me."

"You did an excellent job, Sarah. You might have just saved the Duke's life."

The girl bobbed her head, her face red as a brick. "I hope so, sir."

"Babs," he said turning to her, "I don't suppose you'd like to work for a lawyer."

"No, thank you," she said with a secret smile. "I'm keeping an eye on your wife."

"Is the house still being watched?"

She nodded. "The house. You. And a government man is watching the watchers."

"Well, don't leave her alone. I know we expect a threat first, but I don't want to take chances."

Progress, he thought as he sat down at his desk to scribble a note to Drake. New players. A reference to a verse, which Diccan's sixth sense told him was the object Evenham had told him the Lions were waiting for. A possible way into the Bentley home for a fresh search.

Maybe this could be the way to break the case. Maybe it would mean that he could be excused from seeking the Lions' attention. Maybe, just maybe, he could actually have the time to get to know his wife. He thought of their ride today and hoped so. It had only been an hour, and he was already anxious to match her skills again, to make her laugh so he could see that dimple.

Long experience, though, told him not to count on it.

For Grace, that day was a harbinger for the next sennight. She began each day with a bruising ride and ended with a quiet dinner in their parlor. During the intervening hours, Diccan disappeared into his clubs, and she either to Kate's for education and house-searching, or the Army Hospital to care for her men. Once her evening dresses were ready, Diccan even accompanied her and Kate to a few functions, not disappearing into the card room until he'd spent at least one dance by her side.

He had even listened to her when she told him she'd seen that same man watching the hotel again. She told him she trusted him when he said he was taking care of it; actually, she did.

She began, tentatively, to hope. The more time she spent with Diccan, the more she liked him. The more she wanted to know about him. Diccan seemed interested in her as well. He seemed to relish their rides together. Bolstered by her new, more colorful wardrobe, Grace felt herself beginning to enjoy her role as wife and companion. She saw hints that Diccan was doing the same as a husband, and tried her best to patiently abide until he felt comfortable enough to return to her bed.

It was a difficult wait. Her body rejoiced each time he lifted her onto Epona, his strong hands sure on her waist, his eyes twinkling. She went weak at the brief brush of his hand against hers as he helped her into her chair or down the stairs. She felt her heart thud and her blood heat when she saw his eyes unexpectedly darken when they met hers, when she saw his nostrils flare, just a little, like a stallion scenting a mare. She began to look for it, to wish she knew how to incite it. She wanted him to touch her. She wanted him to do all those amazing things he had done to her before. She wanted to feel his hands on her breasts, his breath against her throat, his moan against her mouth. She wanted to find out if she truly had felt that full, if the heat of him inside her had truly splintered into stars.

But he remained the perfect, languidly polite gentleman, and she didn't know how to demand more. So she did what she did best. She worked hard on being what he needed, and she began to hope that it would be enough.

Her first triumph was finding the perfect house. Situated on Clarges Street around the corner from Kate's house on Curzon, it was a simple white townhouse with wrought iron balconies, tall double-hung windows, and fanlighted doorway. When she showed Diccan through the high-ceilinged, clean rooms, she felt a real sense of pride. Here would be her salon, she said, and here the morning room and here, with its bookcases and French doors onto the back garden, Diccan's office.

"It will be your private space," she promised, a hand on his arm. "I won't even let the maids in."

He smiled at her. "No one would believe I could be this domesticated," he said. "Robert swore I'd spend the rest of my life in a hotel."

It was her one regret, that no matter what, she couldn't seem to entice Diccan to open up more about his childhood, his family, his hopes and disappointments and dreams. He never revealed more then the most superficial information. Soon, she kept hoping. When he felt more comfortable with her.

He finally took her to her first grand ball, given by Lady Castlereagh, who had taken a young Grace under her wing in Ireland when Grace's father had supported Lord Castlereagh, then Lord Lieutenant.

"Well, Mr. Hilliard," the grande dame announced, taking Grace's hand. "You have done better for yourself than I'd expected. If anyone can keep you in check, I believe it is Grace."

Diccan, quite on his mettle, bowed low. "You have given her a thankless job, ma'am."

Lady Castlereagh's smile was knowing. "So I have, Hilliard. I'll see you both at Almack's?"

From that moment on, even Grace's limp failed to constrain her. She had not disgraced Diccan, here where it was most important. She was on his arm, and she was dressed in the most beautiful gown she had ever owned, a V-necked robe of bronze lutestring and spangled gauze she felt displayed her shoulders well. For the first time in her life, she didn't feel like an inconvenient accessory.

It helped that her Grenadiers made a showing, there to support her when Diccan eventually wandered off to the card room. It helped even more that Kate and Lady Bea had been so generous in their lessons. For the first time in her life, Grace felt almost elegant, and people seemed to respond. She felt a new purpose fill her. She *could* be the wife Diccan needed. Now all she needed to do was be the wife he wanted. Because as hard as she tried, she couldn't delude herself. She was falling in love.

Standing at the edge of the ballroom, watching Grace laugh with her Grenadiers, Diccan battled a growing sense of frustration. It had been eight days, and nothing had happened. No one had approached him, or threatened him, or offered him an opportunity to secure his future. Thornton was a toad, Smythe was a lizard, and their friends were worthless. And yet, while his wife devoted her hours to injured soldiers and furniture warehouses, he was forced to waste his at cockfights, gaming hells, and whorehouses.

She was helping form charitable groups, and he diced with strangers.

He was unsettled by the fact that he'd underestimated the effect his wife would have on him. More and more he found himself wanting to see what she was doing, hear what she thought of something. He wanted her reflections on the case, when he knew he had no right to drag her into it.

The best he could do was step aside and let her spread her wings. Because Grace Fairchild wasn't quite the ugly duckling everyone—including him—had assumed her to be. She was not pretty. She never would be. But she was growing into her new role, until no one really noticed her lurching gait or unseemly height. She was still too pale, too gawky, often too quiet. But once a person saw her on horseback, it didn't matter. Once they got to know her, they couldn't help but respond to her quiet decency and dry wit, just as he found himself doing.

What worried him the most was that he was losing distance. How could he convince anyone that he didn't care for her when all he wanted to do was be with her? When had his hands begun to itch for the feel of her hair and the slope of her hip? When had he decided that she was more interesting than his work? How could he protect her from his enemies if he couldn't even protect her from himself?

He made his biggest mistake when he found himself kissing her. Mostly at the edge of dance floors where it would be commented on that Hilliard was making the best of a bad situation. Once in the morning room of their new home as he helped her pick out wallpaper. Quick, impersonal pecks that never satisfied him.

Then, that very morning, he'd come perilously close to disaster. They were out by Richmond, where the gleaming

Thames spun out across the rolling green fields like a carelessly tossed ribbon. Harper had yet to catch up to them, and Grace was laughing with delight at her filly's success in catching Gadzooks. As for Gadzooks, he was nuzzling Epona like a callow boy with his first love.

Maybe that was Diccan's inspiration. He didn't know. He just knew that as he lifted Grace off Epona, he let her slide down his body until their mouths met in an open-mouthed kiss.

He felt her abruptly still, her hands frozen on his shoulders. He could smell dust on her and horse, the faint tang of honest sweat, the smoke of exotic flowers. This time when his cock signaled interest, he didn't object. He savored the slow tide of engorgement as his rod sought the soft haven of Grace's belly. He heard the hum of arousal in his blood and felt it pulse in his throat. He tasted sunshine and excitement on her lips and probed for entrance with his tongue.

He could come to enjoy this, he thought, as she abruptly softened. Opened. Invited. Hands opening and closing against his shoulders, like a cat kneading a throw, she arched to meet him. Heat-to-heat, bodies fitting together more perfectly than he'd ever known. He could even look forward to holding her so that her breasts were flattened against his chest, her toes on the ground, her head tilted to fit more fully against him. Cooperating, initiating, finally finding the courage to send her own tongue out to mate with his, slick and hot and urgent. Welcoming him, as if directing him home.

He *did* want this, damn it. And if someone were watching, they would know. Breaking the kiss with a gasp, he set her away before worse happened.

"Well then, wife," he said briskly, stepping away as if

nothing had happened, not even the obvious bulge in his breeches. "I believe you said you had furniture warehouses to investigate today. We should undoubtedly get back so you don't miss your appointment."

For a second she seemed to weave a bit, her eyes too large, her skin too pale. Then, as if responding to a barked order, she smiled and stepped back, settling her skirts with both hands. "Indeed. I've been privileged enough to gain an invitation to Mr. Wedgwood's showroom."

"You like his work?" Diccan asked, thinking how unexciting jasperware was. Exquisitely crafted, but mostly dusty blues and whites.

"Oh," she said, "I have been assured it is the perfect accessory in the home of a rising diplomat. Kate will go with me to control my more exuberant impulses."

Diccan almost laughed out loud. If there was one thing he would never accuse Grace of—except, maybe, in the saddle—it was an overabundance of exuberant impulses. Or Kate of knowing how to control them. He should say something, he thought. He should ask what she thought of Italian majolica or Venetian glass, bright colors saturated by the sun. Considering the muted tones she wore, he decided he didn't want to know her answer. Maybe he'd just put the majolica in his office.

"Well, then," he said, giving her a leg up, "we wouldn't want to keep Mr. Wedgwood waiting."

Over the next few days as his house took shape, he found that he couldn't argue with Grace's taste. It was unexceptionable, even if it was a bit drab. He might not think his home exciting, but it could be comfortable. The only time he openly challenged her was when he came home to find a familiar face smiling down at him from the sitting room wall.

"What the hell is that doing here?" he demanded, pointing to the most perfect face in Europe as it offered eternal invitation in the guise of Aphrodite, apple in hand and a twinkle in her blue eyes.

Grace looked at the painting, as if not understanding. "It's my mother," she said.

Diccan glared at her. "I know it's your mother. Where did you get it?"

She went still, as she often did, making Diccan think of an animal in defensive posture. "It was my father's. Is there a problem? He thought it was one of Raeburn's finest works."

Diccan, the most suave man in England, couldn't even begin to think how to answer. Was Grace really so blind that she didn't realize that people would only compare that painting to her? That once the *ton* knew about it, they would flock over, just to see how Grace dealt with having her missing mother watching over her shoulder, like a spectre of what she should have been?

"It is the only thing I have left of my father's," she said quietly. "He was never without it."

And in that moment, he almost compromised her beyond safety. Because in her eyes he caught a faint shadow of such pain as he had never known. Loss, hurt. Grief, which he thought was far older than her father's death. And he realized that all he wanted to do was gather into his arms and convince her that somebody did appreciate her as much as she deserved. Somebody loved her beyond what she could do for them.

Good God. What had happened to his objectivity? His conviction that the two of them had no business together, and would do better apart? Was he really changing his mind?

He had to step away. He had to put her off like a dusty

jacket. He couldn't take the chance of betraying himself, not when he was being watched.

Lifting a hand in resignation, he turned away. "I would prefer it in the family suites, then."

Her answer was too predictable. "Of course."

From that moment on, he began to spend less time with her. First a few dinners, then a ride. Late hours and later mornings, excused by the fact that there was a Russian diplomat in town he was supposed to escort. He should have felt relief. He felt anxious and angry, especially when he realized that Grace's Grenadiers could keep her so occupied she probably wouldn't even miss him.

He decided to be grateful. There wasn't anything else he could do. That all changed when he came home to find Kit Braxton in the sitting room.

"Good God," he said when the one-armed ex-soldier got to his feet. "What are you doing here?"

Kit was a particular friend of Grace's, one of the founding members of Grace's Grenadiers. That wasn't what bothered Diccan. What bothered him was that Kit was also a member of Drake's Rakes. In fact, he was supposed to be in France, gathering information for them. To find Kit here meant that something had changed and Diccan hadn't been told.

"I came to see the happy couple," Kit said with a false cheer that sent a new *frisson* of warning down Diccan's back. "Besides, Paris was getting too hot for me. I'm not the dueling aficionado you are, Diccan, and all the French want to do is throw down gloves. It gets old."

Grace had been laughing when Diccan walked in. Now she stood to the side as if waiting for something. "Will you join us for tea?" she asked, hands in their ever-present position at her waist. She almost looked pretty in another of her new dresses, peach sarcenet with spring-green ribbons that looked like a bouquet of roses.

"I'm afraid I can't, my dear. Shall I see you at the opera tonight? It's Gluck, I'm afraid."

"Oh, yes." She turned to her friend. "Would you like to go, Kit? Show off for the ladies?"

"Thanks, Gracie, but I'd rather escort you riding tomorrow."

Diccan felt a shaft of pain, which angered him. "In the morning?"

Grace brightened. "Would you like to come? I know you've been too busy the last few days. Kit offered his escort. Poor Epona has been fretting."

He would undoubtedly be getting in from another late night just as they were leaving. "No, my dear. You don't need my sore head at that hour. Enjoy yourself."

Did she look disappointed? It was so bloody hard to tell with Grace. It wasn't as hard to read Kit Braxton, whose frown was pure displeasure. "Will you have a few minutes for me later, Diccan?"

"If you're at Brooks. Right now I have to meet Thornton."

The frown intensified. "Thornton?"

If Kit didn't know Diccan's directive to befriend Thornton, Diccan wondered what he was doing here. "He hopes to win back the pony I took off him last night," he said, taking a bit of snuff.

It wasn't enough explanation. It certainly wasn't an excuse. Even so, Grace bid him goodbye with equanimity, which only made him feel worse.

So Kit Braxton had made an appearance from Paris. Was it an official visit Drake hadn't warned him of, or was this because of a private concern? Diccan knew perfectly

well Kit would lay down his life for Grace. Was it necessary, and had no one told him? Or was it something else?

He found out not an hour later when he met up with
Thornton on the street in front of Mitchell's, a gaming hell
on Jermyn Street.

"Hilliard, old man," the overstuffed baron greeted him,
hand hard on his arm. "Have I good news for you! Your
penance is over."

A strong sense of unease snaked through him. There was
something about Thornton's smile that presaged disaster.

"My penance?"

Thornton laughed, a high, nasal sound that grated on
Diccan's ears. "That wife of yours. Worthy lady and all;
maybe too much of a good thing, if you know what I mean.
But there you've been escorting her all around town, just as
a gentleman should. Well, my lad, I'm here to tell you that
your virtue has been rewarded." He tightened his hold and
pulled. "Come in and see."

Stepping into the slightly seedy entryway of Mitchell's,
Diccan shrugged off his coat and looked around. There
was little to see; just the usual male company, most of them
intent on cards or dice. The air was thick with smoke, and
the wall sconces flickered weakly, the dimness better to
hide a variety of sins. Diccan had just taken a step toward
the back room when he was hailed.

"Diccan, *chéri!*"

Beside him, Thornton chuckled. Diccan almost shook
his head to clear it of that feminine voice. He turned, suddenly dreading what he would see.

She was in the most delicious silver silk dress he'd
ever seen. Her blond hair was dressed in tousled curls that
clung to her neck. She had breasts like pomegranates and

a smile of pure delight at seeing him. Her hands were out, the wrists heavy with diamond bracelets he had bought her himself.

A sense of inevitability washed over him, and he felt like cursing. Instead, he took those delicate little hands and smiled. "Minette, my love. You've come."

Chapter 13

Grace began to hear the rumors of Diccan's dalliance within days. She might have withstood it better if she hadn't felt so blindsided. After all, she had just had the best two weeks of her life. She and Diccan had shared company and interests and laughter. He'd even kissed her, and not pecks on the cheek. Long, languorous matings of mouth and breath and tongue. She thought he had shared her hope for their future.

It might have even been easier if the rumors had merely been salacious whispers: *Did you hear who Diccan Hilliard was seen with*? She might have discounted those as no more than the irresistible lure of gossip. But this gossip came with patently false looks of commiseration. *Well, it didn't take him long, did it? Poor thing. I hope she didn't expect any better.*

She didn't say anything. After all, Diccan had done the honorable thing and married her. He continued to accompany her to society events, even if he became a bit more distant and tense each day. No one could realistically ask him to do more. He certainly couldn't be held responsible for the crumbling of Grace's unrealistic hopes. Grace was certain he hadn't even realized she'd nurtured them.

So it served no purpose to admit that yes, she had heard that Diccan had been seen squiring his beautiful mistress around town. She was familiar enough with the waters she now swam to know that her admission would offer nothing but more fodder for gossip. No one would care that she spent her nights staring dry-eyed at the ceiling, waiting to hear Diccan's tread on the steps, or that she felt as if something precious and fragile in her had cracked. They had known better than to expect different.

So she once again forced the hurt deep, where it would have to find space with all the other hurts, and she turned her attention to decorating her her home. Kate suggested that Diccan would prefer blues and browns and creams. Grace followed the direction, all the while yearning for the sun-hot colors she had once thought to save for herself. She rode early with Kit, who had become her devoted companion, worked mornings at the hospital, and attended the functions Kate deemed necessary.

She spent afternoons learning proper society behavior, each lesson squeezing her more and more into a role that simply didn't fit, like a bad corset. *Don't gallop in the park. Don't talk politics, especially to a politician. Don't address anyone above you—which meant virtually everyone—until addressed. Don't flaunt your friendships with soldiers. And don't—ever—show emotion of any kind. Not joy or anger or fear or distress.*

Kate could get away with it all, of course. But then, not only was she a widow, she was Kate. Grace was a plain unknown who had thrust herself unwanted onto society's stage. She was an object of scorn and pity, whose husband had already delivered his judgment on her.

If she had been raised any other way, she might have deserted like a coward. But she owed it to Diccan to at least try. She owed it to Kate and Bea not to embarrass them. She owed it to herself to know she had done everything she could to succeed, even though she was beginning to lose faith.

She would do it because she refused to let anyone say that it was she who had failed.

She wasn't so sanguine three weeks later. Oh, she learned Kate's lessons. She decorated her house and staffed it to her satisfaction. She attended soirees and Venetian breakfasts and musical evenings, and even the opera, which she found was surprisingly enjoyable. She was assured she was becoming a pattern card of respectability. She felt as if she was fading away.

The first blow was learning of Diccan's mistress. After that, she couldn't seem to pass a day without losing something else. She was at Kate's, reviewing place settings for a formal dinner, when she learned that Diccan would never live in the country.

"Why can't you use your regular cutlery on a fish?" she demanded, glaring at the little fish knife.

"You can," Kate said with a wry grin, "if you want people to think you're a salesclerk. The point is to separate you from the lower orders who somehow manage to eat with only one fork and knife."

Grace set the knife down with its family. "I will be so glad when the season is over and we can leave the city. The only thing I have to worry about at home is how to get the fish off the hook."

She was startled to hear Lady Bea hoot in amusement. "Cheese bits."

Grace looked up. Kate chuckled. "Diccan is definitely a town mouse. You won't get him more than ten miles outside the city. He says all the dust makes him sneeze."

"Is it true?" Grace asked Diccan later that evening when he led her about the room at a ball. "You really don't like the country?"

He shuddered dramatically. "Abhor it. Except for the odd race meeting, what is there to do? No good company or interesting pastimes. No, madame, you won't find me rusticating for any reason less urgent than outrunning the bailiffs. And my dibs were too well in tune for that."

"But you have an estate."

"And a perfectly good estate agent."

"What about Longbridge?" she asked. "I thought to go there as well."

He nodded to a passing couple. "I've already informed my agent to put it on his list of things to do. Of course, if you want to spend all your time in the country..."

Said as if he would be relieved to see her go. And oh, she was tempted. It had been the dream that had always sustained her. The future she had so carefully constructed in her mind. She would build a small life of contentment: walking land that was her own, riding Epona pell-mell across country. Nurturing the little family she'd gathered, and collecting new friends like flowers.

She wanted to have tea with the vicar's wife and help organize a fete. She wanted to learn how to churn butter and put up fruit for the winter. She wanted quiet and normalcy and the precious comfort of routine. She wanted to set her roots so deep into Berkshire soil that she became indistinguishable from the native flora. Instead she had been sentenced to a life amid the brittle artifice of a society that respected few of her talents and none of her qualities, and where, if she were ever to mean something to Diccan, she would have to stay.

Her heart broke a little more; she could feel it bleed inside of her. But she kept smiling. "Indeed, no," she replied.

The second blow intruded on her gradually. Her watcher was back. Oh, she didn't see him often, and it was often different men. But she'd grown up around strategy, and she recognized the maneuver, no matter that this lurker was in mufti and not in Rifleman green.

"Have you seen the man who lurks on the street around the house?" she asked Harper as they set out for a ride.

Only the man wasn't there. He seemed to slip away every time there was a witness, and then smile when he returned. It was beginning to unsettle her, stealing her comfort. She wasn't mad. But the more she questioned other people, the more they looked at her as if she were. And the more they did, the more she fought the growing urge to keep looking over her shoulder.

Lady Castlereagh didn't see the man either when she stopped by. But she was distracted by the news she had to deliver. "My dear, I'm afraid it has been brought to my attention that you are caring for patients in the Army Hospital," the grande dame said over tea in Grace's new blue salon. "Donating sums is fine, of course, but there has been talk that you care for common men in ways that must shock and dismay any woman of breeding. It's simply not done, Grace."

Teapot in hand, Grace paused. "I am doing nothing different than I did in the Peninsula."

"But now you are married to a rising diplomat," the

sharp-eyed woman said. "He might not have much standing yet, but he has potential. You don't want to destroy his chances."

And so the next day Grace informed the head matron that instead of caring for the soldiers whom the *ton* had forgotten, she must sit in her pale blue rooms sipping tea with women who didn't like her.

It was there Diccan's mother found her four days later, to deliver the worst blow of all. Sweeping into the room like a winter storm, Lady Evelyn barely waited for Grace to order tea before attacking. "I know you can't help it, considering who your mother is," she said in her most arch voice as she settled on the cream sofa. "But I cannot allow you to make the Hilliard name a byword."

Grace felt her ire rise. "I have already quit the Army Hospital, if that is what you mean."

Lady Evelyn huffed impatiently. "I have no interest in your little hobbies. It is your amours I speak of. Even your mother didn't flaunt her affairs while she was married."

Grace found herself blinking, completely flummoxed. "My *what*?"

But she had to wait for the answer. Just then her new butler entered and served tea. Grace saw Lady Evelyn's lip curl when Roberts limped by, his head tilted just a bit so he could see out of his good eye.

It was all Grace could do to keep from giving the woman a piece of her mind. Grace was particularly proud of Roberts. Three weeks ago he had been one of her patients, just as two of the footmen had been. One of the grooms had lost a hand at Vimiero and the gardener, his leg on a ship of the line. And Diccan's mother had the gall to find them distasteful?

"Well, I don't have to wonder why Diccan chooses never

to be home, do I?" Lady Evelyn asked the minute the door closed behind Roberts. "How can you allow such a creature to be in his employ?"

"I wouldn't know," Grace retorted dryly. "Christian charity, perhaps?"

If it were possible, his mother grew colder, her eyes glittering.

"You were speaking about something before Roberts came in," Grace said, rather than have to respond to another set-down. "What was it?"

Lady Evelyn reached for her teacup. "Your behavior. Did you truly think the *ton* would countenance your disappearing every morning with a man who is not your husband?" Her face creased with distaste. "You don't even have the saving grace to have good taste. He is *scarred*. But then, after seeing *that*—" She gestured to the closed door. "I'm not really surprised."

Grace found herself on her feet. "Thank you for your concern, Lady Evelyn. I realize you took time out of your busy schedule to see me. I know how glad you'll be to have concluded your business."

She caught Lady Evelyn with her cup in the air. Grace simply waited, her stare implacable.

Setting the cup down, Lady Evelyn rose to her feet like a queen serving sentence. "You think I won't cut off my son to protect the Hilliard name? Please don't be so foolish."

Which meant that if no one else ruined Grace for her friendships, Lady Evelyn would be pleased to do it herself.

"Since I respect your son so much," Grace conceded, her hands clenched so tightly her knuckles hurt, "when I ride in the country I will limit my companions to my groom, who is an old retainer."

Lady Evelyn responded with a barely raised eyebrow. "Your faithful groom, who would think nothing of accompanying you to a tryst? I think not. *Ladies* ride in the park."

By the time Grace ushered the old besom out five minutes later, she felt as if she'd been run over by a gun carriage. "Roberts," she told the butler, staring bleakly at the closed front door. "I need to send a message to Major Kit Braxton."

Kit came within the hour. Grace received him in the increasingly claustrophobic blue parlor.

"Kit, I'm afraid I won't be able to continue our morning rides. They've been...remarked upon."

He frowned. "I don't understand."

So she explained, smiling as if it didn't matter.

"There isn't a damn thing wrong with our rides," he protested.

Grace shrugged. "Nevertheless, I must end them. I'm trying so hard to fit in, Kit. I can't let Lady Evelyn destroy everything. And she would, without hesitation."

Kit jumped to his feet and began to pace. All Grace could seem to see was his empty right sleeve, the ropy scars along the side of his face and neck that betrayed the terrible injuries he'd suffered at Toulouse. Lady Evelyn would waste not a thought on what her slander would do to Kit. A *scarred* man. One of the most valiant men Grace knew.

"How *dare* she?" Kit demanded. "You're the innocent one in all this."

"Oh, Kit." She actually smiled. "You grew up in this society. When did you begin to believe it was fair?"

His answering grin was a bit bashful. "Point taken. But Grace, I didn't come all the way home to help you just to stand aside."

Grace felt her breath catch. "What do you mean, 'to help me'?"

She realized then that Kit had said more than he'd intended to. An unnatural red crept up his neck. "You need support right now. That's all I'm going to say."

Ah, she thought, feeling even lower. *He thought to protect her from the mistress. Just how much more pitiful could she become?*

Getting to her feet, she took Kit's hand. "If you want to help, do me two favors. Find out who that man is who is following me. And take me for a ride in the park this afternoon."

He searched her face, as if reassuring himself that she would survive. *Oh,* she thought, keeping her smile solidly in place. *She would survive. She always did. But, Christ, it hurt.*

Finally he kissed her cheek. "I'll be by at four."

"If you don't mind, I'd also appreciate the loan of a horse."

That brought him to a halt. "What about Epona?"

She kept smiling by force of will alone. "Epona is going home."

It took her two hours to work up the courage to face Harper with the news. She walked out to the mews to find him grooming her girl.

"You can't really mean to send her back, lass," the Irishman protested, his homely features screwed up in distress.

Grace felt as if her heart were being torn out. Epona whickered, and Grace stroked her silky nose. "I can't keep her here. If I can't give her a good run, she'll waste away. You know that."

She knew he did. Epona lived to race. If Grace limited

her to Hyde Park, she would ruin her. She just wished Diccan hadn't been thoughtful enough to bring her up here. It was so much harder to send her back. Grace thought it might just be the thing that broke her.

"Sure, you'll not let those sharp-nosed tabbies keep you from ridin' altogether," Harps protested, his blunt hand against Epona's withers.

"Of course not. But in the park. Chaperoned. At a walk, just like every other lady of the *ton*."

Harper cursed as if she said she was going to be clapped in irons. She might as well have been.

"I don't like leaving you," Harps said. "Not with himself workin' so hard to shame you."

"I can't trust anyone else to see her safely home," Grace said, staring out to the late flowers in her back garden. "Besides, Harps, there's nothing you can do. I have to work this out for myself."

Harper snorted. "Oh, there's somethin' I can do, all right. I guess 'll just leave it to the lads."

She faced him, her voice unyielding. "Not them either."

He didn't say a word. She couldn't. So she walked away, and thought she could hate Diccan for this. She wasn't sure how much more she could lose. Lady Castlereagh had taken her work, and Diccan's mother had taken her escape. And Diccan? He might very well have taken her hope.

She had been abandoned before, and she'd lived through it. But she'd always had work to occupy her, the open country to soothe her, her horses to set her free. Now she had nothing.

That wasn't right, she thought as she returned to the blue parlor that seemed to have become a prison. She had her friends. But her friends couldn't fill the growing emptiness inside her. They couldn't replace a husband who had suddenly found something better to do than be with his wife. A husband who had made it so much worse by softening her defenses with attention before turning away.

And what was she to do with all that inconvenient longing? She'd been living on hope that soon he would find his way back to her bed. How could he want to, when his mistress had joined him? Grace had seen her once, a lovely armful of blond, as her father would have said. A laughing, sensual bonbon, the type of woman who would make even Kate pale in comparison. How could Grace hate him for wanting her? How could she ever think to compete? How long could she try?

She revisited that thought the next morning when she came down to breakfast to meet Diccan coming in the front door.

"What's this about you sending Epona away?" he demanded. "I just brought her up for you."

He was still in his evening clothing, rumpled and smelling of smoke and brandy, and unbearably appealing. At least, Grace thought wearily, he didn't smell of perfume. She might just have coshed him over the head with one of the brand-new Wedgwood urns if he'd come home smelling of perfume.

"I can't keep her here if I can only ride her in the park," she said, standing a step above him. "And for now, I can't ride her anywhere else unless you're with me. People have been talking."

"Well, *damn* people!" he snapped, throwing down his top hat so hard that it bounced on the black marble floor.

Grace couldn't take her eyes off of it as it rolled toward her feet. "You might want to pick that up," she said, beset by the strangest urge to giggle. "Roberts only has sight in one eye. He'll never see it against the marble."

"That's another thing," Diccan snapped, walking right up to the stairs where she stood. "What are you doing hiring a one-eyed butler with a limp?"

His words, so closely mirroring his mother's, widened the crack in her resolve. "Ah," she said, feeling suddenly hollow and cold. "You see my point about sending Epona home. Just as with Roberts, people must have enough time to overlook my more unsightly flaws before they accept me."

And before he could argue, she swept past him and into the breakfast room, not bothering to mask her lurching gait. She prayed he didn't follow.

He did, damn him. But he came only as far as the doorway. "Grace. I'm sorry. That was ugly of me. It's just...I'm really tied up in something right now, and it's destroyed my patience."

She couldn't bear to face him again, so she focused on settling into her seat. "Of course. Will I see you at the Lievens' tonight?"

For a long moment she was answered only with silence. Then Diccan sighed, as if he had no strength left. "Of course. I have an appointment first, though. Will you go with Kate?"

Benny, the new second footman, arrived to pour her morning coffee.

"I imagine she'll take me up," Grace said, pouring cream into slow eddies in her coffee.

"Wear your bronze tonight," he suggested. "I particularly like it."

Of course she wore the bronze. She wished she had the fortitude to tell him to go to the devil, but she kept hoping. And, just when she despaired, he kept being kind.

She did have a moment of hesitation. It was in the afternoon, when she called for Schroeder to help her change. There wasn't an answer for the longest time, and then Grace heard a knock on Diccan's door and Benny's voice. A murmur, an anxious query, a woman's chuckle.

Schroeder. Grace recognized the timbre of her voice. How had Benny known to look for her in Diccan's room?

Grace stood there for the longest time, just staring at the connecting door. *He wouldn't,* was all she could think. *Not here, in her own house. With her abigail. He already* had *a mistress.* She pressed her hand to her mouth, terrified she would begin to laugh, and that if she did, she wouldn't stop.

Schroeder knocked and came in. Was she looking smug? Was her hair mussed? Would Grace ever know for sure, or would she descend into a world where she could never again look at a beautiful woman and be sure she hadn't been in Diccan's bed?

In the end, Grace prepared for the Lievens as if she were arming for a Forlorn Hope. She simply didn't know what else to do. Schroeder drew her bath and helped her into her beautiful square-necked bronze moiré dress with its spider gauze overskirt and tiny puffed sleeves. Grace wondered whether the abigail noticed that her mistress flinched when she touched her. She wondered how she'd ever be comfortable with her again.

"There's one more thing," Schroeder said, offering Grace a flat, square box. "Mr. Hilliard expressly asked me to have you wear these tonight. He says they were his great-grandmother's."

Grace stared at the box as if it were a snake. An abrupt laugh escaped, making her sound like a lunatic. Oh, God, he hadn't been bedding Schroeder. He'd been sneaking her a gift for his wife. Grace felt so bloody stupid. She accepted the worn brown leather box with suddenly shaking hands. Flipping open the catch, she lifted the lid and caught her breath.

Aquamarines. Not huge, but perfectly matched, the clear saturated blue of water against white gold: necklace, bracelet, and earrings. Grace couldn't take her eyes from them. A person couldn't spend time in India without knowing something of gems. Since her friend Ghitika's father had been a jeweler, Grace knew more than most. These jewels were exquisite.

Her heart beating a staccato rhythm, she handed the box back to Schroeder. "I'll have to thank him. Please put them on."

Though the gems might have been no more than a guilty gesture on his part, suddenly Grace didn't care. It was like his gift of having Epona brought to London: completely unexpected, thoughtful, generous. Whatever else was going on, he was trying to establish her as his wife, and to a society who set store by such gestures, family jewels would be a strong statement.

When Kate came to pick her up, the duchess recognized the jewels right away. "Well, it's about time," she said when Grace settled next to her in the carriage. "I can't imagine how he pried those aquas from his mother's hands. Is the dragon still alive, or did he have to shoot her to get them?"

Grace's smile was quiet. "She was alive the other day when she came to offer motherly advice about my morning rides."

Kate scowled. "How delighted you must have been."

Grace did her best to sound unconcerned. "Oh, after

you've had the Duke of Wellington call you on the carpet, a mere bishop's wife pales. And no, Kate. I don't need you to speak up to Diccan for me."

Kate frowned. "I'm not so sure. Even aquamarines can't make up for blatant neglect."

"No," Grace said and hoped she looked amused. "But they don't hurt."

For once she was pleased to enter a society function, as if the aquamarines gave her extra armor. She even made it up two flights of steps without having her leg cramp up. She was just about to follow Kate and Bea into the Lievens' great salon when Bea suddenly hissed under her breath.

"'Ware, pirates!"

Kate immediately swung around, attempting to follow Bea's gaze.

Grace stared at both of them, but they were caught up in searching the crowd. "Pirates?"

"Oh, yes," Kate answered, her voice strained. "My family crest. A ship in full sail. Which means... ah, yes, there she is. My sister by marriage. Behold, my dear, Her Grace, Glynis, Duchess of Livingston. Now do you see what a bad duchess I am? I don't have nearly enough consequence."

Grace followed Kate's gaze to find Diccan's mother standing at the other end of the salon, looking dyspeptic in jonquil. Alongside her stood a younger version of herself, a blond, blue-eyed ice sculpture with a seeming bottomless well of disdain.

Grace felt like shivering. "*That* is your brother's wife?"

Kate tilted her head, looking amused. "Yes, indeed. You will understand all when I tell you she is Lady Evelyn's niece, and that Lady Evelyn arranged Glynis's marriage to Edwin. Happily, Glynis suits him to a tee. The weight of their combined arrogance could sink Carlton House. Sadly, they do not suit me. I am pleased to say that the feeling is quite mutual."

"Whither thou goest," Bea sang softly beside her, "I will go."

Kate chuckled. "Bea thinks that they're having me followed again."

"Followed?" Grace asked, her focus still on the pale blonde. "Isn't that a bit gothic?"

Kate fussed with one of her diamond bracelets. "Oh, it's very gothic. But so are they. I enjoy the thought that I provide fodder for Edwin's titillation. Edwin claims he is trying to protect the Hilliard name. He is very fond of making dark threats about exile."

Grace found herself staring. "But you're a duchess. Surely he can't force you away."

"Oh, I imagine he could," Kate said airily. "After all, he is a duke, and head of my family."

Grace simply didn't know what to say. If Kate was balanced on such a precarious edge in this society, and she was a duchess, what chance did a soldier's daughter have?

"Surely Diccan would protect you," Grace said instinctively.

Kate smiled again. "Surely he'd try. Wouldn't you, Diccan?"

"Of course I would," Diccan suddenly said behind Grace. "Would what?"

Grace felt the breath leave her body in a whoosh. How could she have not felt Diccan approach? Suddenly he was standing beside her, his body radiating heat like a stoked stove, and she found herself battling the most delicious shivers.

Kate was laughing. "Keep my family from dragging me off in chains to a dark tower."

Diccan shuddered. "I assume that means we are the recipients of the infamous Hilliard glare."

"From any number of Hilliards," Kate assured him, looking unconcerned. "I think your mother may have just spotted the aquamarines."

Instead of looking at his mother, Diccan turned to Grace. "Well, well," he said, reaching out to take her hand and hold it out. "And I thought seeing my mother's purple-faced outrage was reward enough. I was woefully wrong. The stones were made for you, Grace."

How handsome he was, was all Grace could think, examining him in return. Surely formal wear had been invented just to grace Diccan Hilliard. He filled out every fold and crease as if it had been molded to him, his linen crisp and his figured powder-blue waistcoat elegant. Biddle had obviously tried to tame his curly sable hair, but Diccan must have had his hands in it, for it was tumbling again, falling just beyond his collar points. His face was clean-shaven, his jaw a symphony of hard-etched angles, his mouth soft and mobile.

And his eyes. Oh, his eyes, blue-rimmed, ghostly gray. Mesmer should have used Diccan's eyes for his experiments. He could have made people do anything.

"Have I struck you silent, my Grace?" he asked with a lazy smile.

She quickly recovered. "Indeed you have. Here I thought I'd married a mere Corinthian. Instead, I find him to actually be a knight of old, vanquishing a dragon to bring me back treasure."

That won her a hearty laugh and a kiss on the hand. "Then you like my little baubles?"

She fought the shivers of delight his touch inevitably incited. "You know perfectly well I do. They're exquisite. I thank you and your great-grandmother."

"Don't forget my mother, for releasing them before I was forced to do her grievous bodily harm."

Maybe, Grace thought, her hand securely tucked into Diccan's elbow, that was why the old witch had seen fit to threaten her. The necklace. Sadly, it didn't make the woman's threats any less dangerous. Or bring Epona back. Or help protect Grace from disaster two hours later when she found herself listening to her dinner partner discourse about the undeserving poor over turtle soup.

Baron Hale was a smallish frog of a man of about fifty, all protruding eyes and fleshy face on a damp body that smelled faintly of sewers. It was difficult enough for Grace to enjoy her dinner seated that close to him. It became impossible when he began to expound on the need to clamp down on the unrest that was growing around the country.

Grace kept her temper all the way through Corn Laws and Luddites. But when the baron turned his ire on the returning soldiers, she found that patience wasn't an unlimited virtue.

"Good man, Sidmouth," the baron said, shoveling peas into his mouth. "Knows how to contain the rabble. Now if he'd just do something about all those soldiers who litter the streets."

Grace strove for tact. "They have nowhere to go."

"Course they do. They should work for honest wages instead of hanging around street corners, begging or robbing decent people."

"They did work for honest wages, sir. We haven't paid them."

He huffed. "Don't be absurd. They got what they deserved. Can't expect the government to bankrupt itself on every soldier who whines about his lot. I say get off their bums and do for themselves like the rest of us."

"Excellent," she said, unable to help herself. "I met a soldier yesterday with no arms. What job would you like to give him?"

Hale sputtered like a boiling teapot. "Madame, it might behoove you to keep silent on matters you know nothing about. Even Wellington called those men the scum of the earth. They deserve no more than what they've already gotten."

"No, sir, it's you who has no idea. That scum waded into slaughter for three days at Waterloo to keep Napoleon from showing up on your doorstep, and they've returned home to be ignored and abandoned. In fact, they've been wading into slaughter for you for the last ten years. What exactly have you done for England in that time?"

She didn't realize that her voice had risen. She didn't see the faces around her go slack with shock. She saw the fury that climbed Lord Hale's puffy, gaping features, though.

"How *dare* you, madame? What could you possibly know?"

At least, she thought, she had his attention. She was on the brink of telling him *exactly* what she knew when she felt a hand on her shoulder. Whipping around, she saw Diccan standing behind her, his face set and his eyes glittering. "I'm afraid I must leave early, my dear. Would you accompany me?"

All at once, she became aware of the loud hush in the room. She saw the malice on all those aristocratic faces. She heard Lady Bea, far up the table where a duke's daughter sat, sighing, "St. Joan."

And Grace wanted to laugh, because she wasn't sure whether Bea meant that Grace was pot-valiant, or that she'd just asked for incineration. She felt smothered all of a sudden, her heart racing and her lungs on fire. She wanted to castigate every one of self-satisfied people who walked right by those soldiers Baron Hale despised. Brave men all, proud; now blind, legless, armless, mad from the sound of the guns, begging only for the chance to survive. How dare these parasites judge them?

It took Herculean effort, but she rose calmly to her feet and curtsied. "I beg your pardon, Lord Hale. You see, my father was a soldier. A general with the Duke. I find I grow unreasonably emotional when I think on the valiant men he led and with whom he died."

He smiled on her as if she were ten. "Of course, of course. Always make allowances for female sensibilities. But from now on, let your husband guide you. Ain't that true, Hilliard?"

It was Diccan's turn to bow. "Indeed, my lord."

For Grace's part, she leveled a freezing glare on Diccan's hand where it was wrapped around her arm. Diccan let loose of her, and she preceded him from the room, shaken and cold. She knew her outburst could well have threatened his career.

"I'm afraid I can't apologize," she said as they waited for their wraps in the foyer.

Diccan sighed. "I told you never to apologize for the truth. I simply might wish you'd picked a better time to express your views. Hale is brother-in-law to the exchequer."

Grace rubbed the bridge of her nose, suddenly depressed. "Maybe I should go to the country for a while. I could say I'm checking my estate."

"Not right now."

"Why not?"

"Because I say so."

She looked up to see strain in his eyes. "I'm afraid that isn't reason enough, Diccan," she said, for some reason feeling sorry for him, which made her all the more angry.

He collected their cloaks from the footman. "It's all the reason I can give you."

And what about my peace of mind? she wanted to say. *What about my self-respect and happiness?* Happiness, she thought, as Diccan helped her into her evening cloak, wasn't a viable hope. If she could only settle for peace, she'd be content. But as long as she lived this close to her husband and yet stayed so far away, even that was impossible.

He took her elbow to guide her out into the cool night. It was all she could do not to pull away. Her skin sang at his touch. Her heart clamored in her chest. She could have hated him at that moment.

He helped her into the carriage as if she were fragile. Then, just as she thought he might join her, he slammed the door and stepped back. "I'm afraid I have another function."

She felt bereft and hated it. "Of course."

Closing her eyes, she waited in silence for the carriage to start. She was certainly glad she didn't weep anymore. If she did, she wasn't sure she'd be able to stop, and think of the talk that would have caused.

By the time Diccan climbed the steps to his house the next morning, he was so tired he could barely see. False dawn limned the sky behind him. Along the street, maids were washing off steps and polishing railings. Carts rumbled past on the way to market, waking the birds. He couldn't remember how many times lately he'd stumbled home at this hour. Today, though, was the worst.

"Morning, sir," the new butler greeted him, tilting his head a bit to get a good look at him.

"Roberts." Handing off his hat and gloves, he looked around, expecting disaster. All was quiet, though, the rooms still steeped in shadow. "Anything out of the ordinary happen? Is my wife awake?"

Is she safe, or has someone already hurt her?

Roberts frowned as if assessing Diccan's sanity. Diccan could hardly blame him. "Whole world's asleep, sir. 'Ceptin' you and me, anyroad. Well, and that bloke outside."

Diccan had started up the stairs. This stopped him two steps up. "What bloke?"

"Mrs. Hilliard's been seein' him. Said she told you. Almost caught 'im last night."

"What did he look like?"

Roberts shrugged. "Just a bloke. Dressed like he had a shop."

Diccan rubbed at his eyes, suddenly queasy. "And he's been watching the house?"

"Nossir. He's been followin' the missus."

Diccan's stomach dropped. Drake had been right. Grace was under scrutiny. "There are people who disagree with my politics, Roberts. They shouldn't be allowed to worry Mrs. Hilliard."

"They won't, sir. She can count on us."

He nodded and turned for the stairs. "Thank you. Please send Schroeder to me."

Babs arrived, still pinning up her hair, her apron thrown over one shoulder.

"What do you know about a man following Grace?" Diccan asked as he chucked his jacket. "Is it the same man Grace has seen or someone new?"

She didn't pause in her grooming. "Someone new. Reilly followed him. Lost him in Covent Garden. There have also been several ex-soldiers who loiter down by the park."

"And you didn't think to tell me?"

She tilted her head. "You weren't here, were you?"

Diccan pulled off his neckcloth. "That's not your business."

She lifted an eyebrow. "Better tell your valet that. He's ready to gut you with a paring knife."

"He knows better. So do you. If you see anything that looks threatening, you contact me. You understand?" He waited for her shrug. "Who can we trust among the staff?"

"The ones Mrs. Hilliard hired would throw themselves in front of a cannon for her. The rest work for you. Why? You're as twitchy as a cat in a room full of hounds."

He reached into his pocket and drew out a folded paper. "This was in my coat when I left Minette's this morning."

Schroeder accepted the paper and unfolded it. "Ah. The warning you've been waiting for."

He hadn't realized how it would affect him when it finally came, though.

Glad you're enjoying the charms of your mistress. As long as you give her your complete loyalty, you will keep others safe. It would distress us to hurt your innocent wife.

The words were like shards of glass in his gut. He wanted to destroy something. He wanted to lock Grace in the smallest room he could find and guard it until he could guarantee her safety.

"That note has to get to Drake," he said. "Make sure Grace is accompanied everywhere. Arm our people, but don't let her know it. Check and see if any of your staff has picked up any new leads."

"All right," she said, tucking the note into her skirt. "What about you?"

He looked at the bed longingly. "I have work to do."

"You might want to get the whore's stink off you, first."

He stopped, his hands at the waistband of his pants. "That whore has led us to five other people of interest. Last night she convinced me to steal confidential documents for her. She also seems to enjoy sharing details of the Wellington plot. Until we get the rest, I have no choice."

Even so, he yanked his reeking shirt off his head and threw it in the corner.

Babs had been at this too long to argue. "Just be careful," she warned, and reached up to drop a kiss on his cheek before walking out the door.

Diccan had just gotten his pants unbuttoned, when his door opened. "Not now," he barked.

"Yes, now," the intruder answered.

He whirled around to see his wife standing in the same door Babs had just exited, her posture like steel, her eyes winter bleak as she took in his state of undress. "There are things I can control," she said with deadly calm, "and things I cannot. If I ever see Schroeder come out of this room again looking like that, I will fire her without reference and poison your coffee."

Last week he would have argued. Even twelve hours ago, he would have hinted at the truth. But he had been warned.

So he protected her. "Madame," he said, his voice as dry as dust. "My head is the size of a melon and my stomach threatens to disgrace me. If you wish to shrill in that odious manner, inflict it on the staff. I am going to sleep."

She stared at him long and hard, but in the end, she said nothing, just left, not even slamming the door behind her. And Diccan, exhausted and aching and beset by unfamiliar fear, sank onto the edge of the bed and stared sightlessly at the wall, trying to remind himself that what he did was necessary. There was no way he could convince himself that it was right.

Grace wasn't sure how much more she could take. If only she'd waited five more minutes before going down to breakfast, she might have missed seeing Schroeder sneaking out of Diccan's room, half dressed and pinning up her hair. She might have still continued believing in something that didn't exist.

But she hadn't missed it, or the guilty flush on Schroeder's face as she hurried by. She'd threatened Diccan, but even as she said the words, she knew the threat was empty. She couldn't hurt him. She couldn't hurt Schroeder. Evidently the only one she could hurt was herself.

Should she stay? Was there anything really to stay for? She so heartily wished she didn't hear her father's voice in her head. *"Fairchilds never quit! Figure it out and try again."*

It wasn't easy, but she stayed. She returned to her routine, which no longer seemed to include Diccan at all. She tried so hard not to fret. Not to look for him in a crowd, or listen for him coming up the steps late at night. She tried her best to find comfort in her new, more limited life. She counted on the fact that she was finally getting past all the upheavals. And then Uncle Dawes came to see her.

It was midnight when Grace returned home alone from a rare ball with Diccan to have Roberts tell her that her uncle waited for her.

"Uncle Dawes?" She stepped into the fire-warmed salon, not quite believing what she saw. Her uncle was rising from the blue settee, a brandy snifter in his hand. "It's after midnight. What's wrong? Aunt Dawes?"

"She is well," he said. "It's you I'm worried about. It is urgent I speak with you."

Completely bemused, she gestured to the chair he'd vacated. "Then please sit back down."

"No," he said, looking uncomfortable. "Thank you. Did Hilliard come home with you?"

She unpinned her toque and set it aside. "No. He was headed for his club."

"Oh, no," he said, his shoulders slumping, and Grace suddenly felt afraid. "I *hate* this."

He sounded more than angry. He sounded sad. *He looks old,* she thought. "You frighten me, Uncle. Please. Just say it."

He looked away a moment. "He's not at his club. Not now. He had an entirely different destination in mind when he left the party."

Grace was becoming sorely tired of this line of dialogue. "I know about his mistress, Uncle."

"No you don't." Impatiently he shook his head. "You don't know what she's involved in. You don't know what she's involved *him* in."

"Then tell me."

He looked at her, but she wasn't really sure he saw her. "Treason."

Grace just stared. "What are you talking about?"

He sighed. "This very minute your husband is betraying his country."

Chapter 14

Grace wasn't sure how it happened, but within the hour she and Uncle Dawes were pulling up in front of the neat little townhouse on Half Moon Street. She was still arguing with him.

"Uncle, I promise. Diccan might be a rake, but he is not a traitor. Why, not three months ago he helped us get a man out of Belgium who uncovered a plot against the Crown."

Uncle Dawes helped her out of the carriage. "Because otherwise he would have been exposed."

"How do you know?" she asked, looking up at the non-descript row of plain brick townhouses.

"I learned it from the man I'm bringing you to see."

She shook her head. "Unless that proof is the sight of Diccan holding a gun to King George's head, I'm afraid you're wasting your time."

Suddenly her uncle grabbed her arm. "This isn't a joke," he snapped. "People are going to die."

Grace found herself staring. Her Uncle Dawes had never raised his voice to her. He was the one who had taught her to fish during the brief summer she'd spent in England. He'd ridden with her, listened to her bad piano, and laughed at her worse jokes. For the first time, doubt slithered through her.

"All right," she conceded. "Let's talk to this man."

Still, she felt a bit foolish as she walked through a wrought iron gate and up the walk. If only the charge weren't so absurd. If only the night weren't straight out of a Minerva Press novel. It was black and foggy, tendrils of gray wrapping around the lamplights and chilling Grace's ankles. She felt moisture on her face and thought how muffled the sounds of passing horses were. It was as if she had stepped into a cocoon, a cold, unsettling place where she became invisible.

"Did we really need to sneak about like burglars?" she asked, her voice muffled and odd.

"Your husband might question your visiting this man at this hour of the night."

"I'll be surprised if he doesn't question your coming to get me at this hour of the night."

Uncle Dawes knocked on a plain black door and guided her inside. A stone-faced butler met them in the foyer and took their wraps.

"This way, please."

It was an unremarkable house. Flickering wall sconces barely revealed tan walls, heavy red velvet curtains, and mismatched rugs under worn furniture. The air held a faint scent of tobacco and dust, and the decor was bland, except for a wall of encased butterflies. For some reason, that made Grace uncomfortable, bits of iridescence pinned to death in the dark. Following the butler up to the first floor, she felt less sanguine by the minute, as if the house didn't have enough breathable air. Only Uncle Dawes's hand on her elbow kept her moving.

She didn't realize a man waited in the hallway until he greeted her. "Mrs. Hilliard."

He was as unremarkable as the house, with a sharp aristocratic face, thinning blond hair, and ears that seemed too long for his features. His frame had been padded just a bit with expert tailoring. He stood an inch or two shorter than she, but didn't appear to notice her height. Something about him stirred a faint feeling of familiarity.

"And you are?" she asked, stopping well beyond his reach.

He bowed. "Peter Carver of the Home Office. Lord Sidmouth asked me to speak with you."

He led the way into another dim room, this one with some books and a fireplace that sputtered. Even though she didn't feel like it, Grace sat, allowing the men to sit as well.

"I understand you believe my husband is a traitor," she said baldly.

Mr. Carver set his hands on his knees. "I'm afraid so," he said, his voice gentle. "Mr. Hilliard is giving away state secrets that could cause irreparable damage."

"To whom?" she asked. "Certainly no one has the energy or money right now to start a war."

"The threat isn't foreign. It's from within England. Men who seek to use the civil unrest to stoke the fires of revolution."

Grace snorted. "Don't be ridiculous. Diccan is about as revolutionary as the Prince Regent."

Mr. Carver looked regretful. "Mr. Hilliard isn't interested in revolution. He's interested in money. You don't think he supports himself on his government pay? His father cut him off years ago."

"His uncle left him an estate."

"That is crumbling to the ground. I'm afraid he's been doing this for years, for one concern or another. He made a name for himself in some sectors as a man willing to be swayed. For a price."

"Which makes one wonder why he still works for the government."

Mr. Carver shrugged. "He is cousin to a very powerful duke." Clasping his hands on his knees, he leaned forward. "Do you recognize the name Evenham, Mrs. Hilliard?"

She tilted her head. "Lord Bentley's son? The one who was killed in a duel?"

Mr. Carver was shaking his head. "There was no duel. Evenham was shot in the head. Your husband was in the room when it happened. He said it was suicide. We don't believe him. We think Evenham had found damning information about your husband."

Grace felt her certainty slip a notch. "That isn't proof, sir, only another allegation."

"I know. We think he is in possession of restricted files from the Foreign Office and plans to pass them to an operative. We also think he has collected information on his cohorts. I know it's a lot to ask, but we hope you will find it for us. We need that proof, and no one else has managed to get it."

She was on her feet before she could think. "No. I'm sorry, but nothing will convince me that my husband is betraying his country. I'd like to go home now."

Uncle Dawes followed to his feet, begging her to reconsider. Mr. Carver echoed him. Grace remained unmoved.

Finally, when she wouldn't relent, the two men looked at each other.

"She has to be convinced," Mr. Carver said, sounding regretful, as he made a show of checking his pocket watch. "Mrs. Hilliard, I'm afraid I must ask you to follow me."

"There must be another way," Uncle Dawes said, and Grace could see that he was waxy pale.

"Why?" she asked, folding her hands at her waist.

Mr. Carver sighed. "I was loath to take this step, but you need to understand what we're up against. You see, we met at this location for a reason."

Grace couldn't take her eyes off her uncle, who couldn't face her. "What reason?"

"Proof. At this very minute he is with one of his accomplices. We saw him go in. We've arranged for you to see."

Grace found herself looking around, as if expecting Diccan to walk through the door. "Where?"

"The house next door. We've opened a hole between the houses that has been hidden behind a special mirror. Please don't refuse my request until you've seen."

She didn't move. This was absurd. What reason on earth would Diccan have to betray his country? How could anyone think he was involved?

She shook her head one last time. She had no choice. "Show me."

He dipped his head, as if searching for tact. "We will be going up to one of the bedrooms. When I open the door, you must remain strictly silent. You will hear him, but he could hear you, too."

Already her heart was beating faster. She felt the prickle of sweat at her nape and feared for her suddenly queasy stomach. Resting a hand at her back, Mr. Carver opened the door and ushered her through. Uncle Dawes slumped back into his chair.

The bedroom, when she entered it, was dark, with indistinct shadows where furniture should be. She smelled coal smoke and dust and age. Carver led her across the room, where he stopped her inches away from the nondescript red wall. "Remember," he whispered. "Quiet."

She shivered, unsettled by the feel of his breath on her skin, crawling with dread for what she might witness. Then he reached up and slid back a panel, and she could see into the room beyond.

Oh, dear God. She could see.

"No," she whispered, abruptly backing up.

"I'm sorry," he murmured, grabbing her shoulders and forcing her back into place. "But you must look. And you must stay 'til the end. It is when he will betray himself."

She should run. She should give herself away. She should bloody well close her eyes and hide. She couldn't. She could do no more than stare at the sight of her husband making love to his mistress.

They were naked, standing almost directly in front of her, golden firelight pouring over their slick bodies like water. Perfectly formed bodies, exquisitely wrought art come to life. His mistress was a fertility goddess, lush and rounded and soft, even more lovely than when Grace had seen her in Brussels. Her cornsilk hair tumbled over her shoulders in waves, and her great blue eyes were laughing. She was leaning back against Diccan, and he had his hands on her breasts, surely the most perfect breasts ever created; pink-tipped and heavy, milky white moons beneath his long-fingered hands.

Grace's own breasts ached. Her heart stumbled. She

couldn't take her eyes from his hands. Elegant hands, clever hands, cupping those perfect plump breasts. His body was even more compelling than the one time Grace had seen it arced over hers. Taut and muscled and sleek as a seal. The perfect counterpoint to the woman's softness, which he explored with a familiarity that threatened to shatter her.

"I don't like watching a man betray his wife either," Mr. Carver murmured in Grace's ear, setting off fresh chills, his body too close against her back. "I think he hasn't been as kind to you."

Diccan's hand was sliding down Minette's belly, his tongue collecting the scent from her shoulder. He was chuckling, and the sound scored Grace like ground glass.

"I can't get enough of you, *mignette*," he murmured, so clearly that Grace wondered why he couldn't see her standing not four feet away. "It's been too long since I've had you."

"You've had me nearly every day," the blonde sighed, arching into his touch. "You are greedy."

"Not like this. Not naked and tucked away where we can enjoy ourselves for hours rather than hide in back bedrooms and park paths. Not with you ready to do anything for me." He bit down on her earlobe and she gave a little shriek. "Will you?" he asked. "Do anything?"

Grace swore she could feel the path of his hand on her own skin. She struggled to keep her breathing even. To hold still as the two of them turned toward each other, smiling as if theirs was the most delicious secret in the world.

"Haven't I?" Minette asked. "Done everything?"

He ran a finger down her pert nose. "Not quite yet."

She flashed him a coy look of confusion. "You must remind me."

Tangling his hands into her hair, he brought his mouth down on hers. Instantly she melted against him, lifting up on her toes, rubbing her nipples against his chest, moaning into his mouth.

Grace saw how he made love to that woman's mouth and felt the fresh clutch of betrayal. He had kissed her like that, slowly, as if memorizing her, deeply, as if promising, thoroughly, as if incapable of getting enough. It seemed that kiss hadn't been as important as she'd thought.

He had one arm around Minette now, the other hand still savoring the cushion of that perfect breast. Grace couldn't breathe. She heard the man behind her catch his own breath, and thought he was aroused. She was mortified. She couldn't take her eyes from the path Diccan's hands took over Minette's body. She felt heat wash through her, thickening her blood. She ached with envy, knowing he would never want to take her imperfect body like that, measuring her skin like priceless silk.

And then, with a final kiss, he lifted each perfect breast into his mouth to suckle. It was no more than a babe did, and yet the sight of it liquefied Grace. She wanted to move, to stretch, to beg for relief.

"It must be difficult," Carver whispered in her ear like temptation itself, "to watch."

She shivered with distaste, sure that Carver could sense her own arousal. She pulled more tightly into herself, loathing his touch. Wondering at a man who could enjoy this.

"It isn't enough," Diccan moaned. "Hold on, sweet. I'm going to give you the ride of your life."

And without another word, he spun her away to face the four-poster bed and lifted her arms over her head. Pulling his neckcloth from where he'd tossed it on the bed, he quickly tied her hands to the bedpost, waist high.

"Submit," he growled, nesting his erection in the cleft of her bottom. "Tell me you want this."

With a little mewling sound, Minette bent over so her arms stretched out before her, pressing back against Diccan's groin. "Yes," she gasped, writhing. "*Mon Dieu*, yes!"

Diccan growled, bending over and kissing the dimple at the base of her spine. Grace saw Minette shiver. She heard her moan, deep in her throat like an animal in pain. Grace shivered in sympathy. She knew what would come next. She had seen it drawn in pillow books, carved into temple walls. She had always wondered what it would feel like.

"Spread your legs for me," Diccan was saying, as he nipped at the milky white mounds of her bottom. "Let me see how wet you are for me."

Grace instinctively clamped her thighs together. She could feel herself dripping and hot and was ashamed. Behind her she could hear the quickened breathing of Mr. Carver, and that made it all worse. She was desperate to feel Diccan's hand along her spine, the sough of his breath cooling her hot skin. To open herself fearlessly for his invasion.

He stepped back, causing Minette to protest. He laid his hands on her hips, curling his fingers tightly enough to raise bruises. His rod stood out hard and thick and rampant, veins engorged along its shaft and the tip plum-round. Seeing it, Grace was beset by twin waves of arousal and despair.

"You torture me," Minette whimpered, rocking her hips, seeking him. "I have such an itch, and you refuse to scratch it."

Diccan answered by slipping one finger into her. Grace saw the juices on it glisten as he drew back and then slid it in again. She heard the slick passage of it and the low moan from Minette. "Please...oh, Diccan, don't make me wait."

He didn't bother with gentility. He just rammed himself into her. Minette bucked and cried out. Grace pressed a fist against her mouth. Diccan grabbed Minette's hips and began to drive himself into her. Again. Again. Harder and harder, as if punishing her, as if consuming her. Minette began to keen; she threw her head back, her eyes open, her mouth open, her body impossibly bowed to accept Diccan. "Yes!" she screamed, and he bit into her shoulder, a stallion marking a mare, lust at its most primal, and Grace didn't think her own knees would hold her up any longer.

She felt an awful weight in her chest and the laceration of her nails against her palms, and wished she remembered how to weep. She shook with the sin of her arousal, with the gaping wound of loss. She saw Diccan climax; harsh, hard, guttural. She saw Minette take him, shrieking and moaning, and Grace wanted it. She wanted all of it for herself with a greed that was frightening. She saw him rip the bonds from his lover and take her again on the bed, laughing, and wanted to keen with grief.

She stood there for hours, she thought, torturing herself because even though she knew how wrong it was to watch, she couldn't turn away. And when the two finally collapsed onto the bed, wound around each other like old vines, Mr. Carver leaned close once more.

"Now," he murmured. "The bed talk."

For a second, Grace had no idea what he meant. Then she heard Diccan, and she knew.

"I think you still owe me, *mignette*."

Tucked under his shoulder, the blonde giggled. "I have spent it, *chéri*. For what do I owe you?"

"For Wellington's schedule. Wasn't I the only one who knew about his secret trip to Whitehall next month? That should mean something."

"It is not next month you need to worry about, but the one after."

He lazily stroked her breast. "What are you waiting for, auguries from the planets?"

"Everything won't be in place for the perfect act 'til then."

"Tell me, then. So I can enjoy it, too."

"No, no," she murmured, her voice already breathy again with his attentions. "You won't want to play. You'll think it an insult to the great man, and you English, you think so much of him."

Diccan lifted his head. "Wellington?" He laughed. "Dear girl, haven't you heard? The great Wellington and I cordially loathe each other. I stole one of his barques of frailty once. He calls me a waste of good tailoring."

Minette smiled back, looking suspiciously like a contented cat. "Good. Then you won't mind our little game. We merely wish to give him such a little humiliation, him, who won't defend all those brave soldiers who fought his war. They need pay. He wastes his time feting the French instead of insisting his own government pay its debt. Bah! He should be shamed."

"A Frenchwoman worried about English soldiers?"

She stiffened as if he'd slapped her. "A Belgian woman, whose best cousin is married to one of these brave men. She is too proud to rely on me. She should rely on your duke." Then she spit, as if he were beneath her feet. "Belgians died for him, too. He forgets them all."

Diccan was smiling that enigmatic smile of his. "Well then, a worthy cause indeed. But why wait for your revenge?"

"Maybe if we can be ready. But so many need to be involved. It will be very public, this cut."

Diccan gave a casual shrug. "Well then, I suppose I'll just have to get his schedule for October and meet you here again tomorrow."

She ran a nail down his chest. "How can you get what we need so soon?"

"I'll manage." He kissed her, a slow, sultry mating of mouths and tongues that left Grace bereft. "I can't bear to part from you," he told Minette. "I wish I could just move in here and be done with it."

Minette fingered the damp curls at his neck. "What about your wife?"

"The cripple?"

Grace blinked, sure she'd heard wrong. Her heart had surely gone silent as she waited. But he sounded completely indifferent. "She has nothing to object to," he was saying, his focus on Minette's breasts. "I married her. I'll be damned if I have to fuck her."

Grace felt hot and then cold. Her heart thudded against her ribs, slow as death. She was terrified she would sob, and she hadn't done that since the day her mother drove away. That crack inside her widened into nasty, jagged lines. Something she had protected as long as she could remember was disintegrating. Something old and delicate and so worn it would take very little to shatter it. With only a few words, Diccan had almost done it.

She didn't bother to ask Mr. Carver's permission. She

just turned and walked out. He caught her by the arm just shy of the front door. She could hear Uncle Dawes panting down the stairs behind her.

She refused to look at either of them. "I don't know," she said. "I don't know if I can."

For a moment he didn't answer. Then Carver said, very softly, "Trust dies, but mistrust blooms."

Grace shot him a startled look. "What?"

He was studying her, his pale blue eyes oddly intense. His smile, when it came, was curiously mild. "A quote; Sophocles, I think. You realize, of course, that they don't mean to embarrass Wellington. They mean to kill him."

Grace couldn't look away, suddenly afraid of the odd light in the man's eyes. Finally Uncle Dawes caught up with them, wheezing apologies.

Grace broke away from Mr. Carver's hold and stepped back. "If I do this," she said, rubbing her arm. "How do I contact you?"

"I'll contact you. If you need me, though, I ride in the park every day." He waited for her to accept her wrap and opened the door. "One more thing, Mrs. Hilliard. Don't speak to anyone, not even Lady Murther. And I beg you not to go to anyone in the government. We don't know whom to trust."

She didn't even answer. Ignoring the arm her uncle held for her, she walked out.

When Grace finally returned home, she undressed, took down her hair, and slipped on her night rail in complete silence. She was terrified that if she opened her mouth, she would begin to wail like a lost child until the last of her pride and self-respect poured right out onto the floor like old blood.

The worst of it was that she was still aroused by what she had seen. Her body had no discretion. It didn't care for honor or betrayal or shame. It hungered. It hungered for Diccan. So after Schroeder left, Grace closed her eyes, as if she could hide, and, just as her friends in the *zenena* had taught her, she brought herself relief, all the while seeing Diccan mount his mistress like an animal. Only there was no relief. She lay awake the rest of the night, not moving, lest she lose the last semblance of control and shatter into shards of pain.

How could Diccan have done that? How could that man make her watch? How could she ever face Diccan or Uncle Dawes or anyone else she knew, with Diccan's words still echoing in her head like a death sentence? *I married her. I'll be damned if I have to fuck her.*

It wasn't until late the next morning that her intellect finally began to worm its way through the crippling pain. She had taken her coffee out into the small back garden, hoping to avoid Diccan, and was sitting on the wrought iron bench that rested against the back wall. From here she could see late roses and ash tree that had begun to turn, and almost imagined she sat in the country.

It might have been why her mind calmed enough for the first, tiny voice of reason to assert itself. Yes, she thought, Diccan had betrayed her. That would never hurt any less. It could never be forgotten, and she wasn't at all certain it could be forgiven. But had he betrayed his country?

Uncle Dawes had obviously believed it to be true, or he wouldn't have been party to that little visit. Grace trusted her uncle. She knew the man and she knew the soldier, and she couldn't imagine anything that would compel him to hurt her unless it was vital.

But she also knew Diccan. At least she knew him well

enough to know he had sacrificed comfort for honor. He could have backed out of their marriage. No matter what he'd said, the onus wouldn't have fallen that heavily on him. But he had refused to allow Grace to bear the brunt of disgrace alone. And before that, back in Belgium, he had flawlessly and discreetly managed to get Jack Wyndham and his information safely back to England.

Until Uncle Dawes had arrived at her house, Grace had never once thought to suspect Diccan of anything more than wasting himself on frivolities. Even after hearing him offer his services to his mistress, she couldn't quite believe that he would actually harm his country.

The person she did not know in all this was Peter Carver, and the accusation of treason rested on his shoulders. He said he worked for the Home Office, but she would be a fool to act without making sure of him. Which meant she had to get off this little bench and do something.

Her first instinct would have been to go to Kate. But Uncle Dawes had echoed Mr. Carver's warning. "She is Hilliard's cousin. We can't trust that she won't go right to him with the story."

As much as Grace hated to admit it, he was right. Kate would go right to Diccan, who would undoubtedly throw up a smokescreen the size of a London fog before Grace could learn the truth.

But Grace could tell Kit Braxton. Kit had also played a part in saving Jack Wyndham and in capturing the Surgeon. She knew too well his sense of patriotism. Kit was the heir apparent to a dukedom. But rather than enjoy his prospects, he'd bought a commission to fight and had almost died for his country. Grace could rely on him to discover the truth, and to do it discreetly.

"A spy?" he asked when she broached the subject as they walked through Hyde Park later that day. "Hilliard?" He began to laugh.

"This isn't funny, Kit. I saw him myself, and it looked as if he was telling his mistress things he shouldn't have been."

Kit abruptly stopped, his face hard with outrage. "Saw him? Saw him where?"

Of course she blushed, a hideous red that undoubtedly spread to her toes. "Half Moon Street."

For a moment, he couldn't even formulate a response. "What the hell were you doing there?"

And so she told him about the night before. She revealed everything except Diccan calling her a cripple. There was no reason to, she decided, no matter what it might have revealed.

By the time she finished her story, they had come to a halt by the Serpentine. Kit stared out over the gray water and rubbed his injured shoulder. "Bastard," he muttered.

"Maybe," Grace answered. "But is he a treasonous bastard?"

"She told you *what*?"

Diccan was once again sharing his rooms at the Albany with the Rakes. At Braxton's accusation, he came to his feet. He couldn't have heard correctly. Images of the night before spun past his exhausted brain. Visceral, mindless rutting. Callousness that would have shriveled even a strong woman. And Grace had seen it? She'd heard it? She'd heard what he *said*?

"It's impossible," he insisted, needing to be told that

Braxton had been mistaken. That, please God, he was lying.

But Braxton was braced before him like a fighter waiting the bell, his expression hard, his fist clenched. "That you did it, or that she saw it?"

"Oh, badly done," Chuffy said from the settee, giving his head a ponderous shake. "One thing to have a mistress, Hilliard. Quite another to make the wife watch. It's perverted. I think the French do it."

There were five of them this time: Chuffy and Braxton, Drake and Alex Knight, who worked in the War Office. And Diccan, called from a bout with Gentleman Jackson, undoubtedly too soon. He still felt an overwhelming need to hit something.

"You heard me," Braxton said to him. "What do you think you're doing?"

Diccan battled a blinding rage. "What the Foreign Office asked me to, damn it!"

"And you've brought us good information," Drake acknowledged, handing him a glass of his own brandy. "Especially this last lot. We'll alert Wellington first thing."

Diccan glared at him. "How the hell could Grace have seen me?" he demanded, thinking that Drake seemed far too unconcerned. "Don't you have that block of houses secure?"

"We should have." Drake shook his head. "I'll find out what happened."

"You're too bloody right you will!"

"Who did Mrs. Hilliard say escorted her to this private viewing?" Drake asked Braxton.

Still glaring, Braxton finally sat. "Her uncle. He evidently handed her off to a Mr. Peter Carver from the Home Office. Ever heard of him?"

"Alex," Drake asked. "You're our eyes in Whitehall. Ring a bell?"

From the depths of Diccan's best leather armchair, Alex nodded his curly blond head, making him look like a cherub accepting grace. "Newish man in Sidmouth's office. Secretary, I think."

"Well, if he arranged last night's travesty," Diccan snapped, "he's more than a bloody secretary."

Again the memories assailed him. Minette's earthy laugh, the scent of musk. The blind exhaustion of a hard climax. And Grace had seen it all. She'd heard him call her a cripple.

He dropped onto the couch and threw back his brandy, needing the heat. He felt as if he were caught in a nightmare. He had spent last night making sure no one thought Grace was worth hurting. And why should they have to? He'd evidently done a bang-up job of it all by himself.

Christ. He thought he'd be sick. Why had he ever listened to that bastard Thirsk?

"I hear your mistress has come to England looking for you," the peer had said when Diccan met him at his nondescript office in Whitehall the day after running across Minette at McCarthy's. "Respond."

He'd responded all right. It had been shamefully easy at first. After all, he'd been celibate for weeks. He had begun to feel a real regard for his wife, but how could he think of touching her, when he'd been told it would put her in danger? What could it hurt, he'd told himself, to relieve a little tension? After all, he was doing it in the service of his country, wasn't he?

The pleasure had been short-lived. Oh, he could still fuck his former mistress. Minette could make a dead man come. But pleasure had long since metamorphosed into frustration and guilt. How could he have known that his shapeless, colorless wife would so thoroughly work her way into his regard? That he would come to value sense over seduction? Wit more than sensuality?

He almost laughed. The idea that Grace had no sensuality was ludicrous. All a person had to do was see her on a horse.

"You can't do this anymore," Kit Braxton said. "Give the whore to somebody else to turn."

Chuffy raised a hand. "Happy to help."

"I can't," Diccan said, hating those two words more than any he'd ever spoken.

How could he face Grace, Diccan asked himself, knowing he would see his betrayal reflected in her eyes? She wouldn't even challenge him about it. She wouldn't think she had the right. And he couldn't correct her.

"What do you mean, you can't?" Braxton demanded, back on his feet.

It was Drake who answered. Diccan couldn't manage it. "Somebody slipped Hilliard a note. If he doesn't cooperate with Minette, they'll go after Grace."

For a moment there was a stricken silence. "Can't allow that," Chuffy finally said. "Not to her."

"But what are we going to do?" Braxton demanded.

It was left to Drake to tell the awful truth. "Nothing."

Braxton looked even more stricken than Chuffy. Diccan knew just how they felt.

"There is something else you need to know," Drake said. "Diccan's household brigade paid off."

Diccan lifted his head. "Babs didn't say anything."

"You haven't been home. She got her girl Nancy into

Melvin's home as a maid. Melvin's Evenham's lawyer. Nancy overheard Melvin speaking to someone about the verse Bentley was supposed to have."

Now even Chuffy was sitting up, alert. "The one we're looking for?"

Drake nodded. "Seems it's been found. The visitor, who Nancy didn't see, said distinctly, 'The whore has it. So we know where it is when we need it.'"

Diccan felt his stomach drop. "The whore. Minette?"

Drake shrugged. "Who else? Nancy said it sounded like they couldn't implement the main part of their plan without the verse. Which means we need to find the bloody thing before they do."

Diccan glared. "Search her house."

"We did. You need to search her."

"Shouldn't be hard," Chuffy mused. "Ain't in the habit of wearin' a vast amount o' clothes."

Diccan thought of the pile of luggage Minette seemed to need. "It could be anywhere."

"Well, find it." Drake climbed to his feet. "In the meantime, I'm sending Ferguson off to keep an eye over Wellington in Paris. Chuffy, you're still chumming it up with the Evenhams, and Alex, you're keeping your ear to the ground at Whitehall. Check on this Carver chap."

He got nods from everyone but Chuffy, who was pulling on his ear as if it would help him think. "If the government's compromised," he mused, "just who can we trust?"

"Drake's Rakes, Chuff. Nobody else."

That seemed enough for Chuffy.

Diccan rose to his feet. "And my wife?"

"You have to tell her," Braxton objected. "You know you can trust her. Need I remind you just who she is? Or that she helped get the information on the Lions in the first place?"

"I will allow that she's brave," Drake said. "But we can't count on her to keep from giving herself away. The Lions have to think she has truly been deserted by Diccan, or they'll use her for leverage. Would you bet her life on her ability to pretend?"

Even Kit, Grace's most loyal Grenadier, couldn't say yes. Which meant, Diccan thought bleakly, he would have to find a way to hurt her even worse.

"The only thing more important than her safety," Drake said, "Is the country's."

"Need to do that," Chuffy said suddenly. "Keep her safe. Still, Diccan. Not the thing."

Diccan agreed. It was not the thing at all.

Grace was dressing for a rout at the Wildes when Diccan slammed through the door to her boudoir. "Out," was all he said to Schroeder.

The abigail glared, but she complied, leaving Grace sitting in nothing but her chemise and stays.

Diccan didn't seem to notice. He was swaying a bit, as if the ground were uncertain. "I have just learned that you were at Half Moon Street last night."

Disappointment bore her down. "Did Kit tell you?"

"Braxton? You've talked to *Braxton* about this?" He stepped right up to tower over her, his eyes glowing with a peculiar light that sent chills racing through her. "Do you want to tell me why you shared our private business with Kit Braxton?"

She sat absolutely still, afraid she would unleash all of

her pain on him. It would be pointless and humiliating, and solve nothing.

"You haven't answered me, Grace," Diccan sneered, his words a bit slurred. He'd been drinking, Grace thought, surprised. She couldn't imagine Diccan Hilliard ever being in less than perfect control.

Well, except the night he'd made love to her. Maybe he simply couldn't abide her sober.

"You didn't expect me to ask you, did you?"

For a moment, she thought she had hurt him. Instead of turning away, though, he leaned even closer, his eyes glittering. "Did you enjoy watching, Grace? Were you satisfied by what you saw?"

It was all she could do to hold still. Her stomach turned. Her hands were clenched so tightly she thought her palms would bleed. She'd be damned, though, if she gave him the satisfaction of reacting.

"Are you?" she asked instead, never looking away from him.

He blinked. "Am I what?"

She tilted her head. "A spy."

Diccan quirked a chilly eyebrow. "My dear girl, I barely have the energy to be a diplomat. Where would you get such a ludicrous idea?"

"Actually, my Uncle Dawes. He's the one who took me to that house."

He looked away a moment, his laugh harsh. "At least he has proof I'm not a nancy boy. What exactly did you see?"

Her heart sped; she couldn't tell whether from fear or, damn him, arousal. "Besides the obvious?"

For a split second, she thought she caught pain in his eyes. It was gone too quickly to know.

"You were telling her Wellington's schedule," she said.

"Because her brother is the French liaison for his office."

"And the 'little humiliation'?"

He sighed, as if she were tiresome. "Nothing more than boasting. What else?"

"How did Bertie Evenham really die?"

The question surprised even her. But she saw that she'd hit a nerve. Diccan straightened, his face slack with surprise. "What in God's name does Bertie Evenham have to do with anything?"

She rose to her feet, tired of feeling the supplicant. "How did he die?"

"He died in a duel," Diccan said, sounding bored. "You know that."

She stepped up to him. "No. I don't. The man from the Home Office said he was shot in the head. That you were there when it happened. Were you?"

This time she saw a change in him he couldn't mask. His eyes went bleak. He stiffened, as if bracing himself, and looked away from her.

"Yes," he said, his voice rough. "I was. I saw him kill himself."

Shock buffeted her. She reached out, but he didn't see her. "Why?"

Diccan finally turned. For the first time, Grace thought he looked brittle. "Gambling losses. But I didn't see any reason to tell a grieving mother that her son said that he didn't deserve to live just before putting a gun to his head."

She pressed her hands against her chest, the anguish searing her. Diccan had regained his expression of calm. For some reason, though, Grace thought a storm raged beneath that glossy veneer. It made her ache for him, which made her angry.

"On your honor?" she asked, stricken.

Diccan glared at her. "On my honor. Now will you leave it be?"

She couldn't answer for a long moment. Something felt wrong, and she couldn't think what it was. But she had just suffered one too many shocks and felt bothered by it.

"I don't know," she admitted, surprising herself.

Sighing, Diccan dragged a hand through his hair. "What will it take to satisfy you?" he demanded. "What do you want me to do?"

And before she knew she was going to do it, she told him. "All those things I saw you do to your mistress last night?" she said, trembling with the enormity of her audacity. "I want you to do them to me."

Chapter 15

Diccan opened his mouth, but he couldn't think what to say. He was sure he'd heard wrong. There was no way in hell Grace could have said what she just did. Not pragmatic, practical, self-effacing Grace. But she stood unsmiling before him, and he realized his heart had begun to race. His breath seemed to be caught in his chest. He felt as if he'd been tossed into a racing tide, and was tumbled head over heels.

"Would you like to explain yourself?" he asked, very quietly.

"I've had time to think," she said, her voice as smooth as dark silk, her hands clasped loosely at her waist, her head up. "And I have come to the conclusion that celibacy is overrated. Since you seem disinclined to alleviate that condition for me, I felt it incumbent on me to ask. All things being equal, I would much rather not have to go elsewhere to have my ... itch scratched."

She looked so bloody calm and cool, a barefoot warrior queen in nothing but stays and chemise, her hair tumbled about her shoulders. Before, he might have mistaken her stillness for indifference. He knew better now. Her tension was betrayed by her shallow breathing, the blotchy red that spread from her chest, the way she clasped her hands before her as if taking tea with his mother.

She couldn't be more distressed than he. She'd seen him, seen exactly what he'd done with Minette. By God, she'd *heard* him, and what he'd said was unforgivable. And he couldn't explain.

He felt as if the room were closing in on him. "You want me to do to you what I did last night."

She nodded, back stiff as a lance, knuckles bone white. He rubbed the heel of his hand against his eye, his exhaustion dissipating like a rank mist. His brain might know better than to acquiesce to her request, but his body didn't give a damn. He was already half hard.

"Don't be absurd, Grace," he said, halfheartedly hoping the insult would fend her off. "You don't know what you're talking about."

She lifted her head, as regal as a queen. "I also find that I'm growing unbearably weary of men telling me I don't know what I'm talking about. If last night was any indication, I don't think you're physically unable to accommodate me. Unwilling is another issue, of course, which I do understand. But if you can dredge up the interest to get the thing done, then I believe I would like my fair share."

He had to say it. He had to chase her away. "Why? You know it won't change how I feel about you."

She looked as if he'd backhanded her, stark and ashen and frozen. Ah, and he hadn't thought he could feel worse.

"Maybe," she said quietly, making his punishment complete, "I just want to pretend."

He couldn't answer her. Hell, he couldn't breathe. Those few quiet words had lodged in his chest like a serrated blade, and he swore he was bleeding. How could he keep hurting her like this?

He had to. The Surgeon was out there.

"And when would you like this to happen?" he asked.

He could see the pulse jump in her throat. "As soon as possible, I think. I understand, however, if you need a bit of time to work up to it."

"Talk like that again," he threatened, "and I won't accommodate you at all. You'd better be damned sure, though." Images tumbled through his head, unpardonable sins against his wife. "What exactly did you see?"

She tilted her head, sending that colorless waterfall of hair swinging past her waist. For some reason he couldn't take his eyes from it. "I seem to have missed the disrobing," she said. "But considering how littered the floor was, I imagine it didn't take long."

He couldn't seem to keep from goading her, as if he needed to flay himself with the pain in her eyes. "Not long at all."

Her eyes widened fractionally. "All right."

He felt his breath catch in his chest. "Just like that? All right? You give me complete license."

He saw her pupils dilate. Her nostrils flared just a bit, and he felt his groin tighten. He felt as if he were drowning, and every word pushed him farther under.

And then, not even realizing it, she gave the fatal push. "You won't hurt me."

She meant it. By God, she *meant* it, when he had served her up such pain already that she should have wished the Surgeon on him. Fighting to hide the searing guilt, he stalked over to the door. "All right then. Be ready tonight." He stopped, his hand on the handle. "And when we meet again, you'd better be on your knees."

He waited only long enough to see the impact his words had on her. Then he opened the door and walked out. He didn't know how, but eventually he found himself walking in Green Park. Hands in pockets, head down, oblivious to the other occupants, he stalked the paths as if tracking crime. Nannies pulled children out of his way, and acquaintances gave him wide berth.

He couldn't keep this up. Once he had found his work for Drake exciting, challenging. That was when he'd had no one to worry about but himself. When his bed partners had all played by the same set of rules. No guilt. No attachment. No histrionics. He hadn't even minded if one of his conquests tried to mine him for information while he was mining her. It was only a girl doing her job, after all.

But the moment he'd opened his eyes to find Miss Grace Fairchild in his bed, the landscape had changed. In his new life, guilt had become a familiar companion. Shame, regret, revulsion. He'd hated to be saddled with a wife. He resented the hell out of the fact that she'd been forced on him. And yet, he found himself wanting to spend more time with her. He couldn't think of a sound more musical than Grace's laugh or a sight more stirring than her throwing her heart over a fence along with that elegant filly of hers.

He hadn't meant to become attached to her. God knows he'd meant to do his duty and then find a way out. But she'd grown on him. She'd revealed an amazing courage, an unexpected wit, a mind that was sharp as glass. She had worked hard to make his life comfortable and asked for precious little in return. She'd even managed to make a devoted slave not only of his valet, but of his horse.

He couldn't even call her a martyr. He got no long-suffering sighs from her, no pitiable looks of misery. She'd never even called him to account for his behavior, which made him feel even worse.

Damn her. He still couldn't call her beautiful. Not even pretty. But she was compelling, with her honesty and humor and loyalty. She was, God help him, arousing.

He shook his head, smiling as he thought of her bleeding and covered in mud as she serenely explained how, after everything she'd faced, it had been the sight of her own blood that had made her faint. Wouldn't it be wonderful to once again break through that magnificently calm facade?

Did he dare? Drake would say if he granted Grace's wish, he would be putting her in jeopardy. Diccan knew that Drake was right. But would one night tip the balance? She hadn't professed undying love. She'd asked for relief. Could he cooperate without making her think she meant something to him?

By the time he walked up the steps to White's a good hour later, he still hadn't decided.

No one who saw Grace at the Wildes' rout would have called her agitated. She smiled and chatted and sipped champagne with her Grenadiers. She laughed with Kate and strolled with Chuffy Wilde and his brother Brock, whom, according to Chuffy, she had saved after the battle of Croydon.

"A few centuries off," the handsome blond Brock said.

"Oh, that's right," Chuffy said with a triumphant smile. "Corunna."

Brock smiled. "Ciudad Rodrigo, actually."

Chuffy looked crestfallen. "Blast. Now I'm going to have to start thinkin' all over again."

Diccan never came, and people had finally begun to comment in Grace's hearing how seldom he was seen in her presence. Chuffy and Brock protected her, Lady Bea sang a little ditty about a sailor and his parrot, and Kate won a drinking contest with one of her cicisbeos. And Grace, for whom all these antics were performed, felt more isolated than ever.

For the first time in her life, she couldn't speak the truth. She couldn't let down her guard. She couldn't even hide herself off in a corner anymore. Everyone knew her name now, knew who she was and whom she had married. Most had even taken sides, the *ton* favoring Diccan and her Grenadiers defending her. She felt rather like a shuttlecock, and she knew the worst was yet to come.

At least, she thought, sipping a glass of warm lemonade, she didn't dwell on what had passed in her boudoir. Her heart still ached from the words that had been said; her body thrummed with the residual electricity that always passed between her and Diccan. But she knew better than to expect Diccan to follow through. No matter how much she might have wanted it, she simply couldn't see herself in Minette's place. She didn't have the courage. And Diccan, she was sure, didn't have the interest. He would find more excuses to avoid her, and she would lack the courage to challenge him. In the end they would go on as before, drifting farther and farther apart until they became strangers again.

She was proven quite wrong when she returned to find Diccan lounging in the wing chair in her bedroom, a snifter of brandy in one hand and a riding crop he tapped against his thigh in the other.

"I thought I told you that when you met me again you would do it on your knees," he said, running his gaze up and down her cream silk dress.

Feeling as if all the air had been sucked from the room, Grace came to an uncertain halt just inside the doorway. "What are you doing here?" she asked stupidly.

She even looked around, just to make sure she hadn't walked into the wrong room. But no, it was hers, done up in hues of warm wood and pale blues and creams; a most respectable bedroom. Trying to maintain her calm, she laid down her reticule.

"Stop," Diccan said when she began to pull off her glove. "You don't have permission to undress yet."

She halted, her fingers still hooked into the white kid. "Pardon?"

She noticed, suddenly, how bright the room was, with light not only from the fire, but from a score of candles that had been lit around the room. The effect was magical. The soft, flickering light gilded the reclining Diccan, who wore no more than a linen shirt and black pantaloons.

"Did you or did you not want to play a repeat performance of last night's entertainment?" he asked, his voice rasping along her nerves.

For a second she couldn't get a word out past the sudden anxiety in her chest. Anxiety? Maybe not. Maybe a bittersweet soup of longing and fear.

"Yes, I did say that," she said, still not able to move.

"Except for the conversation. I find I didn't like that nearly as well."

She thought she might have seen chagrin flash across those pale gray eyes. But it was too quickly gone, to be followed by a languid humor. "I find that words add to the enjoyment," he said, taking a sip of brandy. "But I believe I can come up with other topics of conversation. Such as your disobedience. Why aren't you on your knees?"

She knew exactly what he meant. Still she couldn't help looking around, as if clueless. "Why would I do that?"

His smile grew into the most erotic art Grace had ever seen. "That's right," he said. "You missed the first part of the evening. So I'll pardon your ignorance."

He was amused, she thought. He was also suddenly hard. For some reason that excited her almost as much as the promise in his eyes.

"Exactly, you said," he murmured.

"Yes." She dragged in a rasping breath. "I did." Fighting to keep her hand from shaking, she pointed at the crop. "Is that involved? If so, you might want to take a minute to remove the gun from beneath my pillow."

He lifted an eyebrow. "You keep a gun beneath your pillow?"

Even as her knees began to melt, she maintained her poise. "Of course. You never know what rogue might try to force his way into your bedroom."

"I see." He tapped that riding crop gently on his thigh like a metronome. "Well, I can't deny I'm a rogue, so I guess it's up to you."

Her heart began to thud in her chest, and her fingers tingled, as if anticipating the feel of his skin against them.

So, he was giving her the final choice. It made the moment even more exciting. Strolling over to her bed, she reached beneath the pillow and pulled out her Bunney muff pistol. Refusing to surrender completely, she moved it no farther than her bedside table.

She should have known better. She only made him smile. "Well met, madame wife," he said, calmly sipping brandy.

"It wouldn't do to become confused."

He nodded. "Good point. I believe we'll vary the program a bit, then. I don't want to find myself wondering exactly who I'm fucking."

Grace felt as if someone had dumped icy water on her head. "Funny," she said, deliberately stepping back and pulling up her glove. "I don't remember you deliberately insulting the woman you were with last night."

Tap. Tap. Nod. "My apologies. I simply don't want you to get the wrong idea."

She let out a dry laugh. "That you'll fall in love with me? No, Diccan. There's precious little chance I'd make that mistake."

She would have said a shadow passed across his eyes, but she knew better. Her wish for his affection could not create it. She had to settle for pleasure. And she knew he could provide that.

"Pull out your pins," he said abruptly."I want to see your hair down."

She hesitated only long enough to make him understand that she would not stay past another insult. Then, slowly, she raised her arms and began to pull out her pins. Any other time, she would have carefully collected them into her cloisonné box. Tonight she let them drop, the only sounds in the room the little plinking noises as they hit the hardwood and the syncopated rasp of breathing.

She couldn't look away from him. He might not love her. He might not really desire her. But he still managed to look as if he wanted to pull her down on the floor and take her right there. He didn't move, except to tap the crop against his thigh. But Grace felt crowded, suddenly short of breath, as if he had used up all the air in the room. She felt hot and cold and shivery, and her hands began to shake.

"Now spread it out," he said.

Winnowing her fingers through her hair, she pulled it out of its tight twists, shaking it until it fell unfettered down her back. She was surprised to see his pupils dilate at the sight. A melting warmth woke in her belly and seeped into her legs.

"Pull one lock over your breast."

She did. "Like this?"

His breathing was growing shallow; she could see it. He nodded. Grace stood still, her hair a curtain over her back, a curling invitation over her suddenly taut breast, silk on silk. She was mesmerized by the growing bulge in his pantaloons.

"Hmmm," he murmured, resting the tip of the crop against his mouth. "A nice picture, certainly, but I think that lock of hair would look better against a naked breast. Disrobe."

She went still. "No."

His smile grew a bit cooler. "Then you don't want this after all."

She might have complied if he had touched her, or even smiled. "Not if it means I must demean myself," she said, wishing her voice sounded stronger. "I don't intend to spend the next few minutes having you remind me of how little I measure up to your mistress. Enjoy the illusion, Diccan. The reality pales in comparison."

His brow lowered. "I thought I told you not to speak like that. I want to see you naked, Grace. It is my right. Especially since you asked."

She flushed, hot with frustration. Frozen with indecision. Her body cried out a need to obey, to do anything to keep him here. Experience told her he wasn't nearly drunk enough. Pride kept her silent.

"Grace," he said quietly, his expression giving nothing away, his body perfectly still. "I've seen your legs before. Besides, I promise you'll be naked soon enough."

She raised her chin. "Not this way."

For a long, terrible moment she heard nothing but silence. She struggled to stay where she was, to seem impervious to this shame. She waited for his inevitable departure.

"Well," he finally said, and relaxed back in the chair again. "We could move onto the next bit, where you get on your knees."

"Indeed." She met his gaze. "And why would I do that?"

He raised an eyebrow. "Minette didn't ask why."

"Minette probably didn't have to."

He gave her another lazy smile. "Because," he said patiently, "if you truly want to do everything we did last night, then you need to kneel between my legs and open the placket on my pants. You need to slip your hands inside and pull out my cock."

His voice slowed and deepened as he compelled her with his gaze. She felt herself flush and chill, her skin alive. She wanted to squeeze her thighs together again to keep the juices from dripping down her leg. He aroused her that quickly, with only a look and a few salacious suggestions.

"And then, Grace," he said, daring her to look away, to flinch, "you'll open your lovely mouth and swallow my cock whole."

For a second all she heard was him say was that her mouth was lovely. Then the rest of the command sank in. She sucked in a startled breath, the image so clear she could almost feel that tumescent flesh against her tongue. She licked her suddenly dry lips. She saw Diccan's eyes follow the progress of her tongue, and she was surprised by a sensation of power.

She had seen this act before, of course. She'd always thought it debased a woman. Kneeling like a beggar, offering pleasure without receiving it. Subservient in every way.

Suddenly, though, she began to see the other side. He didn't just demand she do this. He wanted it. He needed it. She looked down to see that his buttons were straining. He didn't move, but she felt the sudden tension in him even five feet away, a pulsing energy that bathed her like sunlight. She saw that his hands were fisted against the arms of his chair, and she felt a thrill of control.

"And then what?" she asked, her voice breathy and small.

Slowly, deliberately, he spread his legs, more dare than invitation. "Then, you pleasure me."

She could barely get in enough air. Her heart was slamming against her ribs; her palms had begun to perspire. She felt hot, so hot. She was trembling down to her toes, waves of heat searing her skin. She almost threw herself on the ground right then, furious to feel that hard velvet rod against her lips, against her teeth, against the tender curve of her throat. She longed to roll her tongue around that lovely rounded top, to lick the drop of moisture from it, to see if she could make *him* scream.

She stood perfectly still. "And when is it my turn?"

His smile darkened. His eyes were all but black. The riding crop was motionless in his hand. "Oh, don't worry," he said. "It will be soon enough, and if you think you climaxed that first night, you have no idea what's in store for you tonight."

His words pierced her deep, a searing lightning so intense she almost folded beneath it. She wasted a moment just enjoying it. The last time he'd taken her she'd been blindsided. Overwhelmed. She hadn't had any time to appreciate the sensations he'd unleashed. Well, she would tonight.

Slowly, deliberately placing one foot in front of the other, she approached. She felt suddenly liquid, swelling and pulsing, life pouring through her like water. She felt feminine, as if her acquiescence imbued her with the instinctive understanding millennia of women possessed of how to give pleasure, how to receive it. She felt her hips sway as she walked, as if she were really rounded and soft and as sensual as a cat. She heard silk slither over her legs and delighted in its breezy caress. She saw the sudden fire in Diccan's eyes and knew that whatever else, his response would set this night apart.

"Like this?" she asked, lowering herself as gracefully as if she were curtsying to the queen.

The rug was soft beneath her knees. She could smell brandy and the citrus tang of soap. And beneath it, the subtle musk of his arousal. She could see the candlelight slither down his throat as he swallowed. Her body responded; softening, swaying, swelling to meet him. She laid her hands on the insides of his thighs and pushed them farther apart. She didn't imagine his surprised gasp. She never took her eyes from his as she slowly ran her hands up toward his groin, and swore his buttons would pop from the pressure. Savoring the sensation of iron muscle beneath the soft slide of wool, she edged her hands up to the placket and felt the scorching heat beneath. She felt his shaft throb and twitch, as if instinctively seeking her mouth. Her attention. Her domination. She was on her knees, but he was the one who would soon be helpless.

With a slow smile that told Diccan just that, she ran her fingertips around each button, and was rewarded when his hips came off the seat. "Grace," he growled, looking fierce.

"Diccan," she growled back and flicked open the first button.

Then the next. And the next. She didn't have to reach in. He was already so hard she could barely get that last button free. In the end, she just yanked at it, sending the button pinging faintly against one of the bedposts. She barely noticed, for there, springing right into her hand like a prize for her perseverance, was his engorged rod.

For the first time she took her gaze from Diccan's. She sated herself on the sight of his erection. The essence of power, of pleasure. Of life. She'd been right before. Temple art had nothing on Diccan Hilliard. He was magnificent. She couldn't help it. She giggled.

"You find my cockstand amusing?"

"No," she said, unable to keep from running a finger up and down his length. It felt so silky. She hadn't expected that. "I was thinking that you must have posed for the erotic temple art I saw in India. It's the only way to explain the size of some of those phalluses."

His smile was quite satisfied. "I hope you're impressed."

Ah, there it was, that pearly white drop trembling on the tip of his penis. She slowly licked it off, tasting salt and smoke. "I'll reserve my judgment until it's my turn for pleasure," she said with a saucy grin.

She did slip a hand inside his trousers now, savoring the dark heat that met her, and cupped his balls, the sacs heavier than she'd imagined. She ran her other forefinger over the top of his rod, fascinated as much by his reaction as by the smoothness of it. He was bucking a bit, as if he couldn't keep his body from its pleasure. His lips thinned and his nose flared. It made her smile. It made her want to torment him to death. With one more smile up to him, she bent her head, letting her hair cascade over his belly, and she slowly wrapped her lips around him.

Mmmmm, soft; earthy. She raised up on her knees and took more of him into her mouth, sliding forward until she could feel him pressing against the back of her throat. He was hot and throbbing and silky, and she was becoming obsessed with the texture of him.

One hand holding his sacs, she pulled back on his penis, then slid down again. She heard a startled groan and relished an astonishing sense of power. She began to suck as she pulled back, drawing him more deeply into her mouth. She realized she was humming in her throat, savoring how he throbbed against her tongue, how he jerked when she left little love bites on his tender skin. How he was lifting to her mouth, as if incapable of staying away.

"Enough," he growled, grabbing her shoulders.

She ignored him, pulled harder, anxious to know how

this would end. Her world had diminished to the taste of salt and sweat, the scent of arousal, the sound of gasps and the wet sucking of her mouth. She didn't want to stop. She wanted to make him mad.

She almost did. But just when she thought she'd triumphed, he pulled out and pushed her onto the floor. In one fluid movement, he shoved her skirts up and her knees apart, and he drove into her.

Not a kind word. Not a caress. His eyes were closed and his hands were fisted in her hair. She swore he was growling, and the sound reverberated in her chest. She felt impaled, split, the pressure of him inside her unbearable. Yet her body tightened, seeking him, reveling in his loss of control. She lifted up, arching to fit him inside of her. She closed her eyes, all her focus on the unbearable fullness, the sliding, searing pleasure of him as he pumped into her, the abrasion of cloth and buttons and stays as he took her on the hard wood floor.

Almost before she could comprehend that she'd been usurped, before her body could catch up to intense pleasure, he gave a harsh cry and spilled himself into her, deep against her womb, where she could feel the heat of his seed pulsing into her, life-giving warmth. Life-affirming communion. Life-altering power. And then, just as before, he collapsed on top of her, gasping.

After a moment when he made no more move, she felt compelled to prod him. "It doesn't seem to take long," she said, her arms wrapped around him, as if she could keep him close, "does it?"

He lifted his head to glare at her. "It's your fault."

She blinked. "Me? How could it be me?"

He scowled. "I don't know. But I've never been this impatient before."

Was she wrong to feel absolute delight at his words? Could he possibly mean such a thing? Could he even know what it meant to her?

She decided not to enlighten him, in case it would frighten him away. Instead, she lifted her head to lick the sweat that beaded in the little hollow in his throat. She wanted to say, "What's next?" She still didn't have the courage. After all, they were still dressed.

Evidently, she didn't have to. Without prompting, he lifted his head and gazed down at her, and she thought his eyes were softer. He didn't smile, exactly. But he didn't need to.

And then he was kissing her. Edging off her chest a bit so she could breathe, he laid his hands on either side of her head, and bent to take her mouth. It was a kiss for the ages, a slow mating of lips and tongues and murmurs that seemed to last for days. Grace slanted her head to meet him more fully. She slipped her hands around his neck so she could finger the damp silk of his curls. She relished the feeling of her body reacting to him, her breasts aching and swelling, the nipples tightening almost painfully, especially when she rubbed them against his chest. Her heart had found a new rhythm that seemed to match his, quick and full. Her body seemed to be melting, molding to his as if they were warm candle wax. She swore her womb contracted.

He began to nuzzle her ear, and then her throat, sending sharp chills cascading through her. She arched her neck to give him better purchase. He cupped her breast in his hand, and her body instinctively lifted to meet him. Oh, she thought, gasping for air at the exquisite sensations his fingers wove, this is what I've missed. This is what our lives would be if he returned my love.

It was when she admitted it, finally. It had probably been inevitable from the moment she'd first tucked herself in a corner just to watch him. He fascinated her. He amused her. He confounded her. He was such a contradiction, but at heart, he was a man who could see greatness in the ungainly Gadzooks. He had seen Grace, and even though she knew she was the last person he would choose to make love to, he made love to her. And he did it with passion and enthusiasm. He was a man she could love.

He was a man she *did* love.

Even as she felt his weight on her, she ached for its loss. She felt his clever hands unlacing her stays and thought she would do anything to insure their return. She felt her body warming, opening, hungering, and she wanted to feel that all the time. She wanted to have the right to feel it.

She wanted Diccan to feel it for her.

Then he took her breast in his mouth and she forgot about love. She could only focus on pleasure. "Oh, my," she gasped, grabbing his head and pulling him to her, "that's quite . . . lovely."

He smiled against her. "Glad you like it. I admit some chagrin that I didn't realize your breasts were quite this nice."

She found herself looking down at herself and realized that somehow he'd slipped her dress down to her waist. "Kate's chef insisted I needed to put on some weight," she said stupidly, impatient at his absence. "Would you like another taste?"

He chuckled this time, his attention on the nipple he took between his fingers. Pleasure shot through her and she arched against him, groaning. "Please, Diccan."

Somehow that stopped him. His hair was rumpled, his

eyes languorous, his expression thoughtful as he looked down at her. "No," said, dropping a kiss on her forehead. "If we stay down here, I'm just going to take you again, and that's not fair."

Grace huffed, her body already chilling as he sat up. "I don't think I complained."

He climbed to his feet and held out a hand. "You said you wanted everything. Now, come on."

Still lying on the floor, she glared up at him. "You're making me feel like a child you have to drag through the fair."

His smile would have melted steel. "Oh, but I assure you you'll enjoy this fair as much as I."

And oh, she did. Accepting his assistance, she got to her feet, where he kissed her again, his hand against the back of her head to hold her close as he leisurely explored her mouth, his arm around her waist to keep her from collapsing back to the floor. She insisted on undressing him, using the excuse to explore his sleek, toned body with her hands and eyes and mouth. She almost dropped to her knees to take his rod in her mouth again, but he laughed and hauled her back into his arms where he kissed her some more; playfully, deeply, seductively, until she couldn't stand up. He pulled her so tightly against him she could barely breathe, and when he stepped back, somehow her clothing had joined his on the floor.

"I see you've washed the dye out," he murmured.

She almost fled. He couldn't want to see all of her. She tried to pull away, but he caught her back to him again. "Am I going to have to tie you down?" he asked.

"You don't want to . . ."

He grinned, and she felt her knees turn to mush. And

suddenly his neckcloth was in his hands and he was tying her hands together, just as he had with Minette.

"Thank heavens for neckcloths," she snapped, pulling at the bonds, her nakedness forgotten, "or your partners would keep getting away."

His grin was positively salacious. Spinning her away from him, he pressed his body full length against her back, his rod throbbing in between the globes of her bottom, his mouth right against her ear. "Oh, you don't want to get away."

Her body flared to life with the barest whisper of his breath against the shell of her ear, with the remembered feel of him pressing against her. This time, though, was better. This time he chose to be here; he surrounded her with himself, and she felt unbearably cherished.

"What now?" she whispered, breathless and unnerved.

"You must tell me," he murmured. Lifting her small breasts into his hands, he began to knead them, teasing the taut nipples with his thumbs until she wanted to wail with impatience.

"Tell you what?" she asked, her voice thin. "I'm tied up here."

His head still just next to hers, he kissed her exquisitely sensitive ear, licking her shell and then blowing on it until she couldn't breathe at all. Her entire body was on fire, freezing, chills chasing one after another all the way to her core, beyond to her legs, her feet, her toes.

"Do you want me to be polite?" he asked, his voice a deep rumble against her back, "or do you want to know how a mare feels in heat?"

Another flash, this of lightning, jagged and blinding. She didn't want polite. She wanted to know he couldn't help himself. She wanted to make him lose control again.

"Take me," she moaned, letting her head fall back.

He took hold of her hands and tied them to the bedpost. He nestled right up against her, so she could feel the entire length of his erection against her bottom. She was trembling now, pulling in air in gasps, her entire body thrumming with anticipation.

Then he did something she'd never expected. He wrapped a blindfold around her eyes. She jerked back. "You didn't do this before."

"I know. But aren't you feeling adventurous?"

She felt as if she stood balanced on a sharp precipice. She was naked, vulnerable, submissive. He was behind her, not touching her, close enough, though, that she could feel the heat radiate off his skin. She was thick with arousal, taut with uncertainty. It was her choice. Did she trust him?

"Yes," she said, relaxing into her bonds. "I am feeling adventurous."

"Spread your legs."

She shook with excitement. She spread her legs and felt the air tease her wet core. She saw blackness and thought how easily she could hear the rasp of his breath, the slide of his feet on the floor.

"Bend over."

She bent over.

"Ah, beautiful," he murmured. "I can see the the pink of your netherlips, and they're already wet. Tell me you want this."

She found herself even more aroused by his words. More uncertain. More fragile. He hadn't even touched her and she felt as if she'd splinter into shards of glass. The air swirled gently around her. She could hear nothing now but her own breathing. Her own heart. But she smelled him, sharp sex and dusky night. Secrets and satisfaction. Suddenly she felt the pressure of one callused finger against her.

"Tell me."

She gasped, the touch burning her; she arched, seeking a deeper touch, a sharper contact. Just that one, tiny friction from his finger was igniting a firestorm in her.

"I want this," she said, trying not to groan. "I want you."

He reached around with his other hand and caught her nipple. He rolled it, stretched it, and she moaned. "Now?" he murmured. "Do you want it now?"

"Yes," she hissed, furious with waiting, with not knowing.

For a second his hands disappeared. She pulled against her bonds trying to get to him. She couldn't even hear him. She held her breath, desperately seeking proof of him in the darkness. God, she was so close to just whimpering, and she refused to show such need.

Then she felt his hands on her hips, no more. She jumped when he ran his tongue right there at the little dimple at the bottom of her spine. She felt his breath cool the place he licked, and she shuddered. She heard the rumble of his chuckle.

"Damn you," she rasped. "Will you just fuck me?"

And he did. Driving in so hard she gasped, unsure how she could take all of him, feeling impaled, invaded, pummeled. He held her with steely hands and he thrust into her, a stallion claiming his mare. He slowed, pulling almost all the way out until she bit her lip to keep from protesting, then drove in again.

This time he lasted longer. This time he murmured words of encouragement, words of endearment as he marked her, as he destroyed her concept of who she was. Her body was consumed with sensation; sharp, hot, swirling, a pleasure–pain she had never even known could exist. She panted like a runner. She reared back to meet him until they were pounding at each other, no sound in the room but the slick slide of his cock, the slap of skin against skin, their frenzied breathing. And then he found her nubbin, and he took it between his two fingers. It was the spark that lit the explosion.

Grace's body seized. Inside her, light splintered into fireworks and waterfalls and cannon fire. She heard herself keening, a high, wild sound of exultation that filled the room. She heard Diccan's breathless laughter and felt his seed pulse into her, his hands clenching her so tightly she knew she'd be bruised in the morning. She felt him bend close over her, as if he couldn't bear to separate his skin from hers. He was shaking, and she was once again swept by the feeling of pure power that she, Grace Fairchild, could bring Diccan Hilliard almost to his knees.

She came within inches of telling him that she loved him; that this would be a moment she would cherish for the rest of her life. She almost betrayed an unbearable truth. That in that moment, she would do anything for the chance of having this again.

But worse was to come, for after such primal, explosive lovemaking, Diccan untied her, tossed away the blindfold, and carried her to the luxurious four-poster bed where he made thorough love to her again, this time with gentleness and tenderness and a smile that could capture the heart of a stone.

It captured hers, the bits that hadn't already succumbed. And when she fell asleep, still in his arms, she knew she had made a grave error. She had wanted him too much to protect her heart. She had pretended it didn't matter that only one of them had meant the love they'd shared.

She could pretend no longer. Which was why, in the end, she would have to leave him.

Chapter 16

She might not have left after all if Diccan hadn't made love to her again. They had awakened deep in the night, still wrapped around each other, and sleepily, easily, slipped into the touches and murmurs and kisses that bespoke intimacy. They made love like friends. Diccan taught her how to ride him, easily lifting her so she could impale herself on him, as if it were something she should be used to.

Even in the last of the firelight he must have seen her blushing, because he grinned up at her. "Come now, my Grace, you can't still be shy."

She couldn't quite raise her head, her excuse, the fascination of seeing her hair pool amid the ridges of his belly. "I'd rather not be on display," she muttered. "Scrawny women don't like it."

He actually shook her. "Grace. Stop it. You aren't scrawny, damn it. You're a horsewoman. Didn't it ever occur to you that you're lean because you've spent your life in the saddle?"

She looked up, surprised. Oddly, he seemed just as startled.

"Good Heavens," he said with a huge grin. "It never occurred to me! I actually *have* married a warrior queen."

She snorted, but she sat a bit straighter, finally able to relax enough to enjoy the amazing fullness of him inside her. "Does that mean I have your obedience, sir?"

He chuckled, moving enough to remind her who was impaling whom. "I'm yours to command."

They laughed and played and teased their way to climax, to sleep, to comfort. And as she lay in his arms, replete and easy, he stroked her hair. "Isn't your friend getting married soon?"

"Olivia? Yes. I was hoping to go."

He nodded against her. "Excellent idea. I'll see if I can get some time off."

They didn't say any more, just drifted back off to sleep, tumbled together like puppies beneath the sheet. When Grace woke the next morning, she felt oddly lethargic and warm, as if she were lying out in a noonday sun. It was still early; she could tell from the pink light against her closed lids. She was alone, but she could still smell Diccan on her skin, the wonderful contrast of citrus and smoke. A tang of brandy, the sharp bite of sweat. Earthy, real scents, familiar to her from her years with the army.

But there was one scent she had never really known: the scent of lovemaking, as if the sea had washed over her and left a residue of salt. An energizing, life-affirming scent. She inhaled the compelling bouquet and rolled onto her back, stretching her arms over her head. How could anything feel more wonderful than a well-loved body? How could any memory be better than a man's smile as he made you his? How could a woman want for more than that strange, wonderful, overwhelming intimacy that united bodies and cemented souls? It was as if Diccan had painted a black-and-white world with bright, primal colors and invited Grace to bathe in it with him.

It occurred to her then that what she had hoped for had actually happened. Her hours with Diccan were the most intimate she'd ever known with another human. Until Diccan had wrapped his arms around her, she had never known how cherished one could feel. Oh, Breege and Harps cared for her, but it was the gruff affection of shoulder claps and cheek busses. Her father hadn't known how to do even that. And her lads had known to keep a respectful distance from the general's daughter. Now, finally, she knew that she could close her eyes in someone's arms and feel completely safe.

It was at that moment, of course, that she heard it again in her head.

I married her. I'll be damned if I have to fuck her.

The memory propelled her right out of that comfortable, tumbled bed to stand on the bare floor, naked and shaking. He had sounded so angry when he'd said that; so disgusted. Had he been lying? Or had he lied last night when he'd held her as if she were precious to him? She simply didn't know, and the thought sent a flood of cold washing through her.

Not knowing what else to do, she pulled on a wrapper. Her body still seemed to glow. She could almost feel Diccan's hands on her again. She wanted so badly to believe that he'd lied to his mistress, that it had been a facade. Yet a lifetimes worth of experience told her differently. No one would choose her over Minette Ferrar. And yet, Diccan had at least made her feel as if he had.

He had been kind. She had fallen in love.

When she heard a rustle of movement in Diccan's room,

she had to restrain herself from running in and begging to be held. To be reassured that the night before had meant as much to him as it had to her. No, she thought. It would demean her and embarrass him. She would stay where she was.

Somehow she found herself at his door anyway. Maybe, she thought, she could prove something to herself if she greeted him with a smile and sent him off with a joke. Maybe she could prove something to him if she let him go as easily as before.

She really should have known better. When she opened the door to Diccan's room, it was to find Schroeder standing in the middle of the floor, a porcelain bowl of soapy water in her hands.

The pretty blonde flushed as if Grace had caught her *in flagrante*. "I was just cleaning up."

"Indeed." Grace was proud of how calm she sounded. "Biddle is indisposed?"

Schroeder clutched the bowl so tightly that water sloshed onto her apron. "He is with the master on their way to Brighton. The prince, you know . . ."

Grace felt as if her heart had stopped. She managed a nod. "Ah."

He hadn't even thought to wish her farewell. Grace decided that was answer enough.

"Is there anything I can do for you, madame?"

Grace saw pity on Schroeder's face, and oddly enough, that was the last straw. "I'll be getting dressed, Schroeder." Turning away, she walked out and closed the door behind her.

There was no note, of course. Only Schroeder, who laid out a pretty *eau-de-Nil* figured muslin for her. "I hope this is acceptable," the abigail said in strained tones. "You have your lessons with Her Grace this morning. And then the primrose sarcenet for tea this afternoon with Lady Haversham?"

Grace nodded. She kept nodding, even as Schroeder helped her wash off evidence of the night before and change into chemise and stays and muslin. She couldn't seem to breathe. Each layer of clothing made it worse. She kept replaying the night before in her head. She thought how much trust it had taken to close her eyes in Diccan's arms. How much it had meant to her that she could.

Thank God she hadn't told him.

"Will you have breakfast, madame?" Schroeder asked. "Cocoa, perhaps?"

Just the thought made her queasy. "Not this morning, I think."

Long after Schroeder had left, a bemused frown on her face, Grace stood in the middle of her bedroom and thought of what her day would be. What all her days would be, slipping into progressively tighter and tighter stays, boxed in by society and convention and the casual oppression of the *ton*, all so she could hold on to a husband who didn't want her.

A husband who would come to her sometimes and make her feel as if she meant something to him. Who would define her days without ever knowing it. And Grace would end up doing anything...*anything*...for those brief moments with him. She would learn to excuse his infidelities, his inattention, his casual tyrannies. She would become one of those pitiful women who suspended her life upon her husband's sporadic attentions.

Standing there in the middle of her uninspiring blue

room, looking out the window to where the early sunlight washed the rooftops and strawberry vendors sang in the streets, Grace came to the most momentous decision of her life. She wouldn't do it. She *couldn't*. She had given up everything for him. Everything she'd wanted. Everything she'd once hoped to be. All she had left was her self-respect, and she was about to peddle that away for a look. A kiss. A casual glance across a room. She would once again sentence herself to the periphery of everyone else's lives for nothing more than Diccan's notice.

By God, it wasn't enough.

For a long time Grace could only stand there, watching the street come to life, a hand clenched against the grief that crowded her chest. In the end, though, she turned away and tugged on the bell cord. When Schroeder answered, she asked her to pack a bag and arrange a post-chaise. She ignored the astonished looks her staff gave her as she personally packed her red Guards jacket and riding boots.

She was pulling on her gloves in the foyer when, as if to put a final punctuation on the day, Kit Braxton walked in the front door.

Grace stopped, her mouth open. Good Lord, she'd forgotten. "Kit," she greeted him.

Kit was accompanied by another gentleman she knew from the war. Shorter, with the sweet face and the curling white blond hair of a cherub. "Hello, Alex," she said. "Why did Kit drag you over?"

"Moral support," he answered with a rueful smile, hands in pockets.

She nodded and turned for the salon. "I only have a moment, but why don't we sit?"

She was ashamed to realize that she'd forgotten Kit's

mission. The night before had pushed everything else from her mind.

Kit waved Alex and her into the salon. "We need you to stay silent about your suspicions," he said bluntly, shutting the door behind him.

Grace made it a point to offer the men seats before settling herself onto her cream Sheraton settee, the perfect society matron. "We who?"

Kit exchanged a brief glance with Alex as they took up the matching navy blue chairs across from her. "Those of us who love you," he said.

Grace considered him a moment. "Bollocks. Who?"

Kit frowned. "You don't need to know. You just need to listen to me."

Grace almost cursed again. There was a sheen of perspiration on Kit's forehead, and he kept clenching his hand. She might never understand society, but she knew soldiers. Kit didn't want to be here, but he was on a mission. Suddenly beneath his words she heard echoes of unnamed men trying to figure out what to do with her, a surprise pawn in a chess match.

"Did you wait for Diccan to leave for Brighton?" she asked, "or is this simple serendipity?"

The glance Kit and Alex exchanged was answer enough. The timing of this visit was no accident. The question was whether Diccan had had a part in it. Grace fought a sudden flush of shame. Had the night before been an attempt to do the same thing? Keep her off balance? Focused on something beside the greater question of just what he was involved in?

"Are you telling me Diccan is a traitor after all?" she asked.

Kit looked down at his clenched hand. "There are questions. The government is looking into the allegations right now."

She quirked an eyebrow. "You mean to say he's a traitor."

He shook his head. "It isn't my judgment to make."

"It's just your job to warn me off."

"You came to me, Grace," he reminded her gently.

She sighed. "Yes, I did. Oddly enough, I'd hoped for answers."

"This is the answer."

She turned away a moment, her focus out the front windows onto the tidy world of Mayfair. "What about Mr. Carver? Is he who he says he is?"

It was Alex who answered. "He works for the Home Office."

It was a blow, but she refused to let them see it. "And what do I do when he and Uncle Dawes come to me for information?"

"We'll take care of it," Alex said, his pale head bobbing.

"Who?" she asked, knowing that Alex, the man dubbed the White Knight, had as much trouble lying as Kit. "Those who love me, or the government? I assume they're the ones making these allegations."

"Both."

She nodded absently, her anger hardening. "I see."

"You must understand, Grace," Kit insisted. "It could be dangerous."

He actually made her laugh, a dry, sharp sound. "I might forgive you for that if you hadn't lived two tents away for the last five years. Tell me, Kit. Am I too stupid to understand or too frail to act?"

Kit actually looked as if he were the one who'd been hurt.

He moved over to sit alongside her. "Gracie," he said, reaching for her hand. "Please understand. It's complicated."

She neatly pulled away and came to her feet. "Oh, I imagine it is," she allowed absently. She wasn't quite certain how, but she found herself standing before the window, as if it would give her a better perspective of the problem. "Are the Lions involved?"

It took him a moment to answer. "We owe you that much. Yes."

She turned. "And you think Diccan is a Lion, even though he protected us from them not three months ago. Or would it be my uncle, the man who fought with Cornwallis, who is betraying his country?"

He sighed. "I told you. We don't know. It's more likely Diccan is after money. Reports from his various posts claim he amassed quite a small fortune performing shady tasks for local governments."

Grace shook her head. No. Against all evidence, she couldn't believe it. But again she thought of the sneer in Diccan's voice when he'd been with his mistress. Of his laughter the night before. Diccan was, indeed, a liar. A very good one. She just wasn't sure about what.

"And you don't want me to search for suspicious documents."

Kit stepped up to her. "No. We want you out of it."

Turning back to the almost bucolic scene out the window, where a nanny strolled by with her charges and a pair of matrons chattered beneath their frilly parasols, Grace struggled with the new information. They would expect her to simply back away, she knew. Leave everything in their capable hands. What, she wondered, should she do? What did she *want* to do?

"All right," she said, turning back to Kit. "I take myself out of it. You lot can deal with my uncle and my husband and the Home Office. Just know that if anyone I love is hurt because of this, I swear I'll see you in hell."

"Now, Gracie," Kit protested.

"Don't patronize me again, Kit." Walking to the door, she opened it. "Now, gentlemen, I am late for an appointment. I wish you good day."

Kit looked almost grief-stricken. But he gave her a quick bow and followed Alex out. "I'm still here if you need me, Gracie."

Grace couldn't bear to do more than nod. Kit had just taken away her last refuge. If Kit couldn't tell her the truth, no man would. He should know better, though, than to think she would calmly retreat into the arms of society. She would search for answers on her own.

She was turning from showing him out the door, intent on doing just that, when Schroeder approached, Grace's bonnet in hand.

"I don't understand," the woman said, her features pursed. "You don't wish to take me along?"

Grace took the bonnet and set it on her head. "Thank you, no, Schroeder. As a matter of fact, I find I won't need an abigail at all. I'm going to the country, you see, where your talents would be wasted. Thank you for your help. I've left a letter of recommendation for you."

For a moment, she wasn't certain Schroeder would leave. In the end, of course, the abigail dropped a curtsy and departed, leaving Grace feeling even sadder than before. She tried to turn away again. Again she was interrupted, this time by Benny, the second footman.

"Excuse me, ma'am," the fresh-faced Cornish veteran

said, his posture rigid. "We've taken a vote downstairs and decided that I'm to go with you."

Grace wasn't sure how to react. The thought was so sweet, even though she could probably take Benny in a fair fight.

"You aren't even going to have your abigail," he insisted, hands clasped behind his back, his face red. "You should have someone to do for you."

"Thank you, Benny," she managed, her throat thick with emotion. "I appreciate it."

There was only one more thing she needed to do. Drawing a calming breath, she strode over to Diccan's office and opened the door. For a second she faltered badly. She could smell him in this room; citrus and smoke and the faint tang of something purely Diccan. She saw the evidence of his life; racing journals, a small pile of dog-eared books, and a framed map of the Ottoman empire he'd hung on the wall. Paintings she didn't recognize and silhouettes of people she didn't know.

Another reminder, if she needed it, of how little she really knew him. Was Robert here? What about the sisters she'd never met? How had she fallen in love with a man who had shared so little?

But she was here for paper and pen. Striding to his elegant walnut desk, she opened the top drawer. She was reaching inside, when something glinted at the back of the drawer. She picked it up.

A dagger, exquisitely wrought in gold over steel, obviously the work of master artisans. Mohammedan artisans. Grace would recognize the style anywhere. But that wasn't what caught her attention. It was the fact that the perfectly balanced handle was encrusted with gems: rubies, emeralds, sapphires, peridots, pearls. Surprising for a man who professed a loathing for all things ornate. Too-convenient evidence for those who claimed he was a mercenary, especially since he'd spent those years in Constantinople. The jewels alone could have kept Longbridge running for five years.

But then, Grace knew better than most how lavish gifts tended to be in the East. For just a second, she saw herself at fifteen, her hand out as a necklace was poured into her palm, a glittering waterfall of sapphires, hot green enamel and 24-karat gold, all crafted in intricate designs: peacocks and lotus flowers and spirals, a swirling symphony of color and whimsy and wealth. It had been the jewelry of a mughal's bride.

She had tried to give it back. She knew it was too much. But her friend Radhika's father had wanted to say thank you for shooting the tiger that threatened his son. Grace had tried to tell him that she hadn't seen his son. She'd only seen the tiger, all hot yellow eyes and wide, snarling mouth, heading straight for her. Her shot had been instinctive and lucky. Her reward had been six necklaces from Jaipur's premier family of meenakari jewelers. One measly dagger paled in comparison.

She weighed the dagger in her hand. A weapon of deadly beauty. Not something she could take, though. She put it back and wrote her notes to Lady Kate and Olivia Wyndham. And then on the way out, she impulsively picked up one of Diccan's riding crops that lay on the leather wingback by the fireplace. Running it through her fingers, she thought of him sitting in her bedroom chair, slowly tapping it against his leg. She didn't even nod. She simply turned, the crop and letters still in her hand, and exited the room, closing the door behind her. It was time to go home.

• • •

For the second time in a week, Diccan found himself staring stupidly at someone, certain he'd heard wrong. "What do you mean Mrs. Hilliard isn't here? I have brought guests."

Guests whom he'd rather have left somewhere else, preferably in a ditch. The Thorntons, eyeing the house as if totting up the cost of the furnishings; Geoffrey Smythe, leaning against the front wall as if he hadn't the energy to stand alone; and, waiting in the carriage, Minette, who had insisted she wait outside while he informed his wife of his progress from Brighton to Newbury for the races.

He had spent the last week with Minette, trying to figure out just where she might have hidden a verse. Trying like hell to figure out exactly what the verse was. He'd come up with nothing but an endless headache, a new loathing for French perfume, and a surfeit of Thorntons.

The only success he did have was to learn that the Lions' ultimate goal was to set Princess Charlotte on her grandfather's throne, fully expecting her to yield to their wishes when they did. Considering the fact that the princess was only nineteen and had been kept in virtual seclusion much of her life, Diccan couldn't discount the possibility of success. According to Smythe, they had already succeeded in scotching the engagement Prinny had arranged for her to wed Prince William of Orange, and now they had another candidate in the wings whom they felt to be more sympathetic.

All good information. Nothing, though, that told him anything about that bloody verse. Or just how the Lions planned to put Princess Charlotte on the throne, besides murdering Wellington.

For now, though, he had to deal with a disaster of his own. "Where is Mrs. Hilliard?" he asked.

Roberts looked down his prodigious nose at Diccan's party, as if he hadn't been raised from fifth gunner to butler in the course of a day. "Madame did not share her destination with me, sir," he said.

He wanted her here, where she was safe. But if she refused, at least Babs was with her, Diccan thought.

"Who went with her besides her abigail?" he asked.

Diccan swore the damn butler gloated. "Schroeder was let go the day you left for Brighton."

Diccan felt the ground drop away. "Who went with Mrs. Hilliard?"

"John Coachman and Benny, the second footman."

Diccan wanted to throttle someone. The only comfort he'd had in the last week had been the belief that at least Grace was safe. She was surrounded by people he and Babs had vetted. But she'd run off from them, not knowing that she was in danger. He had to move. He had to get her back here. He had to pretend it wasn't for her safety, or Smythe would become suspicious.

Giving a long-suffering sigh, he turned to his companions. "Why don't you enjoy a bit of sherry in the salon. I'm sure I won't be long."

Lady Thornton giggled, patting his cheek on her way by. "It seems your wife needs a bit of discipline, Diccan. It's good you enjoy dispensing it."

Diccan kept himself from flinching by will alone. He was so tired of his borrowed persona. So ready to take Grace and disappear where no one else could find them. But it would be fatal to repeat that amazing, miraculous night he'd spent with her in his arms. If he found himself in Grace's bed again, he damn well didn't think he'd leave.

"Longbridge," the first footman suddenly spoke up from where he stood in the shadows by the closed study door. "She said she was going home."

Diccan recognized the man as one of the people Babs had secured for him. He stepped closer. "What happened to Schroeder?"

The man shrugged, his handsome face perfectly passive. "Mrs. Hilliard said she wouldn't need an abigail no more."

Diccan just nodded, rubbing at his eye again. He had to get a message to Babs, who was undoubtedly making free with his bed and brandy. He damn well had to find Grace. She couldn't simply go off as if life were normal. Surely Braxton had delivered the warning. Surely he was keeping an eye on her at least. It had been an entire bloody week.

"Why didn't you go with Mrs. Hilliard?" he asked the footman. "It's what I hired you for."

The man shrugged. "Took the new second footman. Another ex-soldier. We figured he'd watch her." Leaning to the side, the man scanned the area. "Another thing, sir," he said, reaching in his pocket. "Note came for you."

The note changed hands. Diccan read it and cursed.

Checked names from other night. Carver clean so far. Gen. Dawes has questionable contacts, including Bentley. Be careful. Drake

And just what the hell was he supposed to do with that? He sure as hell couldn't tell Grace. It would devastate her. But if he kept it from her, she could be in even greater danger.

"Doesn't do to have a wife who's a loose cannon," he suddenly heard.

He turned to see Smythe leaning against the doorway into the salon, a glass of whiskey in his hand. A blunt-faced man about Diccan's age with smallish brown eyes and thin, mousy hair, Smythe proferred a lazy smile. Diccan felt the subtle threat of that smile to his toes. If he couldn't control his own wife, how could they trust him to keep their secrets?

"Happened to one of my neighbors," Smythe continued, sipping at his drink. "Couldn't deal with her odd starts. Had to put her away for her own good. Baroness Sanbourne. You've heard of her?"

He had. A gracious, quiet woman who had been devoted to her husband. Diccan had attended a funeral for her. Could Smythe be saying there was more to it?

"Grace isn't unpredictable," Diccan drawled. "Just tedious. I know how to handle her."

Nodding, Smythe straightened. "We'll go along for moral support. Should be excellent sport."

It wouldn't be sport at all. It would be pure disaster. She'd left him. There could be no other reason for summarily letting Babs go and fleeing to Longbridge. If it had been any other time, he might have given her the space. God knew she deserved it. But she needed to be protected. And, selfishly, he couldn't focus on his task if he constantly worried for her. Besides, Smythe was watching to see how he reacted to Grace's move. He was walking a tightrope.

And that was how Diccan wound up with witnesses when he next greeted his wife. He wanted to forewarn her. To explain, apologize. To beg, if necessary. But when he rolled through the gates of Longbridge ten hours later, he was accompanied by his so-called friends, including Minette, who kept acting as if she couldn't imagine how she'd come to be in this position.

"She is a cripple, yes," the pretty blonde said, nibbling at her lip like a callow girl, "but I do not wish to hurt her, me."

"Don't fret about it, my dear," Letitia Thornton said with a pat to the knee and a satisfied smile. "She knows who you are. And this saves time, since we're already on the way to Newbury."

"We don't have to take the chit with us, do we?" Thornton asked, inhaling a pinch of snuff that ended up all over his puce waistcoat. "I cannot enjoy sport with a fish-faced woman in my business."

"We'll see when we get there," Diccan said.

Longbridge itself was a surprise. When Grace had told him she'd been left the estate by an aunt, he'd envisioned the kind of place his Aunt Armitrude inhabited: dark, pinched, as precise as a Dürer etching. Longbridge might have been an abbey at one time, but a series of additions had muddied its provenance. Not the look, however. Made of buttery stone, it had been expanded with whimsy.

The main block rose three stories with long mullioned windows, a colonnaded balustrade, and flanking wings constructed with gothic arched dormers and a forest of chimneys. The gardens were a bit overrun, but in the gravel forecourt, a Neptune fountain sent spray into the air.

"Oh, well done, Hilliard," Smythe said, following Diccan down from the carriage. "It's far more grand than your place. And look at those pastures."

How could he miss them? Fences enclosed emerald green grass that swept across the gently rolling Berkshire landscape right down to the River Kennet. It would be the perfect place to breed and raise horses. Was that what Grace wanted? She had never really said.

Another thing to tuck away for later, he thought, as he strolled up the steps to the pedimented doorway. His heart had begun to thud, and his stomach ached with dread. He didn't want to be here, especially now that he saw how special it was. He didn't want to sully Grace's home with the people who called him friend. All he could hope was that in the fullness of time, Grace would forgive him.

The door opened before he even reached it, to reveal the bandy-legged Harper glowering at him as if he were the vanguard of an attacking French brigade.

"I wish to see my wife," Diccan said.

Harper took a scathing look at Diccan and blocked the doorway with his considerable shoulders. "And why should I let you do that, now?"

Diccan came within a hairsbreadth of picking the little man up and tossing him against the wall. "Because I'll make sure you and your wife never see my wife again if you don't," he growled low enough that only the two of them heard.

Harper's glare hardened, but he stepped aside. Diccan strode into an Elizabethan hall with linenfold walls and a checkerboard marble floor that glowed with light from the windows. "Where is she?"

Harper nodded toward the back. "Great gallery. If you hurt her..."

Diccan lifted his quizzing glass and stared him to silence before exiting toward an arching doorway, through which he could hear women's voices. He didn't have to look to see that his friends followed. He could feel them like a miasma at his back as he walked past a polished oak staircase and walls of gleaming weapons. He could distinguish the women's voices now: Grace and an Irishwoman; Mrs. Harper, he assumed. And someone else, another woman with an exotic, lilting accent.

Walking down a short hallway, he stepped into the soaring, bright gallery that spread across the back of the house. His boots echoed hollowly off the creaking wood floor. Above him stretched a brightly frescoed barrel-vaulted ceiling. Windows lined the white-paneled south aspect, portraits and chairs, the north. A charming, inviting room that, oddly, seemed to fit his surprising wife to a tee.

She was halfway down the room with two other women.

"Greetings, madam," he called, pausing at the doorway.

At the sound of his voice, Grace jerked up from the packing crate she had been inspecting. Dressed once again in her ubiquitous gray clothes and an oversized apron, she had been laughing. The light in her eyes died the minute she realized who had come.

"Diccan," she said, stepping before the crate as if protecting it.

A woman almost as broad as Grace was tall took up a stance next to her, arms crossed.

"So this is y'r man," Mrs. Harper all but accused.

"Not mine," Grace said quietly.

The two words hurt more than he'd thought they could. Just beyond Grace stood another woman, slight and dark and exquisitely beautiful, clad in a floating turquoise silk of the salwar kameez style worn by Indian women. She couldn't seem to meet Diccan's gaze, but kept her attention on the crate she had been inspecting.

In fact, the hall was full of crates. It looked like the packing room of an import company.

"I didn't expect to see you here, Diccan," Grace said.

"No?" he asked. "What did you expect?"

She shrugged, the light glinting oddly off her hair. "I expected you would enjoy your life, as always. I thought it would be a good time for me to retreat to my home here and settle some things."

"Run away, you mean?"

Another woman would have flinched. "I might have chosen the word *escape*, but I imagine we understand each other. I simply needed to reacquaint myself with something that was all mine."

He didn't have to hear his companions enter. He saw it in the minute changes in his wife's expression. If possible, she grew in size and dignity. And he was about to diminish himself further in her eyes. He was about to cement his reputation with people he loathed.

"Yours?" he asked quietly, not acknowledging the fact that they were no longer alone. Lifting his quizzing glass, he made it a point to consider the room. "Exactly what is yours, madame?"

Grace never looked away. "Longbridge," she said quietly. "My aunt left it to me."

He nodded, struggling to maintain his composure. He was about to commit an unspeakable atrocity against this grave woman. And there was nothing he could do to stop it.

He twirled his quizzing glass. "And you married me. I see it hasn't occurred to you, yet, my dear. But then I imagine slogging through the mud of Spain isn't conducive for learning marital law." He sighed, as if bored. "What was yours is now mine, Grace. Your money, your horse, your servants, your house. You have nothing, Grace. *I* have it."

He saw the blow strike home. He could almost smell it

on her. She had truly thought she could have a refuge from the inhospitable world of the *ton* in this bright, comfortable place. She had thought he would understand.

"You can surely afford me this much, Diccan," she said, her voice suddenly thin.

Diccan thought he would never forgive himself for that. He tilted his head, tapping his glass against his chin as if considering. "I can afford disobedience and humiliation? I think not. How would it look if, after all I've sacrificed for her, my wife simply walked off? Why, it could ruin my reputation as the most desirable man in Europe."

Behind him, he heard a smothered titter and knew that when this was over he would personally destroy Letitia Thornton.

"I won't punish you this time, Grace," he said. "Your friends may stay. The house can't be left empty, after all. But you will return home. When I get back I will make up for my unforgivable lapse and examine the details of your dowry with your solicitor. And that includes whatever it is you've been hiding from me in those crates."

She backed up, as if guarding a baby from a wolf. "No."

Diccan lifted an eyebrow. "No?"

"Are you sure she hasn't been stealing from you?" Smythe asked in languid tones. "Maybe she thought to meet her lover here and spirit your valuables to the Continent before you knew it."

He would destroy Smythe right after Lydia Thornton. "Grace?" he asked.

She straightened, a soldier facing a firing squad. The two other women came to her side and took up similar stances. He had eyes only for Grace. Was he ridiculous to hope she saw through his words? That she would just believe he didn't mean any of this, even though there was no proof?

"You may take the house," she said quietly. "You may even have Epona, although she'll never let you on her back. But I've spent my life gathering what's here. It's mine, and I'll burn it before I give it to you."

"Oh, for God's sake, Grace," he snapped, losing patience. "What can you possibly have that's worth such melodramatics?"

"Silver," Thornton said, his voice thick with delight. "Gold. The Hilliard family jewels. Smythe's right. Better take a look."

Diccan didn't answer. He stalked up, suddenly as curious as his friends to see what his wife thought worth defending as if it were an infant. Pushing her aside, he reached into the crate, wanting this at an end. Wanting desperately to be away from her stricken face. Grace tried to shove him back. She actually cried out. He grabbed the first thing he felt and pulled it out.

A pillow.

An emerald green silk pillow with gold tassels and an ornate gold needlwork peacock. Diccan stared at it as if would explain itself. He threw it down and reached into the crate again, only to come out with more of the same: pillows in jewel tones, a sinfully soft gold paisley Kashmiri throw, seemingly endless lengths of silks in hot colors: orange, pink, chartreuse, yellow. He walked to the next crate, and the next, only to find them precisely packed with more pillows, more fabric, glints of brass and beads and bangles. He even saw a girdle worn for belly dancing.

"What the hell?"

He recognized it all, of course. The booty of an oriental

merchantman. The interior of a vizier's tent. The color and texture and sounds of exotic lands most people could never even hope to see.

He stepped to the next crate to find beadwork. Basketwork. Fringed doeskin so soft and white it seemed like something out of fairytale. Furs and feathers and fabrics from America. Lifting out a red woven blanket, he stepped back, his breath caught somewhere in his chest. He looked to his wife and saw the jagged edge of grief in her eyes, and he knew. He had just violated her in the most terrible way. He held in his hands the secret heart of Grace Fairchild.

Grace, who had spent her life in grays to support her father, who had squeezed herself into pastels and propriety to please him, kept her true soul hidden away in closed packing crates in the middle of Berkshire.

Color. Texture. Richness. The jewels of the earth and the arts of humankind, handmade in lands far from England. Boxes and boxes of them, lovingly gathered, packed away over the years until she could recover them. And he had not only exposed that frail beating heart to the vultures, he had tossed it thoughtlessly on the floor.

"Good Lord, Hilliard," he heard Thornton sneer. "It's worse than burglary. I think your little wife is going to set up shop."

Diccan saw the words impact Grace like a fatal blow. Dropping the blanket, he slowly turned, quizzing glass once again up. "I believe I told you once before, Thornton. There are certain things I simply cannot allow." His eyes narrowed as Thornton stiffened. "Surely you understand."

The fat peer flushed. "Quite. Quite. Just fagged, don't you know. Lot of driving. Parched."

"Excellent thought," Diccan retorted, arms out to

shepherd all the guests back out of the gallery. "Sadly, Grace isn't a tippler. But I saw a snug little inn back in the village that will do."

He had to get them out of here before he gave himself away by losing his temper. He had to have the time and space to make sure Grace went back to London.

"Discretion and valour, my dears," he said, chivvying them back outside. "You can enjoy a late lunch while I finish this with my wife."

"It looks to me like you're in full retreat, Diccan," Letitia simpered.

Diccan quirked an eyebrow. "I simply reserve the right to deal with my wife in private," he said as he guided her outside. "You understand, Letitia. After all, how would you feel if Percy here chastised you in public for that latest little gambling lapse?"

Thornton went puce. "Gambling? Letitia, what have I told you?"

Letitia glared daggers at Diccan, but she said not another word. That was left to Minette, when she saw them outside. "She doesn't come with us, the cripple? Oh, that is good. It hurts me such the most to look at her."

He didn't even bother to answer.

"You do need to settle this," Smythe said gently so the others couldn't hear. "You need all your concentration soon for the honor I'm about to bestow."

Diccan went very still. Every one of his instincts told him that he was about to receive the payoff for all those weeks of hell. "Honor?" he asked, striving to sound intrigued.

Smythe smiled. "I could do no less for a friend. Especially one who hates Wellington."

"And one who can be trusted to control his own family?" Diccan asked.

Smythe chuckled and Diccan joined him as they both climbed into the coach. Diccan knew without doubt that the entire mission balanced on Smythe's invitation. And yet, he couldn't focus on it as he should. His mind was on his wife as he'd last seen her, posture regal, eyes desolate. How could he ever make it up to her? How could he expect her to allow him to?

He had an inkling of how successful he was going to be at that when he returned to Longbridge an hour later on a job horse. He was still a hundred yards from the house when Grace made her opinion known in no uncertain terms. He heard a sharp crack, and his hat flew from his head.

His horse shied. He hauled it to a stop, nervously scanning the horizon for enemies. He shouldn't have wasted the effort. His wife, decked out in her Guards jacket, was standing on the roof reloading a Baker's rifle. Standing shoulder to shoulder with her, all armed, were the Harpers, the frail Indian woman he'd seen, and a dark man in purple turban and magnificent beard who dwarfed them all.

"Grace," Diccan called, sitting very still. "Stop being petulant."

She shouldered the gun. "I'm not being petulant, Diccan. And you're not getting my house."

Chapter 17

If Grace hadn't been armed, Diccan might have laughed out loud in pure frustration. Of all the outcomes of this trip, this was the last one he could have envisioned. But then, he was dealing with Grace, and when had he ever expected her to follow the rules?

All the time, he admitted to himself. It had been his greatest mistake. Nudging his horse closer, he kept his eyes on the various weapons that were being brandished on the roof. "If you're all up there," he challenged, "who's keeping me from the front door?"

Harper let loose a shrill whistle. Immediately the front door swung wide to reveal a pack of men in a variety of tattered uniforms, brandishing everything from Brown Bess muskets to pitchforks.

"They're helping me with the gardens," Grace said.

Of course they were. The idea of law wouldn't hold sway with men who owed Grace their living. She'd probably had them all eating out of her hand within five minutes of meeting her. And Diccan couldn't explain why she would be safer in London, because she probably wouldn't be. But if she was away, he'd worry constantly. If she were home, with his people, at least he had marginal control.

"Grace, please," he called, bareheaded, so she could presumably see his sincerity. "We can't talk like this for all the county to hear."

She tamped a bullet home and pulled the ramrod up out of the gun, her actions smooth and quick. "I don't remember expressing a desire to talk," she said evenly.

"I can have the constable here in twenty minutes to force you out."

It was her turn to smile, and he saw that warrior in her again, which aroused him more than anything had in a week. Lord, it even seemed as if her hair was redder. "Would you like another demonstration of how proficient I am with a rifle?" she asked.

"I suppose it was another thing your father's men made you practice."

She smiled. "95th Rifles. They trained me to pip an ace at four hundred yards. If you don't return to your friends, I'll be happy to show you."

"They're not my friends."

"What?"

He pressed his knuckles to his head, as if it would ease the ache behind his eyes. How could he make her do what he needed, when he was on her side? When he thought she looked bloody magnificent up in the sunlight in her old red Guards jacket? God, he could still see her deep in the night, riding him like a hunter heading for a fence, her head thrown back, her eyes wide, laughing. He'd seen her dimples again, those shy twins that only peeped out when she let down her guard.

She'd let down her guard. And he'd punished her for it.

"Grace, please. You know that everything isn't always as it seems. Can I at least explain?"

"Will you tell the truth?"

He almost winced. "Of course."

She nodded absently, tucking her gun under her arm like a man on the march. "Well, that will be a novelty. I don't think I've been told the truth since the bishop pronounced us man and wife." She paused a moment, seemingly struck. "You don't think he lied, too, do you?"

"No, Grace." It was Diccan's turn to smile. "No matter how it grieves you, Cousin Charles is far too cognizant of his stature as Archbishop of Canterbury to go about performing illegal marriages. You are, indeed, my wife."

She nodded slowly. "And I stand on the roof of your house. On your land. Eating your food. I did get the message, Diccan. Even so, if you try and force me out of this house, I'll put a bullet in you."

Diccan looked up, ready to argue, when he caught the hollow look of loss in Grace's eyes. It struck him, a physical blow to the gut. He wanted so badly to tell her he understood. That he never would have allowed that carrion in the house if he'd known about her treasures. But he couldn't say a word. Not out in the open.

"Can we call a truce until I can speak to you?" he asked. "I promise not to notify the constable if you promise not to let one of these lads skewer me with a pitchfork."

For a long moment, he wasn't sure she'd answer. She just stood up there, the sun glinting brightly off her hair, her eyes narrowed in concentration, her friends silently watching.

Finally she sighed and set down her gun. "Don't move."

With a battalion of old soldiers holding him in their sights? Not likely, he thought.

Within minutes, the group in the doorway parted to let Grace through. Diccan swung from his horse and met her at the bottom of the stairs.

"All right," she said, her calm belied by the high color on her face. "I'm listening."

She was suddenly so close he could smell the exotic floral scent of her soap. She'd lost weight, and she looked paler. At the same time, she had a curious glow to her, a life he hadn't seen before, as if London had been sapping it away like a pernicious leech. He wanted to hold her and tell her that he liked this Grace. That he would never hurt her. He wanted to make love to her again. Not sex. He'd had sex with Minette. But he doubted Grace would stand still while he explained the difference.

There was so much he needed to say that he couldn't think of anything. He cast a quick look to the roof. "Who are your friends?"

She blinked. Then she, too, cast a quick look up. "Harper you know. And Breege, his wife. Radhika and Bhanwar Singh. Bhanwar is my chef."

"Nonsense. I recognize the turban and beard. Bhanwar is a Sikh warrior."

"That, too."

"He must be devoted to you to have left India behind."

She shrugged. "It was better than being killed for taking the local mughal's concubine."

Had she spent her whole life taking care of people, he wondered? Had she ever wanted anything for herself but the security to open those boxes inside her house? Suddenly he wanted to know. He wanted to know everything he hadn't thought to ask before: what her dreams were, her desires, her solace. What excited her and what eased her soul. He was ashamed to admit that even after these last weeks, he really didn't know any of it.

God, he wished he could just take her hand and walk in that house, and the hell with the Rakes and the Grenadiers and the blasted government. Let someone else risk their lives to protect England. Leave him alone to become acquainted with this complex, compelling woman.

It made him feel no better to know that he couldn't. More was at stake than his peace of mind, or even his wife's. So he had to force her back into this bad fit of a marriage and slog on until the time he could explain it all. Until, he hoped, she forgave him.

Bending his head back, he gave the Sikh on her balustrade a considered look. "When were you going to tell me about this little set-up?" he asked. "Or did you plan to keep all your secrets?"

She never took her eyes from him. "I don't know. Did you plan to keep yours?"

He gave her an unflinching look. "Come back to London and I'll tell you mine. Every one."

She was already shaking her head. "I don't think so. I don't think I'll take well to being shuffled off into a corner so I won't bother anyone."

He opened his mouth to argue and realized Drake had asked him to do just that. "Grace," he said, the pain squeezing his chest. "Your secrets affect your friends. Mine affect Britain."

Diccan saw the remaining warmth leach from her eyes. "I see. You're fucking the Frenchwoman for the good of Mother England. Or was it me you fucked for the flag?"

Again she'd sneaked in under his guard. This time she

almost leveled him. "I won't discuss that, Grace," he said, wishing to God he could.

"Not to my satisfaction, certainly. Go back, Diccan. I won't bother you. I won't even speak to my uncle again. You're safe."

"It's not enough."

She actually looked tired. "I'm afraid it has to be. I can no longer survive like this. And tell the truth. You don't need me."

He said it before he even thought. Before he considered how dangerous the words were. "But what if I want you?"

He hadn't known how bleak laughter could sound. "You are kind, Diccan. But we both know better. Please leave me a bit of dignity."

"Don't argue with me, Grace."

"I'm not arguing, Diccan. I'm simply not going."

He found himself rubbing the damned headache. Then, inspiration struck. "If you won't do it for me, do it for Kate."

She abruptly stilled. "Kate? What does she have to do with anything?"

"Her family is having her followed again. They've caught wind of a rumor that she's being painted as Aphrodite coming out of the sea."

He saw Grace deflate a bit. "Nude, I assume." She shook her head, sighing. "Dear Kate, she never does anything by halfs, does she?"

"They'll yank her back to Moorhaven Castle faster than you can shoot. And if they get her there, they won't let her out again. They won't hesitate to lock her up rather than risk possible scandal."

Grace peered at him. "Can they really just kidnap a duchess?"

"Yes. And if you think she can appeal to her late husband's family, Bea's the only one of them who'd throw her a rope if she were drowning. The only reason they haven't been able to get to her yet is because she stays barely on the right side of propriety. One nude painting would put an end to it."

For a long moment, all Diccan could hear was birdsong and distant cowbells, the muffled shuffling of feet on the roof. Smythe was waiting for him back at the inn, possibly to reveal enough to stop the attempt on Wellington's life, and all Diccan could seem to focus on was Grace.

"You're telling me the truth?" she finally asked. "On your honor?"

Well, at least he could say this with a clear conscience. "On my honor. I ran into the Duke and Duchess of Livingston at the Pavilion in Brighton."

Grace winced. "Vile woman."

"Please, Grace. Kate needs you. Get her to burn the damn thing or have some clothes painted on it. You're one of the few people she'll listen to."

"We're supposed to go to Olivia's wedding," she said.

"I'll try and meet you there."

She spent a moment looking out over the trees, as if seeking support. Finally, though, she shrugged and sighed. "Of course. Now, go on back to your friends. I have to make preparations."

"Thank you, Grace."

She looked back at him, and he saw the warrior again. "Oh, don't thank me, Diccan. I don't think you're going to like how this all comes out."

His heart thudded with relief. "I know. Thank you anyway."

He wanted to embrace her, at least drop a kiss of affection on her forehead. But she wouldn't believe it was sincere. So he stepped back and gave her his best court bow.

"My thanks, madame wife. I'll see you soon."

He was just turning back to his horse, when Grace stepped forward. "Diccan, one thing."

He turned back to see honest concern in her eyes. "That Mr. Carver," she said.

"Yes?"

"He frightens me. Be careful."

He stepped forward, immediately afraid. "Did he threaten you?"

She seemed to consider that, which made Diccan even more nervous. "No," she finally said. "I just think that for some reason this is...personal with him. He can't wait to arrest you."

Diccan stood frozen for an unconscionably long time. If he'd had a decade to consider it, he never would have anticipated Grace's warning. But then, he didn't know too many people with such an unwavering sense of honor. Diccan swore Grace was going to rip the heart of out of him.

"Thank you," he said. "I'll be careful."

Then, wishing he had any other choice, he swung up onto his horse and cantered off.

Grace stood in the drive so long that Harper called down to her, "You all right, then, girl?"

Startled, she looked up to see them all still ranged on the balustrade, the garden staff and Benny still crowding the front door. "Oh, yes, Harps. Thank you for your help. I think we're finished now."

"You would wish me to follow the sahib and chastise him?" Bhanwar asked from the roof, his great black eyebrows pursed into one, his sword cradled threateningly in his arms.

Grace found she could still smile. "Thank you, no, Bhanwar. I would far prefer a lovely biryani for dinner. Then I must pack for London."

He gave her a magnificent bow and held his hand out for his tiny Radhika. Grace watched them follow the Harpers from the roof and ached like a lost child for what she would never have. For every half-formed dream that had died in the driveway this afternoon, every hope that looked oddly like those two mismatched couples on her roof.

Before she knew it, she was limping off over the lawn. No one needed to be around her right now.

"Grace?" she heard Breege call.

"Leave her go," Harper answered. "She needs to walk this one off."

Walk it off. Yes, she imagined she did. It was what they'd done on the Peninsula when the carnage and pain had overwhelmed them. Picked up a gun and walked into the dry brown hills. It hadn't mattered then that by the time she returned her knee hurt so much she had to soak it all night. It didn't now. This had been one blow too many. She had to give motion to the pain.

These fields were a world away from those spare, sere hills she'd walked in Spain. This land was gentle and wooded and oh, so deliciously green. Verdant green. Life-giving green. She could smell the green, felt as if she could roll in it and have the color come off on her.

When she'd walked the empty hills of Spain, she had kept a place just like this in her mind, her reward for services rendered to country and family. A home that would be hers alone, where she could be what she truly was without being pitied or chastised or scorned. She'd known within five minutes of stepping out of the coach to see this place that this was that home. *Her home.*

Only it wasn't.

Epona saw her limp by and cantered along the fence, throwing her head and whinnying to get Grace's attention. Usually Grace laughed at the antics. Usually she had a treat for her beloved friend. But her friend wasn't hers anymore either. Nothing was. She could no longer pretend that any part of her life was really hers. Not her home or her life or her dreams. Not even her treasures, lovingly gathered piece by piece over long years in exile, valuable to no one but her, but inextricably interwoven with the dreams that had sustained her.

Diccan had taken it all away from her. He knew she'd have to go back to London, if only for Kate. He knew she would nail her boxes shut and put them away again, because they simply didn't belong in his world. Only this time Grace had the feeling she would never be able to open them again.

She found herself leaning over the parapet of the stone bridge that gave the property its name. She loved the mellow old structure. She loved the way the Kennet slid beneath with barely a murmur. She loved the time she spent sitting beneath the willows that edged the bank, wrapped in quiet green and insect song as she fished the day away. What she had cherished most had been the feeling that finally, after a life wandering to far and alien places, she had finally come home.

She felt the the crack in her control splinter wider, all

jagged edges and sorrow. She felt lost and angry and afraid, and she knew it would only get worse. She had done everything she should have. She'd been a good daughter, a good woman, a good friend. She had spent her life holding off her dreams so she could be those things. Was it funny that she had actually expected to be rewarded, if only with a home where she felt wanted?

Diccan had been very nice to say what he had, but she knew better. He didn't want her at all. Even so, he would never let her go. Not now. Especially not if what she suspected was true.

She laid a hand against her flat belly, and the acid vanished from her chest. Would it be so bad? She could surely trade a place of her own for a future she could never in her life have dreamed of. Ever even imagined. If she'd never even imagined a wedding, how could she have foreseen a child?

Emotion filled her again, but this time it was an exquisitely sweet pain. A baby. Could it really be true? Certainly her courses were late, but she had never known them to be regular. But for the last week she'd been sick, vomiting up anything stronger than soup and bread. Breege had begun to look at her askance, and Radhika, who had her own babe, smiled.

Yes she thought. She would give all this up, and gladly, if indeed Diccan had given her a child. Someone who was hers, who would love her and look to her for joy and comfort and peace. A small warm body to enfold. She never passed up a chance to hold Radhika's daughter Ruchi, even now that the girl was seven and smarter than anyone else in the household. She remembered the wonder of having that wee babe nestle under her chin, a tiny hand wrapped around a length of her hair, the minute heart a soothing flutter against her own. She remembered the terrible yearning for that babe to be hers.

She knew better than to hope. But, unforgivably, she did.

And so it was that she nailed the lids back down on her precious crates, packed her Guards jacket yet again, and took her Aunt's creaking old traveling chaise back to London. *A week*, she kept repeating to herself. *Only a week until I can escape again. Until I can travel to Olivia's wedding and at least have my friends to support me as I try and untangle my life.* And by then, maybe she'd know for certain what that life would be.

One thing she did do for herself was bring along Mr. Pitt. If Diccan wanted to know what he now owned because of his marriage, let him find out. Within twelve hours of arriving at Clarges Street, the monkey, a rather cantankerous black-faced langur, had shattered Diccan's favorite globe, bitten the first footman, and pelted Diccan's bed with ripe fruit. Grace just reminded everyone on staff that this was now Diccan's pet and that they would do well to remember it. To a person, they grinned.

Leaving the monkey perched atop the curtains in Diccan's study, she donned bonnet and pelisse and left for Kate's. Grace kept her promise. Over tea she alerted Kate to her family's latest threat about the painting. Predictably, Kate laughed. "Good Heavens, how creative. I suppose I must consider myself honored that they're expending such energy to bring me to heel. Sadly, I cannot oblige."

Grace saw the tears rise in Bea's eyes. "Un...*worthy,*" the old woman spat, and Grace knew she wasn't speaking of painters.

Reaching over, Kate took a distressed Bea's hand in her own. "My darling Bea, you and I both know it will come to nothing but more humiliation to be poured on Edwin's head."

"Counterfeit," Bea protested, her face screwed up in worry, her free hand fluttering.

"If there actually is a painting," Kate said, "it is most certainly counterfeit. Which, sad to say for Edwin, is easily proved."

It was something Grace hadn't even considered.

"He wouldn't."

Kate chuckled, still holding tightly to a clearly distraught Bea. "He would. Well, Glynis would. Edwin doesn't have the cunning for it. He would think it a brilliant idea, though, wretched little snirp."

Grace wished she were finished with bad news and could just enjoy her tea. She couldn't, though. During her ride back to London, she had made a decision. Secrets were too dangerous to keep. She needed help; she needed to share her information about Diccan. She'd already sent a note to Olivia, asking her to keep an ear open to the investigation into the Lions. She should have known better than to keep it from Kate. If nothing else, Kate had a knack for deadly insight.

"There is worse, I'm afraid," Grace said, setting down her cup. "It's about Diccan."

Kate must have seen Grace's distress, because she set aside her own cup and settled back, hand on Bea's arm, her expression calm. Bea kept sipping. Focused on her own tea, Grace told them of the accusations against Diccan. Because she knew how much they both loved him, she had to tell them everything, even what she'd seen at Half Moon Street. Grace related it all as unemotionally as she could, leaving the room in stark silence.

Then, suddenly, Bea came abruptly to life. "Bollocks!" the old woman snapped, setting her cup down so hard the tea sloshed.

Grace looked up to see that her friends did not look accusing or outraged, but sympathetic.

"Why didn't you come to us?" Kate asked, taking hold of Grace's cold hand.

Suddenly Grace was trembling with reaction. "I was told not to speak to you. And then Kit told me that Diccan was under investigation and to keep out of it. I've decided I can't do that."

Giving Grace's hand one last squeeze, Kate retrieved her tea. "So a man from the Home Office says that Diccan is a traitor, and Braxton, who I suspect runs with Drake's Rakes, says that Diccan might be a Lion. Bea's right, of course. It's all bollocks. Oh, there are mysteries to Diccan. But it's absurd to think he'd be a traitor." Reaching for a seed cake, she shook her head. "For the record, his uncle's estate is in the condition it's in because he was a notorious pinchpurse. He left Diccan swimming in lard. But you never thought to ask Diccan, did you?"

"Why?" Grace said, at least this one thing in her life certain. "It wouldn't have changed my opinion of him. The question is, is this all connected with the incident in Canterbury?"

Kate let loose an abrupt laugh. "Grace, only you would call scandal and a forced marriage an 'incident.' But, yes. I imagine it might be. The question is, why? Who benefits from his ruin, and how?"

"Ten paces," Bea suggested, while she was picking seeds from her cake.

Kate nodded absently. "Yes, he undoubtedly has enemies

from those duels, but this is not simple revenge. It is more Byzantine. More...pernicious. There are certainly easier ways of blackening a man's name than arranging to have his wife watch him tup his mistress."

For a moment, Kate's expression lost focus and she picked up another cake. Bea must have seen something. "Impolite girl," she warned with a smack to Kate's hand.

Kate's grin was impish. "My curiosity is my besetting sin. But you can't tell me you didn't think just for a moment how much you'd love a peep through that window yourself, you naughty wench."

Bea's chuckle was telling. Grace, who had not succumbed to blushes for a long while, blushed. She could only hope Kate thought it was because of her own speech. Grace simply could not discuss something that intimate, even with her friends. Especially since she still didn't completely understand what had happened herself.

"I think it's the Lions," she said, desperate to turn the conversation. "I think Diccan is more important than we know. He was in such a hurry to get to London after our marriage. Could it not be that he carried information from Europe that someone wanted to see discredited?"

"Like the information Jack Gracechurch brought back?" Kate asked, brows pursed. "If that is the case, why not simply kill him? It's certainly what they tried to do to Jack."

Grace's stomach clenched; it was a thought she'd tried to avoid. "I'm not certain they still won't try. They certainly haven't ruined him. Diccan is received everywhere, and I refuse to betray him."

Kate nodded absently. "And you say you've already sent a note to Olivia about this."

"I thought that if anyone could find out what's going on,

it would be she. After all, she's worked the hardest to get Jack's memory back. Jack can hardly tell *her* she has no right to the information."

"He can certainly try and *protect* her from it. Heaven knows it is men's favorite pastimes. Keeping women in the dark for their own good."

Bea sighed. "Nannies."

"Indeed," Kate said with a pat to Bea's hand. "Amazing, isn't it? It's as if they think we've suddenly forgotten what it took to uncover the Lions in the first place. Well, we'll just keep trying."

"Any ideas?" Grace asked. "I seem to have struck out."

"Orange blossoms," Bea said distinctly.

Kate grinned. "Grace is already married, dear."

But Bea shook her head. "Sussex."

"You think we should wait until we get to Sussex for the wedding?" Kate sipped her tea, nodding slowly. "You might have a point. Jack Gracechurch is a charter member of Drake's Rakes, which means that Marcus Drake will probably be at the wedding as well. Certainly Diccan will. Maybe if we get all of them together, we can find a way to force them to share information."

Grace didn't want to wait. She felt unsettled and fretful, nagged by the feeling that she was missing something. She acquiesced, though, and over the next few days, she returned to society with Kate and Bea, only to feel more smothered than ever before. Everywhere she went she faced renewed whispers and sly glances, and seemed to always be biting her tongue.

Still not able to voice her suspicion about her own condition, she lived on bread and soup and ignored her maid's raised eyebrows when Grace lost enough weight to require taking in her gowns. The only comfort Grace had was being able to hire Kate's maid Lizzy as her new abigail, also letting the staff know that Lizzy's baby girl was to be accepted as well. Oddly enough, Mr. Pitt took to guarding the baby like a dog, which enchanted everyone.

The one thing Grace refused to do was allow Schroeder back, even after receiving an edict from Diccan by mail. She wrote him back: *You must be on premises to discuss my staff. Enjoy the races.*

The next day she asked Kit Braxton to investigate her watchers, only to have him tell her that they were government agents sent to protect her. She nodded, but the answer didn't reassure her. Something about the story didn't ring true. The watchers seemed too...casual, too surreptitious. And then, on her third day in London, she thought she found her answer. She was riding in the park and pretending she wasn't in London, when she saw her Uncle Dawes.

"Where's that prime filly of yours?" he demanded, side whiskers bristling as he pulled his great gray warhorse to a shuddering halt.

"In the country, where she can run," Grace said, pulling up alongside on a perfectly acceptable black gelding of Kate's named Barney.

She'd known she would have to face her uncle. She just wished she could have waited a while longer.

"Need to go somewhere to talk," the general barked, casting a suspicious glance at the moon-faced George, who was placidly following Grace on a lumbering bay.

"George is the soul of discretion," she said, rather than tell her uncle that Kate's groom had the intelligence of a child.

The general wasted one more glare on George before turning back to her. "Well, girl?"

"I'm sorry, Uncle Dawes," she said, truly sorry she must disappoint him. "I will not betray my husband."

For a moment, she feared for his health. He turned beet red, so agitated that his mount skipped back a bit. "After what you saw?"

She felt even more sad. "How could you take me there?" she asked quietly, the pain still sharp. "How could you make me watch that?"

He blustered a bit, and his face grew redder. "It was for your own good," he barked. "Need to know what he is."

"I know what he is, Uncle Dawes. He is by no means perfect. But neither is he a traitor."

The general leaned over and grabbed her arm, his expression truly distressed. "Don't you realize that you put yourself in danger? He must be stopped, girl."

She lifted her free hand and patted his. "But not by me."

He just kept shaking his head, his gaze unfocused, his forehead creased. Grace felt so sorry that she had to disappoint him. She knew he would never understand. To his mind, she had failed him.

"You don't know what you've done," he said, as if to himself. "You simply don't know."

"Does that man really work for the Home Secretary?" she asked, getting his attention. "Mr. Carver?"

The old man yanked his hands back. "Now you accuse *me* of lying?"

"No, I'm warning you that all might not be as it seems." And looking at his dear, familiar face, so tight with anxiety, she made the decision to tell him about the British Lions. Uncle Dawes would be just the type of man they might fool, and she couldn't bear seeing him hurt. "Are you perfectly certain Mr. Carver is who he says he is?" she asked at the end.

For a moment he frightened her, his eyes going flat. "Are you certain your husband is? Have you ever wondered where he gets his money? His father disowned him ten years ago, you know."

"Yes. I heard. I also know that his uncle wasn't as strapped as everyone thought."

"That's what he wants you to think."

She sighed and reached out to him again, laying her hand on his arm. "Uncle Dawes, I know you care for me. Please, for me, be careful. I think these men are ruthless."

. He offered no answering gesture of affection. Before she could even beg his pardon, he wheeled his horse around and thundered off down the path, leaving her with a heavy heart. She was about to set off again, when she suddenly realized that Mr. Carver had been following her uncle.

"He worries for you," the man said, pulling up alongside on a hack.

Grace had to calm her horse, who didn't like his proximity any more than Grace did. "I'll tell you the same thing I said to him, Mr. Carver," she said, wishing the man would move a bit farther away. "I won't help."

He sat still for a long moment, seeming to assess her. Then, as if making up his mind, he smiled. "You will, you know," he said, making her feel even less easy. He looked smug, as if her surrender were a foregone conclusion. Pulling out a small case, he handed her a card. "Contact me here."

Grace glanced at the card to see his name and an address in Lincoln's Inn Fields. "Why not Whitehall, Mr. Carver?"

"I told you," he said, still, oddly, smiling. "There is a leak. I trust no one."

She nodded. "You're wrong, you know. It isn't Diccan."

He looked off toward the trees, as if his words weren't important. "It is," he said. "Be on your guard, Mrs. Hilliard. You don't know as much as you think."

With a tip of his hat, he too set off, leaving Grace behind with an unsettled mind and an unremarkable calling card in her hand. She perused it again. Something about it unsettled her.

"Miss Grace?" George spoke up behind her. "Who's he?"

Grace looked up to see George's normally placid features screwed up in thought. "A man who works for the government, George."

His attention on Carver's departing back, he shook his head. "Don't think I like him."

Grace looked the same way and slowly nodded. "Neither do I, George. Neither do I." She put the card away, though, not wanting to lose it. Not 'til she figured out what about it bothered her.

She was followed home by another of those interchangeable watchers, which failed to make her feel a bit more safe.

"Make sure the house is locked up tonight," she told Roberts as she headed up to bed that evening. "I don't need any more surprises right now."

She did get a surprise, and it was an intruder. Just not one she ever could have anticipated.

She didn't know how long she'd been asleep when she heard something. It wasn't much, a whisper, as if the air had been disturbed. It was enough. Suddenly she was awake, her heart thundering in her ears. There was someone in the room with her.

Trying to stay as quiet as possible, she reached beneath

her pillow and opened her mouth to scream. The scream died in her throat. Her seeking hand came up empty. Her gun was gone.

Suddenly a hand was over her mouth and a body was on top of hers. Her heart all but exploded in her chest. She bit down hard on the hand. He held on tighter. She bucked. He pressed closer. She thought her lungs would burst with terror. And then, from one heartbeat to the next, she knew that the danger was far worse than she feared. She recognized that body.

She'd already given up the fight when she heard a too-familiar voice in her ear. "Grace," it murmured, sounding amused. "There seems to be a monkey in my bed."

Chapter 18

Where is my gun?" she asked when he lifted his hand away to stroke her shoulder.

She should shove him off of her. She should kick him where he'd never forget it. She arched her throat, baring it. He kissed her just below her ear, sending chills down her neck.

"I didn't want you to mistake me for a rogue."

"I didn't hear you being invited."

He leaned over her again so she could barely see the outline of his face in the shadows. She could feel the heat shimmer off his body, though. It seemed to sap her anger, like a debilitating drug.

"You really mind that I'm here?" he asked, his hands already moving down her arms.

"Yes," she managed, wondering where the outrage had gone in her voice. "I do. Just what are you doing here?"

He leaned his forehead against hers. "There was a small argument that needed settling."

The very scent of him wrapped around her like smoke,

pulling her inexorably toward him. She thought her throat would close with mingled fury and arousal. "What argument?" she managed, lying perfectly still, as if that could protect her.

"The one about whether I want you or not."

He reached for her hand and pressed it against his groin. Grace gasped. He was hard and hot and throbbing. She itched to dive in beneath those buttons and wrap her hand around him. To hold on and never let go. She ached for the taste of him, slick and salty against her tongue.

"What does this prove, Diccan?" she asked, struggling to hold on to her sense, even as she forgot to remove her hand.

She couldn't simply succumb to him again. She would be putting herself back on her own path to ruin. But it was so hard to stay strong when she felt how hard he was. When she realized that what she heard in his voice was urgency, need. Sweet Lord, he was all but trembling, as if he hadn't had a woman in years, even though she knew better.

"I want to be in you, Grace," he growled into her ear, lifting his hand to pull away the covers. "I want to feel your body melt around me. I want to hear you laugh again."

She tried to pull away from him. She really did. But he had her caught hard against him, and he wasn't letting her up. And somehow she forgot what it was she was fighting.

"Just how many women do you need to rut with in a day?" she demanded, knowing her voice sounded unforgivably weak.

"I only *want* to make love with you." He lifted his head again; she could see heat and humor and something else, something she didn't have the courage to hope for. "We could, of course, pass the hours discussing my sartorial brilliance, although I have just destroyed the *trone d'amour* Biddle worked so hard on. We could talk about your new charity for returning soldiers. I love talking to you, Grace. I love to see you laugh. But I am in sore need of seeing you laugh in pure, giddy pleasure. Please..."

She didn't let him finish. Reaching up, she pulled him to her and met him open-mouthed and hungry. He wrapped himself so tightly around her, she could feel his heart pounding against her chest, she could smell the smoke of his sandalwood soap on the night air. She tasted the essence of Diccan; no brandy, no cigars, just sweetness and spice.

She wanted to make a banquet of that taste, of the rough invasion of his tongue, the unbearably soft assault of his lips. She felt her body ignite beneath him and knew that she would take everything he had to give her, and she would give back more. She would tell him she loved him the only way she could, whether he heard or not. Whether he acknowledged it. And then, tomorrow, she would collect the broken pieces of her defenses and try and shore them up all over again.

She tried one last time to pull away. "I need to talk to you," she insisted. "It's urgent."

"In a while," he murmured, dipping his head to her breast. "Promise."

There was no more arguing. Not one more word was said by either of them. She felt him pull her braid loose and spread her hair out like a fan. She held on to him and kissed him back, testing and taunting and tempting him to lose control. She felt the juices collect in her at the mere thought of him driving into her until he spent himself. The thought of him losing control ignited a sweet pain that felt like Heaven itself. She couldn't wait to betray herself.

He shattered her reserve with one kiss. He destroyed every defense with his hands. Grace felt his elegant, clever fingers on her like dreams; skimming, sweeping, nipping, yanking the bedclothes away and dispatching her night rail as if it had been no more than a suggestion.

She shivered as the night air kissed her fevered skin, already dampened by Diccan's tongue. She couldn't see Diccan; she could only feel him, hear him, smell him, the heady scent of male in her arms. It was enough to make her mad. It was enough to make her forget.

She pulled his shirt over his head and sought the sleek planes of his chest and back, rippling now with effort. She satiated herself with the smooth sweep of his shoulders, the delicious hollow at the base of his throat, the rumble in his chest when she licked his nipples. She felt his body strain for her, and thrilled in it. She felt her own body respond, swelling, seething, singing with his as they met in a dance as old as life, and she followed it. She heard the rasp of her own breathing in counterpoint to his, and heard music. She returned to the buttons that held back his shaft and began to set them loose.

Diccan never stopped his exploration of her with hands and mouth and tongue: her shoulders, her arms, her belly, her breasts. Oh, her breasts, aching in anticipation, swelling under his touch. Tightening long before he took them with his mouth.

And when he did, she bucked with the shock of it. She swore he tried to devour them, his tongue flicking against the tender skin, his teeth grazing her aching nipples. She arched to meet him; she yanked at his buttons, desperate to be at him. She heard that curious keening again, and realized it was she, her need overflowing into sound. She heard him chuckle and groan when she finally freed that last button and was able to collect the whole of him in her hands, and she smiled. She nudged him to lift his hips and pulled his pantaloons off. Now she had all of him to explore, muscle and bone and the delicious rasp of hair against her fingers. She could almost taste him on her tongue.

He never gave her a chance. Wrapping his arms around her, he flipped her on her back. He tangled his hands in her hair and rubbed his erection against her belly, marking her. His body was taut and slick, his breath coming in rasps. Grace curled her hands around his bottom, pulling him to her, and felt the thrill of victory when he dropped his head against her throat and groaned.

He never asked. She never begged. He simply shifted and she spread her legs to welcome him home. He kissed her again, long and deep and wicked, and then he drove into her, and she forgot everything else. She forgot needing or belonging or having. She forgot pride and self-respect and a lonely woman's despair. For these moments he was hers, and she let him be. She braced her feet against the mattress and lifted to meet him, taking him in, all of him, to the very hilt of him, welcoming him to the edge of her womb. She panted for air, for patience, for strength, because the fire he ignited had begun to overtake her. Not gently, like music. Their meeting was a primal force, both of them straining, arching, gasping, laughing, their bodies slick with sweat, their eyes open in the darkness, their hunger met and matched.

A storm swept over Grace, crashing through her, pulling her under. Lightning, sharp and deadly and blinding. Thunder and wind and fury. She felt her body succumb to it; tightening, darkening, disintegrating. She threw back her head and wailed with the force of it. She felt Diccan follow, heard him call her name as he pumped heat and life into her, his own body taut and urgent, and she laughed. She laughed until they fell, spent and silent, to sleep curled in each other's arms.

She woke to birdsong and knew she'd lost her chance to speak to him. He was gone again, as silently as he'd sneaked in the night before, evidently forgetting his promise to speak to her. She hadn't asked why he'd come or where he was going. She hadn't told him of her suspicions or warned him of his foes. She hadn't even forbidden him entry into her bedchamber again.

She had exhausted herself on him and come back for more. She had listened to his words of affection and let herself believe him. And now, she had to start to repair her pride all over again.

Damn him. Damn *her* for giving in without a fight. Had her trip to Longbridge been nothing more than pretense? Had her decision meant nothing? She had vowed to walk away from him, to reclaim her pride and person. It had taken one kiss to show her up for the hypocrite she was.

For a long while she lay there, her arm over her eyes, as the light strengthened. How many more times would she wake like this and vow not to do it again? How many more times would she excuse Diccan or worse, herself, for their lapses? When would she begin to rely on his appearance?

She already did.

She spent the day preparing to leave for Olivia's, all the while feeling as fragile as a fine porcelain plate, carelessly balanced on the edge of a table where the only outcome could be a terrible crash. She found she couldn't eat at all, even soup, and hoped the next long months wouldn't be like that. She knew she should see an accoucher, but until something was settled with Diccan, she couldn't help holding this one little secret to herself.

She didn't know what to expect from him. She didn't know how to hope. Would he pity her or scorn her, or would he simply walk out again, more interested in his other life? Did it matter, really? She would have the baby. They could get along just fine in the country, where he could run and ride and fish with his mother, and learn to love the land he would one day own. She never thought it might be a girl. She'd never been around enough girls to be comfortable with them. But she knew little boys, and she could see herself raising a fine boy.

Right now she saw Diccan in the picture. But right now, she wanted to bask in the newness of her situation. She wanted to believe in this future. She *wanted* to hope for something she'd never believed could happen. She wanted to tell Diccan and get it over with so she would know how to go on.

She was so distracted by her worries that she became vague, impatient, weary. The trip was worse. Even though she once again rode in Kate's luxurious, well-sprung coach, for the first time in her life, travel made her ill. She knew her friends suspected something, but they were kind enough to remain silent. Her footman Benny was not so sanguine.

"Cook and Mr. Roberts'll have me head if'n you go poorly," he protested as he and Lizzy helped her into the bushes by the side of the road. "Won't you take some of cook's tonic?"

The thought of drinking anything threatened her still

unsettled stomach. "In a minute," she gasped, crouched over, "I appreciate the concern, but I'm not sure it will help."

Her hand on Grace's other arm, Lizzy chuckled. "Not for another two months or so, I'd say."

Grace shot her a glare. "Not a word to anyone, Lizzy."

"Closed as a clam, missus."

She took the tonic to salve Benny's feelings, and felt no better, although she kept that to herself. She didn't know why she was being so circumspect, especially since anyone with a calendar and a pair of eyes could guess what was happening. But the possibility was still so new to her, the feelings so private, that she simply didn't want to have to share them yet.

So it was that when they reached Oak Grove the next day, Grace stepped down from the carriage as if pale green were her normal skin tone. She smiled and chatted and held herself together with will and fear. She simply refused to mar her reunion with her friend by being ill in her forecourt.

The house itself was lovely, a mellow brick Queen Anne home with tall sashed windows and stone parapet that had been given a place of honor at the end of a straight drive lined in oaks. But for Grace the best feature was waiting on the front steps; Olivia and Jack, hand in hand.

"Finally," Bea said with a wide smile at seeing them.

Grace nodded. "It is good to see them so happy and well, isn't it?"

Olivia and Jack had been through so much, their first marriage shattered by betrayal and lies, their lives all but ruined. They had been through even more since they'd found each other again, and the scars showed. Jack had barely survived Waterloo; Olivia had barely survived the

Surgeon. The slash down the side of her face was still red and angry. But as Grace saw the peace in eyes once so care-worn and sad, it didn't matter.

"You're here!" Olivia cried, running down to meet the carriage, her primrose jaconet dress floating around her legs, tendrils of blond hair wisping about her face. "Oh, I've missed you!"

"She's driven me mad for days," Jack said, looking fit in a hacking jacket and doeskin breeches.

He looked healed, Grace thought, as he bussed her cheek, with weight back on his tall, lean frame and life in his sea-green eyes. He was a lucky man to have been afforded a second chance. And a smart one for taking it. But then, Grace couldn't imagine a man turning away from Olivia.

Hugs were exchanged, greetings given, and appearances commented upon. Grace stood back a bit, content to simply enjoy the unmoving ground, wondering suddenly how she could share her fears and hopes and questions even with her friends. How could she explain how earth-shattering the changes were in her life, when any other woman would expect them by right.

How odd to suddenly be shy with the three women she knew best.

"Grace?" Olivia was frowning. "You're so quiet."

Grace found it wasn't hard to smile after all. "I'm tak-ing it all in. I'm so happy to see you both."

Olivia's big gray eyes filled with tears as she reached up to share a hug. "No more than I am to see you. You can't imagine how much I counted on you all to witness my wedding."

"Well, it's only fair," Kate offered wryly, "since we wit-nessed the preliminaries."

"Midwife," Bea added with a nod.

Even Jack laughed. "A very good description of your role. But I'm certain I don't want to rehash it all in the front drive." Turning his wife to the door, he waved her in. "We have tea in our renovated south drawing room." He frowned. "Or is that the Red Salon? Olivia keeps changing the name."

"It's going to be the drawing room where Jack loses his head, if you aren't careful," Olivia retorted amiably, as she allowed him to wrap his arm around her.

Just as they were climbing the steps, a veritable herd of children came thundering around the corner of the house, shrieking with glee as they chased a barking shaggy behemoth of a dog. Grace picked out six youngsters in the melee, ranging in age from three to maybe ten, closely followed by a pretty young woman with curly blond hair.

"Like to introduce my sister Georgie," Jack drawled as she sped past with a wave of the hand in their direction. "Her brat Lully is the one leading the pack. The urchin on her heels is our son Jamie. I have no idea who the rest of them are. Georgie collects brats like Diccan's mother collects dogs."

Grace felt a clutch of wonder at the sight of those raucous, laughing children. It was as if her hopes had crystallized right in front of her. Happy, healthy children, tumbling around the lawns like pups, their laughter bright as the morning. Her throat grew thick with a surge of unfamiliar joy.

It only took a moment to come back down to earth. They had just about reached the steps when Jack stopped and looked back. "Where *is* Diccan?" he asked. "I can't imagine a carriage ever beating Gadzooks anywhere."

Grace's delicate stomach dropped. "He...will try and be here."

Jack peered down at her. "Diccan miss the social event of the fall? Nonsense. I'm convinced he had three waist-coats made just for the weekend."

Grace knew her smile was weak. "And a quizzing glass made of gold. But he was delayed."

By his mistress. Or the Lions. Or a writ for his arrest for treason.

Or all three.

It didn't take Grace long to settle into her beautifully appointed room. Decorated in spring greens and yellows, it was on the southeast corner, with windows on both sides that looked out over sweeping lawns and thick woods. Grace helped Lizzy unpack and then sent the girl to check on her own baby, who had accompanied them and seemed to be missing Mr. Pitt, who hadn't.

Once her own nausea eased a bit, she needed to find Olivia. She knew that this would be her best chance to get private advice on her condition. After all, Olivia had a child. Surely she had gone through the same thing. Would she share her story with Grace?

Grace, though, felt unaccountably shy. It was a discus-sion she'd never thought to have, news she didn't know how to deliver. She was relieved of at least that by the simple expedient of being bent over the chamber pot when Olivia slipped into her room.

"Grace?" she heard from the other side of the dressing room door. "Is that you I hear?"

Grace was in no position to answer. She must have made

enough noise to locate her, because suddenly Olivia was on her knees next to her with a damp rag in the cramped little room.

"Oh, my stars," Olivia said, "what's going on here?"

A silly question, Grace thought. She was on her hands and knees over a chamber pot. She nodded all the same. "I think...I think..."

She simply couldn't say the words out loud, as if they alone had the power to burst the delicate soap bubble that was her hope. It was something too great and too ephemeral at once, as fragile and wondrous and mysterious as the babe itself.

Amazingly, her friend understood. Reaching over to wipe at Grace's forehead, Olivia began to chuckle. "Oh, I remember this all too well. I thought I would end up seeing my liver in a bucket, I was so sick. But it passed. It always does."

"I hope so," Grace managed, eyes closed as she commanded her stomach to settle. "I feel like one giant cramp. Even my fingers hurt."

Olivia was still smiling. "You have simply been clutching too many chamber pots, my girl. Surely you've tried ginger."

She nodded. "I believe I've consumed every grain in London. I pity the housewife who yearns for spice cake this week."

Chuckling, Olivia handed her the rag and exchanged pots. "Well, then, we'll have to think of something else. Have you seen someone?"

Grace merely shook her head, grateful for Olivia's brisk common sense.

"Well, that won't do," Olivia said. "We'll call my own

physician, a wonderful man. Trained in Edinburgh. Once you see him, I think you'll feel better about things."

"I feel so overwhelmed," Grace admitted, sitting back, the damp rag to her forehead. "What did you feel?"

Olivia plopped herself right down on the floor next to her. "Oh, Heavens. Excited and amazed and terrified and certain that this had never happened to another woman in history."

Grace nodded, hearing her own jumbled emotions put into words. "I can't imagine going through this alone, as you did, Olivia. You are the strongest woman I know."

"Fiddle. You spent your life in the army. You know I'm not the only one who had a less than ideal time of it."

To call Olivia's ordeal "a less than ideal time of it" was the pinnacle of understatement. Olivia had been four months gone when she'd been cast out of her home and forced to wander the back roads looking for work to support herself, although she was a countess. There were times Grace still wondered that Olivia could forgive Jack for being party to it.

"Have you told Diccan yet?" Olivia asked.

"Not yet. I wanted to be sure, and...well, I wanted to speak with you, and we all needed to know what was going on with the Lions."

Abruptly Olivia climbed to her feet and held out a hand. "Well, about that, I know precious little more than you, except that there are men patrolling the estate, and Jack won't let me leave the grounds alone. But we can discuss that later. Right now, we need to speak about you." Helping Grace to her feet, Olivia steered her for the bedroom. "We'll get Dr. Spence over first thing tomorrow. After that, you need to tell Diccan, and we can go from there."

Grace sighed. "That's if Diccan comes. He wasn't certain."

Olivia sat her on a chaise by the window and draped a rug across Grace's knees. "Which is, I'm sure, another subject we'll need to address. I'll also want the whole story on how you ended up married to Diccan Hilliard. I imagine it's a pip."

"Yes." Grace sighed. "I believe it is."

Feeling wobbly as a three-day-old colt, she submitted to Olivia's cosseting, for once too miserable to object. She completely forgot her objections when Olivia arranged for a pot of tea and biscuits and settled into a nearby chair for a comfortable coze. They talked for almost an hour about what was really important: how lucky Grace was, no matter how perilous her stomach was.

Grace had hoped that her talk with Olivia would help settle her feelings. Instead it made them worse, sharpening her hope and strengthening her fear. It was all becoming too much, a balloon of possibility that swelled to bursting inside her. She didn't know how to contain this much emotion.

Over the years, she had nurtured her own small dreams like a garden; tilling, planting, weeding, so that each dream had a bit of room to grow. But this dream had been dropped full-blown into their midst, like a rock among fledgling plants, crushing many, disrupting their orderly arrangement. She didn't know if she could adapt the rest of her garden to it. Too many of her little dreams were solitary ones. But maybe, she thought, she could save a few of those old, small dreams to support her in this unknown venture.

Venture.

A baby.

Just the word took her breath away.

By the next morning, she thought she would explode if she didn't work off some of her anxiety. She felt even sicker than the day before, but she thought maybe it was the dreadful anticipation of seeing both the doctor and Diccan. She felt achy and ill and so tired she wanted to lie back down for a week, her fingers cramping again. She swore her skin had taken on a slightly green hue.

Surely not. She just felt green. She loathed feeling like that. So, just as she always had, she countered it with activity. She wished she'd thought to have Epona brought to Sussex. A good ride might put her in a better frame of mind to face the next few days. And even if she was... well, she'd never known a healthy woman to suffer from an easy canter. So she limped down to the stable, collected George, and headed off on trails the stable lads pointed out. And ran smack into Mr. Carver.

She had been enjoying her ride. The morning air was unseasonably warm, and thick, boiling clouds had begun to collect above the hills. There was weather coming, and it sent a bracing wind sweeping before it that whirled among the first falling leaves and cooled her overwarm cheeks. Harps would have taken one look at the sky and warned of Wellington weather, those drenching storms that seemed to accompany Wellington's actions. The turbulent weather matched Grace's mood.

"Rain'll hold off," George had said when he'd given her a leg up. "This'll be an afternoon rain."

She liked George. He was calm and quiet and watchful, and he had a smile like a child's. Even better, he never insisted on knowing what she was thinking. She wasn't thinking anything. That was the point of a good ride.

Grace had just turned back at the River Arun, which

formed the eastern border of the estate, when her horse shied. She quickly compensated, figuring the skittish mare had been spooked by flying leaves. But she saw what the horse had sensed. Another horse was tucked in a stand of alder trees.

George immediately urged his horse up next to her. The rider sat unmoving in the shadows.

"Mr. Carver?" she asked, slowing. "What are you doing here?"

He didn't seem at all perturbed that she'd seen him. "Watching."

She gave George a quick look, to see him frowning. She knew how he felt. There was something very wrong about seeing Mr. Carver here.

"You're on private property, sir," she said. "I'll have to report this to Lord Gracechurch."

"Do and I'll have you arrested for interfering with a Crown investigation," Mr. Carver said, sounding no less amiable. It sent an odd shiver of loathing down her spine.

"Why? Because I won't let you break the law of the land?"

"Because I need to watch your husband without interference."

She turned, as if expecting to see the house from here. "Diccan's here?"

"This half hour. Didn't he tell you he was coming?"

Facing Mr. Carver, she straightened, which put her almost a head taller than he. "Oddly enough, Mr. Carver, I don't believe part of my wedding vows included sharing marital conversations with bureaucrats. But if that should change, I'll be sure to alert you right away." And touching her riding crop to her shako, she wheeled her horse around and headed off.

Diccan had indeed arrived. She could tell the minute she walked into the house. It wasn't simply the increased level of activity that announced more guests; she could *feel* him, a snatch of lightning that flickered along her nerve endings. She swore if she sniffed the air, she could scent him.

It was Biddle she saw first, crossing the hall with a stack of shirts in hand.

"Biddle," she greeted him with a smile. "It is good to see you. How have you been?"

Biddle turned distressed eyes on her. "I have been well, madame," he said, sounding mournful. "Busy, of course." He tilted his head, just a bit. "I seem to be having quite a bit of trouble with Master's neckcloths. They insist on becoming scorched."

Grace wasn't certain whether she wanted to smile or frown. How sweet. He was objecting to Diccan's behavior in the only small way a servant could. If only she wasn't beginning to feel very unwell again, she would stay and share ideas for revenge. But she thought that she had dealt with one too many traumas today, so she briefly laid her hand on the little valet's arm.

"Biddle," she said, so very tired of being pitied, "I would be sorely distressed if I learned that there had been a dimming of your reputation as the finest valet in the British Isles. I would be even more distressed if I thought I bore any responsibility for it."

For a moment, she was actually afraid the stiff-rumped little man might weep. After everything she had tolerated over her life, she stood in fear that this one thing could undo her. "Please, Biddle."

His bow would have been worth of a royal introduction. "You are everything kind, madame."

"Yes, Biddle," she sighed, running the riding crop through her fingers, "I believe I must be. Or I would have given you suggestions on how easy it would be to make starch into a penance."

She smiled. He smiled. He didn't mention the fact that Grace's riding crop had Diccan's initials stamped into the leather. She didn't ask after Diccan's health. Maybe later, she thought, turning for her room. When she felt better. For now, it was all she could do to make it to the chamber pot. She meant to climb into bed, but it seemed too far, and she was too tired. She'd just rest on the floor for a moment.

Diccan wasn't certain he could feel worse. He was exhausted, he was frustrated, and he was in sore need of counsel. On top of that, his valet had turned on him, which meant that he couldn't appear in anything that would require a neckcloth. And he loathed Belcher neckerchiefs.

Not that he didn't understand. Not that he didn't sympathize. Biddle doted on Grace. In fact, the entire staff doted on her. Hell, *he* was beginning to dote on her. But he hadn't found the bedamned verse yet.

He couldn't imagine one other item of Minette's that he could possibly search. He couldn't think of another way to get her to betray just where the verse was. And he was getting damned tired of trying.

"Well, *there* you are," he heard from the doorway to the study he'd slunk into.

Of course it was Kate, and she wasn't looking pleased. He couldn't even raise the energy to be cautious. "How nice to see you, Kate. You look magnificent as ever."

She swept up, glowing in a salmon frock that sported

more feathers than his mattress. "I look furious, and you know it. Where the bloody hell have you been? Don't you know what you're doing?"

He was on his feet so fast she took a surprised step backwards. "Don't," he commanded, a finger in her face. "Just...don't."

Anyone else might have listened. Kate snorted like an overheated horse. "I kept my mouth shut when you started catting around with that whore," she said. "I didn't even say anything to you when Grace gave up everything she loved just for you."

"Everything she loved? What are you talking about?"

She tilted her head, obviously disbelieving. "You mean you didn't know that she quit her volunteer work at the Army Hospital? Or that she's been yearning for the country?"

"I told her she could live in the country."

She looked disgusted. "I'm sure you told her you'd be happy to accompany her."

He didn't have an answer to that, and she knew it.

"I do know you found out about Epona. Why bother bringing her horse when you deserted her so fast she couldn't ride her? You don't see her having to face down the *ton* tabbies every time you don't accompany her. She has to pretend that her husband isn't publicly humiliating her by being seen with a two-penny whore."

"Kate," he objected, turning away. "I'm much too tired to be berated for something I can do nothing about right now."

He hadn't known. Not really. He'd been trying to pretend it wasn't so bad, because if it was, he wouldn't be able to continue being such a bastard. He would be consumed by the pain he was causing her. He'd grab Grace and run, just like she wanted, far into the country where no one could follow, and he'd make it up to her.

Kate sighed. "I don't suppose you could just tell us what's going on."

"Nothing," he ground out, "is going on."

"Causing more trouble, Katie?" a dust-dry voice asked beyond Kate.

She spun around as if the devil himself had spoken. "Why, Harry," she greeted him, venom dripping from her voice. "How did I know you'd be mixed up in this mess?"

Lidge stepped forward, his hands tucked into his pockets, a hacking jacket replacing his Rifleman's uniform. His glare was only degrees cooler than Kate's. "Mixed up?" he asked, one eyebrow lifting skyward. "The only thing I'm mixed up in, *Your Grace*, is seeing a friend married."

Kate waved him off like a pesky fly. "Oh, bollocks. If you're here, you are, whether officially or not, a member of Drake's Rakes. Just when do all the men casually drift off to Jack's office so you can plot in peace over whisky and those vile cigars you brought back from the Peninsula?"

"It's really none of your business," Diccan suggested.

Kate spun back on him with a vengeance. "It is when it is destroying one of my dearest friends. I don't know what game you all are playing, but Grace doesn't deserve the humiliation and pain you're serving her. Do you even know where she is right now?"

Diccan looked around. "I assume she came here with you."

"She's upstairs seeing Olivia's doctor because she hasn't held down a decent meal in ten days. Not that you should care, of course, except for the fact that it's undoubtedly your fault."

"*My* fault?" he echoed. "I haven't done anything to..."

And then, it clicked. His stomach plummeted. Oh, sweet Jesus. Kate couldn't be serious.

Harry leaned against the wall, a half-smile on his face. "Are congratulations in order, old son?"

Diccan pressed knuckles to his eyes. He didn't need to count. He would never forget that first night they'd made love. He hadn't even had the courage to call it that. He'd called it sex. He knew better now.

Could this have happened at a worse time? Smythe had drawn Diccan farther into the group, promising a wonderful chance if he'd just attend Jack's wedding and report back to them any new memories Jack had recovered. If Smythe found out Grace was pregnant, it would put her in his sights.

"Where is she?" he demanded, already walking.

"I'll go with you," Kate said. "I'm beginning to think somebody needs to protect her from you."

He sighed, really tired of this. "Don't be daft."

Kate didn't say a word. She just led the way. He could only follow. He didn't need to ask which room Grace occupied. Olivia stood outside the door, whispering to one of the maids.

"What's going on?" he demanded.

Olivia turned placid eyes on him. "We should find out any moment, although I'd hope you'll let Grace be the one to tell you. I think she's terrified you won't be pleased."

It came out before he could think. "I'm not."

He wasn't, for so many reasons. Because he didn't want to satisfy his father's misplaced dynastic expectations. Because he was still involved in business too dangerous and subversive to consider a family. Because he simply damn well did not want children. And Grace knew that. He'd told her that right after he had, evidently, impregnated her.

If all that was true, though, why was he suddenly feeling so oddly elated? Why the sudden need to hold Grace?

He wanted to groan. He wanted a stiff drink. He wanted, suddenly, to be with Minette, where he knew to a button just what his responsibilities were. More importantly, what his feelings were.

"If you so much as *hint* to that poor girl that you are displeased," Kate warned him, getting right in his face, "I will serve a vengeance on you that even your sainted father couldn't envision on his most biblical days."

"Don't, Kate," Olivia begged, a hand out. "We need to think of Grace. The poor thing is so sick we found her on the floor. This isn't going to be an easy time for her."

He was swinging around to demand an explanation, when the door opened. Everyone in the hall turned to see a robust young country gentleman in tweed and eyeglasses follow a maid out into the hall.

"I think it's time to decamp," Harry muttered, making to go.

His words caught the doctor's attention. "I think you should stay."

His expression jolted Diccan to his toes. The man was afraid.

Suddenly Diccan wanted to shove him aside, to go rescue Grace from whatever it was that was wrong. Was the pregnancy bad? Was she to lose the baby? How could he be so terrified at the thought?

"Who is the husband?" the doctor asked, wiping his hands on a towel.

Kate snorted again. Diccan took a tentative step

forward. "I am. Is there something wrong? She's all right, isn't she?"

The doctor's eyes were a piercing green, and they pinned Diccan like a frantic butterfly. "No."

Even the women gasped.

"Mr. Hilliard," the doctor said, pulling off his glasses and rubbing at his eyes. "There is something seriously wrong here."

"What, damn it?"

Again, the doctor met his gaze, and Diccan felt even more afraid. "Your wife is not pregnant, Mr. Hilliard. She's being poisoned."

Chapter 19

Grace wasn't sure what to do. The doctor had been kind and gentle and thoughtful. He had listened to her symptoms and answered most of her questions, and then, smiling, asked her to dress and wait for his return. But he hadn't given her a verdict. Was there a babe? Was the babe in jeopardy? She felt increasingly ill, as if being swamped by a wave, and her stomach had begun to cramp. Even so, the doctor had assured her not to worry; he would take care of everything. But what did that mean?

Lizzy helped her dress and then carried away the latest chamber pot. Left behind, Grace curled up on the bed, feeling abominably weak and wondering when the doctor would return, what he would say. He said that her symptoms were indicative of breeding. He had even offered some new suggestions for the nausea. But in the end, he hadn't really given her a real answer. She was just about to gather her courage and get up, when there was a tap on the door. For some reason, it made her heart thud.

"Yes?"

She couldn't seem to uncurl, the anxiety overwhelming her. She clenched her hands at her waist to give them something to do as she lay there, not at all certain she could rise, even for Dr. Spence. But it wasn't Dr. Spence. It was Diccan.

Grace blinked. "Oh."

Diccan smiled and closed the door behind him. "Hello, Grace."

He looked as handsome and urbane as ever, which didn't help Grace's anxiety. She felt sick and ungainly and smelled of sweat. She couldn't bear the comparison. Marshalling her strength, she climbed to her wobbly legs and smoothed down her dress. "It's…nice to see you, Diccan."

His smile was stiff. "You, too. Can we sit for a minute? I was just speaking with Dr. Spence."

Grace opened her mouth, uncertain how to answer. Of course if Diccan were there, Dr. Spence would tell him first. But somehow it felt like a betrayal. This was *her* baby, not Diccan's. She was the one who wanted a herd of noisy, rambunctious children tumbling over her lawn at Longbridge, shrieking with glee when they sat their first ponies, creeping like red Indians through the woods when they collected butterflies and bugs, looking like improbable angels when they slept. She was the one who wanted all that. Diccan didn't.

But Diccan was her husband, and he had the right to be told first. So she took a calming breath and dropped into one of the yellow wing chairs by the window. Diccan took the matching chair. Before he said a word, he reached over to collect her hands. His hands were cold. She almost pulled hers away.

"Grace," he said, looking down at her hand. "I saw Dr. Spence."

She nodded. She felt sick again, but she thought it was just fear. "I would have told you..."

He shook his head. "I never gave you the chance. I'm sorry. But I'm here now. But, Grace..." He too took a breath, and it suddenly made Grace afraid. "Things aren't as you think." His smile was fleeting. "I'm sure you'll be glad to hear that you won't be forced to put up with my butterstamp."

The words seemed to lodge like barbs in her chest, and she wasn't sure she could breathe around them. "What?"

Surely she wasn't understanding. He was just being witty, and the rest of the joke was coming.

But his gaze was steady, and it was troubled. "You're not going to have a baby, Grace. You're sick because you're being poisoned."

Later she would think of those words as the cannon shot that toppled the fortress wall. Now, she just stared. She shook her head, as if that would change Diccan's words. As if it could negate them.

"We think it's arsenic, Grace," he was saying, leaning closer, as if that made any difference. "The doctor thinks it's been going on for a while, now. We're going to give you something to counteract it, of course. I hope you like garlic, because that seems to be one of the remedies..."

He kept talking; Grace knew, because his mouth moved. But she didn't hear him. She didn't feel his hands anymore, even though she saw that he still held hers. She couldn't seem to draw in any air, and surely that was her heart careening off its base.

Poison. She was being poisoned.

There would be no baby.

She yanked her hands away. She stood and almost fell over. But when Diccan jumped up to help her, she pushed him away. She turned, not really sure why, not sure what she meant to do, but feeling a terrible need to see the green outside. Her verdant green. The green she had allowed herself to dream of, when peace and comfort had seemed so far away. When she had been too afraid to dream.

"Grace?"

She heard his voice and it seemed far away, too. She kept rubbing at her chest, certain it was on fire. It was being scoured with acid, filling so fast she couldn't breathe, she couldn't breathe, she couldn't *breathe*.

Oh, God, her babe. Her babe.

Her verdant green.

"Grace, sweetheart, please."

She opened her mouth, but there weren't any words. Only a noise, and it was terrible. It was the sound of her defenses disintegrating. She was sobbing.

She shoved a fist against her mouth to hold it in. She couldn't weep. If she started, she would never stop. She would end up wailing like a madwoman, and it would destroy her.

Another sob breached her hand, though, spilling out like water over a weir. Another. Deep, anguished cries, dredged up from her very soul. Not a woman's sobs, but the sobs of an animal, a harsh guttural keening that seemed to be gathering in her chest like an unstoppable tide, too vast to hold back. It was just too much.

Too much.

The tide broke loose.

"Grace . . . Grace, look at me."

But she couldn't. She couldn't do anything but sob. She sobbed until tears clogged her nose and eyes and soaked her neck and dress. Until she crumbled beneath the weight of the tears and found herself on the floor, curled into herself, fists jammed against her gaping mouth, wailing like a madwoman.

She spent herself on that bedroom floor, drained her life away in salt and water until only a husk of her remained. Only a husk, because everything she had filled it with had been illusion. She was nothing but lost wishes. Spent dreams. Duty and honor and responsibility, the bitter ashes of hope.

Finally the sobs died away, but the silence that followed was worse. It was empty.

Diccan shook as if he had the ague. He was so cold, sitting on the floor with his back against the wall, his Grace in his arms. She slept now, her chest heaving sporadically with left-over sobs, like a child exhausted from pain. Her hands were clenched at her middle. Her face was flushed and damp, her hair straggling over his hands. He should get up and wash her face. He should put her to bed so she could rest. He should go away where he couldn't hurt her anymore.

He couldn't bear this. He wasn't made for it. No one had trained him to suffer this kind of devastation. His shirt was soaked with tears: Grace's tears. His tears. He felt shattered. He couldn't even imagine what she felt. He hadn't realized until this minute that he had never suffered real pain in his life, because he had never suffered for someone he loved.

He loved her. What kind of a dolt was he that he hadn't realized it within moments of meeting her? How could he not have realized that hidden beneath that plain wrapping lay the most precious of gems? What exactly had been so vital to him that he couldn't admit how much he wanted her, how much he enjoyed her, how deeply he respected her? How he would move Heaven and earth to keep her from being hurt? There would not be a day in his life he would be able to close his eyes and not see the wasteland in Grace's eyes when her life finally fell apart.

When he pulled it apart.

How had he not noticed how strong she was to withstand all she had suffered? How could he not have seen how fragile she was, a woman so sure she deserved nothing that she asked for nothing? Who had suffered her greatest blow when she had finally allowed herself to hope for more?

He had done this to her.

"Diccan?"

He didn't even bother to look up. He had cursed at every person who'd tried to breach the door, knowing that they wanted to take Grace from him. But this was his task. This was his penance for a life lived on the edge of humanity. He had to protect Grace from exposure, to cushion her fall, to bear her grief. He knew that his Boadicea couldn't have borne revealing her weakness to her friends, which was how she would see her tears. So he had collected them himself and hidden them away for her.

He'd thought they would send in Kate, but it was Olivia who crouched before him, her hand gently resting atop his. Pulling in a harsh breath, he finally looked up to see the fear and compassion in Olivia's eyes. "What have I done to her?" he asked.

And oddly, Olivia smiled. "Don't be so full of yourself. You aren't responsible for everything, you know. Grace had suffered the world long before you pushed your way into it."

"But I used her."

Olivia sighed. "We all did. It's so easy, isn't it? Do you know she never even took the time to cry for her father? She was too busy caring for everyone else."

His laugh was sore as he brushed a damp lock of hair from Grace's ashen forehead. "I think she just did. My poor girl."

He couldn't seem to stop stroking her cheek, as if he could reassure her, ease her, even in her sleep. "What are we to do?"

Olivia climbed to her feet. "We need to get her to bed. You need to find out who it is who's been trying to hurt her."

He looked up, anguish tightening his throat. "Besides me?"

Olivia frowned. "Now you're becoming maudlin. Come, Diccan. We need your brain. The rest of the Rakes are downstairs trying to figure this out. Your footman Benny is missing, and Jack found a half-full bottle of arsenic in his room."

He shook his head, certain that would mean something soon. "No. My place is here. She's going to be very sick, isn't she?"

"I think so. But I don't think she wants you to see her that way. Give us a chance to take care of her for a change. You spend your energies where you're good: plotting, scheming, and investigating. Until we can untangle this mess, Grace is still in danger. All of you are."

He kept running the backs of his fingers down Grace's ashen cheeks. She was finally limp, deeply asleep, and he didn't want to disturb her. No, to be honest, he simply didn't want to leave her. He had to help her recover. He had to tell her he loved her. Most of all, he had to beg her forgiveness for every harsh word she'd heard. He had to make her understand he hadn't meant one of them.

"Isn't it odd?" he asked, once again running his hand down the tangled locks that tumbled over her shoulders. "Her hair actually looks more red. Is that something the arsenic did?"

Olivia laid her hand on his arm. "We'll ask later. Come, now, we have work to do."

In the end, he carried Grace over to her bed, where the women waited like a clutch of anxious nannies. Before he left, though, he bent down and kissed her, wishing he knew what to do now. How to heal this. How to prove to her that she hadn't just lost everything.

"Go ahead and get her ready," he said. "I'll be back. Right now I need to contact her staff at Longbridge." Giving his sleeping wife a smile, he kissed her and murmured, "We'll see what this crowd thinks of your Sikh warrior."

Diccan did come back. And Grace was sick. Deathly sick. So sick that by the next morning Diccan despaired for her life. He never left, even as they purged her and bled her, even as she cried out with vicious cramps. Even as, deep in the night, she began to seize.

He had already had her in his arms when it began. She'd never really woken, even as she lost every ounce of fluid they tried to force into her. And then, suddenly, deep in the early morning hours, her body stiffened, arced, shuddered, right there in his arms.

"Hold her," the doctor demanded, for he'd never left. "Gently."

Shredded with panic, Diccan gathered in her poor, flailing limbs as if he could hold her together. As if he could protect her from her own body.

"She's dying!" he cried. "Do something."

The doctor, looking as calm as a prelate, listened to her racing heart and shook his head. "I was hoping this wouldn't happen."

Diccan held her close, her limbs battering him. "What do we do?"

Straightening up, the doctor frowned. "Keep her safe," he said, sounding less sanguine. "It's all we can do 'til the poison works its way through."

"It doesn't seem to be doing that," Kate said from the corner of the room.

The doctor actually shook his head. "I know. To tell the truth, I've never seen anyone fail this quickly. I think she's been much more ill than any of us realize."

Diccan felt himself stumble at the edge of a great, dark chasm, even as the seizure began to wane. "What are you saying?"

The doctor met his frantic gaze, then looked back down at the once-again-slack Grace. "I'm saying that she has to be the strongest woman I've ever met to have held off these symptoms so long. But even strong women have their limits. If she's finally given up, then she won't survive."

Kate huffed. "Don't be ridiculous. Grace has never lacked for courage."

But Diccan knew it wasn't about courage. It was about despair.

"She won't die," he said simply, his voice threaded with his own despair. "I won't allow it."

He didn't. He fought with her; he fought *for* her, all through the night and the next day. He slept in the bed with her, beset by the fear that if he lost touch with her he'd lose her altogether. He helped change her when she soaked nightgowns and sheets with sweat. He cleaned her when she needed it. And all through those terrible hours, he fell more deeply under her gentle spell. Not the kind of spell a woman exudes to seduce. The kind of spell a courageous woman weaves without even meaning to.

He wanted to be there when she woke. When she opened her eyes and smiled and said, "Oh, that was uncomfortable. But I'm better now." But the longer he stayed in that closed, fetid room, the less he believed it would happen. And if it didn't, he simply didn't know how he could go on.

"Please, Grace," he whispered into her tangled, damp hair, trying so hard to force life into her, to force hope into her. "Don't leave me."

But in all those hours, she never answered.

Chapter 20

Grace knew she was sick. She thought she was dying, but it didn't seem to matter. She just didn't have the strength to push away from it. She couldn't find the desire to. She just wanted to rest, to shut out all the pain and grief and effort that seemed to wait for her. She wanted to stop hoping.

She thought she came close. In a vague, amorphous sense, she even thought she created more dreams to comfort her passing; the feeling of warm arms holding her, the rise and fall of voices, one voice. Diccan's voice, calling her back, exhorting her to try. And then, deep in the darkness when it seemed an effort just to remind her heart to beat, she was sure she heard her father.

"What kind of a Fairchild are you?" he barked, as he would when she would cringe from a difficult task. "Fairchilds don't quit."

This one, she thought, sorry to disappoint him, *would*.

Except for one thing. There was something preying on her mind. Something she should be remembering. Something she had meant to warn Diccan about.

Something...

• • •

Diccan was once again lying in bed next to Grace. The sun had long set and the room flickered with firelight. He was so tired. He was cold. He was trying to hold onto his last vestige of hope.

"Diccan...Diccan?"

He felt as if his eyes were full of grit and his arms full of lead. "What?"

"There's something..."

That was when it finally kicked in. That small, scratchy voice was Grace's. He shot up so fast he almost banged his head against the bedpost. "Gracie?"

She looked like hell. Even in the soft candlelight, she was waxy white, with deep purple bruising beneath her eyes, and her hair was a rat's nest. He thought she'd lost a good ten pounds, just in the last two days. He couldn't remember ever seeing anything so beautiful in his life.

"Grace?" he asked, laying a hand against her cheek. "How do you feel?"

She licked dry lips and looked around, as if surprised to find herself in bed. "Is it malaria?"

He hated to even say it. Grabbing a glass of water, he lifted her head to drink. "Don't you remember? Someone tried to poison you."

The faint light in her eyes died a little. "Oh, yes."

"Grace." Setting down the glass, he gathered her into his arms. "You aren't going to quit now. Tell me you aren't going to quit. I have so much I need to tell you."

Her eyes were growing vague, and he could feel the strength waning in her. "What kind of Fairchild would I be?" she asked.

This time, though, when she faded back to sleep, he felt

something different; a kind of peace in her that hadn't been there before, as if she had finally made up her mind.

"You'd better decide to stay," he threatened her, pulling her to him so he could listen to her heart beat, so he could share his heat and will and *want*. To give her what he could while she let him. He didn't realize that his own tears were now soaking her hair as he wrapped himself around her.

He must have fallen asleep, because the next thing he knew, someone was tapping his shoulder.

"Diccan?"

He jerked awake to see Kate leaning over him. "She's better," he said, and looked down at Grace to make sure. She was still sleeping, but he swore there was more color in her face. He needed to believe there was more color.

"Good," Kate said, "then you can get a quick wash-up and go downstairs. Biddle is waiting to see to you."

Carefully disengaging himself from Grace, he climbed to his feet and stretched out the kinks. It was when he realized that the sun had risen quite some time ago. It warmed the soft yellow and green colors of the room and washed a bit of gold into Grace's skin.

"No, thank you," he said, watching her. "Grace needs me here."

Kate picked up the jacket he'd discarded three days earlier and held it out with two fingers. "Grace needs you coherent and smelling a sight better than you do now." When he moved to balk, she scowled. "Diccan, never in my life could I imagine having to say this to you, but you stink. You haven't left this room for three days. Now be a good lad and bathe. You have visitors."

Diccan finally gave in to a small smile. "Well, she is sleeping…"

He was reaching out to retrieve his jacket when he caught sight of Bea in the hallway, peering intently toward the steps, as if afraid of what would come up. Diccan felt a sudden *frisson* of dread. "What visitors?"

Bea shook her head. "Gehenna."

Diccan turned to Kate, who just sighed. "The bishop."

He felt as if he'd been punched. "What bishop?"

Kate scowled at him. "You know perfectly well what bishop. He and your mother are in the Red Salon doing their best to terrify Olivia."

Diccan knew that his brain was sluggish, but he simply couldn't make any sense out of Kate's statement. "What the hell are they doing here?"

"Fire and brimstone," Bea muttered, not moving.

"Besides that." Diccan scrubbed at his face, suddenly feeling every unslept hour. "Jack wouldn't have invited them to the wedding, would he?"

"Don't be absurd." Kate wet a cloth to lay on Grace's forehead. "They came looking for you. Olivia says your father looks frantic."

It infuriated him, but Diccan knew that if he ignored the summons, his parents would wreak havoc on the house party. So he dropped one final kiss on Grace's forehead and headed for the dressing room and Biddle's care.

In the end, it was only half an hour before he presented himself in Olivia's red drawing room, where the poor woman faced his parents alone.

"I think Kate needs you upstairs," he told her, seeing the near panic in her eyes. His parents must be in rare form. It was too bad for them that he had absolutely no patience left to deal with them.

"Mother, Father," he greeted them after Olivia fled, "Have you been terrorizing my friends?"

"Your levity is distasteful," his father said, standing. "This is important or we wouldn't be here."

Diccan bent over his mother's hand. "I don't see my sisters with you. They are well?"

His mother's nostrils flared. "I left them with your cousin the duke, at Moorhaven. I know that Catherine is here. I won't expose my daughters to that...trollop."

Diccan quirked an eyebrow. "And Kate always speaks so well of you."

His mother sniffed. "I refuse to acknowledge that whore's name."

"Eloise," the bishop chastised. "There is no time for that."

"If you have no time to call Kate names," Diccan said, settling himself on the gold settee as his father resumed his own seat, "I imagine the matter is urgent. I am all ears, sir."

"Don't act the idiot," his father snapped, sounding tired. "We've come to save your life."

Diccan refused to show surprise at his father's rather dramatic statement. "Indeed, sir. And how will you do that?"

He was stunned to see his father return to his feet and pace. The bishop never paced. It was beneath him. "The duke has been gracious enough to offer his aid," the bishop was saying, as he walked. "His schooner will meet us at Hove and take you to Jamaica. The family plantations there are in need of help. We thought that surely you could manage that."

"Surely I could," Diccan agreed mildly, even as his heart stuttered oddly. "The question is, why, in all that's holy, would I?"

His father stopped short, scowling. "Because the soldiers can't be far behind us with a writ of arrest. They found the note, Diccan, although how you could be so careless as to leave it behind, I certainly don't know. But they have it now, and it is damning evidence."

Diccan leaned back and crossed his legs. "Of what?"

"Damme, sir, how can you be so flippant?"

"Undoubtedly a moral flaw. You find me no less confused, though. Exactly what note would that be that so condemns me?"

"The one instructing your footman to murder your wife."

Grace heard voices. She was unable to respond, though, too exhausted to do more than breathe.

"How could this happen?" Olivia whispered over her head. "He's your cousin. You must know if there's any truth to it."

"Of course there isn't," Kate retorted. "After the last three days, how could you even think it? And if those vipers he calls parents thought at all, they would have known that right away." She huffed, sounding disgusted. "The very idea. I swear, if I didn't know that the two of them would never think of performing a charitable deed, I'd think Diccan had been left in a basket on their doorstep."

What was happening? What new problem had arisen? Grace wished she had the energy to think about it. "*Always good at puzzles*," she heard her father remind her, and she could almost see him grinning at her in that way he had before he set out to fight. "*Use your brain*."

But that took too much effort, and she was tired. And

yet, she had the most persistent feeling that she knew something important. Something relevant.

It was, finally, what nudged her awake. She opened her eyes to the golden wash of light from an afternoon sun, the scent of new-mown grass, the music of voices in the house. For a long while she merely lay where she was, gathering her wits. She felt as limp as wet linen, and her brain felt battered and useless. But at least her stomach had settled, and the cramping pain had eased to a dull ache.

Looking around at the pretty, springlike room, she was surprised to find herself alone. Hadn't she just heard her friends arguing? She turned a bit farther and saw the lawns stretching out beyond the window, a field of green ringed by trees like a tonsured head, all tinted with the soft glow of sunlight.

Again, she was beset by something she needed to say, and it had something to do with that lawn. How odd. Her last clear memory was of a lowering sky. It had been about to rain. There was nothing happening outside now; the trees lay still beneath a clear sky. She wondered if it had rained after all. Had they had Wellington weather? Had the skies emptied and the ground shaken from thunder? And why did the thought of swirling, cloud-laden sky make her feel impatient and anxious? What was lurking in her memory?

She knew about the babe, of course. The sharp grief of losing even that hope gnawed at her. Now she would never be a mother. Diccan would surely never be so careless again.

"Grace?" she heard, and turned to see Kate stepping in the door. "Are you going to stay awake this time?"

Grace blinked. "I've been awake?"

Kate strolled up. "Off and on. You've been very ill."

Grace reached up to rub at the lingering ache in her head. "Yes, I think I knew that. The arsenic?"

"All better," Kate said, sitting down. "And before you ask, it's been five days."

"The wedding!"

"—Has been put off a few days."

"I'm so sorry—"

Kate waved her off. "Don't be tedious, Grace. After all the nursing you've done, you're due more than a few days in bed. Although next time I'd appreciate it if you'd simply do it to seem interesting. This poisoning business causes the most distressing anxiety. It gave me a wrinkle." Her grin was as brash as ever as she helped Grace sit up. "But I refuse to show you where. Now, how about some lovely gruel?"

Grace groaned. "That, my dear Kate, is an oxymoron."

Could she ask where Diccan was? If he had stayed for the delayed wedding, or just cut his losses and wandered back off to wherever Minette was? Did she dare reveal how vital those dreams of his comfort had been?

"I think I heard you talking about Diccan," she said.

Plumping the pillows behind Grace's back, Kate actually looked away. "Oh, you don't need to worry about him."

Grace frowned. "I think I do. What happened?"

"What happened is that you haven't eaten in five days, and if you show up at Olivia's wedding looking like you do right now, they'll think it's a wake. Now, what can I get you?"

Grace managed a small grin. "I don't suppose you have your brandy."

Finally, Kate grinned back. "Don't be silly."

Reaching into her pocket, she pulled out the sleek

chased silver flask and uncapped it. Grace's hand shook, but she didn't hesitate to take it and enjoy a sip. "Ah," she sighed as the liquid fire bloomed in her stomach. "If there is one thing I learned with the army, it's that there is nothing that can't be soothed with a bit of brandy."

Kate smiled. "A tradition with which I heartily concur. Now then, how about a bath and clean nightclothes?"

Grace was about to answer with an emphatic yes, when she was distracted by the flask. She was recapping it, when it made a curious clicking sound and one of the sides separated.

"Oh, no," she cried, trying to gather the sides back together. "I think I broke it."

That was when Kate laughed. "Have I never shown you its secret?" she asked, taking the flask back and separating the back side.

It wasn't broken; it had a hinged cover that, indeed, hid a surprise. An ivory oval miniature. The painting was exquisite, of a young doe-eyed blond beauty in rather scandalous attire, with the script, *Is not the first fruit sweet, my love?* engraved beneath.

Grace stared at it, suddenly cold. "I thought you said this was Jack's flask."

Kate smiled. "It was. Olivia found it on him at Waterloo. He didn't recognize it, so he let me have it. I never gave it back."

She motioned to the painting. "And her?"

Kate leaned over to catch sight of the painting. "Oh, didn't you ever see this? It's Mimi. Jack's French mistress. You can imagine what poor Olivia thought when she saw it. It's why I considered it a charitable act to take it. She doesn't need to be reminded that Jack wasn't celibate during the years they were apart. Especially since Mimi turned out to be a spy for Napoleon." She chuckled, inviting Grace to see the humor.

But Grace had stopped listening. "That's not her name."

Kate took another look. "Of course it is."

Grace looked up, feeling off-balance again. "This," she said, lifting the flask so Kate could see, "is Minette. *Diccan's* mistress."

Kate went very still. "You're sure?"

Grace gave a sore laugh. "Believe me when I tell you, Kate. I know every inch of this woman. Do you think Diccan knows?"

Kate sat abruptly in her chair. "Who knows? Those men are closed as clams." She kept shaking her head. "Great Heavens. This is certainly a new twist."

"What does it mean?" Grace asked, rubbing at her aching forehead as she contemplated the winsome smile on the painting.

Kate sighed. "It either means Drake's Rakes have been sharing mistresses, which I find rather distasteful, or someone is playing a far deeper game than we thought." She took back the flask. "Which I find even more distasteful."

"I need to talk to Diccan."

"We need to talk to all of them." Abruptly, Kate rose to her feet and slipped the flask back into her pocket. "I'll send Lizzy up to see to your bath and some food. I believe I'll work on herding the men into a room and not letting them out 'til we get some answers."

Kate had almost made it out the door, when Grace suddenly remembered. "Kate? What trouble is Diccan in?"

Kate stopped. "Diccan? Oh, nothing."

"I heard you before. Is he accused of something? You said something about his parents not standing by him."

Her hand on the door, Kate sighed. "He doesn't want you to worry, Grace."

"He failed."

For a moment, Kate seemed to consult the half-open door. Then, she turned to face Grace. "It shouldn't be all that surprising," she said briskly, "especially since the effort was already made to discredit him. This is just another attempt."

Grace's brain seemed to move at the pace of mud, but after a few long moments, Kate's words sank in. She felt the blood leave her face. "Oh, my God," she whispered. "He's been accused of poisoning me. Who? Who could think such a thing?"

She had never seen Kate look so uncomfortable. "A letter has been found from him to your footman Benny. And Benny is missing."

Grace wished she could have another big gulp of Kate's brandy. "Benny? But he's been so solicitous." Always pushing that foul-tasting tonic on her.

Kate shrugged. "It's all I know."

"Don't you know who it is who is accusing Diccan? Surely they would have something to do with whoever had me poisoned. Was it Mr. Carver, that man from the Home Office? I don't think I'd put it past him. He's obsessed, I think."

She remembered now. It was Mr. Carver she'd been fretting over. He was here, and he was watching Diccan. And she could see that he wanted Diccan brought down. "It's him," she said, suddenly energized. "Mr. Carver. He must have given up finding any evidence against Diccan and..."

"No, Grace. It wasn't."

Grace looked up to see a completely foreign distress in Kate's eyes.

"It was your Uncle Dawes."

Yes, Grace thought. *A person's heart could stop beating.* She swore hers just had. "I think he was having Diccan watched," she said inconsequentially. "To protect me."

"He was the one who found the note. His people were investigating your staff, and evidently one of them was suspicious of your footman Benny. They found the note in lodgings he'd taken by Covent Garden. The general called it providential. I call it a bit too convenient."

"You're saying that the general had something to do with my poisoning? You can't think my uncle would deliberately hurt me. If he did, it would mean he is in league with the Lions. My uncle, Kate. A general in Cornwallis's army."

Kate didn't say a word. She just shook her head, which made Grace feel immeasurably worse.

"Let's find out what the men have learned," her friend finally said. "Until then, it's silly to make accusations."

Grace fought the pain of disbelief. "It sounds as if accusations have already been made."

Against Diccan. She had to find out why.

Grace decided that Kate could perform magic. Within the hour, she had managed to corral the resident Rakes into the Grand Salon, an old-fashioned, high-ceilinged, white room with ornate gilded plasterwork, carved alabaster chimney pieces, and corniced doorways. The furniture, collected into comfortable groupings, was soft sage and gold and crafted along simpler lines, as if the room couldn't bear more ornamentation. It was like making your confession in a baroque Viennese church, Grace thought, as she waited for Kate to settle herself next to her on a Sheridan sofa by the fireplace.

"Nothing to say," Chuffy groused as he plopped himself onto a matching chair to her left.

"Maybe you have nothing to say," Kate told the chubby peer from where she sat, arranging her skirts, "but I assure you, we do."

Grace kept quiet. She had survived both bath and food, and felt quite a bit stronger, but right now she was preoccupied with watching the attendees. Jack Wyndham, of course, pouring tots of whisky for the men; Marcus Drake, standing by the windows; Chuffy Wilde, seated by Lady Bea; and Harry Lidge, who was shooting surreptitious glances at Kate from where he stood, whisky in hand, across the room. Every one of them looked stony-faced, schoolboys called to account. Grace suspected that they would be tough nuts to crack.

The women's contingent consisted of Olivia, sitting behind an unused tea tray, glaring at Jack as if he had misbehaved, Kate, Bea, and Grace. The only one missing, it seemed, was Diccan.

"Where is he?" Grace asked without preamble.

The heads of all the men shot up.

"Pardon?" Earl Drake asked, looking ludicrously innocent, decanter and glass in hand.

Grace lifted an eyebrow. "My husband. Where is he?"

"Here," she heard, and Diccan strolled into the room. "My dear, although it's always wonderful to see you, I wish you would have stayed in your room. You still look a trifle pale."

Grace felt the usual rush of pleasure at the sight of him. She felt something more this time, a sense of intimacy, as if her dreams had been real. As if she really had slept in his arms. She thought she saw him betray a quick flash of intense relief when he spotted her. But, as usual, emotion lasted only briefly in Diccan Hilliard's eyes.

"I feel better," she assured him. "Where have you been?"

Diccan delivered one of his patented smiles of lazy amusement as he accepted a whisky from Marcus and settled in a chair across from Grace. "Oh, here and there."

"Did they arrest you?" she asked. "Or just cast aspersions?"

Diccan sent an accusing glare around the room. "My thanks for protecting my wife's peace of mind while I was gone."

Grace felt her temper fray. "My peace of mind was lost when you told me I was being poisoned," she told him. "In fact, I'd say it was lost long before that. And I find I've had enough. Where do things stand, Diccan? Will I be visiting you in gaol?"

"Not while I'm with him," Harry Lidge said quietly. "He has been remanded to my custody for now." His face broke into a wry grin. "You seem to have thrown off the opposition's plans when you survived."

Grace could feel Kate's feathers ruffling and put a calming hand on her arm. "Thank you, Harry." Grace looked around to see that the men wore varying expressions, from wariness to outright dread. "You need to tell us what is going on."

"No, we don't," Diccan retorted. "Not if it puts you in danger."

"Worse danger than arsenic poisoning?" Grace snapped. She had no idea she had that kind of fury in her; it flared hot in her chest.

To Diccan's credit, he flushed. "It won't happen again, Grace. You're being watched."

"I was being watched before, Diccan," she said. "It wasn't enough."

"Agreed," Chuffy said. "Don't think Schroeder is up to form."

Grace swung her head toward him. "Schroeder?"

Chuffy was blushing. "Great help," he muttered. "Heard it myself from Diccan. She heads his army. Still, couldn't know what she was up against."

Grace knew she was gaping. "She was *watching* me?"

"Protecting you," Diccan said. "It's why I didn't want you to fire her."

She thought she'd go mad. "Well, thank God you told me that. Otherwise I might have thought that since I kept catching her in your bedroom that you were tupping her, too!"

He at least had the grace to look chagrined. "I didn't want to worry you."

She wanted to scream. "*Never* say that to me again. How could you think I wouldn't be worried? Olivia has been attacked. You've been kidnapped. I've been poisoned."

"And married," Kate muttered. "Don't forget that."

"Grace," Marcus Drake said, leaning forward. "Try to understand. We aren't allowed to simply spread this information around."

Grace met him gaze for gaze. "In that case, we'll just have to use what we know and look into all this by ourselves."

Diccan jumped to his feet. "I forbid it!"

"You're too late," Kate told him with a bright smile. "We've already begun. And as opposed to you, we'll actually share information. In fact, we have some now." Reaching into her pocket, she drew out the flask. "What do you know about this?"

Stepping away from the mantel, Jack Wyndham frowned. "It's Evenham's."

Everyone stared. It certainly wasn't the answer Grace had expected. "The boy who killed himself?" she asked.

"Evenham's?" Marcus Drake retorted, stepping closer to see. "What the hell is Kate doing with something of Evenham's?"

Kate's smile was purely malicious. "Why, I took it off of Jack. Olivia found it on him when she came across him at Waterloo."

"I think the question is," Marcus said, "why did Jack take it off of Evenham?"

Jack was shaking his head. "I don't know. I don't remember anything about it."

"This might help," Kate offered dryly. Opening the back of the flask, she handed it over. "I assume you know her."

Jack took the flask. "Mimi," he breathed, looking stricken.

"Your mistress?" Diccan asked. "The one who turned you over to the French?"

"Evidently Evenham's mistress, too," Drake mused, "if the miniature came with the flask."

"Evenham didn't have a mistress," Diccan said quietly. "Believe me."

"He had the flask," Jack insisted, "which connects him to Mimi."

"It connects them both to someone else." Grace extended her hand for the flask. Taking one last wistful look at it, Jack handed it to her. Grace passed it to Diccan.

Diccan took one look and blanched. "My God."

His glass hit the floor with a thud and rolled, spilling a rivulet of whiskey. He didn't even seem to notice, his focus on the miniature. The men gathered around him.

"Bloody hell, Diccan," Harry said. "That's Minette."

"So it is," Grace said. "Does anyone besides me find it singular that she has...um, entertained many two Drake's Rakes, who just happen to be investigating the Lions?"

"Two Rakes and a Lion cub," Chuffy said with a shake of his head. "Too smoky by half."

"I'm telling you that she was not Evenham's mistress," Diccan insisted.

"She certainly seemed to know him," Chuffy retorted.

"Admirable stamina," Kate said with a grin.

"Untidy," Bea retorted with a moue of displeasure.

"Diccan?" Grace asked. "What do you think? Is the woman in this miniature just overly friendly, or is something more going on?"

Slowly sitting back down, Diccan kept staring at the flask. Finally, with a harsh laugh, he shook his head. "I have an awful feeling that the hen is really a fox in disguise. And we thought we were all so clever."

"Is she the reason you're being discredited?" Grace asked.

It was Marcus who answered. "I'm afraid he can't say."

"Because we've already been so free with the information we already have," Olivia almost growled. "Even after being attacked and threatened and ruined."

Grace sighed, feeling her strength flag. "We know the basics about the Lions already. We want to know what the risk is to us. To you. We want to know if there is anything we can do to help."

"No," the men all said together.

Kate shook her head, motioning to the flask. "You forget we've just helped. I assume you learned something from Evenham, Diccan. If the Lions found out, why didn't they just try and kill you, like they tried with Jack? Why all the dancing around?"

Another exchanged look. A moment of discomfort. "We don't know," Marcus finally admitted. "Indeed, it seems... inefficient."

"Not really," Diccan admitted, absently running his thumb over the ivory portrait of his mistress. "Not if they can find some other work for me that compromises me even more."

They all looked up at him. Grace felt her heart catch. "What work?"

Diccan took a moment to meet her gaze before turning to Jack Wyndham. "For one, I'm supposed to be reporting back to Smythe about Jack's memory. I'm sure they're terrified you've remembered more names. And secondly..." He looked up with a singularly dry smile. "I think they're setting me up to kill Wellington."

Grace found herself gaping. "The Lions? Just what have you been doing?"

"Just what you said," he said without looking at her. "Fucking the Frenchwoman for the flag."

"Diccan," Jack admonished.

"Finally," Kate muttered. "A particle of truth."

Diccan looked back down at the flask. "Evenham told me the Lions would try to recruit me any way they could. Whitehall thought that I could get near some of the suspects by resuming my affair with Minette. It's seemed to work a champ. They think I've been spying for foreign governments and am amenable to coercion. I've been the perfect patsy." He turned to Grace, his eyes stark. "You should have been safe. I would never have hurt you like that if I hadn't thought it would keep you safe. I'm so sorry."

Grace heard the ragged pain in his voice and suddenly understood what every vile accusation, every seemingly cruel act had cost him. It shook her how much she hurt for him.

"You're forgiven," she said softly.

She was even more shaken when she saw tears in his eyes. Oh, Diccan.

"What can we do?" Kate asked, pulling Grace's attention back.

"Stay out of the way," Harry Lidge said. "This is dangerous business."

"Indeed," Kate said with a speaking look. "Who could imagine?"

"No, no," Chuffy objected. "Worse than the collywobbles. Knives."

"Chuff..."

But Chuffy shook his head. "They should know, blast it. Fellow's out there cutting lines from Shakespeare into people's heads. Well, he hasn't cut any of *us*. It's the ladies he usually goes after. Like Lady Gracechurch."

Olivia went pasty white. "The Surgeon?" she asked in stricken tones. "What about him?"

"Quotes?" Grace asked, suddenly feeling sick again. "What are you talking about?"

No one heard her. They were focused on Jack, who went to kneel by Olivia so he could take her hands. "I'm so sorry, Liv," he said. "The Surgeon has escaped, and no one knows where he is. But we've had you protected. I swear."

The Surgeon. Oh, sweet God. Sweet, sweet God. Grace thought, *they couldn't mean it.*

"The Surgeon is at large?" she demanded, knowing she sounded shrill. "Did you know that, Olivia?"

She knew by the stark pallor of Olivia's face that she

hadn't known. The scar that ran down her friend's cheek seemed to stand out against her pallor like a personal accusation.

"What did you mean about a quote, Chuffy?" Grace demanded.

Chuffy flushed uncomfortably. "Shouldn't have told you. Not a thing for women to hear."

"It's his signature," Diccan reluctantly said. "He... carves a quote into his victims."

A quote. Like something from Sophocles. Grace closed her own eyes a moment, swamped with sudden nausea. "Damn you," she rasped, hitting the chair arm with her fist. "Damn you all. You could have warned us! But you decided you knew best, and you let that monster wander around without telling us!"

"Grace, come," Diccan said, reaching for her hand. "Do you really think I'd let the Surgeon anywhere near you?"

But she batted his hand away, unable to face him. How could she have felt sorry for him? "Kate," she said. "Will you get my reticule, please? It's on my dresser."

"Grace?" Olivia asked. "What is it?"

But she shook her head and kept her silence until Kate had returned with Grace's serviceable knit reticule dangling from her wrist. Unable to give Diccan so much as the comfort of a glance, Grace took it and opened it up. Her hands were shaking.

"I tried to show you," she told Diccan, retrieving the business card she'd kept. "I tried to tell you something was wrong. But you wouldn't listen. You didn't talk to me. You all decided that would be too *dangerous.* So how could I know the Surgeon wasn't safely in prison? How could I have connected the two? You tell me."

She all but threw the calling card at him.

"Grace," Marcus said softly. "What about the Surgeon?"

She didn't answer him either. She felt her heart shrivel inside her. She knew, finally, just how badly she'd been used.

Diccan was reading the card. "Mr. Carver," he said, and she saw the light begin to dawn on him.

"What about him?" Marcus asked, stepping up.

Diccan handed over the card, and his hands were shaking, too. "Mr. Carver gave Grace a card with the address of Lincoln's Inn Fields. Chuffy? What else is at Lincoln's Inn Fields?"

Chuffy's round face scrunched in thought. "Royal College of—"

Marcus was staring at the card as if it were a snake. "Surgeons."

It was what had confused Grace, because she'd known all along that an address on Lincoln's Inn Fields was significant. She wanted to scream with frustration. With outrage. "He's been beneath your noses all along, and you didn't know. Because you wouldn't tell me!"

Diccan looked up at her, and she saw the fear that had blossomed in his once-cool gray eyes. "Where is he, Grace? Do you know?"

"Of course I know. He's been following me more closely than my abigail, telling me I needed to turn you in. Warning me about you. Threatening me with arrest and ruin if I didn't help him. How could I *not* know where he is?"

Again Diccan tried to grab hold of her hand, but she wouldn't let him. "Where, Grace?" he asked. "Where is he?"

Fear bubbled like acid in her chest. "He's here, Diccan. He's at Oak Grove."

She might just as well have loosed a bomb in the room. Suddenly every man was on his feet, and everyone was trying to talk over each other. It took a good twenty minutes for her to be able to tell them her story, to describe the man she'd met time and again, thinking he was a government agent. It took another ten minutes for the men to disappear, scrambling to collect a force to search the grounds.

The grounds that should have been secure.

Grace couldn't seem to move. She kept seeing the cold smile in that man's eyes. She heard the suggestive whispers she had never spoken of to anyone. She felt cold and hot and dirty. She felt afraid. She never allowed herself to feel afraid.

"Come along, Grace," Diccan said when he finally strode back into the room. "I'm taking you upstairs, where you'll be safe 'til we find him."

And without waiting for her response, he swept her into his arms. She should have protested. She should have kept chastising him. She had so much to chastise him for. But the minute she felt his arms around her, she weakened. She held on to him, as if he were all that was familiar. As if he really had held her when she had been so ill. Closing her eyes against the fresh sting of tears, she leaned her head against his neck and submitted.

"It will be all right, Gracie," he promised as he pushed open her bedroom door and carried her inside. "I promise."

"You can't promise that, Diccan," she said. "None of us can. I'll be content if you stay safe. But when this is over, you and I will need to sit down and decide how to go forward. I refuse to continue like this, Diccan. I just…can't."

"I know," he said, and he sounded sad. "But we'll have all the time in the world to deal with it."

"No," came a voice from the window. "I'm afraid you won't."

Diccan came to an abrupt halt. Grace fought a cold flood of terror. She didn't even need to open her eyes to know who was there. She did anyway.

"Diccan," she said, glaring at the man who stood before the open window, gun in hand. "I believe you know Mr. Carver."

Chapter 21

Ah, me," Mr. Carver said, sounding amused. "I was afraid of this. Leave it to you, Hilliard, to show up in your wife's bedroom for the first time in a month. I'm so glad I came prepared for you." He lifted his gun, a top-over-bottom pepperpot two-shot. "You see? I even adapted. You see, I need you both dead, and time is of the essence." He shook his head. "And I had the most lovely verse reserved to carve into your breast."

Diccan was so proud of Grace. He felt her tense at Carver's words, but she kept perfectly passive, as if completely unimpressed. "Verses," Diccan drawled, struggling to keep his own calm, his arms tight around her. "I keep hearing about verses. I think I've had my fill of the damned things."

He got a slow, chilling smile from the assassin. "And you still don't know what it means. Or who has it. Won't you be surprised?"

"I'm sure I will."

"In fact," Carver said with relish, "I think you have a lot of surprises yet to be discovered. If only you had the time.

But you see, now both of you have had a good look at me. It simply won't do."

Diccan's heart was hammering, and his hands were sweating, but he made sure Carver wouldn't know. "You seem a bit self-assured for a man who'll never get out of this house alive."

Carver was still smiling. "Don't underestimate me, Mr. Hilliard. I'll get away. And before I do, I'll recover the verse everyone is so anxious for." His smile grew. "Not from Minette, of course. She never had it. I'm sure, though, that she amply rewarded you for your thorough searches of her."

"Are you going to be tiresome and gloat, now?" Diccan asked. "Are you going to tell me who the man is behind all this, right before you put a bullet in me?"

"Man?" The Surgeon tilted his head, obviously amused. "Grace, if I were you, I would be insulted that my husband doesn't give enough credit to the fair sex. Never assume, Hilliard. It's brought down more than one spy."

"A woman is behind the attempts to discredit me?"

"In a roundabout way."

Diccan held perfectly still. In his arms, Grace kept her silence, as if withdrawing into herself. Diccan could feel the leashed tension in her, though, radiating from every taut muscle. He hoped she was paying close attention, because the next moments were vital.

"Ah, well," he said, coiling his own muscles. "I guess I'll have to apologize when I meet her. In the meantime, if you don't mind, my wife is no sylph. In fact, she's getting damn heavy."

And without hesitation, he tossed her over onto her bed.

"Now then, Mr. Carver," he said, not even watching her land, "let's continue this."

Carver barely spared a look to Grace, where she was bouncing on the bed like a tossed portmanteau. Diccan almost laughed. And Carver had chastised him for underestimating women. Carver never saw Grace reach under her pillow. He saw the gun she pulled out, but it was already too late. Before he could even turn, she shot him.

The crack rattled the windows. Smoke curled up from the gun. Carver, looking astonished, peered down to see a blood blossom at his shoulder. Before the man could remember he was still holding a gun, Diccan charged him. Grabbing the gun, Diccan crashed into the wall alongside Carver, both of them struggling for control. Carver tried to shove Diccan away. He was so close Diccan could see the black flecks in his blue eyes. He could smell the sudden fear on him. He could hear the gasp of surprised pain as he was jostled.

So Diccan butted into his shoulder, hard. Carver grunted, but he wasn't about to go down. He rammed his head at Diccan's nose. Diccan avoided it by an inch, so that their two foreheads cracked. Diccan felt his ears ring. He wrapped his free hand around Carver's throat. Carver did the same. Diccan could feel the breath wheeze in his chest. He backed up and slammed Carver into the wall again, trying to dislodge him. He pushed at the gun, still caught between them. He tightened his own hand around Carver's throat, until he swore Carver was turning purple.

"Push him away!" Grace yelled. "I can get off another shot."

He wasn't about to give Carver even that chance. He held on even more tightly, slamming his body against Carver's in a futile attempt to get free. He heard steps thunder up the stairs and for just that brief moment he let his concentration lapse. Carver took advantage and kneed him in the groin. Agony lanced him. His guts turned to jelly. But he didn't let go. He held on as Carver tried to wriggle free. He turned to get better leverage, spinning them around, each turn throwing them back against the wall.

Letting go of Carver's throat, Diccan slammed the heel of his hand against the man's nose. Carver grunted; blood spurted down his face. He gave Diccan a short jab to the ribs, taking Diccan's wind. They wrestled together, stumbling away from the wall.

"Push him away!" Grace cried again, just at Diccan's periphery.

Diccan tried to do just that. He jabbed at Carver's jaw. Carver stuck his foot beneath Diccan's in an attempt to sweep him off balance. Instead, he sent them both reeling straight into the wall.

But Carver miscalculated. They slammed into the window instead. Glass shattered against Diccan's shoulder. Wood splintered, and he felt the sudden shock of open air. He felt his feet leave the ground. He thought he heard Grace scream. Suddenly his vision was full of Carver and sky and pinwheeling trees.

Oh, hell, was all he could think as he tumbled through the air. He lost his grip on Carver and saw the gun spin by as he slammed into a tree. He heard Carver curse and branches crack as he followed. And then, with jarring abruptness, they both hit the ground, two stories down.

Bones snapped and the ground thudded with the double impact. Diccan couldn't breathe. His head felt like a burst gourd. He thought he heard people yelling in the house. He felt the jagged embrace of boxwoods, and heard a breathy chuckle from next to him.

"You're…not getting…away…this time," Diccan promised, once he could drag in air. It hurt to breathe, but not mortally. He wasn't as sure about his arm, which lay bent at an odd angle beneath him.

From next to him, Carver gave another gurgling laugh. "No," he agreed. "I don't think…I am. But I'll leave you… with…this. I should have…killed you. But who…didn't want you…dead? Who do you know…would…protect you? Even over…England?"

Diccan managed to drag himself up on an arm to see Carver splayed against the bushes next to him. A tree branch stuck straight up through the assassin's chest. Blood frothed at the corner of his mouth, and his legs were already twitching. And, damn him, he was smiling.

"Who?" Diccan asked.

"Is it a…woman?" Carver asked, his eyes beginning to fade. "Or a man? Your…cousin…or…"

Diccan leaned closer, grabbing him by the lapel. "My what?"

But his enemy just smiled. "'The whore…has…the verse.' Who else…would he…speak of…that…way…"

That was all. Bloody froth spilled from Carver's mouth, and his eyes rolled and froze. A desultory breeze lifted his hair off his forehead, and Diccan could smell death. He smelled triumph, too. The Surgeon had taken his secrets to the grave.

The whore has the verse. But not Minette.

Carver had mentioned Diccan's cousin. What would Kate have to do with anything? Diccan kept staring at the slack features beneath him. Carver had made a lot of accusations, some general and one specific. Who could he have been speaking of?

And then, from one heartbeat to the next, he knew. He closed his eyes. His brain whirled faster than the trees had. He wondered whether he'd suffered a fatal injury after all, because suddenly he couldn't get air past the searing pain in his chest.

He wanted to beat Carver, pound on the bastard's chest 'til he woke so he could take back his accusation. Because what he'd intimated simply couldn't be true.

It couldn't be.

"Diccan? Diccan!"

His strength vanishing, he finally let go of Carver and collapsed onto the ground. His arm had begun to hurt. His ribs. His head. He thought by the next morning he would be a symphony of aches and pains, caused by broken bones and bruised flesh—treatable pain. The same couldn't be said of the pain brought about by betrayal.

It couldn't be true.

Harry was the first one to reach him. Dropping by his side, the bluff blond rifleman quickly assessed him. "You going to live, old man?"

Diccan offered a wry smile. " 'Fraid so. Surgeon's come a cropper."

Harry looked over to where the Surgeon lay sprawled over the bush. "Too bad."

Diccan could hear more people following Harry out of the house. Diccan grabbed his sleeve. "Harry. Before anyone else gets here, you have to listen to me."

Harry went still in the way soldiers did. "Of course."

"I think Kate has the verse."

His eyes grew wide. "What?"

"*The whore has the verse*," Diccan quoted. "Minette isn't the only one called a whore. At least by some people I know."

He thought Harry had stopped breathing. "She's involved in all this?"

"I think so. I think that's what the Surgeon just tried to tell me."

Harry shook his head. "Why am I not surprised?"

"She's in danger, Harry."

"She's surrounded by protection, Diccan. How about we take care of you first?"

Diccan didn't get the chance to answer. Suddenly Grace was there, gasping and weeping. "Damn you, Diccan Hilliard. What were you thinking?"

She didn't kneel as much as collapse on his chest, making him wince.

"I was thinking we were still by the wall," he said, wrapping his good arm around her. "Are you all right, Gracie? I didn't hurt you?"

She was still wrapped in high dudgeon. "I reloaded. I could have taken him if you'd just moved!"

He gave her a small grin. "What do you think sent us out the window?"

Her face slackened in dismay. "Oh."

He couldn't help it. "I thought you were the one who could pip an ace at four hundred yards. What happened?"

Ah, there it was. That marvelously unique blush that he knew for a fact spread right up from her toes. She dropped her head, and shuddered. "Harps will never forgive me."

"I don't know," Harry mused. "Looks to me like this dead man has a big gunshot wound to the shoulder here."

Grace glared at him. "I wasn't aiming for his shoulder."

Diccan felt bad when he realized how ashamed she was. "Grace," he said, pulling her against him, "we're fine and the Surgeon is dead. That's all that matters."

Although it wasn't. But he wasn't going to be able to deal with the rest right now. Fortunately, hot on the heels of that thought, the rest of the wedding party arrived, and he didn't have the time anyway.

Diccan knew he should have faced his adversary alone. But he couldn't seem to leave Grace behind. He hadn't realized until now, but she gave him calm. She gave him strength. And God knew he was going to need it by the time this interview was over. He brought Marcus and asked him to wait in the salon, because he knew the interview was not going to end well.

It didn't.

"You tried to have my wife murdered," he said baldly.

They were fifteen miles from Oak Grove in the library of Moorhaven Castle, the perfect place for a family confrontation. Thankfully, his cousin Edwin, the Duke of Livingston, had never questioned Diccan's need for an interview or his request for privacy. Even more fortuitously, as part of their purported visit to the family, Diccan's mother and sisters were off with the duchess, making calls.

The library itself seemed to reinforce the reason for the visit. A testament to male dominance, it was a symphony of rich oak wainscoting, thick Persian carpets, green wall coverings, and overstuffed chairs, all complementing a priceless collection of books that Diccan couldn't remember anyone actually reading. A statement of power and wealth and heritage. The most fitting place to meet his father.

Stolidly seated in one of the brown leather chairs, Diccan's father responded to the accusation just as he would have if a subordinate had questioned his word, with no more than a lifted eyebrow. He was wearing his collar and ecclesiastic cross and chain, as if on his way to some important ritual. Beyond him, Grace sat on a matching leather couch, so still you could almost imagine she wasn't there, even in her pretty salmon day dress. It was a knack she had, Diccan thought, the ability to seem as if she wouldn't even leave an imprint on the couch; to be there yet not be there. Right now, he was grateful for it. He was grateful for *her*.

He was standing in the center of the room, his broken left arm in a sling, his head still ringing and every inch of his body protesting movement. He hadn't been able to wait until he felt better to have this meeting, though. He had to confront his father here, where they could be alone.

"Tell me you aren't that much of a coward, Bishop," he said, his own voice colder than death. "Tell me you haven't waged a campaign to ruin my good name and terrorize my wife."

The Bishop sneered. "Your good name? You have no good name. You forfeited that years ago with your first duel. And now you've had what, four? And how many mistresses? It isn't a surprise you're accused of such crimes. The surprise is that it hasn't happened before."

Not a word of denial. Not an outraged protest that Diccan could even think such a thing.

"We couldn't figure it out, you know," Diccan said, taking a quick look at Grace for reassurance. "After all, when Jack Gracechurch unearthed the conspiracy against the

Crown, he was hunted down like a fox. When I brought evidence to support his claim, though, I was...married. Then I was told to reunite with my old mistress, and my wife was forced into a despicable situation in an effort to turn her against me. And then, Bishop, she was fed arsenic. Slowly. Deliberately. She was used as a pawn in a game she hadn't asked to play." He shook his head, as if still bemused. "It all involved so much effort. So many players. We just couldn't understand why the Surgeon didn't just come after me some dark night and slit my throat."

He saw Grace flinch, but he couldn't react. His focus was on his father, whose expression had hardened even further.

"You mean you ruined an innocent girl, shamed her, and then poisoned her to be free to return to your whore," the old man accused.

"And then," Diccan continued, as if his father hadn't spoken, "you and Mother arrived out of the blue at a home you've never visited, to spirit me out of the country. Any sane person would wonder why you'd pick this moment in my life to suddenly show concern."

That brought his father to his feet. "You're the only son I have left! Do you think I would just let you be destroyed? Do you think I'd let that monster carve you up for the sport of it? I'm your *father*."

Diccan froze, stunned to immobility. He saw such emotion in his father's eyes, and for once, it wasn't disdain. It wasn't disappointment. It was desperation.

Diccan couldn't comprehend it. It was too foreign a phenomenon to digest. His father worried about *him*?

"And Grace means nothing?" he asked.

His father waved off his objection. "She's a soldier's

daughter. She knows some sacrifices are made for the good of all. And you would have been safe. Your reputation might have suffered for a bit, you would have spent a few years in the Indies, but you would have been *alive*. Don't you see?"

He did, and the enormity of it was unbearable. His father meant what he'd said. He had waged his campaign against Grace to save his son from his own allies.

He was a Lion.

"Why?" Diccan finally asked. "What could make you betray your country?"

"Betray it?" his father retorted, rigid with fury. "I'm helping save it! Don't you see what's happening around you? Financial ruin! Riots in the streets! A call for revolution! And who do we have to protect us? A mad king. An incompetent, profligate heir. Whigs, who are trying to pull us into chaos, and Tories who don't really see the danger around them. If we don't do something now, there will be no England to defend!"

Grief pierced Diccan, sharp and sudden. "And to protect England," he said, "You would assassinate one of its greatest leaders?"

His father snorted. "The last thing anyone could call the Prince of Wales is great."

Diccan battled a growing sense of unreality. *They were going to assassinate Prinny, too? Yes*, he thought, after a moment's consideration. *Of course they'd have to kill him. It was the only way to put Princess Charlotte on the throne.*

"He's speaking of Wellington," Grace said, from her place on the couch.

Diccan's father spun around as if she'd sprung out of

the wall. Diccan wasn't surprised. But one look into her eyes revealed the implacable steel at the core of this quiet woman.

"Wellington?" his father retorted with a sharp laugh. "Don't be daft, girl."

"The attempt is going to be made sometime before November," Diccan said. "I heard it myself."

For the first time, his father looked uncertain. He looked around, as if he could find reassurance somewhere. Finally, in an instinctive gesture Diccan recognized, he took hold of his cross. Not as a symbol of his faith, but as a symbol of his power. "That's absurd. Why would they?"

It was Diccan's turn to lift an eyebrow. "Could you see the Duke of Wellington standing patiently by as his country was attacked? Can you not imagine how easy it would be for him to raise the army to battle you? No, Father. He has to be taken care of before the plans are set into motion. The only thing lacking is a verse."

The bishop huffed. "That isn't what the . . ."

Red-faced, he clamped his mouth shut.

"Then you know about the verse," Diccan said, stepping closer. "A verse the 'whore' has. Didn't you call my cousin Kate a whore?"

The bishop bridled. "That woman *is* a whore."

Diccan shook his head. "We'll discuss that slander later. Does she have the verse?"

His father blinked, as if suddenly realizing who it was he was talking to. Not his son, but the enemy. He flushed. He shook his head. Briefly closing his eyes, as if in prayer, he sat back down and turned away.

Diccan went over to kneel before him, a position he'd given up long ago. "Don't you understand?" he asked to his father's turned head. "You could be drawn and quartered for what you've just told me."

His father never turned. "And you would turn me in?"

"I'd have to." Diccan dragged a breath past the jagged edge of sorrow. "I love my country too."

His father said nothing. Diccan waited, but there was no more. He felt devastated. He couldn't even begin to contemplate what this would mean. His father had just admitted to treason. His father, a duke's brother. A Lord Spiritual. Even though Diccan had suspected his father's crime when he'd come, the enormity of it would take months, maybe years, to sink in. His father was a traitor to the Crown.

"Grace," he finally said, standing up, "Would you bring Marcus in?"

Meeting his gaze with one of unwavering support, Grace got to her feet. She never said a word. She just laid her hand on his arm on her way by. It was the only spot of warmth in his entire body.

"Wellington truly is a target?" his father asked, still looking away.

"Yes," Diccan said, walking to the window, where he could see the sky.

"Wait," his father said, a hand out. "You, too, young lady."

Her hand on the door, Grace paused. Diccan turned.

"Before you hand me over to the soldiers," his father said, sounding curiously hollow, "there is something you should know."

Diccan met his father's gaze and saw defeat. "What?"

The bishop looked over at Grace. "She was convenient. Someone with the kind of reputation that could ruin yours if you ran, as any sensible man should have done. But I'd never met her until that day. I didn't realize…" He cast a quick glance at Grace, who now stood stock-still, and returned to Diccan. "She was never worthy of the Hilliard name. You deserve better."

Diccan laughed. "Don't be daft. She's worth more than all of us put together."

"Of course she isn't. Which is why I couldn't allow your marriage."

Diccan felt as if he'd stumbled at the edge of a precipice. "What?"

He fought a surge of nausea, because his father smiled, as if he had just given Diccan a gift.

"You're not married."

Chapter 22

Diccan heard a a small sound of distress behind him, but he couldn't look away from his father. "As a method of revenge, this falls short, Father. If there is anything in all this mess that is unquestionable, it is my marriage."

"Not revenge," his father said, his hand still on his cross. "Don't you see? Even for this I couldn't condemn you to a life with this woman."

"Father," Diccan said, as if instructing a toddler. "Don't you remember? Cousin Charles performed the service. He said the words himself that wed Richard Hilliard to Miss Grace Fairchild. Even you couldn't challenge the Archbishop of Canterbury."

His father was shaking his head. "Not Richard Hilliard. *Robert*. I wrote your brother Robert's name on the license. I knew no one would look closely enough to catch it."

Diccan felt as if he'd been kicked in the gut. Stalking over to his father, he dragged him to his feet. "Tell me you're lying."

His father pulled Diccan's hands away. "I never lie. I

know you don't like to accept anything from me, but when you've had time to consider, you'll realize the favor I've done you. I've set you free."

Diccan couldn't move. Behind him, the door opened and closed. He could actually feel her go, deep inside him where she had taken to living. But he didn't move to stop her. He had no right to. After all, no matter what his father said, he wasn't the one who had just been set free.

Diccan realized in that moment that his father was wrong. It wasn't the marriage that would destroy him. It was the ending of it.

He stepped back, his words an implacable weight. "Lord Evelyn Hilliard, I arrest you in the name of the King."

"I won't go to jail, you know," his father said, straightening the coat Diccan had rumpled. "The government can't afford the scandal."

"That isn't my decision to make."

He tried to turn away. His father grabbed him. "Think of what this will do to your mother."

Diccan refused to face him. "I will look after my mother and sisters."

"Your mother won't let you anywhere near her. Let me go."

"No, sir."

It should have ended there. He should have been able to turn his father over to Marcus and escort Grace away from this house, to somewhere where he could begin to undo some of the damage his father had just done. Somewhere he and Grace could begin to construct a new life. He should have known better.

Marcus had a carriage waiting outside. With apologies to his cousin Edwin, Diccan escorted his now-silent father through the massive old hall to the great oak doors, which were held open by the duke's very correct butler. Marcus followed Diccan outside, Grace trailing silently behind.

After the dimness of the castle, Diccan blinked at the sudden sunlight. He saw the coach at the bottom of the steps, with a brace of outriders waiting to mount. He heard the querulous tones of his cousin as he demanded that the butler shut the door. He led his father down the steps. Suddenly, his father stumbled. In the same moment, Diccan heard a distinctive crack.

"Gun!" he yelled, pulling at the older man. "Everybody down!"

He saw Grace hit the ground, her attention out where the gunshot still echoed over the valley. Marcus charged down the steps. Diccan tried to get his father down, but it was as if the bishop had turned to stone. He stood stockstill, with the most bemused expression on his face.

"Father?"

His father managed to look up, but he was already toppling. Before Diccan could catch him, the bishop pitched over and rolled all the way down the stone steps, to land motionless on the gravel.

Diccan ran to where he lay, Grace following on his heels. Marcus yelled at his outriders to find the gunman.

"Sharpshooter," Grace said quietly, as she dropped to her knees by his father. She pointed toward a stand of trees off to the right. "Over there."

Marcus shot her a wry look. The outriders took off. His heart thundering in his chest, Diccan rolled his father over, ready to do something. Anything.

But there was nothing to do. His father was dead.

• • •

The day before Grace's nineteenth birthday, she had been swept into a rain-swollen river. It had been spring, and her father, then a colonel, was bringing up a battalion of Guards to reinforce Wellington's forces in Spain. Afraid he was going to miss an engagement, the colonel was hard-marching his soldiers and Grace across the difficult terrain of Portugal.

It had never occurred to Grace that she couldn't cross the nameless mountain stream. She had crossed dozens of others, and she was atop her dependable roan, Joker. This time, though, Joker stumbled. Suddenly Grace found herself catapulted headfirst into the roiling, boulder-strewn waters and swept inexorably downriver.

She remembered the terrible feeling of disorientation and panic. The struggle for air, the tantalizing glimpse of sky that kept disappearing before she could reach it. Most of all, though, she remembered the feeling of futility that overtook her as she flailed helplessly in the water, the sense that no matter how hard she struggled, she would ultimately drown.

She hadn't drowned, of course. Kit Braxton had dived in after her and dragged her to shore, a mile downstream. But the memory still gave her nightmares.

She felt exactly the same right now. Tumbled and battered and disoriented. Angry and panicked. Hollow with the growing sense of futility. She had lost Diccan. No. She should be honest. The truth was, of course, that she'd never had him. He had been kind, and he had done his best with the cards dealt him. But his father had been right. He was free.

He would protest, of course. He was an honorable man. He would not want to see her ruined any more than he had before. But Grace could not bear the thought that she would be punishing him to gain security.

They had agreed that they wouldn't tell their friends the truth until after Jack and Olivia's wedding. After all, the atmosphere had been dimmed enough by the death of Diccan's father. The truth about the bishop's death would never be told. Evelyn Hilliard, Bishop of Slough, had been slain when he uncovered a plot against the Crown. That was the story the Arch bishop of Canterbury would give out when he arrived to bless his cousin's passing. It was the only way to protect Diccan's mother and sisters.

Grace had finally met Diccan's sisters, pale, quiet Charlotte and restless young Winnie, looking to their brother for comfort, and at their new sister with suspicion. Grace had wanted so badly to help, but Diccan's mother wouldn't even allow her close. Considering the shape Lady Evelyn was in, it was the least Grace could do to stay away.

Lady Evelyn's reaction had been the greatest shock in a week of shocks. That rigid, superior woman, who looked down on every other human, had been shattered by the bishop's death. Evidently, she had adored her hidebound husband.

"Grace?" she heard in her ear now. "Are you all right?"

"Oh, yes, thank you," she answered automatically. "I'm fine."

She struggled to attend to her surroundings. It was Kate who had spoken. They were sitting side by side at a table in the Great Hall at Oak Grove, surrounded by chatter and laughter and the desultory clinking of glasses and forks. For a moment Grace wasn't quite certain why she was there. Then she heard Jack laugh. Oh, Heavens. She had let her mind wander off right in the middle of Jack and Olivia's wedding breakfast.

She wished she could have blamed her mental lapse on the turmoil of the last few days. But the truth was that she had done it deliberately. She felt so small, but it hurt to see the happiness in Jack's and Olivia's eyes. To see them finally happy, when they'd been through so much.

The ceremony itself had been simple and sincere, conducted by the local vicar in the the little Norman church in Bury. Her eyes shining as she looked up at her husband, Olivia had looked indescribably beautiful in her pale blush dress and straw cottage bonnet. From the besotted look on Jack's face as he smiled at her, he'd evidently agreed. Grace doubted they had noticed anyone else in the church.

Grace wasn't used to feeling envy. She didn't like it. But she envied her friends. She envied them their friendship, their devotion, their hope. She envied them most their joy. Theirs was the kind of marriage she wanted. It was the kind of marriage Diccan deserved.

She looked around, almost expecting to see him. He wouldn't be there, of course. He was attending his mother.

"Grace," Kate chastised her. "At least do your bit to keep Olivia's chef from quitting in a huff. Eat a lobster patty."

Instinctively, Grace put on a smile and picked up a delicacy that she knew would taste like ashes on her tongue. "I should probably save it for Diccan. He hates to miss out on lobster patties."

"If you want to please Diccan," Kate suggested, "toss the lobster to the cat. Cadge him a bottle of champagne."

Grace smiled again, although not as brightly. "I already have. He's had such a bad few days."

"His mother is still...?"

"Silent and hollow-eyed? Yes, from what I hear."

Kate nodded. "Well, tell Diccan that I won't go near the funeral. It would be the last thing that woman would need. Besides, I am in no rush to visit my exalted family."

Grace frowned. "Oh, Kate, no. He needs you there."

Kate took a sip of wine. "Don't be silly. He'll have you."

A fresh wave a pain assailed her. How did she tell her friend that it was very possible he wouldn't? That Grace would be forbidden to attend by the tenets of taste and propriety? Diccan swore that his father had only made that claim about their marriage to hurt him. But Grace had seen the look in that old man's eyes, and she disagreed. She knew her marriage would last only as long as it took the archbishop to arrive with the official documents.

"Well," Kate said, suddenly, settling her fuchsia dress around her as she stood, "it looks as if it is time to send our lovebirds off."

Grace turned to see that Olivia and Jack indeed stood by the doorway, dressed for their short wedding trip to the Isle of Wight. Their son Jamie was jumping up and down, Jack's sister Georgie holding his hand. The rest of the party was gathering to send the newlyweds off.

It was then that Grace saw Diccan. He was just strolling in the door, languid and smiling, his poise wrapped about him like a cloak. But Grace could see the effort it took. He looked gaunt to her, brittle. Was she the only one who saw how tense he was? How weighted down his shoulders? He was laughing with Jack, giving Olivia a buss on the cheek. The couple laid hands on his arm. Grace could almost hear their concern. Diccan gently smiled it away.

She had ached to be able to comfort him, to pull his

head against her shoulder and let him rest. But his mother couldn't seem to abide Grace being about, as if she were a fly someone had let in the window. So she had stayed away.

She knew the minute he saw her. His expression didn't change. But she felt the change in him anyway. Her heart sped up. She felt frozen. She could see in his eyes that something that happened.

She had to last until Olivia and Jack had been seen safely into the Gracechurch carriage for their trip, everyone laughing and throwing flowers, the children running after the carriage like puppies. Then Diccan sauntered over to where she stood with Kate on the top step.

"Well, don't they look smug and silly," he greeted them, his attention still on the departing couple.

"I believe it is a prescribed state of weddings," Kate said easily. "Terrified and nauseous, smug and silly, exhausted and cranky."

"I'm glad you made it," Grace told him.

He gave her one trenchant look before looking away. "We need to talk."

Grace nodded. "Kate suggested I save you some lobster and champagne."

He couldn't even seem to come up with a witty comeback. He just shook his head and smiled. She stepped forward, wanting to help him. To touch him, hold him to her so he could know he didn't face this alone. She pulled up short, though, suddenly uncertain. Everything had changed. Diccan was no longer obliged to tolerate her concern.

Kate had no such reservation. Grace saw her step up to Diccan's other side and take his arm. He looked down at the beautiful duchess, his smile softening. No words were exchanged. Grace knew they didn't need them, and it hurt all the more.

"Come along then, my girls," he said, lifting both elbows for their hands. "There are matters of import we must discuss."

Grace's courage faltered. It was one thing to lay her wounds bare to Diccan. It was quite another to include Kate.

It seemed Diccan could read her like a book. "Come, my Boadicea. 'If it were done when 'tis done, then 'twere well it were done quickly.'"

Grace's heart stumbled. Still she gave him a comical grimace. "That, my dear, was not Boadicea. It was Lady Macbeth."

Kate grinned. "And if anybody is going to be called Lady Macbeth here, I think it should be I."

Kate was not nearly as amused ten minutes later when Diccan filled her in on the situation.

"What in blazes do you mean, you're not married?" the little duchess demanded, actually on her feet with outrage. "I bought you a present!"

They had retired to Jack's study, closing out the noise of the departing guests. Grace sat on the couch, her hands clasped in her lap to give them something to do, her heart withering in her chest. Diccan leaned against the oak desk, his arms crossed. Kate stood between them, glaring.

"We received a messenger from Cousin Charles today," Diccan said, his attention now swinging to Grace, his expression rueful. "He didn't think it would be prudent for us to wait to find out about our marital status until he arrived later this week. He sends his regrets and all that. The name on the license is indeed Robert. You are now a widow, my dear."

Grace wanted to shrink farther into the couch. She wanted to run and run and run. It was only by force of will that she kept her place.

"That's not funny, Diccan," Kate snapped. "We have to get Charles to rectify his mistake the minute he gets here."

Diccan nodded. "He has already said that he will."

"Good." Kate started pacing. "I know it isn't the thing to mix weddings and funerals, but I don't see you have a choice. I imagine Olivia and Jack wouldn't mind if we had another wedding here. I assume the archbishop is bringing a special license."

Finally, Grace could wait no longer. Her hands still clasped, she came to her feet. "No," she said simply, and was relieved that her voice didn't sound as desperate as she felt.

Diccan and Kate turned surprised expressions her way, as if they'd just heard the couch speak. "No, what?" Diccan asked.

"Bugger *no*," Kate said baldly. "You have no choice."

Oh, how it hurt to have to play this scene again. Before Grace had only suspected how she would feel if Diccan broke her heart. Now she knew. "No," she repeated softly. "Your father is right, Diccan. He has given you a second chance. He has given both of us a second chance to choose instead of being forced." She gathered every ounce of courage she had and stood before the man she'd thought was her husband, and she met the denial in his eyes with certainty. "No."

"But you'll be ruined," he said, so gently she wanted to weep.

So she smiled. "It still doesn't matter to me, Diccan. All I ever really wanted was to nest on my little piece of land and raise horses. I don't need a society pedigree to do that. And you don't need the marriage to save your political career. I think it will be quite easy to spread the story that our marriage was a clever ploy to help you unearth traitors."

She saw a world of understanding in Diccan's hypnotic gray eyes. She saw pain and regret and loss. But she knew he agreed. Her poor battered heart bled a little more at his quick acceptance.

"It will help that Marcus is in London to bring warrants against more of the Lions," he said. "We at least have that. My father was arrogant enough to have left evidence in his luggage."

"Your name is cleared?" Grace asked.

"It will be. Marcus promised to talk to General Dawes."

That was another question Grace wasn't sure she wanted answered. What role had her uncle really played in all this?

"What about your role as Apprentice Lion?"

Diccan shrugged. "Minette has disappeared, as has Smythe. I imagine I'll just have to wait and see if someone else approaches me."

"Be careful," Grace said, her hand instinctively on his arm. "Please."

His smile was pale. "I will."

"Excuse me," Kate interrupted. "As intrigued as I am by all of this, I demand we return to the matter at hand. Your marriage. You are not just going to walk away from it. I won't allow it."

It was Diccan who calmed Kate. "Grace is right, old girl. She's been given a second chance. Why should she settle for a layabout like me? If I were she, I'd run back to that sweet estate of hers posthaste."

Grace hadn't thought she could feel worse. She did then, because she realized she would never walk through Longbridge again without seeing Diccan there, reminding her what her life might have been if his father had never spoken.

Diccan took Grace gently into his arms. "You've been trumps, my dear. A perfect lady. I only wish you had been served better in all of this."

Briefly Grace closed her eyes and succumbed to the comfort of Diccan's embrace. "Don't be silly," she said, her voice wavering only a bit. "I wouldn't have missed it for the world. But I think it is just about time for me to retreat."

"Will you stay here for the funeral?"

"If you want me to."

He did. So she stayed at Oak Grove, just long enough to see Diccan's father buried and his mother settled temporarily in the dower house at the castle. She withstood his mother's rancor and supported his sisters and held Diccan's hand when he needed it. And she did it without the help of Kate or Bea, who kept Kate's promise not to attend the funeral. By the time Grace climbed into the coach for the Moorhaven chapel, her friends were already on their way to London.

So it was that she had no friends with her when her life with Diccan officially ended. The mourners were just returning to Moorhaven from the bishop's interment, Diccan in their lead. The archbishop passed by Grace without a word. Diccan's mother hadn't even shown her face. Grace stood on the gravel drive, just about where Diccan's father had fallen, watching as Diccan approached.

He looked so strained, so stretched. But no one else seemed to see it.

"Well, Grace," he greeted her with a sad smile.

She smiled back, knowing it was good-bye. "Well, Diccan."

The mourners passed around them, like a river around rocks, but Grace didn't notice. She was busy memorizing Diccan's features, his scent, his smile. She was saying good-bye without a word. He answered with a nod.

Marcus Drake stood off to the side, as if officiating. "I wonder who that is," he was saying.

Diccan looked up and froze. Grace followed his gaze to see a traveling coach pull to a stop at the end of the lane. She shot Diccan a startled glance. The coach wasn't marked, but all the same, she knew it. She saw that Diccan did, too. She meant to say something. Then the door opened, and out stepped not only Harps, but Breege and Bhanwar, his white robes catching the morning sunlight and his sword gleaming. Pain swelled in Grace's chest; tears threatened.

"Well, it's about time," Diccan groused. Grace looked up to see him smiling. "I'm sorry it took so long for them to get here, Grace. I should have brought them sooner so they could have protected you."

She couldn't think of anything to do but throw her arms around him. People stared. The Duchess of Livingston made a harrumphing noise. Grace didn't care. Diccan had done this last thing for her, and she couldn't even tell him what it meant to her.

"Be happy, my Grace," he whispered in her ear, holding her tightly.

A sob caught in her throat. "You, too, Diccan. You deserve it."

Before she could weaken and beg him to let her stay, she gave him one final kiss and ran down the lane and into Breege's arms. And then, without looking back, she climbed into the carriage and made her lonely way home.

• • •

Thirty miles away in Guildford, Frank Shaw pulled the Murther traveling coach around the corner of the Angel Inn. He was late. It wasn't his fault; the ostlers had had trouble poling up the fresh horses. Not that it would matter in the end. It was his job to be on time. But you'd think that as often as the duchess stopped here, they'd figure out how to move faster for her.

Deftly guiding the four-in-hand through the crowded courtyard, he looked around, gauging the activity. To his right a stagecoach was discharging its passengers. Two middle-aged women in gray struggled with overlarge bandboxes. A couple ushered along three little terrors who shrieked with glee as they raced across the cobbles. A schoolboy, not much older than the terrors, kept pace with a round, red-faced vicar. All hurried toward the half-timbered inn for the meal they'd been promised.

Beyond the coach, a flashy young blade was turning his phaeton into the exit. The lad must have known his business, because he swung through the arch into High Street without a scrape, leaving Frank's way completely clear. He nodded in satisfaction. His horses were fresh and they were prime. Once he was through that same arch, he should be able to get a good run out of them.

Now, if only the duchess wasn't dragging her little feet over tea.

Ah, there she was, just stepping out into the courtyard, a tiny slip of a thing with lots of plumes in her bonnet and big, pretty eyes. She was talking to a grim-faced old biddy who had a good foot on her, patting the old gal's cheeks with a handkerchief. Not so perfect.

Oh, well, Frank thought. You worked with what you got. Skirting the stage, he brought his own restive team to a halt right in front of the women.

"Ho, there!" he yelled to one of the postboys. "Help the lady!"

The boy, a gawky carrottop, scurried up to grab the door. Frank tightened up his hold on the reins. The boy turned to the passengers. Frank eased off the brake. He saw the plumes nod on the duchess's bonnet as she climbed the steps and surreptitiously lifted his whip. The postboy turned back for the old woman.

Now! Frank thought. With a shout, he cracked the whip over the near leader. The horses whinnied and jerked into motion. Frank heard the carriage door slam as the postboy lost his balance. He hoped the boy was all right, because he couldn't stop for him or the old lady who still stood there with her hand out and her mouth gaping. Pulling with all his might, he turned his horses out of the courtyard onto High Street. He was scraping through the arch when he heard the shouts behind him. They were too late though. He had the duchess, and they weren't going to stop him. He had a delivery to make.

Chapter 23

It had been a long day. It had been a long few weeks, ever since Kate's disappearance. Hearing of the abduction, Grace had immediately traveled to London to help any way she could. When there was nothing left for her to do, she'd returned home.

Now winter was approaching, and there was much to do to prepare Longbridge. There was even more that Grace chose to do to make the estate resemble the home she'd held in her mind for twenty years. Today it meant overseeing her cadre of ex-soldiers as they laid a foundation for the stable extension.

Once again tanned and healthy, her soldiers worked hard out under the autumn sun, one old sailor singing a hauling shanty as they laid in the heavy stones. Harper supervised, but this was Grace's future. She helped Bhanwar cook meals for the workers. She stood with Harper as he directed the work, and she bent with the men to set the stones. She had blisters and a sunburn and felt the pleasant exhaustion of accomplishment.

She wanted the stables finished before the snow flew. She had already seen the hay cut and the harvest in. She had helped Breege and Radhika put up the fruit from the orchard. Tomorrow she would stop by the home farm in the morning and spend the afternoon making sure enough wood was cut to keep the estate cozy throughout the coldest days.

It would be her first winter in her home. She needed it to be everything she had ever wanted.

"Dear, have you seen that terrible simian?" a voice called from the pantry as Grace and Breege passed through the bustling kitchen.

Grace smiled. "Mr. Pitt is up watching over Ruchi and Lizzy's baby, Aunt Dawes."

Underneath her old Guards jacket, Grace was wearing black. Two weeks earlier, she had suffered yet another loss. Her Uncle Dawes, hunting right at the front of the Belvoir pack, had taken his best charger over a stone fence and come down on his neck. He had never recovered from the fact that he had unwittingly conspired with traitors. It was only after his death that the government had acknowledged that the greathearted old warrior had acted out of good faith, never knowing that villains had taken advantage of him.

At the funeral, attended by Wellington himself, Grace had invited Aunt Dawes to come live with her. Facing her loss with the kind of gruff courage that had endeared her to her formidable husband, Aunt Dawes had agreed, insisting that Grace needed a chaperone. Surprisingly, she developed an exceptional affinity for Mr. Pitt, so that quite often she and Pitt and little Ruchi could be found together, having tea and decorating hats. It gave Aunt Dawes purpose and Ruchi a grandmother. As for the monkey, he looked surprisingly coy in a cottage bonnet.

"I think I'm early to bed tonight," Grace told Breege as they walked through the green baize door into the front hallway. "It'll be another very long day tomorrow."

Breege harrumphed. "Sure, you know stone layin' is men's work."

Grace couldn't help but smile. "I've waited my whole life for this, Breege. Let me enjoy it."

Breege shook her grizzled head. "A body could enjoy it just as well from a few feet back."

A body could certainly find it less painful, Grace admitted. Her leg hurt. Her back hurt. The blisters on her hands hurt. But it felt delicious. She had worked hard, and she'd done it for what she wanted. The added bonus was that it had also been what her little family wanted as well.

She passed the Red Parlor she had decorated in silk pillows and samovars. The library was filled with artifacts she had brought home from Canada, and the morning room, with her majolica. She had saved the jade for her office, a paneled den she'd painted cream to show off the shelves of luminous green. Her carpets were from Persia and her silk wall hangings from China, every room an explosion of color and texture. And she was only getting started. She still had twenty more packing crates to dig through.

As she passed the front hall table, she centered the small gold painted statue of Lord Ganesha, the elephant god. He was always kept near the front door to bring in good luck. Grace knew she needed it now more than ever.

"You want a bath before bed?" Breege asked.

Grace almost groaned. "No. I'm too tired for even that."

As every evening, she and Breege would part at the great stairway, Breege doing her final rounds before retiring to the housekeeper's suite and Grace climbing the stairs to her own room. Their habit on parting had long been a nod of the head, a pat on the arm. Now Grace made it a point to hug the hefty woman. Breege was still surprised by the gesture, but she hugged back with all her massive strength.

It was the greatest lesson Grace had learned in these last weeks. To never let anything keep you from letting those you loved know how you felt. It was the surest way she knew to keep regret at bay.

God knew she had enough of that. It lay on her shoulders like a shroud, the weight of it eased only by the affection of her friends. But she would never have the chance to tell Uncle Dawes how much he'd meant to her. She would never be able to hug her father and tell him she loved him. She would never have her Grenadiers back, the friends she'd lost to countless battlefields without ever thanking them for making an ugly, ungainly girl feel special.

But the worst regret followed her right up the stairs and into her bedroom. Lizzy was waiting when she walked into the room, a flannel nightgown laid out on the bed.

"Oh, not flannel," Grace objected. "I'll be in it soon enough. What about my caftan?"

"Well, it'll sure go better with the new furniture."

Grace smiled. She had unpacked her first crate here. She had known from the day she'd walked into that *zenena* at fourteen what her bedroom would one day look like. Her walls were hung in orange and purple silk, the color of a desert sunrise. The chandelier dripped multicolored glass petals, and the windows were draped in gold-embroidered saris. On the bed, a low platform topped with a headboard of carved Ceylon teak, she had created a nest of silk pillows in a rainbow of colors; lime, hot yellow, royal blue, peacock. A symphony of colors, a riot of hue.

She had kept her best artwork for these walls no one else saw. Her father had never realized just what kind of art she'd been collecting in the Indian and Turkish bazaars all those years and had hidden away, or what it was the ladies of the harem had taught her to paint. It was hidden away no longer. Her walls were populated by exquisitely beautiful women and men painted in bright colors, caught in the eternal dance of erotic love. Knowing now exactly what it was those women felt as they smiled up at their paramours, Grace battled a fresh wave of envy. They would forever be locked in the most intimate moment of life, their pleasure at its pinnacle, their world captured in primal colors. While Grace, who had briefly touched that place, had been forced back out into the darkness.

It was here she missed Diccan the most. Oh, she missed him other places. She thought of him every time she rode Epona. She saw him lifting his quizzing glass at some of her renovations and putting on his best manners when asked to tea by Ruchi and Aunt Dawes. She heard his laughter and smelled his sandalwood, and it stole some of the joy from her new life.

"Will there be anything else, Ma'am?" Lizzy asked.

"Thank you, no, Lizzy. Good night."

Lizzy softly closed the door behind her, leaving Grace where she sat at her dressing table, her hair down and her nightwear on. Feeling nostalgic, Grace fingered the sleek royal blue and gold silk of the caftan she'd found in Cairo. She so clearly remembered the day she'd bought it, one of her first forays into the city. She could see the jumbled, teeming alleys of the bazaar, where she'd been forced to duck to keep from knocking down the hanging merchandise: flower garlands, necklaces, copperware, fabric and rope and herbs. She could smell dust and spices, horses and camels, the exotic smoke of incense and the earthy tang of coffee.

Grace had thought it all magnificent: colors washed by the sun, voices raised in a dozen languages, men sitting cross-legged on the ground as they haggled prices. She wished she could tell Diccan about it. She had the feeling that he loved travel stories more than he'd let on.

Outside her open window, a brisk October breeze rustled in the trees. The sky, that peculiar peacock of fall, was lit by a lone star. The sun was gone, and a long night was begun. It was the nights that bothered her most. Diccan came to her in the nights, whispering in her ear, worshiping her body, accidentally scattering futile promises before her like rose petals.

It was in the night Grace admitted that the dream that had sustained her for so long was no longer enough. She had her home. She had her little family. She had every ornament she had collected over the years to comfort her. And yet, the edge was gone from her contentment. The colors weren't as bright nor the accomplishments as satisfying. She couldn't remember how to be happy. Diccan had taken that with him.

"Will you tell me what you're thinking?" she heard behind her.

The voice sounded so real that she gasped. Her heart began to race and her chest tightened. She looked up into her mirror, searching the shadows behind her. She was so afraid she had summoned him, a delusion to soothe her loneliness. Tears stung her eyes and clogged her throat.

It was another inheritance from her short marriage. She wept now. She wept when she got the news about Uncle Dawes, and she wept when she removed her first pillow from its crate. She was afraid she would weep now for nothing more than a chimera in the dark.

"Go away," she said out loud, as if that could scare off her own pitiful dreams.

"And if I don't?"

She squeezed her eyes shut, desperate for sanity. She couldn't seem to stop trembling, though. Her heart wouldn't slow.

"Open your eyes, Gracie," he said, and she couldn't help it. She did.

She braced herself for disappointment. Instead she received a shock. Her heart lurched into her throat, and her insides seemed to melt. He had just stepped out of the shadows.

He looked tired. His corbeau coat and buckskins were a bit mussed, as if he'd been careless with them, something Grace could never have imagined. But his eyes were still that ghostly gray, and his face still missed being handsome by a broad brow. It was all she could do to keep from bowing with the pain of seeing him again.

"What are you doing here?"

"I had a bit of a break, and there was someone I needed to see."

She swore her heart was going to tumble out of her chest. "There was?"

"There was. There's only one problem."

He stepped right up behind her, a dark fantasy reflected in her mirror. "It seems the monkey is still in my bed."

She couldn't help it. She laughed, an abrupt, surprised sound. "Don't be silly. Mr. Pitt has no need for you now that Ruchi and Aunt Dawes feed him teacakes and licorice."

His eyes glinted with amusement and something Grace

was afraid to name. "A sad day when a man can't even rely on his monkey."

"Diccan." He was so close he was stealing her breath. Her body recognized him and began to sing. "Why are you here?"

He stepped right up behind her and bent to rest his head atop hers, dark to light, fierce to frightened. "There still seems to be a small argument that needs settling between us."

She couldn't even answer. Desire was so tangled up with terror that she couldn't get a word past either. It seemed she didn't need to. Without asking permission, Diccan leaned closer and wrapped his hands around her to cup her breasts.

The shock froze her. The sweet pleasure melted her. The impossibility crippled her.

"You've taken to dyeing the rest of your hair to match your maiden-hair?" he asked, his voice a low rumble in her ear.

She sat as still as an animal caught in a hunter's sights. She was trembling hard now. He was nibbling her ear, nuzzling her hair, kneading her breasts. Sapping her reason like a siphon.

Before she could succumb, she yanked away and jumped to her feet, whirling to face him, her caftan swirling around her. Her legs were so rubbery she had to clutch the dresser.

"No," she said as clearly as she could before she couldn't. "I *stopped* dyeing my hair. This is its natural color. 'Whore's red' my mother used to call it. The vicar who baptized me at St. John's in Calcutta called it an abomination. So I bleached the sin out of it so no soldier would get the wrong idea. But I'm not bleaching it back, ever again. This is who I am, Diccan. Now, I want to know what you want."

His eyes widened just a bit, but he was smiling, and it ate at her strength. "Truly?"

She straightened, a pillar of dignity and hard-won pride. "Truly."

Oddly, his smile only grew until it looked curiously relieved. "I assume you've gone on a decorating tear with all your collected treasure?"

She refused to relax, struggling to understand. "I have."

His smile just grew as he looked around. "Why didn't you bring all this out when you decorated the townhouse? I never would have left it."

She realized she was gaping. "You *like* it?"

"Do you think you might have room for some crates I've collected?" Diccan was asking as he looked around at the symphony of color. "Mostly from the Ottomans, but Russia, Finland, and Greece as well. I've had them stored until I had a place that I could call my own."

She kept shaking her head. "Why didn't you *say* something? Do you know how much I loathe Wedgwood?"

"No more than I, I assure you. I'm sorry for that, too, Grace. I thought about telling you when I saw your crates, but things were just too uncertain, and I was afraid to get too close."

She nodded. "I know. I understand."

He reached out a hand to cup her check. He was trembling. "Do you?" he asked, sounding sad. "I don't see how."

She laid her hand over his. "You were trying to keep me safe. Of course, I imagine it would have been a lot easier to bear if you had just told me."

"How could I…" His protest faded. "You're right. I should have told you everything."

She smiled. "I know."

For a long moment, he just watched her. Finally, though, that sly smile reappeared.

"Did I see majolica in your crates?"

"In the morning room." She pulled in an uncertain breath. "Now, you have to leave. We're no longer married, and I don't carry on casual affairs."

"I don't carry on casual affairs either," he retorted. "Not anymore."

He tried to put his arms around her. Grace balked like a green horse.

Diccan must have seen something, because he looked even happier. "I should have known you'd need the whole tradition." Reaching into his pocket, he pulled something out. Flipping it open, he dropped to one knee.

Grace tried to back up. He caught her hand and held her in place.

"Grace Georgianna Fairchild, would you put this silly fribble out of his misery and marry him?"

Her brain froze. Her legs almost gave out on her. She couldn't pull her gaze away from the ludicrously hopeful expression on his face to see what was in the little jeweller's box he held.

"Stop this," she whispered, the pain tearing at her. "Please. I can't..." She pressed her fingers against her mouth, as if it would hold in every hope and dream and fear that threatened to tumble out.

He didn't even seem to notice. "Did I tell you how much I love red hair, Grace? Real red hair, not that faded insult you had when I met you. Hair the color of a sunset over the Pyramids. The color of fire and warmth and life." His eyes looked alarmingly sincere. "I came back before I knew your real hair color, so I guess I must love you without it. But I have to admit that it adds a lovely piquancy to the deal. Don't you think God considered it a huge joke that I fell in love with you before I realized you were the woman of my dreams?"

He'd said it twice. He couldn't mean it. She was afraid she would shake apart with the power of her emotions. Pain, longing, hope, despair.

"You don't think I'm serious," he said, tilting his head in some surprise. He gave a frustrated sigh and put the ring away. "Grace. Do you love me? It's all I want to know."

But it mustn't have been, because he regained his feet and laid his hands on her shoulders. Before she could protest, he had turned her around so that they both faced her little mirror, his face hovering over her shoulder like a wish, her own eyes unpardonably huge, her chest rising and falling too fast beneath the shimmering blue silk.

"Please tell me you do," he said, and damn him if he didn't sound sincere. "I don't think I could survive if you didn't. I certainly couldn't marry anyone else."

She tried to turn, but he wouldn't let her. He had begun to stroke her hair, his fingers winnowing through the fire-red strands and sending cascades of chills down her throat.

"I don't understand," she protested, sounding breathy and frightened. "You were free. You escaped. What are you doing back now? You can see I haven't suffered any horrific scandal."

He kissed the top of her head, as if it were more precious than any artifact she had collected. "I waited until now because I wanted to make sure it was all well and truly over. The documents signed and witnessed and finalized. It is official now. We were never married."

The words pierced her like hot steel. "Yes," she whispered. "I know."

He nodded. "And you definitely said that I didn't have to come back to marry you out of any sense of obligation."

This time she could only nod.

His smile grew wide and bright. "Good. Then it must mean that I came back because I wanted to. Did you even bother to look at the ring I went to so much trouble to obtain? It's the Hilliard emerald, you know. Goes well with red hair, or so I'm told. Worth a bloody fortune. I was hoping that if you weren't sensible, or madly in love, or mad as mud, at least you might be a bit mercenary and accept me for the ring."

She was shaking her head again, wondering if he was the one who was mad as mud. "You can't want me."

He quirked an eyebrow. "I can't?"

He ran his hands down her arms, to her hands, up the underside, the slide of his fingers against silk unbearably exciting. Before Grace could think to move, he was unbuttoning the buttons at the neck of her caftan.

"Curious garment," he murmured, dropping little kisses along the side of her throat. She couldn't bear the whisper of breath against her skin. Still, she seemed to need to arch her neck to give him better access.

"It's a caftan," she whispered. "I had to get…a… man's. Too tall."

He began to slide the silk off her shoulders. "I beg to differ. You are the perfect height. With the perfect mouth and the perfect shoulders and the perfect, delicate feet."

"Don't be…"

The caftan fell away and she was naked before him. Grace squeezed her eyes shut.

"Oh, Grace," he murmured against her. "Are you so afraid of me?"

Yes, she wanted to say. *No. I'm afraid of me.* "You can't possibly want this." She didn't think she'd have to explain. She knew he could see perfectly well what she meant, displayed right there in the mirror.

She felt his mouth on her shoulder, her back, his lips skipping over the ridges of her neck. "Again, my dear," he said, his hands sliding up her sides, "I beg to differ. Admittedly a horsewoman's body might be an acquired taste. After all, not every man can appreciate the special pleasure of being able to cup a pair of breasts entirely in his hands."

To demonstrate, he wrapped his long-fingered hands around her breasts. She shuddered again, pleasure shearing straight through to her toes.

"Too...small."

"Grace," he sighed, and she almost found herself smiling. "Tell me. Am I not known throughout the *ton* for my exceptional taste?"

She wanted to giggle, but couldn't get the breath in to do it. "Biddle certainly thinks so."

Lower. His hand was slowly sweeping over her hip, marking pelvis and navel and the slope of her belly.

"Exactly. Then you can't dispute my word when I say I find something beautiful."

She was glowing; she swore. His breath was on her neck, his fingers dipping into the curls at the juncture of her legs. Her breasts were suddenly taut and tingly, her limbs trembling so badly she simply wanted to sink to the floor.

"Open your eyes, Grace," he commanded.

And she opened them. She opened them and saw *his* eyes, almost black with arousal, languid with delight, soft with...no, she could never hope for that.

"I love your body, Grace," he said, as if he heard her. "I've missed it fiercely these last weeks. I can't get the taste of you off my tongue, or your cries of climax out of my ears. I want to hold you as you fall asleep and slip into you when you wake. I want to see what you're going to do with those great stones you've laid out in the stableyard and inspect every room you've decorated." He closed his eyes, nuzzling his face against her neck. "I want to recreate every painting on your wall."

This time she did giggle, because he had found her netherlips and was skimming his fingers over them. "It would take an awfully long time."

He licked her ear, and she gasped. "Not so," he disagreed. "There are only what, thirty or so? No more than a week's worth."

She panted with the red heat that swirled up through her. "More in ... storage."

He nipped at her neck. "How many?"

Head against his chest, legs spread, she chuckled. "Years."

He chuckled back, the most delicious sound in the world. "Naughty minx. Please, Grace. Marry me so we can do this every day. Twice a day."

"You're sure you aren't doing this out of ... obligation? You don't really need me."

He stopped, and Grace could feel how still he became. "I think you deserve more than to be needed, Grace. I think you deserve to be wanted. I want you. I love you. I suddenly find myself visualizing little girls with red hair and gray eyes." He stood so quietly, a suggestion in the shadows. His eyes were real, though, clear and bright and anxious. "Let's have a pack of children to make this place echo with noise. Let's raise horses and babies and be the most bucolic couple in England."

Dear, sweet Lord, she thought, stumbling over the possibility. He means it. He loves me.

"What of your career?"

"Let's do that, too. I've been offered a post in Calcutta. I don't suppose you want to see it again."

Her head came up so fast she almost cracked his chin. "Really? India?"

He chuckled. "So the horses will have to wait. Unless you wouldn't mind bringing them both along. I hear they have a wonderful racetrack in Calcutta."

She nodded. "Oh, they do."

"Then marry me. Truly make me the happiest of men."

"Yes," she said before she lost her courage and failed to ask for what she really wanted. She would ask about other details later, because the details didn't matter. "I love you. I want you. I'll marry you."

He seemed to have stopped breathing. "You mean it?"

She met his gaze for the first time without flinching, sure her heart could match a hummingbird's. "With all my heart."

He seemed to deflate, as if he had braced himself for her refusal. It was such an alien thought that she fell even more deeply in love. Fortunately, she had a chance to express it. Turning her to him, he pulled her into his arms and kissed her as if he'd been starving.

"Good," he said briskly." "Then I don't have to drag Gadzooks away from Epona again. He bit me the last time."

"He's in love."

His smile was salacious. "I know just how he feels. I tried to bite Biddle, but he was too fast for me. I'd love to drag you down to town to wake the vicar, but I think we learned our lesson last time. First we'll go see a lawyer to make sure you don't just willy-nilly give Longbridge to the first husband who comes along. And then I'll give you the emerald so you can show it off. My mother assures me it's a far greater treasure than any you've ever seen."

She wanted to laugh. "I'm sure." She couldn't take her eyes from the almost boyish enthusiasm on Diccan's face. She couldn't believe it. He truly looked younger, as if all the ennui and posturing had been stripped away by one word.

Tears crowded her throat again, but this time sweet ones. "Diccan."

Her voice seemed to pull him back from somewhere. "Yes?"

She smiled. "Now that we've agreed on the important details, do you see that first painting on the wall by my dresser?"

He looked, and his eyes, if possible, grew darker. "Yes."

"Can we reenact that one tonight, do you think?"

He pulled her off her feet so that they landed in a mound of pillows. "Oh, yes."

Diccan and Grace's second wedding took place in the little stone church in the village of Longbridge. The local vicar, a gentle young man named Sharp, presided, and the neighboring ladies provided flowers. There were no guests, only Grace's staff, with the Harpers standing up for them. The last wedding had been for the benefit of everyone else. This wedding was theirs alone.

"I think our girl's about to be surprised altogether," Sean Harper said beside Diccan.

Diccan hoped so. He'd spent hours debating whether to

reveal his own secrets. But if Grace could have the courage to show her true colors, why couldn't he? No matter how Biddle wept.

"Not nearly as much as she's surprised me," he said. He couldn't believe it, but her hair had continued to brighten, until it was a sun, a beacon, a conflagration he could spot all the way to the horizon. And as her hair had brightened, so had Grace. She was like a flower planted on friendly soil that lost no time in blooming. No longer could she ever be mistaken for that grave young spinster in the gray dresses.

"Well now, will you look at that?" Harper murmured beside him.

Diccan came to attention. He looked down the aisle toward the back door. He felt his breath whoosh out of his chest. "Well, bugger," he chuckled. "And here I thought I'd surprise *her*."

He should have known better. When had Grace ever let him get the upper hand? But he'd thought that the Turkish wedding costume he'd unearthed would at least have impressed her, with its belted gold-and-white brocaded tunic and salwar. His head was covered in a great white turban, adorned with two heron feathers, and his shoes were kid, with appliquéd arabesques. He even wore a jeweled knife at his belt. It had been liberating to toss that damn black-and-white to the floor and don gold. It had been comfortable. It had been decadent.

Not as decadent as his bride.

Gliding up the aisle as if on air, Grace was draped in a gold-embroidered scarlet sari, her arms adorned in red and white bangles, her sandaled toes ringed, her throat circled in no less than three wedding necklaces of priceless gemstones and 22-karat gold. She had a *maang tika* of gold and sapphires and rubies in her hair, and matching chandelier earrings that brushed her shoulders as she walked. Diccan could see the intricate pattern of henna tattooing up her arms. Sweet God, she was exquisite.

And then she lifted her demurely downcast eyes and got a look at him, and she burst out laughing.

"Well," Mr. Sharp greeted them both with twinkling eyes. "This is certainly a new look for our church."

"How can a girl compete against such beauty?" she asked with glowing eyes when she stopped by Diccan, the silk of her garment whispering like a promise against the stone floor.

Diccan took her hand and raised it for a kiss, the Hilliard emerald winking right alongside his ruby signet ring. "How could a man be so lucky as to have such a singular woman take him on?"

He wasn't joking. His once-plain Grace looked exotic and sensuous and alive in her adopted attire. The sari, thrown over her loose-flowing hair, framed a face still too long, too strong, too unremarkable for traditional beauty. But to Diccan, it was a face of courage and whimsy and joy. It was a face he couldn't wait to see reproduced on his children and lying on the pillow next to his until the day they failed to wake.

In fact, he was so enchanted with her face that he almost missed the fortune she'd hung around her neck. "I don't suppose all that gold and gimcrackery is exceptionally good paste."

She chuckled. "A bit of incentive, husband."

He found himself frowning. "It's no incentive at all. You're worth more than every stone and karat you own."

He thought he might have actually surprised her. He

thought he might enjoy doing it frequently. His Grace had a lot of catching up to do in the appreciation department.

"As this compliment comes from a great Caliph," she said, her voice suspiciously wobbly, "I believe I'll accept."

"You like it?" he asked, showing off his attire. "I believe it will be three times as difficult to squeeze back into that vile black-and-white."

"Then don't."

He smiled over at the vicar, who was still patiently waiting. "*'Her price is far above rubies,'* isn't that so, Reverend?"

"I couldn't put it better myself," Mr. Sharp answered with a smile.

Diccan still smiled at his wife. "You've freed me, my Grace. You've liberated me from the prison of perfection."

For a moment, he thought perhaps she hadn't understood him. She just stared, her eyes wide. Then, subtly, her expression changed, warming, widening, blooming into a delighted smile.

"Obviously that amuses you," he challenged.

She was shaking her head, the gold tinkling in her ears. "Intrigues me," she said. "I just remembered standing at our last wedding and thinking that your evening attire was a kind of uniform, like my gray. I was just thinking that today we've changed those uniforms for new ones. But I was wrong. We weren't in uniforms at all; we were in disguise."

Anyone else would have challenged her, for what was Diccan Hilliard but his reputation, his attire, his wit? But from now on, he intended to be a happy husband, an ambitious diplomat, and an exemplary country gentleman. Grace had finally given him permission to be himself. She had, in a way, pulled him from his own crate and set him free.

"Should we make it part of our vows?" he asked, holding on tightly. "That we'll never allow another disguise between us as long as we live?"

Her smile was incandescent. "I think we just did. I love you, Diccan."

He kissed her. "I love you, Grace. Now, since nobody needs us to do it, let's get married and live happily ever after, shall we?"

It was just what they did.

Passion flares when Lady Kate Seaton
is locked in a deserted castle...
with the man who betrayed her.

Please turn this page
for a preview of

Always a Temptress.

Chapter 1

If there was one thing that showed Kate Seaton's life up for what it was, it was a wedding. Kate loved weddings, especially if good friends were involved. She loved the flowers and thumping organ music, and the sloppy sentiments that brought out handkerchiefs to be waved like white flags of surrender. She especially loved the smiles. Everyone should smile at weddings. Everyone should have a wedding to smile about.

Which was why once she ate her surfeit of lobster patties and succumbed to the obligatory hug from the happy couple, she escaped as fast as a thief purloining silver. After all, the sentiment expressed on such a nice day should never be envy or cynicism.

So it had been this time. She had attended the wedding of two very good friends, friends whose happiness she could hardly resent, friends whose joy was hard-won and universally celebrated. Jack had looked handsome and stalwart as he'd said his vows, Olivia lovely and honest-to-God glowing, as every bride should. Kate had joined wholeheartedly in the celebration. And then, at the first opportunity, she had run.

At least, that was her excuse. She refused to think how she had abandoned her cousin Diccan and her friend Grace to their problems. But maybe, she kept thinking, without her to smooth the way, they would learn to rely on each other and rebuild their marriage.

Pulling on her gloves, Kate stepped out of the door of the Angel Inn and into the gray afternoon. Guildford was bustling, as always, situated as it was on the main London-Portsmouth road. Of Guildford's two coaching inns, Kate had always preferred the smaller Angel on High Street with its cozy half-timbered facade and efficient staff. It never took longer than twenty minutes to change out the horses—just enough time for her to down a cup of tea.

Today seemed to be different. When she stepped out into the cobbled yard, her coach was nowhere to be seen. A stage was being unloaded, with much shouting and banging, and behind it a curricle waited. Kate tapped her feet, impatient to be away.

From her left came the sound of a muffled sob. She smiled. "Bea," she gently chastised her companion, laying a hand on the older woman's arm. "It is perfectly bourgeois, to continue crying over a two-day-old wedding."

If Kate enjoyed the pomp of weddings, Bea positively wallowed. She hadn't stopped crying since they'd walked into the tiny Norman church of St. Mary in Bury to find it bursting with friends and late summer flowers.

"Odysseus and Penelope," her friend inexplicably answered, dabbing determinedly at her eyes with one of the aforementioned flags of surrender, this one edged in the honeybees Bee so loved to embroider on things.

"Yes," Kate answered, giving her a squeeze. "It was particularly satisfying to see Jack and Olivia married, after all the years they'd been apart."

"Devonshire," Bea said, casting soulful eyes down at Kate.

This meaning Kate had to work for. "Devonshire? The duke? Was he invited?"

Bea glared, which on the elegantly silver-haired woman, was formidable. "Georgianna."

Kate frowned, wondering what the late Duchess of Devonshire could have to do with the newly minted Earl and Countess of Gracechurch. Georgianna had been married to a cold fish who'd kept his mistress and children in the house with his legitimate family. All Jack had done was divorce his wife and take five years to rectify the mistake.

"Unfair?" Kate guessed.

Bea beamed.

"To whom?" Kate asked, now cognizant of the looks that passed among the various travelers and ostlers cluttering up the courtyard. She had to admit, following Bea's unique conversational style could indeed be distracting. "Jack and Olivia? How could it be unfair that they're finally happy?"

This time Bea gave Kate an impatient huff, and there was no mistaking her meaning.

Kate, who never got misty-eyed, nearly succumbed. "Oh, Bea," she said, wishing she were tall enough to give her stately friend a smacking kiss. "How can you think my life is unfair? What more could I want than money, freedom, and my very best friend to share it with?"

Bea sniffed. "Half loaf."

"Not at all, darling. Or is it you?" She leaned close and

whispered. "Do you long for an amour? Mayhap a young cicisbeo who would squire you about on his arm? General Willoughby would snap you up in a minute, if you just let him."

Bea's laugh was more a snort, but Kate saw the pain behind the humor. Bea thought no one would want her, no matter her impeccable lineage and bone-deep aristocratic beauty. Not only was Bea into her seventies, but a few years earlier, her brain had suffered a terrible injury that left her speech so tortured that many days, Kate was the only one who understood her.

But Kate also knew that, like her, Bea couldn't tolerate coddling. So, with brisk fingers she took Bea's signature handkerchief and dabbed away the last of the old woman's tears. "Now, then, my girl, we need to be going. After all, you're the one who committed us to Lady Riordan's memorial service tomorrow."

Immediately Bea's expression folded into pity. "Poor lambs."

"At least Riordan has finally accepted the truth and declared her dead. Now maybe the children can move on." Kate shuddered. "I can think of few things I find less appealing than drowning. "

Just then, the coach clattered around the corner, the house of Murther crest shining against the black lacquered panels. The horses were unfamiliar, but they were handsome bays that seemed to be pulling hard at the reins.

"Your Grace," one of the postboys said, bowing low as he opened the door.

Kate smiled and let him hand her into the carriage.

She had just settled and turned to help Bea, when suddenly she heard a shout, and the coach lurched. She was thrown back in her seat. The door slammed. The horses whinnied and took off, as if escaping a fire.

Furious, Kate tried to right herself without success. How dare they abuse the horses that way? How dare they leave Bea stranded in the coaching yard, her hand out, her mouth open, still waiting to get into the coach?

Kate righted herself with some difficulty. The coach turned on two wheels and skidded through the archway. Kate could hear the clatter of the horses' hooves against the cobbles, the scrape of stone against the coach sides. She heard the urgent cries of the coachman and thought, suddenly, that it didn't sound like Bob Coachman.

She pounded on the roof to get his attention. No one responded. The coach didn't slow; in fact, it sped up. It didn't occur to Kate to be frightened. She was still too angry, too anxious for Bea, who simply could not be left alone at a coaching inn.

"Blast you, stop!" she shouted, pushing at the trap. It was wedged shut. She pounded again on the roof. The coach sped on, rocking from side to side and throwing her off balance. She already felt bruised. She couldn't imagine what injuries she would collect before the idiot driving her coach finally brought it to a halt.

That was the thought that finally gave her pause. What idiot? Brought it to a halt where? Why hadn't anyone paid attention to her? Why weren't they so much as slowing through a busy town? She could hear shouting outside, and feared for nearby pedestrians. She tried to pull open the window shades, but they wouldn't budge. She heard a crash and more shouting and cringed.

"Are you mad?" she cried, rapping again against the roof. "Stop immediately!"

There was no response, except for the sound of the driver urging on the horses.

Kate began to feel unsettled. Whoever was driving her coach had no interest in listening to her. In fact, he seemed intent on spiriting her away as fast as he could. Kidnapping? She was wealthy. But who in their right mind would think anyone would pay to get her back? Certainly not her family. Her stepson loathed her as much as she did him. Her own family was even worse, especially her brother.

Her brother.

Suddenly her mind shuddered to a halt. Oh, God. Edwin. He had been threatening to restrain what he considered to be her profligate ways. According to him, she was an abomination, not fit to share the exalted Hilliard name with the Duke of Livingston. He never tired of telling her that the only place for her was a lunatic asylum.

He wouldn't.

He would.

Kate refused to be terrified. She categorically refused to believe that her brother had the power to incarcerate her for the simple sin of escaping her family's clutches. And when she saw him, she would tell him so.

On the other hand, it would probably be better all around if she didn't have to face him at all. She needed to get back to her friends, who could protect her against him. She needed to get back to Bea, who would be frantic without her. She needed to get free before Edwin managed to wield his not inconsiderable power and have her locked away.

The coach was moving too fast, its balance precarious. She was holding onto the strap, and still being battered around. She would probably kill herself if she leaped.

She laughed out loud. There were worse things than a split head, and this trip threatened her with most of them. She would happily jump and take her chances.

She was still too furious to really be terrified. Which meant it was time to act. Pulling in a steadying breath, she crossed herself like a Papist and reached for the door handle.

It didn't move. She jiggled it. She yanked. She tried the other one. Nothing. Somehow they had secured the doors, preventing her from escaping. She was truly imprisoned.

For the first time, she was beginning to realize how desperate her situation was. Damn Edwin to hell. She needed to get word to Diccan. He would intercede. He could at least threaten Edwin with the kind of public disgrace her brother loathed.

Diccan was thirty miles away burying his father. Too far for a quick rescue. Much too overwhelmed to have any attention left for Kate.

She sighed, hating the shaky sound of it. She hated being out of control. She had long since sworn that she would never again be at the mercy of another human being. She would never again know the feeling of helplessness.

She should have known better. She'd never had that kind of luck before. Why should it start now?

"Please," she whispered out loud, knowing it was a prayer that wouldn't be heard.

Back at the inn, people were just beginning to realize that there was something wrong. The ostlers had certainly seen carriages speed through the archway before. There was an entire generation of young bucks who refused to leave any other way. The bystanders weren't even particularly surprised to see the elderly lady standing flatfooted by the door, her hand still out, her mouth open and emitting garbled noises that made no sense. Obviously the young lady she'd been talking to had departed mid-conversation. Unsettling even for people who weren't dicked in the nob, like the old gal seemed to be.

A few people frowned when the old woman turned back and forth and cried out, "Sabine women!," her hand still pointing toward the departed carriage. A few more shook their heads, sorry to see such a pitiful thing right there in public.

But when she started to sing, everybody stopped and stared. It wasn't that she was singing Cherry Ripe, which shouldn't have ever been heard on the tongue of such a dignified old lady. It wasn't even that she was singing the wrong words. It was that even with the wrong words in a tune she shouldn't know, it was beautiful.

"Thrasher, come!" she sang, head back, hands out. "Thrasher, come! Lady Kate, follow the way! The carriage has her! Follow the way, Thrasher come!"

And just as if she were making any kind of sense at all, suddenly a motley gaggle of men in blue and gold livery came thundering around the corner from the stables and headed for the old woman.

"That way I say!" the old woman sang, waving toward the street where the carriage had just disappeared. "Four horses black, a driver strange. Follow the way, Thrasher, go!"

And darned if one of them didn't respond. A thin, sharp-featured boy, without even pausing in his tracks, waved at the old girl and took off after that carriage like a hare at the sound of a gun. As for the old lady, she just stood there, tears running down her cheeks as the other men circled her, her own mismatched army. She stopped singing, though. The people who had stopped to listen shook their heads and went back to their business.

"Well now," the head groom said, turning back to his stable. "Wasn't that somethin'?"

Kate began to frantically search the coach. Not for escape; she knew the coach was too well-made to be easily pulled apart. For weapons. It was almost impossible, and she knew she'd be bruised from head to toe from trying, but even as she was thrown around, she rifled through the cushions and side compartments, ripping and tugging until the inside of the coach looked as if a mad animal had been caught inside.

Not so different, she thought, feeling more frantic as she failed to secure so much as a rusty spring with which to defend herself. She was left with a hat pin. Luckily, she had used hat pins to great effect on more than one occasion.

If only she could rip through enough of the coach to see daylight. The coach was beginning to close in on her, all the daylight barricaded away, leaving only shadow and speed. Even throwing herself under the wheels seemed to be a better option than simply surrendering herself to the dark.

Bastard, she kept repeating to herself, although of any insult she could rain on her brother's head, that would certainly be the most unlikely. He truly was the one and only Duke of Livingston, holder of all titles and privileges, born to the strawberry leaves, and certainly happy to remind you if you forgot.

He was nothing like their father, who had been a good duke. A responsible man loyal to his people and generous to his community, that duke had truly been mourned when he died. When Edwin went, Kate had the feeling there would be a lot of show and no sincerity.

The problem was, he still had the power. And that meant, since he was head of her family, he was legally in charge of her life.

She worked for hours, tearing the coach apart like a starving woman looking for the last bit of cheese. She unearthed two blankets, a writing desk, a tiny bottle of scent she didn't use anymore, three vinaigrettes from Bea's stash, and a stale hunk of bread from behind the cushions.

To that pile she added a handful of coins and a small sewing kit she'd been looking for since the Countess of March's soirée six weeks ago. No weapons. No escape. No hope. Except she refused to consider that. She would go mad if she considered the places Edwin might want to incarcerate her.

She must have finally fallen asleep, sitting in the well with her head on the ruined seat. All she knew was that when she woke it was deeply dark. It took her a moment to realize that the change of speed had alerted her. They were slowing and turning.

Had she been brought to Edwin at Moorhaven? Would he have the effrontery to drag her back home kicking and screaming just as he was burying his uncle in the family vault? For heaven's sake, the Archbishop of Canterbury was supposed to preside. If it was Moorhaven, though, Diccan would be there. It was his father they were burying, after all.

Closing her eyes, as if that could keep the darkness at bay, Kate assessed her options. She loathed the idea of putting her fate in someone else's hands. Especially a man. That had never exactly worked well for her in the past. But she could trust Diccan. No matter the risk to his social standing, he would speak out against Edwin.

The coach ground to a halt. Kate could hear the jangle of harness as the horses settled. She heard men's voices, and the creak of the coach as the driver swung down from his perch. She heard the hollow caw of a raven.

And then, nothing. No movement. No voices. No appearance by someone who would offer explanation. Obviously a move orchestrated to heighten her terror. Considering how dark it was inside the coach, it was working. Already her heart was running an erratic race. Her hands had begun to sweat inside her calfskin gloves.

Well, she'd be damned if she showed him how frightened she was. Even as her stomach threatened revolt and her hands shook, she straightened her clothing and tucked up her hair. She repinned her cottage bonnet and pulled on her gloves. Stuffing the horsehair back into the cushions as well as she could, she perched herself in the center of the seat, a duchess come to call.

And still no one came.

"Edwin!" she called, injecting the proper amount of impatient disdain into her voice. "Games are childish. Let me out so we can battle this out face to face."

Suddenly the door was yanked open. It was all Kate could do not to jump. She didn't, though. Proud of her composure, she turned to face her brother, or whatever henchman he'd sent to represent him.

She froze. It wasn't Edwin at all. For a moment, she couldn't say a word. She could only stare, sick with betrayal. Not him, she thought. Not again.

"Harry," she drawled, hoping he didn't see how lost she suddenly felt. "Imagine seeing you here."

Harry Lidge made it a point to look around the disaster she'd made of the carriage. "What the hell have you been doing?"

Kate didn't bother to look. "Redesigning. You know how easily I bore."

He offered a hand. "Get out."

She didn't move. She hated the fact that his hair gleamed like faint gold in the lamplight, that she could see even in the deep shadows that his eyes were sky blue. He had grown well, filled out into a strong man. A hard man who had survived the wars with fewer scars than most. He was no longer the boy she'd known, though, and it showed in more than the web of creases that fanned out from the corners of his eyes. It showed in the unforgiving rigidity of his posture, the impatient edge to his actions.

But maybe that was just for her.

No, she thought, furious that it mattered.

"I don't think I will," she told him. "Not until I understand why. Are you working for Edwin now, Harry? I certainly hope he's paying you as much to kidnap me as my father did to desert me."

His expression, if possible, grew colder. "You don't get to ask questions, Your Grace. You get to answer them. Now, get down before I drag you out bodily."

"Go to hell, Harry."

Harry didn't answer. He just reached in and yanked her out of the carriage. When she shrieked and fought, he tossed her over his shoulder and turned for the building Kate could see only as a deeper shadow in the darkness.

"What do you think you're doing?!" she shrilled. "Put me down!"

She managed to land a particularly good kick to his chest, briefly taking his breath. He reached up and swatted her on the bottom.

She was breathless with rage. "Damn you, put me down."

"When I'm finished."

She saw legs on the way by, and one woman's skirt. So Harry had staff here. Was that good or bad? Was he to keep watch over here, or simply desert her?

What was she going to do?

By the time she could think to argue, Harry had hauled her into the house, up a dim, grimy set of stairs and into an even grimier bedroom, where he proceeded to dump her on the bed. She bounded back as if the mattress were on fire and scrambled to her feet. She was suddenly afraid and disoriented. This made no sense. She couldn't even think of what to ask first.

"When did you start doing Edwin's bidding, Harry?" she demanded, settling her skirts so she couldn't dwell on how her voice had begun to rise. "Are you under the hatches, or do you need another promotion?"

"I don't work for Edwin," he said, his voice dripping ice. "I work for the government. And I have the dubious pleasure of keeping you here until you give us some answers. Where is it, Kate?"

Her hands stilled on her skirt. Kate found herself blinking like a child. "The government? *Our* government?" She laughed, even angrier that she sounded shrill. "Pull the other one, Harry."

He took a threatening step closer, his rugged features as hard as granite. "Oh, I think you know perfectly well what I'm talking about. Just before he died, the Surgeon told us. You're mixed up with the Lions. Do you have it,

Kate? Do you have the verse with you? Because if you do, we'll find it."

"The verse?" she echoed, stumbling back from him, only to have her knees fold and land her back on the bed. "The verse we've been searching all over creation for like a lost Easter egg? *That* verse?"

He merely tilted his head.

"I don't have your bloody verse," she snapped, still feeling pathetically overwhelmed. And then, the second betrayal sank in. "You really believe the Surgeon? The man whose favorite pastime was carving poetry into people's foreheads? Are you mad?"

"Not as mad as you if you think I'll fall for your stories again." He stepped back toward the door, and it was all Kate could do to keep from reaching out to beg him not to lock her in.

"Don't," was all she could say.

Harry stopped, his eyebrow quirked with disdain, but she couldn't get another word out. "What?" he asked. "No clever quotes? No Latin or Greek or German, Kate? I'm disappointed."

From the bottom of her toes, she scraped up all that was left of her self-respect. "Latin, Harry? You must have me confused with another one of your prisoners. A dowager has no reason to spout any foreign language, except, occasionally, French."

"What happened?" he retorted. "No more ignorant farmers to impress? I would have thought you'd find a head other than mine to hold your book learning over."

He couldn't possibly believe that. Hadn't he heard her at all?

"Now then, Your Grace," he said, his voice a razor. "You

can make this easy or you can make it hard. Your luggage is being searched even as we speak. If we don't find it there, you'll be searched. You can cooperate or not." He shrugged. "It really makes no difference. We'll find it. Until then, you can consider yourself my prisoner."

Kate couldn't seem to form words. She couldn't seem to comprehend what Harry was saying. She didn't even recognize this Harry. She'd known him once; an open, easygoing son of the earth with a brain too big for farming. She had loved him once, with the passion reserved for a first love. She'd seen him as the hero who would save her from the future her father had planned for her.

But he hadn't been her hero. He had betrayed her. And over the last ten years, grown into this implacable, humorless, spiteful man.

She was, to put it bluntly, at his mercy. God help her.

"I don't have it," she repeated, rising to her feet like a doomed Mary, Queen of Scots. "I wouldn't recognize it if it came up and asked me to dance. Now, stop being such a bully and let me get back to Bea."

She was furious to hear a note of pleading creep into her voice. It stiffened her spine, at least, so she could brace her feet on the floor and confront the enraged stranger she'd once known so well. Or thought she had.

"The verse," was all Harry said, crossing his arms and leaning against the door. "Give me the verse and you can go...well, maybe not. If you have the verse, then you're a traitor. Maybe I should just lock you in the cellars right now and be done with it."

It was all Kate could do to keep her composure. She could only hope that Harry didn't understand how much that threat terrified her. She could barely stand in this room. It was infested with shadows and dark corners, just a candle away from darkness. She refused to imagine what would happen in a cellar.

She couldn't let Harry know that or he would make good on his threat. She could no longer trust his basic decency.

"You don't understand," she said, taking a step forward, closer to freedom. "Bea can't simply be abandoned. She isn't strong. She'll fret herself to flinders wondering where I am. I have to get back to her."

Harry took another step back toward the door. "Give me the verse and we'll see."

Her temper snapped. "I don't *have* the bloody verse!"

He shrugged. "Then tell me where it is." He stepped through the door. And then, as if daring her to argue, he waited there with one foot in the room and one in the hallway, taunting her with his freedom to move.

"Diccan will kill you for this," she snarled.

He stopped, his stare implacable. "Diccan was the one who told me to do it."

Kate wondered whether shock really had a sound. She thought she heard a whirlwind; she thought she heard the echo of a cold void. "Don't be absurd."

Diccan would never do this. He would never threaten her with Harry, much less darkness. He knew...no, she realized, he didn't. Only Bea knew. But Bea wasn't here.

She snapped out of her reverie just in time to see Harry back through the door. She grabbed him by the sleeve. "A candle!" The one in this room was short and sputtering.

"The verse," he answered and turned away.

"You bastard!" she almost screeched, pulling him back. "I don't know what game you're playing, but you know perfectly well I don't have the verse. Now let me get back to

Bea before she makes herself ill. Or have you also taken to torturing old women?"

It was as if she'd snapped some restraint in him. Suddenly Harry spun around and advanced on her, forcing her across the dark room until her back was pressed against the peeling, dingy wall. He kept pressing forward, crowding her with his body, battering at her with the fury in his eyes.

Her first instinct was to cower, to throw her arm up to protect herself. Her second was to hold herself perfectly still. She knew too well that cowering only made it worse.

"I told you," he said, his voice suddenly low and insulting. "Give me the verse and you're free."

She had nowhere to go. Harry loomed over her, heating the air between them. She wanted to spit at him, to simply laugh and walk away. But inexplicably, caught like cornered prey, her body suddenly remembered. It wouldn't move; wouldn't fight. It began to soften, to open, to *want*, and she hadn't wanted in so long she'd forgotten the feel of it.

Even if she didn't want Harry, her body did. It remembered how she'd hungered for the scent he always carried, horses and leather and strong soap. It remembered how he'd touched her with the raw wonder of an explorer. It remembered how it felt to trust those guileless blue eyes enough to offer him her virginity.

It only lasted a moment, that sense of elation, before she remembered exactly what it was she had once wanted. Before she fought the urge to curl into herself and hide. And that made her angrier than ever.

Somehow she must have betrayed her momentary weakness, because suddenly he was smiling like a wolf. "On the other hand," he murmured, leaning even closer, too close, only small inches away, "maybe you want me to find it myself. Shall I look for it? Should I strip you myself until I can see every inch of milky white skin? Should I search you, slipping my hands under your breasts to make sure you haven't tucked it inside, where it would be warm and damp?"

She couldn't breathe. She couldn't tell if it was fury, fear, or arousal, even though her nipples tightened with his words and a light flared in her belly. She couldn't breathe because he was taking the last of her air. She couldn't think because he was too close.

"I could do it," he whispered, his mouth next to her ear. "All I'd have to do is kiss you, right here behind your ear. You'd let me do anything, then. Wouldn't you, Kate?"

Reaching out, he pulled a pin from her hair, loosing a thick curl. Kate shivered, frozen with memory. Suddenly she was fifteen again, standing on the edge of womanhood. Trembling with possibility, with wonder, with hunger. For the first time in ten years she remembered what it had felt like to anticipate, and shredded her control.

And then, Harry made his mistake. He took that last step as if he had the right. As if she would never defend herself, or maybe simply succumb to his pressure. "Or would you like to offer me a bit of incentive not to look?" he murmured into her ear. "I'm sure it wouldn't be too difficult a task. From what I hear, it's your favorite thing to do."

He was too close. He wrapped one hand around her throat. Not squeezing, just controlling. It was enough. It was too much, and she had nowhere left to run. She felt the familiar wings of terror beating against her chest. She did the only thing she could. She rammed her knee straight up into his bollocks.

Wheezing out a strangled cry, he went right over on his knees. Head down, hunched over, as if folded into the position of supplication.

It took a moment for Kate to get enough air into her lungs. Her legs had gone liquid and her belly hot and shivery. She almost lost her lunch over Harry's bent form. Her body was shaking so badly she was amazed she could take a step.

But she did, using every ounce of strength she possessed to pull herself up into perfect duchess posture. Projecting an air of bored disdain, she stepped past him. "I knew you weren't honorable anymore," she said, pulling open the door. "I didn't know you'd also lost your manners."

She had meant to run down the steps and out the front door. One look into the hallway stopped her. It wasn't the hulking pair who stood, arms crossed, five feet away. It was the fact that she recognized where she was.

Hanging in the stairwell was a portrait of a grim-faced stick of a man in bagwig and black serge. Great Uncle Philbert, who had willed Diccan what was left of his ramshackle estate when he died. Kate knew. She'd toured the place with Diccan right after he'd inherited. They'd had a lovely day making absurd plans for its renovation into a premiere spa or even more expensive madhouse.

Harry hadn't lied. Diccan had told him to kidnap her and bring her to this dilapidated pile of stone in the middle of nowhere to torture information out of her she didn't have. She had no one to go to for help.

Turning back into her room, she stepped aside so Harry could limp past.

"You're not going to get out of here until you admit your guilt," he rasped.

She tilted her head, sure he could smell the despair on her. "I would be tempted to tell you that the only thing I'm guilty of is being too naïve when it comes to men. But it would be such a cliché."

"Well," he said, walking out. "You've certainly made up for lost time."

She couldn't imagine how she could still be hurt by anything Harry said. But she was, the wound sawing against the other emotions that roiled in her chest. And then Harry slammed the door and she heard the unmistakable screech of a bar being slid home. She was left staring at the scarred wood, her brain frozen. She was closed into a house with a man who hated her enough to torment her with her own body. She didn't even want to think of what he would do if he found out about her fears.

She could feel the darkness begin to grow around her, swelling against the pitiful light of the candle. She turned, searching for the windows, to find them shuttered, and the shutters nailed shut. Harry had prepared well. She wasn't getting out of here. And she couldn't give him the verse, because she didn't have it. She didn't even know what it was. And from what she'd heard, no one else did either.

Until they did, she was locked in a dark room in a dark house, imprisoned by a dark man. Edwin himself couldn't have come up with a better torture.

THE DISH

Where authors give you the inside scoop!

From the desk of Roxanne St. Claire

Dear Reader,

I know it's right out of the *Romancing the Stone* opening credits, but I do usually get a little teary when writing the final scene of a book. Maybe my heart and head are fried from months of storytelling, maybe the looming deadline gets the best of me, or maybe I just adore a good Happily Ever After and can't resist writing one that tugs at my heartstrings.

But when I wrote SHIVER OF FEAR, I admit I shed some *serious* waterworks—and not just because the hero, Marc Rossi, has found true love after never believing he could again…and the heroine, Devyn Sterling, is finally part of a big, happy family after a lifetime of loneliness. I was emotional because I set the scene during *La Vigilia*, also known to Italian families as The Feast of the Seven Fishes. What better place for a happy ending than around the dining room table during a meal that has deep personal meaning for me and for most members of a big Italian clan? No, I'm not Italian by descent, but my husband is "first generation"—the son of an immigrant and, therefore, deeply entrenched in some of the country's best customs. I have no doubt that the fictional blended family that peppers the pages of The Guardian Angelinos series would embrace this time-honored tradition as we do.

No one really knows the origin of the required "seven" fishes that are served on Christmas Eve in Italian families. Some say the number reflects the seven sacraments and others believe the "fishes" represent the seven hills of Rome. It doesn't matter, because most of us go way past seven that night. From the scungilli salad to the baccala amalfi and all of the salmon, swordfish, clams, scallops, shrimp, lobster, and calamari in between…it's a night to celebrate the gifts of the sea and the season. I rarely make it through the evening without looking around at my loved ones, blinking back a tear of gratitude, and going back for seconds on the lobster.

During an earlier scene in SHIVER OF FEAR, I used Marc's description of the evening to highlight Devyn's aching for a family and intensify her belief that she isn't destined to have that kind of love in her life. While he takes the tradition for granted, she is left to imagine the magic of that night and the warmth that comes from celebrating with food and family. Most of the story is set in Northern Ireland, where Devyn and Marc are on a hunt to find her birth mother and discover a hornet's nest of terrorist activity along with an unexpected attraction that soon blooms into love. But when it came time to give the reader the ultimate *dolce* moment—the sweet dessert of a lifetime together—it seemed natural to set that scene on a snowy Christmas Eve with the loud, laughing, loving Angelino and Rossi families gathered to celebrate.

So, I wiped a few tears when I typed "the end" of SHIVER OF FEAR and hoped that whatever traditions my readers honor and celebrate, they can relate to the atmosphere of joy that fills a home during The Feast of the Seven Fishes. If nothing else, I'll send them all out in search of good seafood!

Best,

Roxanne St. Claire

www.roxannestclaire.com

♥ ♥ ♥ ♥ ♥ ♥ ♥ ♥ ♥ ♥ ♥ ♥ ♥ ♥ ♥ ♥ ♥

From the desk of Eileen Dreyer

Dear Reader,

Marriage of Convenience. Those three words alone will convince me to buy a book. I can't think of anything I enjoy more than a romance where two people who would never have chosen each other find themselves having to negotiate a marriage neither one wanted. So when I had the chance to write historical romance, I knew that it wouldn't be long before I wrote a Marriage of Convenience book.

NEVER A GENTLEMAN is that book. Diccan Hilliard is known among Society as *The Perfection*. Suave, smooth, sophisticated, with a taste for only the most beautiful women, he has a keen wit and rapier tongue. The fact that he is also a member of Drake's Rakes, a group of aristocrats caught up in espionage, is a well-guarded secret. That secret, though, leads to marriage vows, when he wakes to find that his enemies have left him naked in bed with Grace Fairchild, the woman known to his friends as *The Most Notorious Virgin* in Britain.

Poor Grace. As tall as a man, painfully plain with an ungainly limp, Grace has spent her life following her father around the world with the army. She has no female accomplishments, no wish to mingle in a society that has long since shunned her, and even less desire to be shackled to a man who did not choose her, especially since she has long been fascinated by him. But Grace has secrets too. The question is, will those secrets help her gain Diccan's love, or condemn her to loneliness? And will Diccan's secrets cost them not just the chance at a lasting love, but their very lives?

Do you like Marriage of Convenience books as much as I do? What draws you to them? Let me know at my website, www.eileendreyer.com.

Enjoy!

Eileen Dreyer

♥ ♥ ♥ ♥ ♥ ♥ ♥ ♥ ♥ ♥ ♥ ♥ ♥ ♥

From the desk of Jill Shalvis

Dear Reader,

Writing a romance called THE SWEETEST THING, which centers around a decidedly *not* sweet heroine, amused me. Tara Daniels is wound a little tightly and likes things her way. She's also a former southern belle who appreciates the fact that she's right. A lot.

The Sweetest Thing? Not exactly.

But her heart's in the right place, always. And, as it turns out, there's a man who melts her like butter on a hot roll. Not only that, but he can soften her in a way that she isn't sure she likes. See, Tara thinks she has it all together, but it turns out she doesn't. She doesn't know a lot about herself. About all she has is the fact that she can cook like nobody's business. Oh, how she loves to cook.

Tara was a challenge for me because—here's where I must admit it—I got a lot of her recipes from my husband. True story. I'm married to a big guy who works with his hands and is the ultimate Alpha Man—and yet he can cook. Don't try to figure him out; it'll hurt your brain, trust me.

Good Morning Sunshine Casserole is all his. Just don't tell him I "borrowed" it and am telling the world that it's my heroine's. It would just go to his head.

Happy reading and cooking!

Jill Shalvis

www.jillshalvis.com

Find out more about Forever Romance!

Visit us at
www.hachettebookgroup.com/publishing_forever.aspx

Find us on Facebook
http://www.facebook.com/ForeverRomance

Follow us on Twitter
http://twitter.com/ForeverRomance

NEW AND UPCOMING TITLES

Each month we feature our new titles
and reader favorites.

CONTESTS AND GIVEAWAYS

We give away galleys, autographed copies,
and all kinds of exclusive items.

AUTHOR INFO

You'll find bios, articles, and links to personal websites
for all your favorite authors—and so much more.

GET SOCIAL

Connect with your favorite authors, editors, and
other Forever fans, and share what's important to you.

THE BUZZ

Sign up for our monthly romance newsletter,
and be the first to read all about it.